# 1812
## THE LAND BETWEEN
## FLOWING WATERS

# 1812
## The Land Between Flowing Waters

By

Ken Leland

*Fireship Press*
*www.FireshipPress.com*

1812: The Land Between Flowing Waters by Ken Leland

Copyright © 2013 Ken Leland

ISBN-13:978-1-61179-251-5: Paperback
ISBN 978-1-61179-252-2: ebook

BISAC Subject Headings:

FIC014000FICTION / Historical
FIC032000FICTION / War & Military
HIS028000 HISTORY/ NATIVE AMERICAN

Cover Work: Christine Horner

Address all correspondence to:
Fireship Press, LLC
P.O. Box 68412
Tucson, AZ 85737
Or visit our website at:
www.FireshipPress.com

# Dedication

My most heartfelt appreciation goes to Susan, my wife, and to our daughter Meegan, for their patience and support during the years of research and writing.

# Acknowledgements

I wish to thank the past and present members of the Bloor West Writers Group for reviewing the manuscript while it was under development and for offering many useful and insightful comments. I also thank the First Nations Elders, particularly those who so graciously shared their culture and wisdom at Dodem Kanonhsa in Toronto. My thanks also extend to Jane Zavitz-Bond of the Ontario Quaker Archives at Pickering College in Newmarket, Ontario, for assistance in my efforts to research Quaker society during the early 19th century and the effects of the War of 1812 on Friends living in Upper Canada. Thanks are due to the staff of the Niagara Historical Society Museum for invaluable assistance in researching primary materials, and for a century of published historical information. My profound thanks go to the staff of Fireship Press for their expert assistance in preparation of the manuscript.

# List of Contents

# The Principal Characters

The **Benjamin** Family – Black Loyalists
**Ben** and **Sarah**, the elderly parents.
**Matthew**, 29, teamster.
**Janie (Roberts)**, 23, married Jeremy Roberts after rejecting Alexander Lockwood's plea that she wait for him. Business partner with Miriam Lockwood. Janie and Jeremy have a two year old son, Ethan.

The **Lockwood** Family – White Loyalists
**Lois** and **Asa**, the elderly parents.
**Ruth**, 30, leaves for England with her husband Colonel William Mayne early in the story.
**Miriam**, 27, friend and business partner with Janie (Benjamin) Roberts.
**Alexander**, 23, Captain in 49th Regiment, Brock's spy, Janie's rejected lover.

At Niagara
**Jeremy Roberts**, 23, school friend of Alexander Lockwood, husband of Janie (Benjamin) Roberts.
**General Isaac Brock**, 42, President and Administrator of Upper Canada/Commander of British forces in Upper Canada.
**John Ellis**, 10, ward of General Isaac Brock.
**Major John Baskerville Glegg**, 35, Aide-de-camp to General Isaac Brock.

Among the Neshnabek
**Kshiwe**, 39, widower, war leader of Shishibes Lake, Bear Clan.
**Senisqua**, 15, his daughter.
**Shkote**, 8, his son.
**Hannibal**, 13, Kshiwe's adopted black son.
**Nanokas** and **Mishomes**, Kshiwe's companion-wife and infant son
**Kmonokwe**, 42, a Midewiwin shaman: a religious leader and healer.
**Menomni**, 34, the village Okama (leader) of the Shishibes Lake community.
**Mukos**, 15, a hunter.
**Ashkum, Maukekose**, village elders.

<u>Among the Quakers</u> – The **Babcock** Family

**Henry** and **Margaret** Babcock – the parents, 52 and 49 years of age.
**Patience**, elder daughter, 19.
**Hopestill**, elder son, 17.
**Dinah** and **Nathan**, 14 and 12.


# Place Names

<u>In 1812/Today:</u>
Black Rock/Buffalo, New York State
Brownstown/Gibraltar, Michigan
Maguaga/Trenton, Michigan
Niagara/Niagara on the Lake, Ontario
Oxford/Woodstock, Ontario
Raisin River/Monroe, Michigan
Sandwich/Windsor, Ontario
York/Toronto, Ontario

# Translation of First Nation Names/Terms

Haudenosaunee – Longhouse People, Six Nations, Iroquois
Kmonokwe – Rain Woman
Kshiwe – Buffalo Bull, the male buffalo that leads the herd
Main Poche – (French) Withered Hand
Maxinkuckee Lake – Big Boulder Lake
Midewiwin – Neshnabek/Three Fires healer and religious leader
Menomni – Rice Gatherer
Mishomes – Grandfather
Mukos – Young Beaver
Neshnabek – the Potawatomi People
Nanokas - Hummingbird
Okama - leader
Senisqua – Bright Shining Pebbles (Woman)
Sheyoshke – Bird Flying Fast
Shishibes Lake – Little Duck Lake
Shkote – Fire
Tenskwatawa – The Open Door

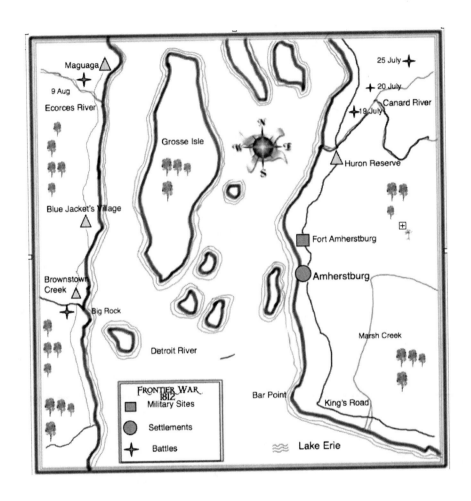

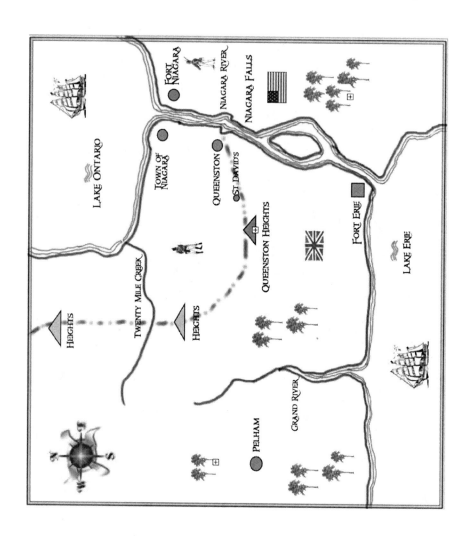

# Prologue

## Thursday, September 4, 1806

Janie Benjamin strolled happily along King Street, Niagara Town. In years past, her father drove the wagon home from the schoolmaster's door, but now at seventeen she thought it more grown-up to walk. Besides, dark-haired Alexander Lockwood was escorting her. That wasn't how Alexander would describe what he did; no, he'd just say it was more convenient to stable his horse at the Benjamin's, and then walk to school and back with Janie. Alexander carried their books as the sun slanted down toward five o'clock.

The plank sidewalk along King ended at Gage, but there were still three more blocks to the John Street corner. The last finger on Janie's left hand held the smallest finger on Alexander's right as they stepped down onto the narrow, grass-lined path. Neighbours might sniff disapprovingly at public displays of affection, but only the most sharp-eyed villager would notice that the black school girl and her white companion were holding hands. As they came to a puddle, Alexander and Janie each stepped wide but held on, one to the other: their hands linked over the water. Alexander smiled as they nudged closer.

"You'll come out early, then, on Sunday?" he asked.

"About ten, but you mustn't plague me when I get there. Your mother and Miriam and I will have lots to do."

"Maybe I can plague you after dinner," Alexander whispered.

"Really! What a pestiferous nuisance you are, Alexander Lockwood."

The lot at Centre Street was double length, two acres of soaring oaks and maples where children imagined themselves deep in Indian country. A black squirrel scolded from high above.

1

# The Land Between Flowing Waters

"We could cut through here," Alexander suggested. He bumped gently against Janie's hip to guide her onto the woodlot path.

"Not today, Alex," she decided quickly.

"But it's such a beautiful woods," he teased.

When Alexander said that something was beautiful, Janie heard a special message. She remembered the spring when they were both thirteen, on a bright morning, sitting in this very wood among white and red trilliums, reading from a history of British monarchs. As they sat face to face, their knees almost touching, she would read a paragraph aloud and then pass the book to Alexander to scan the next. After reading one passage, Janie looked up to find him staring at her budding breasts. Through the winter, woollen sweaters and jackets had concealed what Alexander now found so fascinating.

"You're worse than Jeremy Roberts," Janie had scolded. She crossed her arms to conceal the objects of his attention.

"You'll be such a beautiful woman, just like your mother," Alexander declared.

Janie brought up her arm for a roundhouse punch, aiming to bloody the miscreant's nose for the third or fourth time in their young lives. But instead of leaning back to dodge, Alexander rocked in closer. His lips brushed her cheek as her arm swung behind his head. For half an instant Janie considered what he'd said, and then she turned to kiss him. Alexander had leaned to her lips, even as her long, slim black fingers settled upon his shoulder.

After a time, Alexander stood. Then he reached down with both hands to lift her up.

Janie remembered how at thirteen she had loomed over him; now Alexander could kiss her brow, and often did, without tilting his head.


"Afternoon, children."

Janie's father lounged on the front porch swing reading the *Upper Canada Gazette*.

"Father!"

"All right then, how about...Hello, Mr. Lockwood? Hello, Miss Benjamin."

"Oh, Papa!" Janie groaned as she stomped inside.

# Ken Leland

Alexander called out, but when she didn't return he balanced her schoolbooks on the porch rail and sat on the swing beside Mr. Benjamin.

"Dad asks you all to come to Sunday dinner. Ruth's bringing her new baby."

"And what does your Mother say?" Mr. Benjamin asked with a laugh.

"Mom hopes Janie will come by early to help cook."

"Tell your folks we'll be there about noon. Did you ask Janie?"

"Yes. She'll come."

"That's fine then, Alex."

The Benjamin and Lockwood families had been fast friends since fleeing the American Revolution, a quarter century ago.

Alexander leaned forward to peer past Mr. Benjamin, hoping Janie might stop pouting long enough to say goodbye. Then he sighed and slumped back against the swing.

"Alex, your horse is in the barn."

"Yes, I know, Mr. Benjamin."

"I mean, it's time to go home now."

"Oh. Yes, Sir."

Alexander stood just as Mrs. Benjamin emerged in a long, flour-dusted apron.

"We'll see you Sunday, Alex," Sarah Benjamin said. Then she reached out to pat his shoulder as he said goodbye.

\*\*\*\*\*

On Sunday morning, Alexander watched for Janie from his front porch. Across the lane, just beyond the milking barn, was the apple orchard where he and his father had spent the last three days propping up fruit-heavy branches. The pear and peach harvest were long finished, but the apples still had a few weeks to run. Alexander's older sister, Ruth, carrying her week-old daughter, sat on the porch lounge and draped a shawl over her bosom.

"What do you think of your niece?" Captain William Mayne asked Alexander.

"Hard to believe she'll be like those two someday," Alexander said nodding toward his two young nephews romping in the barnyard.

Uncle Will agreed. "She's sweet, but awfully small. I have to tickle her to keep her awake."

3

# The Land Between Flowing Waters

"Will," Ruth said, as she opened her dress beneath the shawl. "Duty calls."

Alexander watched as Uncle Will rubbed the sole of one tiny foot.

*****

Eight years earlier, in the fall of 1794, Ruth had decided she must take pity upon the utterly smitten Captain William Mayne. She was a farm girl with straw-blonde hair, who danced like an angel at Niagara's subscription balls. In her mother's opinion, Ruth did not possess a serious mind. But the death of the family's older son changed the Lockwoods in many ways. He had died fighting, with the Indian Nations, against a Yankee army at Fallen Timbers. The parents, Lois and Asa, were devastated, and younger sister Miriam fell into a year-long depression. Ruth herself realised the obvious truth; she loved a soldier, and it was cruel to deny him any longer. Shortly after the terrible news, she announced they would marry as soon as possible – that she'd not chance losing Captain Mayne without first giving him a son. Lois was amazed at how quickly her daughter had matured, and overrode any qualms her husband Asa harboured about the marriage.

In their grief the family tended to overlook its youngest, Alexander, but Captain Mayne saw that Alexander was forlorn. It was Mayne who filled the sudden gap in the boy's life. Together, they tramped the ramparts of Fort George. It was Mayne who brought home a regimental drum on which Alexander practised all through one winter, and a bugle the following spring. Asa found the well-remembered drumming barely tolerable, but he could not abide the strangled bugling. Asa banished his son and the bugle to the attic, then quickly to the barn, where the livestock were panic-stricken, and then finally to the root-cellar beneath the summer kitchen, with the heavy plank door shut tight.

Mayne, now Uncle Will, insisted that education was the stuff from which military officers were made. For indeed, at an early point, Alexander decided he would be a soldier – like his father, like Uncle Will, like his vanished big brother.

"But your brother wasn't a soldier," Janie said gently one day when they were small. "My daddy says he was a fur trader, and that he lived with the Nations."

Janie was right, he realised. The lives of Uncle Will and Alexander's deceased brother had mixed together in his mind. But as a child he had told Janie indignantly, "Momma says he fought to protect his friends. That's what a soldier does! That's what I'm going to do!"

*****

That Sunday afternoon, Ruth and Captain Mayne seemed to have forgotten that seventeen-year-old Alexander stood beside the open farmhouse door.

"That's all she'll take," Ruth said as she rearranged her dress and patted her infant daughter on the back. "How in the world can we tell Mother we'll be leaving soon?"

"I have to go home, Ruth," Mayne said. "Napoleon will surely invade England in the spring."

"This is home, William. And the fleet will never let him across the Channel."

"You and the children could stay..."

"No!"

Mayne leaned closer to brush a finger across his daughter's cheek. The tiny creature blew milky bubbles, and then relaxed into sleep on Ruth's shoulder.

"You're right, darling," Mayne said. "How could I ever leave you here?"

"Indeed. So we'll all stay."

Her husband shook his head sadly. "Ruth, you agreed when I asked for the transfer. I can't hide in this Upper Canada backwater any longer."

Ruth stood, only to see Alexander standing open-mouthed at the door. Fixing her younger brother with a steadfast gaze, Ruth approached him to balance her sleeping daughter along Alexander's arm. Nestling the little one's feet in his left hand, she drew his right hand securely onto the baby's chest. "A useful skill even for a soldier," she declared, "but I'll be the one to tell Mother about leaving, when the time comes."

A few minutes later, Janie drove a gig up the farm lane. She wore a full-length apron over a fine, cream-coloured, linen dress that she and Miriam had sewn, and as she stepped down she untied her white bonnet. Her black, tightly woven hair glistened in the morning sunshine. With a glowing smile, she embraced Mrs. Lockwood who came from the summer kitchen.

"My folks won't be along for a while, Mrs. Lockwood. Matthew's still asleep."

"Let your brother sleep," she laughed. "Miriam's only just got the roast in the oven. You and I still have to bake a couple of pies, pick the beans and clean the sweet corn."

Janie darted over to kiss the baby in Alexander's arms. With a bright smile and a meaningful glance, she then pecked Alexander's cheek before rushing after Mrs. Lockwood.

"And don't you take that as encouragement, young man," Mrs. Lockwood admonished her son. "We've all got too much to do this morning for any foolishness."

As Alexander guided Janie's horse to the barn, the lowing of impatient milk-cows reminded him that his mother was right.

# Ken Leland

## The Departure
### Monday, October 27, 1806

"We'll leave in a fortnight. It's the last ship before winter," Captain Mayne said as he finished his announcement to the Lockwood family in the front parlour.

In tears, Miriam retreated to the second floor sewing room. Asa gathered his grandsons for a walk along the river, while Ruth and her mother wept in each other's arms in the winter kitchen. Mayne and Alexander sat abandoned by the hearth.

"That went down well," Mayne said as he filled his pipe.

"About as expected," Alexander allowed.

"Before we leave, Alex, I'd do something for you – if you wish it."

Alexander leaned forward in the armchair at Uncle Will's words.

"You remember I mentioned the Canadian Fencibles? Well...they're recruiting."

"That's the British regiment for service in the Canadas?" Alexander asked.

"That's it. The muster is in Trois Rivieres. Ruth and I will be passing through on our way to Quebec City."

"Please take me, Uncle Will. You taught me the drills and all the signals. I've always wanted to be a soldier."

"A soldier, yes – but I was thinking you might purchase an ensign's commission."

"How much would that cost?"

"Four hundred pounds."

"Uncle Will! I don't have it. I don't have four pounds. Even if Father sold the farm...but where would they live if he did that? I'll join as a private."

"You have a reasonable education, Alex. You'd be wasted in the ranks."

"But then...how?"

"Ruth and I will be selling our property here in Niagara. There will be enough and a little more."

Alexander grasped Uncle Will's hand in gratitude.

"But maybe we should wait until tomorrow to break this news to your parents."

# The Land Between Flowing Waters

*****

Janie and Alexander sat on the dusty sleigh bench in the Benjamin stable.

"You're leaving in three days?" Janie was furious, wounded.

"Uncle Will wouldn't take me to Trois Rivieres without Father's permission. I've only just talked him round."

"And me! Why tell me so late?" Tears streamed down her face.

"I've come to ask you to wait."

"Wait? My God, Alex, there's no need to wait! We love each other. All you have to do is ask Papa."

"Janie, we can't marry right now; an ensign can't support a wife. But in a year or two..."

"Alex, look at me!" Janie shouted. "Think of what you're saying! A black woman can't be an officer's wife."

On Monday, November 10, HMS *Toronto* set sail from Niagara Town with Alexander Lockwood aboard.

# Chapter One
# Prophetstown

**Five Years Later**
**Saturday, November 2, 1811**
**Kshiwe**

Kshiwe woke at dawn. Threads of smoke rose slowly from the hearth to disappear into the sliver of grey light atop the lodge. Kshiwe's chest brushed against his companion's back as he rose onto one elbow. He saw their baby boy fussing in fevered sleep just beyond Nanokas' outstretched arm. Their fifteen-year-old daughter lay in a bed of furs beside the south wall, and their eight-year-old son slept quietly by the western door.

Nanokas began to cough. Kshiwe pulled the blankets higher over her shoulder, and spooned himself against her back and legs. His right palm circled between her breasts to quiet the spasms. The baby stirred, but did not wake.

Nanokas was exhausted. Kshiwe remembered her waking at least three times in the night to nurse and comfort tiny Mishomes, and twice more their daughter hastened to cradle her infant brother, offering the tip of her finger to suck. The little one was very sick. He could keep almost nothing of the milk his mother offered, and now Nanokas seemed to be falling ill as well. We need a Midewiwin, Kshiwe thought, but the traveling healers seem fewer every year.

Kshiwe gently rubbed his companion's throat and chest until her coughing began to subside. In her sleep she leaned back fondly as he kissed her ear and bare shoulder. He felt himself begin to stiffen against her hip, but after a moment he rolled away

9

carefully. Kshiwe tucked the blankets close around her, and then rose from their bed. Nanokas would appreciate sleep more than love-making after such a night. Kshiwe dressed, then bundled their youngest warmly in rabbit fur. Carrying the infant in the crook of his left arm, he opened the eastern door to the cool autumn morning.

Early fog swirled over the lake, and the mist drifted ashore to rise a short way uphill. The oak branches, now clothed in curled brown leaves, floated high above the fog. Kshiwe lifted the bit of fur from his son's face, now so pale, so pinched and wrinkled as if from long starvation. He walked the hundred paces up through the forest to the plateau above the lake. Here the late-rising sun struggled to burn through clouds, and no mist covered the village pasture. The brightening fields extended out to the east and west, empty now after harvest.

Kshiwe sat cross-legged in deep yellow grass and propped Mishomes inside one knee so that the son might watch his father. With closed eyes and bowed head, Kshiwe quieted his mind and heart. As always, he prayed thanks to the Master of Life that his family had lived to see another morning. There was much to be thankful for, even in these times of sickness and terror.

Fleeting pools of sunlight rolled across the fields, warming Kshiwe's face, and then moved on to leave cool shadows. When he opened his eyes, Mishomes was awake. His son did not cry, only watched intently.

"Mishomes – Grandfather," he said to the infant, "I've missed you for so very long. I don't know if this tiny form that Nanokas and I have made can endure, but I am so very glad you have returned, if only for a little while."

The baby boy pushed weakly with his legs, straining from side to side as if he might wail in anguish – but then, as Kshiwe began to sing a Morning Song, Mishomes settled back against his father's knee to listen.

Kshiwe carried his son through the forest that skirted the village but did not visit any other lodges. With the coming of sickness, the People had scattered a little way apart. Kshiwe took the infant from place to place, naming for him each kind of tree, each kind of berry bush, and even his favourite horses in the village paddock. For a time Mishomes was diverted, but then he began to sob from hunger. Senisqua, Kshiwe's daughter, followed the sounds of the baby's howls.

"Mother is awake now," Senisqua said to her father. "She pretends to be angry you left with Mishomes."

Senisqua took the infant and tucked the finger she had coated in maple syrup into his mouth. The baby quieted.

"Thank you," she said leaning her forehead against Kshiwe's shoulder. "Thank you from both of us."

Fishing was always poor from Turkey Moon until the ice hardened, but even so Kshiwe paddled to the north side of the small lake. At a likely spot, he wedged the canoe into a stand of cattails.

Shishibes Lake was long and narrow; through shallows choked with weeds, it was part of a chain of sparkling lakes. As he fished, he watched the tree-lined slope where his lodge stood. His heart sank as Mishomes' thin, tortured cries floated across the water. A little later he saw Senisqua pacing with crossed arms along the path above the lodge, and then, as if in response to Nanokas' unheard call, Senisqua sprinted back inside as her baby brother went quiet. Fearing the worst, Kshiwe took up his paddle to return.

At that moment he heard the warning yips of a messenger rider. The rider was painted in red and black, and he whipped his horse along the trail between the lakes. He splashed down into the shallows and then charged up the northern slope.

From across the lake he heard Shkote, his eight-year-old son, calling "Father!" As he paddled, Kshiwe's face streamed with tears. *Surely*, he thought, *Mishomes has left us*. As he neared shore, Shkote called again.

"Father, a tobacco rider has come. The People are gathering at Okama Menomni's lodge."

*****

The young messenger waited with ill-concealed impatience. The villagers were scattered and slow in gathering. Each time he began to speak, Okama Menomni held up his hand and said, "We must wait for the rest." The messenger fingered a red-painted tobacco leaf, folded until it fit into the palm of his hand. He showed it to each Neshnabe hunter, as the villagers arrived in twos and threes. They came from lodges and cabins along the chain of lakes, and from the banks of the Yellow River some hundreds of paces to the south. At the council fire, Kshiwe took his seat to

# The Land Between Flowing Waters

Menomni's right. Village Speaker arrived to sit on Menomni's left. As elders joined the inner circle, young men found a place outside the ring, then women and children farther out still. Women's Okama sat between Kshiwe and Menomni; Youth Leader found a place just behind the ring of elders. Maukekose and Ashkum, past leaders of their own villages, took places of honour beside Kshiwe.

When Calumet-Carrier formally entered the circle, the tobacco rider stood and shouted, "The Prophet calls everyone who is a man to war! Take up the scalping knife! Mount your horses and follow me to kill the Long Knives!"

The elders were clearly appalled at such an interruption. Ashkum and Maukekose hid smiles behind their hands. Kshiwe glanced toward Village Speaker, who simply shook his head and stared at the ground. Menomni and Women's Okama sat stone-faced. One of the elders shouted, "Young man, who is this Prophet you speak of? The Black Robes' Christer? Main Poche? Handsome Lake? Who?"

Youth Leader stood. "Who are you, Messenger? Why should we follow you anywhere?"

"Better you begin again," Women's Okama directed.

Messenger stomped his foot in frustration. Clearly these villagers were primitives. "I am Swago of the Wolf Clan. My message is from The Shawnee Prophet, Tenskwatawa. The white chief Harrison leads a thousand Long Knives to attack the Prophet's town on the Wabash River. There is great danger! Please come quickly to help fight them off."

"That is a little better," Village Speaker pronounced, "but not much." He motioned for Calumet-Carrier to come forward to open the council. "We have no Midewiwin with us, so Calumet-Carrier will lead us in opening prayers."

As the afternoon wore on, many elders spoke in favour of aiding The Prophet. "We are Bear Clan, defenders of the People," one old man avowed. "How can we not go to the aid of Tenskwatawa?"

"Perhaps, dear Brother, it is just because we are Bear Clan. We are sworn to protect the Neshnabek, not the Shawnee," another venerable hunter replied.

"Red is red," rejoined another.

"I will follow Kshiwe as War Leader," Okama Menomni announced.

The old okamas, Ashkum and Maukekose, were quick to agree. There was a general murmur of approval from many of the senior Neshnabe men. The Grandmothers nodded too.

"I will lead if any will follow," Kshiwe agreed. He turned to Youth Leader. "If there are young men who have never gone to war, send them to me before morning. I will tell them what is expected if they wish to join."

## Wednesday, November 6, 1811
## The Wagoner

Tom's freight wagon was heavily laden with officers' travel beds, tables, and camp chairs, and there were two live steers hitched to the back gate. As he loosed the brake, ropes wrenched the animals' necks, pulling them down the creek bank after the Conestoga wagon. Then, in midstream, Tom shouted and whipped the horses up the opposite slope. A dozen commissary wagons had already churned the water to a black, muddy stew. Tom was glad he was near the front of the baggage train; teamsters behind would find it harder and harder to cross. It was dangerous for Tom, a slave clamped in leg irons, to jump down if the wagon was mired in a bog.

One of the cattle bawled as Tom slowed the horses to a walking pace. He glanced back to check for a broken leg. A maimed steer would be steak for supper.

Then he looked back again, at the left rear wheel.

The baggage train wound between oaks too massive to fell. Iron-rimmed, shoulder-high wheels cut into the blanket of brown leaves. Dry branches as thick as Tom's wrist snapped like rifle shots beneath the grinding wheels. Far out to the left, through the bare autumn trees, was a long line of blue-coated regulars. Close in, dragoons guarded the supply column and to the right, toward the river, were companies of the Indiana Territorial Militia in brown homespun jackets and fur caps – a thousand soldiers, more or less. A man, even one with Tom's well-deserved reputation as a runner, would find it hard to disappear in the midst of such an army on this bright November afternoon.

The army had marched for over a month, stopping only once to build a redoubt of wooden blockhouses. Planning for disaster, Territorial Governor William Henry Harrison thought, was prudent when fighting Indians – particularly when surprising the

# The Land Between Flowing Waters

Indians was not possible. As they trekked north from Vincennes, Redskin spies glided furtively through the forest; and then, after his men forded the Wabash, they were shadowed by riders from prairie hilltops.

With Tecumseh away, fomenting trouble elsewhere, Governor Harrison was determined to seize this opportunity to clear away a batch of ungovernable savages. Watching their destruction approach slowly would make the heathens anxious, and anxiety would lead to mistakes by Tecumseh's younger brother, Tenskwatawa, The Prophet. The Prophet was a reformed drunkard without military experience. Harrison thought Tecumseh's absence could hardly be more propitious.

Harrison, with aides and gentlemen volunteers, rode at the head of the central column, just in front of the artillery and supply train. After an hour or two, the army emerged onto an expanse of prairie. There, on a rise at the northern horizon, was the usual cluster of mounted savages. But this time, one barbarian carried a towel-sized white cloth tied to a lance. At a little distance were several bare-chested youths with a lengthy string of ponies.

"Stop here," Harrison ordered. Bugles sang out and the three columns lurched to a halt. "Lieutenant Fowler, take a sergeant and go find out what those bastards want."

Harrison dismounted as regular army and militia officers clustered around the tall, finely-tailored Governor. They watched as Lt. Fowler rode out at a walking pace to parley.

"Bring up the furniture," Harrison ordered. "It looks like we'll be here for a while."

Tom carried camp chairs in each arm as he limped with iron-measured strides. All around, orderlies and servants scurried to lay campfires, raise a canvas pavilion against the sun, close crop the prairie grass, and position a writing table between American and regimental flags. Colonels, majors, and captains, with swords dangling, gathered beneath the canvas. They formed an intimidating array behind the Governor's chair. Lt. Fowler rode in slowly with half a dozen Redskins in tow, then more slowly still, until Fowler could see that all was ready at the Governor's tent.

Harrison stepped forward to drape his right hand over a finely crafted, plush chair. His left fist gripped his sword pommel as he stood stiffly erect. "Stand over there, Hannibal," Harrison said, nodding to a young black servant of about thirteen years. The youngster balanced a water pitcher and a single crystal drinking-glass on a silver tray. Gingerly the boy moved through the freshly mown grass to a spot beside the writing table. Tom, the wagoner, watched his son from behind the line of officers.

"Governor Harrison," Lt. Fowler said, "This Shawnee Chief is called White Horse. He says he speaks for Tenskwatawa."

Harrison noticed that The Prophet's ambassador was dressed as if white men had never touched North America. In place of the usual flowing cloth shirt and colourful head-wrap, he wore a buckskin vest over a bare, heavily tattooed chest. His head was shaved to a scalp-lock to which a feather was tied with a leather throng. Even his tomahawk was of stone instead of fur-trader's iron. Clearly this man was a disciple.

"Tenskwatawa sends greeting to Governor Harrison," the translator began for White Horse. "Though you come with an army at your back, we offer you the hand of friendship and assure you..."

"Enough of that," Harrison growled as he sat down. The line of officers behind him took their seats as well, leaving White Horse standing alone, a petitioner. "I have told every delegation from the Shawnee charlatan the same thing, but I will say it one last time. We want the murderers of the Illinois settlers, and the horses they stole. The Winnebago, the Kickapoo, and all strangers to this Territory must leave Prophetstown and return to their own villages. Turn the marauders over to us, tell the strangers to go home, and we will leave you in peace. We have come to remind you that murder has a price."

The Prophet's ambassador clenched his teeth but only pointed toward the ponies held by a handful of young Shawnee men. "Here are twenty horses. Is that enough?"

Harrison ordered Lt. Fowler to inspect the herd, and then waved toward the young slave to bring him water. Harrison sprawled back in the chair, swirling his drink in the sparkling glass. He said nothing, nor did he look at White Horse.

"No brands," Lt. Fowler reported.

"So, these are not the horses that were stolen," Harrison concluded. "But perhaps those men are the murders, eh?" he said, pointing to the Shawnee drovers. White Horse began to reply, but Harrison cut him off.

"No?" Harrison continued. "Always no. Perhaps you think I'm a fool."

"Main Poche led the raiders who killed the settlers," White Horse insisted. "Main Poche is not of our People. He is not here, nor are his warriors. He lives far to the north, in the Illinois country."

"Stories for children," Harrison spat. "Well, sometimes I discipline my children. Tomorrow the discipline will begin."

"Wait. Tomorrow, Tenskwatawa will come to speak to you, Governor Harrison."

"Be sure that he does. And be sure he brings the murdering cowards and the stolen horses. My patience is at an end."

*****

As Tom carried camp chairs back to the wagon, the young servant Hannibal hurried after him.

"Daddy," Hannibal said, "I ain't seen you for three days."

"At night, now, they chain me to the wagon."

"I'll come see you."

"No, I got an idea for tonight. You stay clear."

"Daddy, if you run again, they'll whip you."

"Maybe I can get us some help."

"Oh, Daddy. Who's goin' to help us way out here?"

*****

Rain clouds darkened the early autumn evening. Army guides found a wooded ten-acre plateau, surrounded on three sides by low prairie and a modest creek along the western edge. Harrison directed the artillery and baggage train into the woodlot's centre. As the troops lit bonfires, servants emptied the wagons of tents and furniture. The foot-soldiers threw their backpacks into the wagons and then arranged themselves along the perimeter in a shortened, rectangular box. With Prophetstown less than two miles away, the troops prepared to sleep, fully-dressed, beside their weapons on firing lines. As thunder rumbled in the distance, Harrison did not order that trees be felled to form barricades. The inferior axes the civilian commissioners provided had broken daily since they left Vincennes, and there were hardly any left. The men would be uncomfortable enough in what promised to be a cold, wet evening without blistering their hands uselessly.

# Ken Leland

Water dripped from the pavilion's edge as Hannibal circled Harrison's crowded supper table. The boy poured Madeira as the officers tucked into a supper of roast prairie chicken.

"A happy change from pork and steak," a Kentucky major laughed.

"Catfish last week was a treat," said the Fourth Regiment's Commander. A score of officers fell to as the courtly Virginian, Governor William Henry Harrison, presided.

Later, over cigars, there came a break in the conviviality. The newly joined commander of mounted riflemen remarked, "Your Excellency, Chief White Horse is probably right about Main Poche leading the killers."

"Oh, almost surely he is," Harrison agreed.

An awkward silence descended.

The young commander marshalled his courage. "What then, Sir, do you expect The Prophet to say tomorrow?"

"What will he say? Oh, my dear Sir, it hardly matters."

Barks of laughter sprang from both sides of the supper table.

Harrison chuckled. "Commander, you don't imagine we've gathered all these men, came all this way, just to go home again?"

"Kill the bloody bastards!" was the drunken call from the table's end.

"Oh, yes indeed, we most certainly will," Harrison smiled.

Hannibal leaned in to refresh the Governor's coffee. Thunder crashed like a man's full-throated roar. Hannibal stared out through the torrent, toward the wagon park.

"Damnation, boy! Watch what you're doing!" Harrison shouted. Hannibal ran for a towel to sop the stained table cloth.

Earlier that evening, as Tom drove into the bivouac, another teamster cursed him when he whipped his team toward a particularly level patch of ground. The Quartermaster Sergeant slapped a crop against his blue striped trousers. "What you think you're doin'? Get back in line!"

"These are the Governor's things, Mr. Sergeant. He'll want 'em directly."

When the Quartermaster turned away, Tom scanned the ground for flat rocks. Moving as fast as the shackles allowed, he stopped the Conestoga's wheels with square wooden blocks, then unhitched the team and led them to the horse-lines. Rain began to fall as he emptied the wagon of chairs, tables and straw-padded boxes of Madeira. He dared not speak to Hannibal as he carried the supplies into Harrison's tent.

An hour later, the Quartermaster returned with an iron lock and a short length of chain.

"Too wet to run tonight, Tom," he said. "All them Injuns out there – those nappy curls would make a helluva scalp for somebody."

"Evenin', Sir," was all Tom said from his dry spot beneath the wagon. The Quartermaster reached down as if to chain his leg irons to the left rear wheel.

"Please, Sir," Tom asked in a panic. "Please do like last night and use the axle. That way I'll be drier."

"Aaaah," the Quartermaster groaned as he crouched lower to reach the wooden pole that ran between the two back wheels. "You're just a goddamned nuisance. Maybe I'll feed you to the Redskins. Bet they'd like black meat for a change." He draped the chain over the axle and locked Tom's leg-irons into the loop. Then he groaned again as he rolled out from beneath the wagon, back into the pouring rain.

*Injuns don't eat people*, Tom thought. *Do they?* Then he realised he would be counting on them for a lot more than that.

Later, the Quartermaster brought Tom a plate of pork and beans, floating in rainwater. After supper, the army's soldiers sought shelter beneath canvas tarps at the firing lines, leaving the baggage park unguarded in the storm. The ground under the wagon was still mostly dry as Tom pretended to sleep. In the early evening, thunder began to crash and Tom glanced all around. He stretched to grab the flat stone wedged behind the right front wheel, and then he crawled over to retrieve the second rock. The back wheels were stopped by solid wooden blocks. Tom slid his shackles to the very end of the axle beside the rear left wheel. Then he positioned the stones and one wooden slab, atop them, beneath the middle of the axle. He braced his back awkwardly to lift the mostly empty wagon bed, just enough to slide the second wooden block onto the stack. Now the wheel was a finger's width off the ground, supported by the blocks. Tom bent double to reach around it, out into the rain to grasp the metal ring holding the wheel's hub to the axle.

Last night, after being twisted with all his strength, the ring had turned a fraction of an inch. In desperation, Tom almost loosened the wheel entirely before realising that the unsupported wagon would crash onto his legs if the wheel fell free. Tonight Tom was prepared. The wagon bed stood supported on level ground. All he needed was to unscrew the ring, push off the wheel, and slide the chain from the axle. Tom twisted the ring, but his right hand slipped on the rain-slick metal. He thrust his hand into the drier soil beneath the wagon and tried again. This time the whole wheel rotated. Tom gripped a spoke with his left hand, fearful now, that he might roll the wagon off the supporting blocks. Again he twisted with all his might, grit tearing his palm on the ring. Nothing. With a gasp, Tom collapsed back onto the sodden ground. Rain washed his face as lightning streaked overhead. *My son will die a slave if I can't do this*, Tom thought. He breathed deeply, and again dug his hand into the dirt. *Please, Lord. Help me.*

The muscles in Tom's right arm strained to bursting. He screamed as thunder rolled through the glen.

The ring moved.

The wheel was loose now. Tom waited for the next deafening flash and then pushed the wheel free. It fell unnoticed in the returning darkness. Tom slipped the chain from the axle and began to crawl through the camp toward the picket line.

*****

Near midnight, the last rain clouds scudded across the waning moon. Village Speaker half rose from a crouch.

"Look there, Kshiwe. Don't you see it? Out by the Long Knife camp."

A dozen Shishibes Lake warriors waited soundlessly behind Speaker.

"There's nothing there," War Leader Kshiwe objected.

"No. Speaker is right," Okama Menomni said. "See! It just fell down."

"It did that before. Now it's up again." Speaker was standing now and pointing. "It's a man coming this way."

"Do you see him?" Kshiwe turned to ask Youth Leader, who was several paces back. Youth Leader just shook his head. Now the five boys with him were bobbing up and down like prairie dogs.

"Yes, there!" Mukos, the youngest boy, said, pointing out into the patches of moonlight.

# The Land Between Flowing Waters

Kshiwe looked again. Finally he noticed movement through the tall grass.

"Youth Leader, take your warriors and capture him. Don't kill unless you have to."

Youth Leader spoke quietly, and the boys spread out in an arc, just as they had practised, leaping forward like wolves in pursuit of a deer.

Kshiwe watched with concern. The Grandmothers would blame him if he failed to bring home even one of their precious youngsters, but if the youths wished to be warriors he could not protect them forever.


"Look! Look! He's black," said the youngest warrior, Mukos. "Feel his hair. What a funny scalp!"

Kshiwe peered at the large man the boys held tightly by both arms. The prisoner did not call out or thrash about in fear. In a hush, he kept repeating words Kshiwe didn't understand. In the mist shrouded moonlight, he did look black.

"He's covered in war paint," Kshiwe speculated.

"But it doesn't come off!" another Neshnabe youngster said, rubbing the prisoner's face.

"Everyone, back to Prophetstown. Hurry."

Village Speaker led off, with the veterans following swiftly in line. Kshiwe motioned impatiently for the youths to proceed, but the prisoner fell almost immediately.

*We'll need a smith's tools*, Kshiwe thought, as he hoisted the prisoner onto his back. "Watch if he tries to strangle me," War Leader Kshiwe admonished the boys, and he began the long jog back to the Wabash village.


Kshiwe puffed and blew when finally he dropped the prisoner onto his own feet, just outside the log barricades surrounding Prophetstown. The man patted Kshiwe's shoulder and spoke in tones that might have been gratitude. Mukos and the other youngsters led the prisoner through the maze gate, and along the path leading to the Council Lodge.

Speaker fell into step beside Kshiwe as they passed through the crowded, anxious town. "He must be what settlers call a slave."

"You don't make much of a horse," Menomni teased as they passed Tenskwatawa's medicine lodge.

# Ken Leland

The chains..." Kshiwe mumbled in exhaustion.

"Will be broken by the time we get you to the Council Lodge, old man," Speaker promised.

The Lodge was almost empty when the Neshnabe warriors arrived. The building was nearly fifty paces long; its roof rose to three times a man's height and was supported by many pillars. In the torchlight the boys now squatted in a half-circle, watching as the prisoner spread his feet as far apart as the manacles would allow. Ringing metallic blows fell until the chains parted.

"Ho!" the young men exclaimed at the smith's skill, and speculated on how many furs it would take to trade for a hammer and chisels.

The prisoner, his ankles bleeding and raw, staggered to his feet and approached Kshiwe. He pointed out into the night, then to himself, then – surprisingly – to Mukos, the smallest of the warriors, and then to himself again, all the while gibbering in the settlers' tongue. Then he knelt below a torch and patted the soil smooth. He punched four holes in the dirt to make a box, then two more holes in a line flowing out to the right, and then a seventh mark above the opposite side of the box. He pointed to the seventh mark, and said a word again and again. Kshiwe looked up to the roof.

"Does he mean the sky?" Kshiwe asked the others.

"He's drawn the Great Bear," Village Speaker suggested.

"Can he mean north?" Okama Menomni puzzled. Then, "I'll go find someone who will understand him."

An hour later, the Lodge was crowded with leaders from half a dozen Nations. The Shawnee chief, White Horse, struggled to keep the Council in order, but arguments and objections flew from the hundreds of warriors surrounding Kshiwe's small band of Neshnabek. Tenskwatawa sat watching from the corner as turmoil swirled. Finally, the one-eyed prophet of the Shawnee stood in his place outside the ring of warriors and surveyed the room.

"Brothers, we are agreed. If we do nothing, the Long Knives will attack the town tomorrow. The Master of Life cannot give us victory against cannons. Our companions and children will be no more. What then are our choices?"

"Run," a Winnebago chief said in disgust. "Or fight tonight!"

"Yes. This is the message the Master of Life sends," The Prophet agreed. "We must attack tonight."

21

White Horse rose again in the torchlight. "This man is a slave of the Long Knife chief," he said pointing to Tom. "That is a condition to which Harrison would lead us all, my Brothers."

The silence into which this statement fell did not indicate disagreement.

"I am thinking he can lead us to Harrison's tent. If the Long Knife chief dies in his bed, his warriors will be lost."

"I will kill Harrison," a Kickapoo warrior volunteered, "if the black one will show me the right tent."

"And why would he do that?" a Wyandot war-chief asked.

"He will do that," Tenskwatawa replied, "because you will free his son. Then they can both go north to King's Country, or wherever they wish. But Harrison is a dangerous man."

"I didn't suppose I would return from the Long Knife camp," was the Kickapoo's quiet reply.

"Then someone else must try to steal the boy," suggested White Horse. "A few moments after these men slip into the camp, all the warriors will attack. In the confusion, there is a chance of escape. With Harrison dead, victory will be easier."

"Now," Tenskwatawa asked, "who goes to help bring out the boy?"


## Thursday, November 7, 1811
## The Drinking Gourd


In the hour before dawn, Kshiwe crawled the last hundred paces across the forest floor. The settler's jacket he wore was torn and rain-soaked, and the fur cap kept sliding down over his eyes. The ground was cold. *Maybe I'm getting too old for this,* Kshiwe thought, as he lay motionless in a drift of leaves. He rested his chin on his arm to watch the picket line. He could smell the tomahawk's wet leather throng. He had traded his axe for an old fashioned, river-stone club; the rock would kill but not catch in a rib or skull. *Tenskwatawa is right – sometimes the old ways are better.*

The black man edged up even with Kshiwe's right foot. Tom was unarmed. Three times he had picked up a long butcher knife at the Council Lodge, and three times laid it down. *He thinks to carry his son away in his arms,* Kshiwe thought, *not to fight.*

# Ken Leland

Kshiwe glanced to his left. The young Kickapoo warrior crouched in the greater darkness beside a tree. He, too, wore a jacket and cap. A knife sheath hung around his neck.

Behind them was a thin line of scouts, leading five-score warriors armed with muskets and rifles. *My friends are back there too*, Kshiwe thought. *And our boys only have bows. Rifles would be better.*

Up ahead, a few soldiers were awake in the Long Knife camp. Bonfires glinted through the trees. Shafts of light winked out and reappeared just as quickly. Kshiwe watched and counted slowly. To slip between the sentries, they would have to get closer. Kshiwe signed to the warrior, then back to the man at his heels. *It's meaningless to him*, Kshiwe thought, *but at least he knows to watch me.*

Kshiwe led the way as they crept forward. From beneath a thornbush at less than a half dozen paces, Kshiwe watched as a sentry crossed from right to left. The militiaman balanced a musket on his arm as he peered out into the darkness. At the count of twenty, another guard followed. Both wore buckskin jackets and fur caps. Kshiwe watched as more guards passed. Then they began to cross from left to right, but at the same intervals.

Kshiwe pulled in a deep breath, counted, and half-rose to scurry across the line. Tom and the Kickapoo warrior were right behind. Windblown trees and brush formed a low barricade just ahead. Light from the campfires glinted from rifle barrels laid atop the logs. In the darkness, the Kickapoo turned quickly to grab Tom's left arm. Kshiwe clasped his right, and then Tom fell limp between them. Cautiously they began to drag Tom toward the barrier. Bonfires blazed in the camp's centre beside the officers' tents and wagon park. As they neared the line, a blue-coated officer stood and raised his pistol.

"Who goes there?" he snapped.

"Oh, Lordy, Mr. Officer Sir, it's just me, Tom. And these here fine gentlemen who come help me when I got lost in the woods."

Kshiwe's cap shaded his face. He hoped the Kickapoo's nerve would hold.

"They's just helping me back to my wagon, Sir." The officer was a regular; not one of the Indiana militia.

"Drunk, are you?" the officer laughed as they weaved past.

"Well...well, some do say. Some do say." The other infantrymen behind the barrier still slept undisturbed.

23

# The Land Between Flowing Waters

As he feigned drunken stumbling, Tom led the way toward Harrison's pavilion. Kshiwe kept his eyes on the path as they skirted a long horse-picket, then the artillery and wagon park. Tom guided them around an iron-rimmed wheel lying beside a tilting wagon. Up ahead, in the light of a bonfire, Kshiwe saw a large tent with a broad canvas awning. Flags hung from poles planted at the tent's corners. Two yellow-jacketed militiamen stood with muskets grounded beside the tent flap. "You take the one on the left," Kshiwe signed to the Kickapoo as they came within fifty paces.

The Quartermaster walked stiff-legged into the torchlight beside the tent. As he paused to adjust the buttons at his groin, he glanced toward the shadowy men holding Tom.

"Hey!" the Quartermaster shouted, "How'd that slave get free?"

"I just...we been..." Tom sputtered.

"Who're you?" the Quartermaster growled as he tried to see the faces of Tom's captors. The river stone club slid down Kshiwe's sleeve.

"Guards! Guards! Injuns! Injuns in the camp!"

The young Kickapoo on Kshiwe's left dashed forward, pulling his hunting knife from beneath his jacket. He dodged past the Quartermaster, toward the lowered muskets of Harrison's guards. Now Tom was yelling at the top of his lungs and sprinting forward.

"Hannibal! Hannibal!"

The Quartermaster tackled the slave, who yelled again and again. As the men rolled on the ground near the bonfire, Kshiwe swung at the Quartermaster's head. The deadly blow sailed through empty space when Tom rolled the soldier onto his back and began to pummel his eyes and nose.

Kshiwe rushed after the Kickapoo warrior, but Harrison's guards both trained their muskets on the young man with the knife and fired. The buckshot charges plowed through his jacket to tear clusters of holes – one group below his throat, the other into his ribs. He lurched forward screaming to fall onto the bayonet of the militiaman on the left.

The guard on the right swung toward Kshiwe, as the first guard grappled with the man he had impaled. Kshiwe cut loose a war whoop and charged with club raised. His strong forward swing knocked away the probing bayonet, and his backhand sweep destroyed the second guard's face.

24

# Ken Leland

The first sentry was shrieking now. He could not loosen the bayonet; perversely, his victim held the musket barrel tightly as he died impaled. Kshiwe lunged at the terrified guard but tripped over the legs of the man he had just killed. As Kshiwe hit the ground, a rumble of musket fire swept through the grey morning air, and war-cries lashed the camp. The first guard dropped his musket and fled as Kshiwe struggled to his feet.

A half sized, black-skinned figure in white pants burst through the tent flap, collided with an unbalanced Kshiwe and sent him tumbling onto the ground again. Kshiwe grabbed the boy's foot before he could join the two men, yelling and wrestling next to the bonfire. As they scrambled on the ground, the boy kicked Kshiwe in the face and tried to crawl to his father. Kshiwe seized the other foot and held on. Now there were officers with swords, and soldiers with muskets, running in from all sides. The pile on top of Tom was growing. Kshiwe lurched upright, and with an open hand smacked the panic-stricken boy sharply in the face before throwing him over his shoulder. He bent to retrieve his cap, and with the boy's body now shielding his face, Kshiwe edged through the crowd of white men rushing to defend Governor Harrison. Through the pandemonium, Kshiwe balanced his burden and headed toward the soaring war-cries.

Near Harrison's tent at the northwest corner of the bivouac, the Long Knives were being pushed back from the low barrier at the camp's edge. A few soldiers were running in terror to the presumed safety of the wagon train. A double line of regulars formed across Kshiwe's path. The first line fired a volley into the gunsmoke billowing from the trees, then knelt to reload as the second line fired over their heads. Companies of militia began to form on their flanks, extending the line. Kshiwe sidled to the south, hoping to find a break in the defense. From behind him, horses screamed as they broke loose in terror. Kshiwe dodged the stampede and then followed quickly in hopes the herd might open a gap in the Long Knife line.

Kshiwe ran almost the length of the camp with Hannibal draped over his shoulder. Then, straight ahead, there was heavy gun fire as warriors probed that side of the camp. The panic-stricken horses recoiled, closely followed by companies of dragoons and buckskin-clad Territorials running back toward the bivouac's centre. Kshiwe hid beneath an artillery limber as the Long Knives retreated, leaving Kshiwe and Hannibal outside their line. *Now,* Kshiwe thought, *all I have to worry about is getting killed by the Shawnee and Winnebago coming up from the south.*

# The Land Between Flowing Waters

The boy was stunned, or pretended to be. Kshiwe crawled out from beneath the limber. Praying furiously that the warriors would not fire at someone carrying the slave boy, Kshiwe raced back to the northwest, back toward the spot where he entered the camp. As he ran, suddenly his leg burned as if he had been stung by a hornet. He ignored the pain and raced onward. When he neared the log barrier, he crouched behind a tent. He watched as a line of Wyandot and Neshnabe warriors rushed forward to the barricade to fire a ragged volley almost into Kshiwe's face. Then they retreated into the trees to reload, before coming forward again. Hannibal was moaning now. Kshiwe shucked his settler's jacket and threw the fur cap into the weeds. Again he picked up the boy and timed the warriors' retreat. As they turned to withdraw, he raced into the gunsmoke, yelling at the top of his lungs.

"*Bozho! Bozho! Bozho!*"

As he dashed by, Okama Menomni reached out from behind a tree to spin Kshiwe into Village Speaker's arms.

"Who is still alive?" Kshiwe panted as he scanned the brush for the dozen Shishibes Lake warriors sheltering there. "Where is Youth Leader? Where are the young men?"

"They're 'guarding us from a surprise attack' out on the prairie," Speaker said. "It was the safest place we could think of. They don't even have muskets."

"Neither will we, if we keep this up," Menomni confided. "I'm almost out of gunpowder."

"I'm going back for Tom," Kshiwe said, "and for the Kickapoo lad. He's dead, but we can't leave his body there."

"What will you do with this one?" Speaker asked as he knelt over the slave boy.

A trembling cry sounded from the Wyandot war chief in charge of that part of the line.

"We'll be back in a moment," Menomni said, as he rose to head for the firing line. "Why don't you take him out to the prairie? Then do as you must."

Sometime during the trek out to the prairie, Hannibal stirred. In the morning light, Kshiwe could see the boy watching him through mostly shuttered eyes. Kshiwe was ready when the youngster rolled out of his arms to run. He grabbed Hannibal's

26

arm, but suddenly the boy fell limp at the sight of Kshiwe's gore-covered war club.

"*Bozho! Bozho!*" Kshiwe was nearing the spot where he expected the young Neshnabek to be watching.

"This is your new brother," he informed the astonished Mukos, and then to each of the others. "Hannibal," he said carefully, again and again.

*When was it,* Kshiwe wondered, *that I decided to adopt this boy?* "I think the fight is almost over," Kshiwe said. "Take him to Prophetstown. Don't lose him!"

Village Speaker and Okama Menomni were unhurt, but two of the other Shishibes Lake men were sorely wounded in the last desperate rush against the Long Knives. Stubbornly, the army lines did not break, and the Nations men withdrew. Now, in the morning light, the soldiers would see just how few warriors ringed their camp. With empty powder horns, the warriors slipped from the forest, out onto the prairie, to trudge back to Prophetstown. For the rest of the day, the Long Knife army waited behind their barricades for another attack that did not come.

Shawnee, Wyandot, Kickapoo, and Winnebago warriors, some four hundred survivors in all, carried their dead and wounded across the autumn-seared grasslands. Kshiwe limped beside the stretchers of two Neshnabe wounded. A rifle bullet had passed though the fleshy part of Kshiwe's upper right thigh. The other two men were in much worse shape. One had a long sword-gash across his face; the second had suffered a buckshot wound in the stomach. As the war-band retreated, Kshiwe held the second man's hand and talked of happier times.

The Neshnabe youngsters waited beside the partially built village walls. Mukos sat atop his new black brother. Thirteen-year-old Hannibal was yelling and doubtless making threats against the fifteen-year-old Mukos, whose bottom pinned him face down in the grass.

"He wants to run back to the Long Knife camp!" Mukos panted in amazement.

The other young men peered at their wounded clansmen as the little band stood aside from the long lines of dejected warriors filing into the town. The youngsters conferred quickly before racing away.

"I expect Hannibal wants to find his father," Kshiwe told Mukos. The older Shishibes Lake warriors gathered round.

# The Land Between Flowing Waters

"Tom?" Kshiwe mouthed the word awkwardly. Instantly the boy stopped struggling. Kshiwe handed the bloody war club to Village Speaker as Hannibal leapt to his feet.

"Tom?" Kshiwe said again.

The boy nodded eagerly and poured forth words that almost surely asked where his father was, and whether he was still alive. For the first time, Hannibal realised that the presence of both his father and this Indian outside Harrison's tent was not a coincidence.

Kshiwe held out his right hand. Hannibal stared at it for a moment then reached out to grasp it. *This isn't quite right*, Kshiwe thought. The handshake is a sign of taking a captive – but most times, captives become family. Menomni and Speaker, all the village men, had seen the offer and Hannibal's acceptance. There was no turning back.

Kshiwe gathered pebbles and smoothed a patch of earth. He arranged them into the shape of the Great Bear and then placed the seventh pebble above the open side of the box.

"Nord," he pronounced carefully, pointing at the top pebble. Then "Nord" again.

"North?" Hannibal asked. Kshiwe nodded. Then he pointed to the boy: "Nord." And then, a bit reluctantly, at himself. "Nord."

Hannibal asked, "Tom. North?"

Kshiwe just shook his head and gazed at the ground – then said, "Come." With his leg burning like fire, he gestured for the boy to follow. "I'll have to teach you to speak, but first we must tend to the wounded." Kshiwe smiled at the solemn black face. "And tend to me, too," he added as he limped into the village.

Prophetstown was in turmoil. Everyone gathered on the lawn outside the Council Lodge. Tenskwatawa and the war chiefs argued as everyone listened. Should they stay to defend the town, or flee? What would Tecumseh advise if he were here? As Tecumseh's younger brother, Tenskwatawa argued that they must scatter to fight another day. Now that the white chief Harrison no longer hid his hatred, Tecumseh could strengthen the alliance and lead all the Nations in defense of their homelands. In the early afternoon it was decided that Prophetstown would be abandoned before nightfall, before the soldiers could recover their courage and attack. In the afternoon The People, the women, children and elders, packed what they could and hurried to leave.

# Ken Leland

The dozen Shishibes Lake warriors waited in an empty lodge. Youth Leader and the youngsters were missing. Surely, the men believed, Youth Leader would not let the boys fall into great trouble. The Neshnabek had waited for the villagers to decide their fate; now, as the sun slanted into the west, they watched families turn refugees as they streamed by the open door. Young matrons pulled ponies carrying baskets, heavily laden with food and toddlers. Children and old women carried what they could. Everyone followed the sons, fathers and grandfathers armed with bows, lances and empty muskets along the paths to the town gates. From there the refugees sought trails leading east or north. Prophetstown was emptying quickly; even the dead were leaving.

By late afternoon, Kshiwe was fevered and could no longer stand. The man with the fiery sword gash was in great pain, and the third Neshnabek was delirious. Hannibal slid from one patient to another with a water bowl and a moistened cloth. The war band would have to make its own decision very soon. Menomni stood outside the lodge and peered along the deserted streets in every direction. Speaker was out searching. Where were Youth Leader and the boys?

In the last hour before sunset, Menomni came to kneel on the lodge floor beside a dreaming Kshiwe and nudged his shoulder. "Our young men have returned. They found a woman in The Prophet's gaol – a Midewiwin shaman. They are bringing her now."

A few moments later, a tall figure appeared and announced, "I am Kmonokwe of the Whitefish Clan. I am third-level Midewiwin. Where are the wounded?"

A woman in her early forties stood at the threshold. Kshiwe watched from his elbows as the healer, in a blue sheath dress, shawl and embroidered leggings, glanced at each man in the lodge. "Is there a village okama among you?" she asked imperiously.

"I am Okama of Shishibes Lake," Menomni replied.

"I see you. Please suggest that your people do as I ask."

"Yes, as you will," Menomni conceded.

She knelt beside each injured man, examining them quickly, and then from her knees she turned to Youth Leader. "Please send one young man to steal a cook pot, another to find clean water, another to boil the water and another to bring my medicine bundles from Tenskwatawa's lodge. We must hope he hasn't already burned them."

"We do not steal, Kmonokwe," said the offended Youth Leader.

29

# The Land Between Flowing Waters

"Of course, you don't. But only just now, your men stole me from Tenskwatawa's gaol. I have no time to argue. Two of these men are dying."

Youth Leader recognised wisdom when he heard it. He turned to issue a stream of directions that sent the youngsters flying through empty streets.

When she moved back to Kshiwe's side, he asked softly, "Surely, I am not one of the two?"

Her long black hair was gathered with a silver clasp and her hands were smooth as doeskin on his bare leg. She did not answer him.

Kmonokwe probed the entry puncture on the front of his right thigh, sending lancing pain that he locked behind clenched teeth.

"Sorry," was all she said.

Hannibal helped roll Kshiwe onto his side so she might examine the exit-wound. Then she pronounced firmly, "Excellent."

She spoke again, addressing a fondly observant veteran who was seated against the wall. "For this one, I will need half-a-dozen clean stalks of straw. And for all three, as many clean cloth strips as you can find. Could you do that for me, dear Uncle?"

Her smile dazzled. The old warrior rose indulgently, and motioned for a friend to help.

"Okama?" she asked without turning. "I presume you already have three travois in the making? We must leave by sundown."

"Yes. Yes, indeed," Menomni murmured as he stirred the remaining veterans into action.

In the lodge, now empty but for the patients, Kmonokwe whispered above Kshiwe's ear, "No, dear Brother, you are not one of the two."

Before treating her patients, Kmonokwe quickly painted her face in the red and green patterns of a third level Mide. As she knew it would, it comforted and reassured the injured men. By torchlight Kmonokwe worked quickly, sewing the warrior's swordslashed face with a thin needle, then packing Kshiwe's clean puncture with potions and straw; but to probe for the buckshot buried deep in the third warrior's belly was pointless. His gut already smelled of death. Poultices, powders, hot and cold draughts, soporifants, and prayers to the Master of Life, she did her best. As the moon rose, Hannibal and Kmonokwe propped Kshiwe on a travois and raised his leg so that the wound might drain from the straws. When the other two wounded were ready,

30

the Neshnabek set out from an abandoned Prophetstown into a freezing, white night.

They travelled with two outriders ahead and one on each side, everyone bundled in blanket coats and hoods. Three senior warriors lagged behind, watching and listening for pursuit. Okama Menomni, Village Speaker and the others rode in the centre with the litters. Sometimes Kmonokwe would ride beside Kshiwe's travois in the trek north, but mostly she stayed beside the two gravely injured men. The jolting of the litter poles over prairie hillocks was almost more than the wounded could endure. After moonset, they stopped to rest for only a few hours, and then rode out again. An hour after dawn, a low-hanging smoke cloud rose far behind them in the south. By midmorning, the sky was overcast. Scattered snowflakes settled on Kshiwe's face as he lay in great pain.

There's the river," Kmonokwe said, shortly before midday. Her green-and-red-painted face was confident.

Kshiwe stretched up to see where she was pointing. On the eastern horizon was a meandering tree-line that marked the course of the Tippecanoe. *Maybe she does know this country,* Kshiwe thought. *I wonder who she is.* Instantly, he thought of his companion, Nanokas. This woman was a little older but almost as lovely.

"Head for the river," Village Speaker called over the grasslands, and the outriders angled to the east. After an hour, they made camp beneath white barked sycamores. Hannibal broke through the ice at the river's edge and started water to boil, then accompanied Kmonokwe to each wounded man as she cleaned and changed bandages. After a while the scouts brought in a dozen fat rabbits, and the boy returned to Kshiwe's small fire to prepare dinner.

"The Grandmothers will not scorn you, War Leader," Kmonokwe said as she changed Kshiwe's dressings. "You bring back their grandchildren and all but one of the warriors."

"Who has died?" he asked anxiously.

"The man with the belly-wound has awakened. I gave him another draught, and now his pain is almost gone. We have been talking of the Land of Peace. He thinks he is lucky to be going there so soon."

Kshiwe looked a bit dubious.

# The Land Between Flowing Waters

"Oh, you know he's right," Kmonokwe insisted. "His old father and mother wait there in joy for him, and he has a brother and a child to welcome him home as well."

"You do know the Elders' ways."

"Of course. That's why the Prophet imprisoned me. He is the new way, and will brook no other." She laughed. "If Harrison had not attacked, I'd probably be with the Master myself."

"Why did you ever go to the Prophet's town?"

"Oh, it wasn't by choice," Kmonokwe said. "I canoed down the Eel, then along the Wabash. I would have gone up the Tippecanoe to reach home, but I was caught a few days ago. The Prophet's people do not bide with Midewiwin. Unfortunately, I didn't know that when I left."

"You are going home? Where is that?" Kshiwe asked.

"Maxinkuckee Lake. I am Whitefish clan."

"Yes. Yes," he said, understanding at last. "That is why you know our village. But the people at Maxinkuckee are —"

"Yes, I know," she interjected. "Still, I'm going home."

They were quiet for a while, then Kmonokwe made as if to rise from the fire. Hannibal scrambled up quickly. Kshiwe could not let her go so soon. "I have a companion," he said tentatively.

"I never doubted it. A man so well kept as you could hardly be without." She pointedly eyed the modest roll of comfort at his waist.

"And our younger son is only a few months old."

"Yes," she said, settling again beside his litter.

"When I left, both were ill. I fear Mishomes may be with the Master by now. I should never have gone to war."

"Are you Mide, then?"

"You know I'm not."

"Then by staying home, could you have saved your son?"

Kshiwe did not bother to shake his head.

"But by going, you bring back almost everyone — even one new person to balance the loss."

Hannibal did not know what they said, but he had no doubt of whom they spoke.

# Chapter Two
# Upper Canada

Major-General Isaac Brock
to Lt. Colonel George
Robertson, Canadian
Fencibles
Government House,
Niagara, November 19, 1811

Sir Francis Gore's departure for home occasioned the Governor General to cast about for some poor soul to take on the civil administration of this province. As I'm sure you've heard, his gaze fell upon your correspondent. I pretend no qualifications, but nevertheless, I am charged to do my best until Sir Francis should return. At this point you are saying to yourself, what favour does Brock want?

You are quite correct. I do need a favour. More particularly, I wish to second one of your Upper Canada born officers; a First Lieutenant Alexander Lockwood.

I met Lt. Lockwood two years ago during my time as inspecting officer for...

# The Land Between Flowing Waters

## Tuesday, December 17, 1811
## Niagara

HMS *Royal George* heeled gently to starboard. A morning snow shower drifted across the horizon.

"Port ahoy!"

Precariously, 23 year old Alexander Lockwood made his way forward at the lookout's hail. His boots slipped on the ice-coated deck.

"Our luck's held, Sir. You're home for Christmas." The ship's First Officer smiled, and then turned to a passing sailor. "Bo'sun, my compliments to the Captain. Tell him Niagara Harbour is in sight."

"Will you winter here?" Lockwood asked.

"One more passage back to Kingston, and we'll be home too. Shipping's done for this year."

As Lockwood grasped the bow rail, his dark hair was speckled by driving snow. The Niagara River lay straight ahead, its waters a broad, pale sheet disappearing into the green depths of Lake Ontario. To Lockwood, the brown western shore looked unchanged. The dock and ageing warehouses of Navy Hall, the white lighthouse, and the taverns on Front Street were all the same. Overtopping the leafless November tree line, he could see two towers dedicated to God – one for Anglicans, one for Presbyterians. Homes and shops lined the streets, a village grown into a town over the years of Lockwood's life. And only a few hundred yards south, on the orchard-ringed Commons were the trenches, earthen mounds and palisades of Fort George. Atop one log-faced redoubt the Union Jack flew from dawn to dusk, marking the border of Upper Canada.

As the ship sailed into the river, the snow-shower swept out over the lake to reveal the eastern shore. There, on a tall point, lay the cut stone walls of Fort Niagara, its parapets lined with cannon, the Stars and Stripes snapping in the wind. The fort had been built by the French, captured by the English, and then ceded to 'Jonathan' – as the former colonists were called – after the American Revolution, for reasons no one now understood. Lockwood turned his back as *Royal George* swung into the western harbour. He shivered in his greatcoat as the ship docked, then followed the season's last few merchant travellers down the ramp onto the wharf. As he expected, a heavy teamster's wagon was parked beneath the freight derrick. Its driver was Janie Benjamin's older brother, Matthew.

Matthew, rising thirty, was a tall black man, a larger image of his father and a lifelong Lockwood family friend. Matthew had taken up the family freight business and was as well known in Niagara as Lockwood himself. Matthew lumbered along the wharf toward his younger friend.

"Do I call you Captain Lockwood now?" asked the towering black man, with a glowing smile and a bear-hug.

"You never called me Ensign or Lieutenant, so why start now?" Lockwood wheezed in his grasp. "How are you, Matt? How're your parents?

"I'm fine. Ma and Pa too." Matthew paused for an instant, and then continued carefully. "We're all fine, Alex."

For the last five years letters had travelled to and fro between Lockwood and his family, but a single line was more important than any other. A year after he enlisted, his mother Lois wrote, "Last Saturday Janie Benjamin married your old friend Jeremy Roberts in the Methodist Chapel at St. David's."

Janie had not replied to Lockwood's letters. She had not waited as he had begged, prayed, for her to do. Thereafter, he made only a few trips home. Lois chided her son gently for his neglect, but now, after the General's staffing announcement in the *Upper Canada Gazette*, Lois thought her son's heartbreak must be mended. Lockwood, too, supposed himself reconciled to Janie's decision.

Lockwood glanced down, his bare frozen hand still buried between Matthew's huge warm paws. "That's good to hear," he said, surprised at the catch in his voice. "Yes, I'm glad of that."

"Last ship o' the season, for sure," Matthew said as he released his friend. Matthew squinted through the latest snowfall obscuring the derrick; in its thick rope net dangled crates of sugar cones and spices from the Islands. Still aboard lay casks of rum and wine, hardware, bolts of cloth, and pallets of English manufactures.

"Are your travel chests still aboard?" Matthew asked. "Should I drive you home?"

"I've got to report to General Brock first. I don't know where I'll be lodging after that."

# The Land Between Flowing Waters

"Then let's go up to the fort now." Matthew waved toward the newly arrived freight. "I'll need a couple of days to deliver all this lot anyway."

\*\*\*\*\*

Smoke rose from the guard-post chimney. Two red-coated privates of the 41st scurried out onto the frozen road leading from the main gate, one soldier still adjusting his shako strap as he ran to the opposite end of the turnstile. Their corporal followed without delay. Normally the guards would not have bothered – though by regulation they should be at their posts to greet every caller, Bristol-fashion. Anyone could see it was only Matt the teamster driving up the road, but the man on the wagon-bench beside him just might be wearing a military greatcoat. The officer of the day would not be favourably impressed if sentries didn't properly greet an official visitor at Fort George's gates. As the wagon approached, the corporal could see that the heavily-cloaked young man did, indeed, have a splash of red uncovered at his throat. The coat fell open as the officer jumped down onto the road.

"Corporal, I'm Alexander Lockwood. You might be expecting a Captain Lockwood, but I'm not dressed for the rank. I'm reporting to the General Staff."

"Sir!" The corporal growled, enunciating a handful of r's. He waved to the closest sentry. "Find Major Glegg. Tell him there's a new staff officer warming himself at the guard-post."

The soldier hurried pell-mell up the path into the fort.

"If ye'll just come this way, Sir, we've a nice fire goin' inside." The corporal turned. "And if you're staying, Matt, you come too."

\*\*\*\*\*

"As I live and breathe, Captain Lockwood!" Major General Isaac Brock exclaimed. "I thought we'd find you frozen on the back of a horse, twenty miles short of York, in January. You must have caught the last sail up from Kingston."

"Indeed, Sir," Lockwood said.

Brock had to stoop to pass through almost any door in Upper Canada, and he was at least a stone heavier than the oversized Matthew Benjamin. At forty-two Brock was florid of face, dark of

36

hair, and enthusiastic of demeanour. He was a lifelong soldier, born in Guernsey, with nine years service in the Canadas already behind him.

"It's as well Major Glegg met you at the gate," he commented. "You'll be reporting to him."

Major John Baskerville Glegg, Brock's Aide-de-Camp, smiled mischievously from behind a small writing-desk. He twirled a goose quill between his fingers as he leaned back to enjoy Lockwood's first encounter with the commanding general.

Brock settled next to a broad oak desk nestled in one corner of the officers' mess, where regimental flags of the 41$^{st}$ and 49$^{th}$ decorated the hall. The Union Jack, mounted on a staff, stood beside his desk. "I remember you from when I was Inspecting Officer for Lower Canada. Want to know why?"

"I suppose so, Sir. Or, maybe not," Lockwood almost laughed. For some reason, he didn't think Brock would be particularly offended.

"You told me you were in the Army to do some good, Captain. You seemed to mean it. Remember?"

"Not really, General."

"Well, I did. Looked into your family when I came here. Colonel Mayne is your brother-in-law, yes? Commands a regiment for Wellington, in Spain. Your father led a half-company of Butler's Rangers during the Rebellion. Most every Loyalist west of Kingston has heard of Asa Lockwood – I asked. And a lot have heard of his son."

"Yes, Sir, " Lockwood said with some incredulity.

"Of course, it's all Simcoe's fault!"

"Sir?" Lockwood asked.

"Old Governor Simcoe. You know what I mean! After the Loyalists, he let in all those Yankees and Dissenters. Now, not one man in five actually fought for the Crown. God knows if a single one would fight today. It fair shrinks my liver to think on it."

Lockwood was aghast. After a moment, he thought to close his mouth.

"Of course, you realise we'll be at war with Jonathan before the year's out," Brock continued. "They've already bestirred themselves to gobble up more Indian land in the West, at a place called Prophetstown. Soon enough, they'll cross the Detroit River, looking for us. God's Wounds, they'll come across the Niagara River to knock on our front door!"

# The Land Between Flowing Waters

Major Glegg smiled as the General ranted. Glegg had heard it all before and knew what came next.

"And do you know who's going to stop 'em, Captain Lockwood?" Brock peered expectantly at the bewildered young officer. "You and I, Captain Lockwood. You and I!"

Brock warmed to his topic.

"You're going to be my eyes and ears, my counselor and spy. That'll be your job, Captain. You'll talk and listen to every man in this province and tell me what he thinks, what he wants, what he fears. The demoralized will complain to you, knowing you have my ear. The loyal will tell you their concerns. And from what you learn, we must somehow cobble together a public resolve to resist what's coming. For the Lord knows, if we're attacked tomorrow, not a militiaman will stand and fight. Upper Canada will vanish in a twinkling."


"You mustn't take it too much to heart, Captain Lockwood," Glegg said later that afternoon. "General Brock has a way of making everyone think what they do is important."

After the meeting in the mess hall, Glegg and Lockwood had retreated to the canvas covered northeastern bastion. They leaned against the parapet to watch sleet falling on the river and the Yankee fort beyond.

"Of course, Brock's right," Glegg said. "The recent immigrants will be completely useless when the fight comes. A good number are Quakers and Mennonites. Some folks, even a few in the Assembly, hope we'll be invaded. And people with even an ounce of allegiance are frightened, frightened they'll lose everything again, frightened of their neighbours who don't care a toss for King and Country."

"I knew it was bad," Lockwood began, "but I never dreamed....What can we do?"

"Not a clue, Captain. Not a clue. We're hoping you can help us with that."

Glegg's laughter rolled down the snow-sprinkled parapet, out toward the river.

# Ken Leland

## Wednesday, December 18, 1811
## The Bay Window

"The Quartermaster had a spare 49th jacket." Lockwood and his mother Lois sat at the kitchen table. She pushed the coffee pot aside to spread out the coat. The facing at the throat and cuffs was green in place of the Fencibles' yellow. The lace bars were different too.

"Twenty pounds!" he complained to his father Asa. "And it fits like a tent. I'll try to get my old jackets made over."

"Miriam can do it," his mother said with a nod.

Miriam Lockwood and Mrs. Janie Roberts were business partners. They owned the Niagara Dress and Tailor Shoppe.

"I thought I'd try at the fort."

"You'd never hear the end of it. Why hurt your sister so?"

The silence stretched on.

"Go see them," Lois said gently. "Go see Janie Roberts. Best get it over sooner than late."

A little before noon, Lockwood rode into town. A cold breeze whipped through the leafless peach orchard at King Street, and the sycamore swayed in the high wind. On the roof of the Benjamin house a puddle of brown leaves nestled outside the second floor window. That bedroom was empty now, but Lockwood remembered when its candle glowed into the night. As he passed, the empty porch swing creaked in the wind.

Down King Street he rode, past the oak woods, then west on Front. The Dress and Tailor Shoppe was a white house of two storeys, trimmed in green, with cedar shingles. Along the wooden sidewalk was a waist-high white fence, wrapped in thorny rose vines. The Shoppe was only a few steps from the street, and passersby could see into the large bay window on the first floor. The glazier's bill had been astonishing, but the window was put to good use – displaying, in season, five-button vests and cravats, camel-coloured pantaloons and fine linen shirts for gentlemen, and for ladies, fur hats, muffs, gloves, and remarkable gowns in recent, if not the latest, London fashions. Lockwood could feel Miriam and Janie's pride shining from that window.

Lockwood carried his bundled military jackets up the gravel path to the front door. In the window, just beside the front steps, was a printed notice:

# The Land Between Flowing Waters

The Religious Society of Friends Welcomes All
To An Evening of Worship and Thanksgiving.
Mrs. Priscilla Cadwallader, visiting from
Indiana Territory, will speak.
Twenty-third day of Twelve Month
The Indian Council House, Niagara.
7:00 PM

Miriam watched him through the display window, and saw amusement growing on her brother's face as he read the flyer. When he glanced up, she motioned for him to hurry inside.

"I take it you don't approve," Miriam laughed as she hugged her brother tightly. Her beribboned braids lay snug against the back of her head. She wore a lovely blue dress, with frilled cuffs of her own design.

In the last five years they had seen each other only a few times. Miriam was twenty-seven and still unmarried. Her eyes were sparkling brown and she had a gentle, playful manner that her brother remembered well. But most of all, he remembered her strength and independence.

They stood on the shop floor, surrounded by tailor's forms and bolts of fabric strewn on cutting tables. Between the fitting rooms was a stairwell leading to the second floor parlour and the bedrooms.

"It's not for me to approve of what you do, Miriam. Mother always says you're the sensible one."

"Are you home for good?" Miriam asked.

"I think so," Lockwood replied, "but I'll be traveling a lot – to Kingston, York, Sandwich, and everything in between. But closer, yes."

"Miriam, who is it?" a voice called.

Shoe-tops swept by a grey wool skirt appeared at the top of the stairs. As their wearer descended, dark elegant hands in cream-coloured sleeves appeared. The first two buttons at her throat were open.

Janie.

She stood erect, her hands clasped at her waist. There was no hint of a welcoming smile. She stared at Lockwood as if he were an ill-formed mannequin.

# Ken Leland

"Janie...Mrs. Roberts, I wish to extend my congratulations...to my best friends...on the happiness they have..." Lockwood managed.

"Yes, Captain Lockwood. Jeremy and I are most happy," she said icily. "But how would you know? No letters, no visits, not a whisper, since we married! What must you think of your best friends?"

Nowhere in his imaginings had he practised a response to such a question. In his visions, Janie was still a girl of seventeen – not this remarkably lovely woman. Her hair was straightened and gathered behind her head, revealing her ears and slender neck. Fine cheek bones and generous full lips, now pressed tight. The cream bodice swelled – and below her heart, Lockwood guessed, were the beginnings of creation.

Her eyes followed as he laid the regimental jackets on a display case. He struggled to find something to say.

"I thought it best...I did not think you would want...that Jeremy and you would want..."

"No. You didn't think." Janie crossed her arms.

A small brown boy came down the stairs. His left hand sliding against the wallpaper, he sat upon each tread, and then lowered himself to the next. When he reached the workroom floor, he was most pleased with his accomplishment. Janie stretched out her hand.

"Come here, Ethan," Janie said as she lifted her son onto her hip.

*The boy has Jeremy's smile,* Lockwood thought, as the youngster clasped his mother's neck and peeked at the stranger. *God in Heaven, what have I done?* He stared at the boy and then at Janie.

"Why have you come back?" she asked.

"I...I'm sorry..."

"Why are you here?"

"General Brock. He wants my help to...to save the province..."

"Oh, Alex. Were you always such a fool?"

Later that afternoon, Janie used a tailor's knife to rip carefully through the seams of the swallow-cut officer's jacket. She sat upstairs in the fading light at the parlour window. In a back bedroom she heard Ethan plaguing Miriam's cat.

"Jeremy will be home soon," Miriam said. She brought in a steaming teapot and sat at the window table beside her friend.

"Hmmm."

"I mean, you could go home now, Janie. I'll finish Alex's jackets tomorrow," Miriam said, pouring tea for them both.

"Miriam, you've done trifles for him all his life. This is my last chance."

Miriam slid the china cup across the table as the cat dashed from the bedroom to hide beneath the tablecloth. She considered Janie's tear-streaked, averted face.

"Time to stop now, my dear. You're ruining your eyes."

## Monday, December 23, 1811
## The Indian Council Hall

The Society of Friends did not seek to borrow a meeting place from their competitors in the Lord's worship, nor was the Freemason's Hall a suitable location, and a tavern dance floor was simply unthinkable for a Quaker service. Instead, the British Indian Department Council Hall was the only, barely acceptable, large venue in Niagara.

"Everyone in town will come *pour le divertissement*," Major Glegg predicted to Captain Lockwood, "and half the farmers for twenty miles round. Just the sort of doings we, or rather you, should be attending."

"Scout the land," Glegg winked. "Put both ears to the ground. You know what I mean!"

Glegg glanced up slyly to gauge the fall of his shot. *Astonishing*, the Major thought as he eyed the straight-faced Captain. *This young man has no humour at all.*

Lockwood, for his part, had learned long ago that laughing in the presence of a superior officer was to balance one's career on a knife edge.

"You should go in that fine, new uniform," Glegg advised.

"Sir?"

"Everyone knows we brought you back to spy on the locals. The scarlet will make 'em think," Glegg said.

"They'll think that we know, that they suspect..." Lockwood chuckled. "Great fun for all."

# Ken Leland

"Indeed," Glegg said, beginning to warm to the young man. "No need pretending to be something you're not. A few people are depending on us. Good for them to see we care."

Torches lined the path to the Council Hall. Farm wagons, with horses blanketed against the lightly falling snow, were parked at hitching rails. Townspeople in muffs and fur coats strolled up King Street. Lit by the moonlight, they turned in to the woodland park just west of the Commons. The Council Hall was a wide, one-storey wooden building with a high-peaked ceiling and many windows. Built to accommodate treaty negotiations, the seating area was large with numerous benches and chairs. In the corners, iron stoves warmed the gathering throng.

There was no dais or pulpit at this service. Instead, a short double row of plain wooden chairs was centred against the wall. Curious townsfolk and farm families hurried in to find seats. With beribboned Miriam on his arm, the brightly uniformed Captain Lockwood searched through the noisy crowd. Momentarily he spotted their parents waving from seats near the wall.

"The Benjamins are here," Miriam whispered as they approached, "and the Roberts too."

One row ahead and a few chairs over, past Ben and Sarah Benjamin, sat Janie with her husband Jeremy Roberts. Janie turned shyly when Miriam called her name. The two sets of parents were too busy chatting to notice the young peoples' discomfort.

"Hello, Alex," the sandy-haired Roberts called over the hubbub. With family members leaning forward, happy in each other's company, the two young men were separated by loved ones. Lockwood raised his hand distantly in greeting, then settled back to scan the throng.

The room was overflowing. People were standing now, two and three deep, at the back and along the walls. Candles burned brightly from wall sconces. With smoke leaking from the iron stoves, and a multitude of bodies, someone would soon start opening the windows.

Lockwood twisted in his seat. More often than he expected, heads nodded in his direction, conversations stalled at his glance, while others smiled broadly to attract his attention. There were smiling neighbours and boyhood friends, noncommittal acquaintances whose names would soon come to mind, and complete strangers showing hard looks of determined suspicion.

# The Land Between Flowing Waters

Then, from the back of the hall, came a spreading wave of quiet as a double row of Friends walked up the aisle to take their seats: a dozen men and women, all clad in shades of somber blue and grey. The men wore cloth coats without collars, and carried black, wide-brimmed hats; the women were in grey bonnets and dark dresses. From just a few yards away, a man whose beard fell to his belt stood aside to make an announcement. His firm, steady voice carried to the hall's edges.

"Good evening, friends. I ask for quiet now, so that we all might listen for the Lord's voice in our hearts. If thou be truly moved by the Spirit, speak freely to share His Grace."

The elder then took a place in the second row. When the Quakers sat down, they disappeared from view to all except those in the nearest rows.

To Lockwood's surprise, the room hushed. People bowed their heads, or at least contemplated the floor boards. For long minutes the stillness extended in the search for the Inner Light, the Voice of God.

After what seemed an ocean of time, Lockwood looked to his right, past his sister Miriam lost in contemplation, past his parents in quietude, to Janie. Her head was bent, her graceful fingers linked. Lockwood was transfixed as he watched her breathe.

"Our Father who art in Heaven, hallowed be Thy name."

At last, overwhelmed by the quiet, or perhaps moved by the Spirit, someone had spoken. Many others joined in the next line.

"Thy kingdom come, Thy will be done on earth as it is in heaven."

Lockwood watched, enthralled, as Janie prayed.

"Give us this day our daily bread, and forgive us our trespasses, as we forgive those who trespass against us."

As the last line was spoken, Jeremy Roberts shivered and began to turn. Lockwood flinched, wrenching his eyes forward through three rows of townspeople, only to fall upon the face of a young Quaker woman.

# Ken Leland

"And lead us not into temptation, but deliver us from evil, for thine is the kingdom and the power and the glory..."

She had seen him watching Janie. The young Quaker locked eyes with his, one brown curl having escaped from her bonnet to dangle toward her cheek. Seemingly, she was angry and appalled by what she had observed. *Whatever must she think of me?* Lockwood wondered. After a moment, the Quaker glanced at the guest preacher seated beside her, worried that her distraction might become apparent. With visible effort she composed herself as the prayer came to an end.

"Forever and ever, Amen."

Lockwood contemplated his boots. *Perhaps she imagines I covet another man's wife.*

Now the grey-bearded elder was on his feet again to introduce the visiting preacher. Priscilla Cadwallader stood and advanced two steps toward the multitude, some of whom were skeptical, some curious. From behind Cadwallader, the Quaker girl again glared at the red-coated army officer in the fourth row.

Cadwallader's voice reached even to the farthest corners of the hall.

"I found peace this morning, dear people of Niagara, in giving myself up to duty, for peace is the reward of obedience to God's will.

"Oh, that I may be favoured to feel that peace which does not consist in, or depend upon, external things, but is vouchsafed immediately from the Father and fountain of mercy, to comfort, refresh, strengthen and animate humble travellers on the way to Zion.

"Lord, be pleased to provide that measure of patience, wisdom and strength that will prove sufficient for the work of my day."

At Lockwood's elbow, his sister Miriam leaned forward with unstinting focus. What did Miriam see in this Cadwallader woman? His eyes found the fierce Quaker girl again. *Peace! Please.*

45

# The Land Between Flowing Waters

"Oh, that I may be preserved and kept from sin, but I sensibly feel, except the Lord keep the city, the watchmen waketh but in vain. Yet it is needful for me to endeavour to keep in the watch tower, yea, to dwell there whole nights.

"The enemy of my soul lays close siege. My mind hath been exceedingly tried with false presentations and motions, the work of the enemy, but he hath been detected and made manifest by the true Light; it is the Lord's mercy that favoured and gave me strength to resist him in his subtle appearances.

"Help, Lord, or I perish; a Saviour be or I die. Lord, look down in mercy, and send help from thy holy place, that Victory over the spiritual enemy of all good may be my happy experience."

*Perhaps*, Lockwood thought, *these people fight greater battles than I supposed.*

Then to the Quaker girl: *Mercy!*

"In God's will I desire to rest; he delighteth in mercy, he afflicteth not willingly, but for my good. He that humbleth himself shall be exalted, but he who exalteth himself shall be abased. Gracious Lord, be pleased to help me to dwell in the depth of humility.

"I feel thankful that my mind is reduced to a state somewhat like that of a little child; O Lord, keep me humble, little, and low in my own sight, for it is the humble thou teachest of thy ways, and the meek thou guidest in judgment."

Lockwood stole another glance at the woman in the first row. She glared no more, but blushed, seeking now to avoid his eyes.

"God is Love. Oh, that my heart may more and more expand in love to my fellow creatures, to desire the present good and everlasting happiness of the whole of mankind; may this love prevail among all the inhabitants of this world.

"Oh Love Divine! A ray wherefrom warms the breast, inflames the heart of the true Christian, to make him love his enemies, and do good for evil.

46

# Ken Leland

"My heart is replete with love to my fellow creatures, with fervent desires for the salvation of their immortal souls. Be pleased, dearest Lord, to turn and overturn until thou comest to reign in the hearts of the children of men. So be it, saith my soul."

Peace, mercy, simplicity, and good for evil: a sure recipe to gall the wicked. *I think it galls both of us,* Lockwood sent to the young woman in the first row.

Cadwallader's address was drawing to a close.

"Do the work of an evangelist – make full proof of thy ministry. This is the language that hath been sounded in the ear of my soul. Lord, thou canst give me wisdom, strength and utterance. Without thee I am nothing.

"This morning, a taste of heavenly bread. Oh my soul, bless the Lord thy God and continue to hope and trust in his mercy, that he who was thy morning light may be thy evening song. Amen."

The Quakers rose promptly to file toward the exit. Conversation and greetings among neighbours washed through the hall as the audience spilled into the aisles. Lois and Asa Lockwood stayed with the Benjamins, waiting for the crowd to disperse. The Roberts were already lost from sight. Lockwood and Miriam navigated the slow-moving crush. Finally, they reached the doors and spilled out onto the wintery Commons. Jeremy and Janie Roberts stood waiting in the torchlight, a few yards off the slushy path.

"Hello," Roberts again called quietly. Miriam rushed to take Janie's arm and they hurried through the chill towards town.

Lockwood reached out to his old schoolmate. "It's been a long time, Jeremy. You're a surveyor now, I hear."

"I stake in good weather, and draw maps in bad."

"Ha!" Lockwood exclaimed. "You were always better at maps and such."

"How are you, Alex?" Roberts gripped his old friend's hand and smiled. The gold braid on Captain Lockwood's right shoulder glinted in the windblown light. "Janie said they made you a captain, to help save the province."

"She doesn't think much of my chances."

"No?" Roberts asked as their hands fell apart. "I guess it depends on why you've come back."

"I'm here because Brock wants me. That's all, Jeremy."

"That's all right, then."

A silence fell between the men. Finally, Lockwood said, "So, you draw maps now, eh?"

"And keep records of who owns the land."

"Really!"

"Yes. Really!" Roberts laughed.

"And these maps that show who the landowners are? Who do I ask to see them?"

"Just me. They're public records. Come by Government House any time."

"Tomorrow morning?" Lockwood asked.

"Of course."

Roberts made as if to follow his wife and Miriam on the path back to town, but then he stopped and turned slowly.

"Come summer, Janie's expecting. So, Alex, I got to say it straight out. We were happy while you were away. I mean, Janie and I love each other. I got to know you're not here to change that."

"I didn't come back to change it, Jeremy. I swear I didn't."

## Tuesday, December 24, 1811
## Government House

A little after 9 A.M., Captain Lockwood stabled his horse behind Government House and walked down the alley to the Queen Street entrance. The red brick building was a rectangular structure of three storeys. Lockwood entered the foyer, and as he hung up his greatcoat he noticed a battered cocked hat on the shelf above the coat-rack.

"Hello, Alex," Jeremy Roberts called from the stairs.

"General Brock's here, I see."

"He and the boy are upstairs in the library," Roberts replied.

"Boy?"

"John Ellis, his son – or his ward, I suppose. Come to the basement. The charts are down here."

# Ken Leland

An hour later, Lockwood was still taking notes from the maps arranged on the broad walnut table in the Survey Office.

"The names on the river townships are the most current," Roberts explained over Lockwood's shoulder. "You must remember everyone along here." Roberts swept his hand over Niagara's town plot, along the farms leading to Queenston and Niagara Falls, then down to the British fort on Lake Erie.

"Most of these men fought with Butler's Rangers," Roberts said, "and lots more Loyalists live over toward St. David's."

"Yes. I know of almost all those families, but I don't know as many names below The Falls, and hardly any over this way." Lockwood pointed west toward Short Hills and Pelham Corners.

"I have the records for Haldimand and Norwich Counties," Roberts added, "but you'll have to go to York for the rest."

"I'll wager last night was interesting. Am I right, Captain Lockwood?"

Lockwood sprang to attention at the sound of Major Glegg's voice. "Sir!"

"Goodness, Captain. It's too early for jumping about." Glegg waved his hand for the young men to sit. He pulled off his coat and fur gloves, and then bent over the work-table. "Names," he mumbled as he scanned the land registry plots. "Names beside every farm. Did last night make you think of this?"

"Mr. Roberts is a surveyor," Lockwood said. "I thought it'd be useful to know where the Loyalists are."

"And where the troublemakers might be," Glegg surmised.

"Yes, that too. By looking at charts like these, I think we can predict numbers for militia turnouts, and how trustworthy they'll be."

"Don't lose yourself, Captain," Glegg said as he headed upstairs. "I'll be back shortly."

Half an hour later, Captain Lockwood was tracing township maps when an auburn-haired boy of nine or ten slipped into the Survey Office to stand at his elbow.

"Whatcha doin', Sir?"

Lockwood held up a paper showing Twenty Mile Creek and its marsh sketched in.

"A map, is it, Sir? The General and I look at maps all the time. Spain and Portugal mostly; that's where Wellington is. But that's not Spain, is it, Sir?"

49

"No. It's not too far from right here," Lockwood replied. "You must be John Ellis.

"Yes, Sir. I'm the bastard John Ellis."

"You don't look like a bastard," Lockwood said. "Is that what people call you when they're angry?"

The boy scowled. "General Brock says I'm a son of the regiment."

"He does? Why does the General say that?"

"My father was a captain in the 49th. He drowned in the ocean two Christmases ago. I don't remember my mother. Folks say I never had one."

"I'm sorry to hear that."

The boy studied another map but put it down again out of place. Lockwood said nothing. "The General says he and the 49th are my parents now."

Lockwood handed John another map. "This is the one for the Falls."

"General Brock took me last summer." The boy returned the map to its proper place. He rested his arms on the table and then looked up. "Do you keep Christmas, Sir?"

For a moment, Lockwood was too surprised to reply. "John, my name is Captain Lockwood."

"Do you keep Christmas, Captain Lockwood?"

"I will this year, John. I'm home for the first time in a long while."

"Could I come? Could I bring the General?"

## Wednesday, December 25, 1811
## Keeping Christmas

A dark infinity cradled the milk-white crescent moon, but to the east and west a thick band of stars stretched across the heavens like a sparkling stream. With harness bells jingling, the sleigh flew past the guard post and headed south on River Road.

"Look up there, John," Major Glegg said as he pointed into the northern sky. "It's the Plough."

John Ellis twisted round to gaze at the stars. In the brilliant moonlight the boy's breath streaked upwards into the night.

# Ken Leland

"On Guernsey, they call it Charles' Wain," General Brock said as John snuggled close beneath the buffalo robe.

"Who's Charles?"

"The man who owns the wagon," General Brock teased.

The road was rutted, with mud puddles frozen solid. The driver eased the team out onto the snow-covered berm. As he loosed the reins, the draft horses snorted with pleasure and broke into a ponderous trot. Glegg wrapped another layer of scarf around his neck and huddled beneath his blankets, while on the opposite bench John hunched under a buffalo robe as his eyes teared against the stinging wind. Moon-shadows lay among the trees between the road and the river gorge. The oak forest slid by until the driver turned into a tree-lined farm lane.

"This is it," the driver called.

John Ellis stood, dragging most of the buffalo blanket with him. A picket fence enclosed the fields as the lane rose gently. Up ahead, a lantern shone from a tall post. Just beyond, centred in the white orchard, was a house and barn. Another solitary lantern hung from the stable door, but the farmhouse gleamed. John saw porch windows alight on three sides. Captain Lockwood stood bundled in his greatcoat outside the front door. Jeremy Roberts stood beside him.


"Relay riders," Major Glegg said. "That's got to be the fastest way between here and York."

Only men remained at the dinner table, recovering from a feast of wild turkey, barnyard goose, and freshly glazed ham, served with potatoes, vegetables and the last of the apples stored in the root cellar. Pastries and cakes were the officers' contribution, delivered earlier from the garrison kitchens.

"A couple years ago, Sergeant Major's crew rowed a launch down from York in half a day," General Brock insisted.

"And blest we are, General, you lived to tell the tale," Glegg replied. "Couldn't happen in winter. How did Colonel Butler manage in the Revolution, Mr. Lockwood?"

"Runners," Asa Lockwood answered.

"Riders?"

"No, runners. Captain Brant organised a corps of message carriers. Trot five miles in an hour, rest for ten minutes, then go again. The Mohawks can cover a hundred miles in a day and a night."

# The Land Between Flowing Waters

The General and his aide just shook their heads.

"Of course, no white man could do that," Asa said, "and a horse would be dead by mid-afternoon. No, I think Major Glegg is right: relay riders are best – if it doesn't rain."

The men sighed. The roads were impassable for two days or more after every storm.

"Father, didn't Governor Simcoe use runners between here and Detroit?" Captain Lockwood asked.

"He did, over the Indian trails. And I don't see how to do it any faster. The King's Road is a swamp, and the Dundas Road is hardly better."

"Well, it's beyond me," General Brock said, "but perhaps not beyond Captain Lockwood, here. If you please, Captain, you and Mr. Roberts shall conjure us a faster courier system – from Sandwich to Niagara, and then on to York and Kingston. I've received a pamphlet about the semaphore Wellington is using in Spain. You might find it interesting."

The men fell silent over wineglasses, with Lockwood and Roberts both lost in thought. After a few moments, pianoforte music drifted in from the parlour.

"Miriam vows that tonight someone besides her must sing for their supper," Asa said. "She will play, but gentlemen, one of us will have to sing accompaniment."

"Then, by all means, let us join the ladies," General Brock said.


Lois Lockwood sat in a deep armchair, her back to the hearth. John Ellis entertained young Ethan Roberts at cannons-and-castles on the carpet before the fire. Miriam, her long brunette hair decorated in ribbons, played as Janie leaned her elbow on the pianoforte. Each young woman was dressed in a fine silk gown of her own creation: long frilled sleeves, cuffed at the wrist, bodices tight to the neck, in the style of the latest illustrated magazines.

Watching them, Lois thought how impossible it was that she had grown old, now grey and a little stooped. It was only yesterday she was as vital and handsome as the two lovely creatures before her. Janie sang a ballad as the men entered.

> 'Tis the last rose of summer
> Left blooming all alone.
> All her lovely companions
> Are faded and gone.

# Ken Leland

Glegg sprawled on the sofa beside the bookcase. The tall General approached the piano in stages, pausing once near the lamp table, then again beside the children, before sliding onto the bench next to Miriam. With satisfaction Lois noticed that her daughter missed not a beat as Brock tried twice before finding an octave. Then, despite protestations to the contrary, Miriam's voice made a third part in the harmony.

> No flower of her kindred,
> No rosebud is nigh,
> To reflect back her blushes,
> To give sigh for sigh.

Lois watched her husband settle into the chair beside her. Each morning this dear old man reached out to caress her with gentle calloused hands, just as he did as a young man. And she opened to him still as if she were that devoted bride of long ago.

"Surely, you know this one too," Miriam said to Brock as she placed new music on the piano stand. Janie came closer to turn the pages.

> You remember Ellen, our hamlet's pride,
> How meekly she bless'd her humble lot,
> When the stranger, William, had made her his bride,
> And love was the light of their lowly cot.

*Alexander and Jeremy seem to have reconciled,* Lois thought, as Jeremy found the chair closest to the piano. Her son pushed aside the curtain to gaze out on the glistening front yard. During the day, the two young men had gathered holly, rose hips and cedar boughs to decorate the Christmas table.

> Together they toil'd through winds and rains,
> 'Til William, at length, in sadness said,
> "We must seek our fortune on other plains."
> Then, sighing, she left her lowly shed.

Snowflakes on the lawn sparkled like stars as Lois watched Alexander patiently holding back the drape. The singers were reflected in the glass. *He's watching Janie,* Lois realised. His mother clamped down hard on surging anger. Alexander, in the unthinking pursuit of his dream, had let a treasure fall from his hands. Lois and her longtime friend, Sarah Benjamin, had always supposed their children would somehow find a way. When that hope died, the mothers had spoken of it only once. Now, sometimes when parting, they clung to each other fiercely, so tightly their husbands wondered at the cause.

> They roam'd a long and a weary way,
> Nor much was the maiden's heart at ease,
> When now, at close of one stormy day,
> They see a proud castle among the trees.
>
> "Tonight," said the youth, "We'll shelter there;
> The wind blows cold, the hour is late,"
> So he blew the horn with a chieftain's air,
> And the porter bow'd, as they passed the gate.

Lois blinked into wakefulness. General Brock was bowing beside her, speaking his goodbyes.

"My most sincere thanks, dear Lady, for sharing your Christmas with us, but I'm promised for cake at three dinner parties in town. And at midnight, the garrison officers will toast the King. It's near 9 o'clock. I must take my leave."

"John Ellis is welcome to stay with us tonight, as promised."

"I've brought his nightclothes. Again, thank you, Mrs. Lockwood. I'll have an orderly come for him tomorrow."

"Send him to us whenever he asks. Asa misses our grandchildren...and so do I."

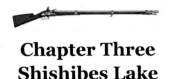

# Chapter Three
# Shishibes Lake

**Forest Moon, Full, 1811**
**(November 30, 1811)**
**Kmonokwe**

When Kmonokwe dropped the reins, her horse meandered to a stop. It began to graze on snow-sprinkled grass beside the trail. She stared down the cross trace leading to Maxinkuckee Lake. It was clogged with bare, arching saplings. Hannibal rode past, pulling the travois on which Kshiwe lay, but then Hannibal stopped beside the trail to wait. The boy watched as Kmonokwe gazed, forlorn, down the forgotten way. Kshiwe, dreaming from the pain of his suppurating leg, snapped awake when the travois lurched to a stop. He too saw Kmonokwe waiting while the rest of the small war party rode through.

"Come with us," Kshiwe whispered unheard. "Please come with us. The dead will wait. Don't you realise how much we need you?"

A few hundred paces south of the Yellow River ford, Kshiwe called out for Hannibal to stop. He struggled from the travois, bracing himself against a pole as he limped forward. He signed for the boy to take his place on the litter.

"What are you doing, War Leader?" Kmonokwe asked. "It would be wiser..."

Kshiwe sprang high, his right leg flying over the horse's back, to land with stupefying pain against its ribs. Almost instantly, blood gushed into his right legging.

"My children will be frightened if they don't see me leading."

# The Land Between Flowing Waters

"Kshiwe and Menomni, they're coming! They're coming!" a youngster shouted, as he galloped past the lodges and down the slope between the lakes. His heels bounced as high as the horse's withers. "The warriors are back! They're home!"

The People gathered on the plain above the lake. Women's Okama led the dash of a dozen spry grandmothers across the cornfield. She could see the warriors emerging one by one from the tree line along the river. Her heart stumbled. They weren't singing.

Women and children, the families of those who had gone to fight for Prophetstown, lined the trail. Grandfathers and hunters stood behind companions and children, no less eager for sight of brothers, fathers, sons.

The watchers counted. At the back, strung out so everyone could see, were Youth Leader and his five young men holding their lances aloft. The Grandmothers smiled. The older warriors were clumped together, but still, Women's Okama counted eleven riders and three travois. Surely, only twelve had departed!

She counted again and scanned faces as they approached. Oh! Thank the Master! One is a woman whose face is striped with red and green. And the boy on Kshiwe's travois is as black as charcoal. Wonders! But a blanket covers the last litter. No, the warriors are not singing.

Among the families there was a commotion. One of the young mothers fell to her knees. Kshiwe rode close to her and struggled to dismount. The black boy hurried to support him as Kshiwe bent over the kneeling woman. Everyone heard his words.

"Your children will never hunger."

Women's Okama saw his blood-filled moccasin. When he collapsed upon the earth, Ashkum, Maukekose and the other Grandfathers rushed to carry War Leader to the travois, and then the Elders escorted all the men to the Warriors' Lodge. In good time, Maukekose will tell Kshiwe of his family, Women's Okama thought. Grandmothers at her back flowed around her to welcome the dismounting Midewiwin shaman, and she hurried to be among the first.

"Beloved Sister, Revered Mother," Women's Okama said, as she reached out to the painted woman. "The Master sends you as his Gift of Life."

# Ken Leland

Kmonokwe relaxed into the welcoming embrace of the strong, stout woman. *How can I ever fullfill such expectations?* Kmonokwe wondered.

"A killing demon stalks among us. We are defenseless against it," Women's Okama said.

"The pox?" Kmonokwe asked in dread.

"No. There are no blisters, and very little fever. There is a deep, hollow, endless cough, and the young ones lose all they eat."

"Take me to those who are ill," Kmonokwe said as she signed for the black boy to fetch her medicine bundles. "This is Hannibal," she told the women as the boy approached. "I don't know what his name means, but we are teaching him to sign and to speak."

All day Kmonokwe and Hannibal visited lodges, along the river and beside the chain of lakes, until Kmonokwe had spent herself utterly. At her request, women and children scoured the forest for sumac and chokecherry, for sassafras roots and the bark from willow and red bud trees. Elders prepared potions to Kmonokwe's instructions.

"This is Kshiwe's lodge," the young torchbearer said that night, as Kmonokwe and Hannibal descended the tree-lined path to the lake. After the torchbearer called out softly and scratched the bark wall, one of the ubiquitous grandmothers emerged from the lodge.

"Bless you, Mother," the ancient said. "War Leader's daughter, Senisqua, and first son Shkote, lie within. They are very ill."

"Kshiwe spoke of his companion and second son. Where are they?" Kmonokwe asked.

"Nanokas carries little Mishomes along the Path of Souls," the old woman said. "Surely, they are Home by now."

After a long day of practice, Hannibal knew the words for firewood, hearth, water, cooking pot, cloth and willow bark. Kmonokwe no longer needed to give directions upon entering a lodge. The boy and old woman worked to prepare what they knew the Mide would require.

Senisqua, Bright Shining Pebbles, lay close to the hearth, and Kmonokwe knelt beside her. The girl's face shone pale and listless in the firelight. From the bowl of warm water that appeared promptly at her hip, Kmonokwe washed Senisqua's face. It was truly lovely, Kmonokwe thought, as the girl fought to bring back her wandering soul. Kmonokwe spoke when the girl's eyes regained some understanding. "I am Mide. I've come to help you and Shkote."

The girl started, her eyes flying wide. "Mother! Mother! I lost her. I couldn't...and Mishomes...I lost him too. Oh, Father, I lost them both."

Senisqua began to sob.

"Hush. Hush," Kmonokwe whispered as she rocked the girl in her arms. "Kshiwe loves you beyond all telling. He will always love you. I know this."

"Where is Father? How is Shkote?"

"Kshiwe is in the purification lodge. He will come to you when he is able. Shkote is only sleeping by the western door."

Kmonokwe hoped this was true, as she watched Hannibal pull back the furs to cleanse the little boy's face and chest with warm cloths.

"Now you are Bright Shining Pebbles," Kmonokwe said, "but I name you Bright Strength. I name you Shining Steadfastness. Kshiwe's Daughter, you must live to merit these names I give you. Your father and brother will need you more than ever."

In the hearthlight, young Senisqua searched the face of the woman who held her close. Then she nodded and swallowed from the cup Hannibal offered. She convulsed then in deep, wracking coughs which stopped only long enough for her to spew forth the water and bile from her long-empty stomach.

*Master of Life, help me*, Kmonokwe prayed. *Must this soul come to you so soon?*


The next day Kmonokwe began at sunrise. She tramped through ankle-deep snow to visit three families living on the westernmost lake, and then travelled along the river to complete the circuit of Neshnabe lodges. Hannibal walked at her side.

"It is not meet that I go to the Warriors' Lodge unless there is great need," Kmonokwe told the boy. "But you could go."

Hannibal looked up quizzically.

She signed as she spoke. "You. Go. To See. Kshiwe. At the Warriors' Lodge."

Hannibal made if to leave her.

"No. No. Tomorrow." She smiled and thumped him playfully on the chest. Then she pulled her ear, and touched her lips. "Now listen and I will teach you what to say."

# Ken Leland

By the end of the day, they found that two children and a grandfather had died in the night; but one young mother, for whom Kmonokwe greatly feared, rallied by late afternoon. Five villagers in three families were newly ill. Perhaps one in four of the People were sick, but some were returning to health. Women's Okama and the village Grandmothers worked through the night, sorting, cleaning, shredding, boiling, and mixing the barks and roots for what Kmonokwe hoped would be a lifesaving potion. After an hour's prayers, songs, and entreaties to the Master of Life, Women's Okama directed the delivery and ministration of the concoction to all those who were ill.

Hannibal was exhausted by the day's work. When they arrived at Kshiwe's lodge, long after dark, Hannibal wrapped himself in furs and lay on the cattail mats beside Kmonokwe. He was barely able to stay awake; but Senisqua, who had slept for hours at a time during the day, was restless now. Her eyes were shaded with hope and worry. Kmonokwe sat crossed-legged beside the fire. Eight-year-old Shkote nestled in her lap, the top of his head leaning back against her chin. Grandmother said he had coughed only a little during the day. A buffalo robe covered them both as Kmonokwe rocked him in her arms. Broth, which vegetables had only swum through, was so far tolerated by both children. Kmonokwe willed them not to suffer the spasms that had wracked them last night.

Senisqua watched the Midewiwin shaman as Kmonokwe began to sing the evening prayer. Hannibal rolled closer, so close his forehead touched her knee. Shkote yawned.

"Shkote," Kmonokwe asked the little boy, "Have you heard all the stories about Raccoon?"

"Oh, never even one," he teased with a wan smile.

There was a sparkle now on his big sister's face. Hannibal pulled down the furs from around his ears at the sound of Kmonokwe's voice. Grandmother smiled happily as she tended the fire.

"Well, then, here's a story you don't know. This is how it goes.

"Everyone knows that Raccoon is a terrible trickster," Kmonokwe said. "He isn't naughty at heart, but sometimes he just can't help himself. One day in summer, he was most terribly hungry, as he almost always is. As he loped through the forest, not too far from here it was, he came upon the lodge of three old women living together. Their companions had walked the Path many years gone by, and their children were all grown and moved away to live their own lives, and so the women stayed by themselves and talked of younger days. As Raccoon lurked at the lodge door, he could hear them boasting inside.

"'I was so beautiful,' one old crone said, 'that all the young Bear Clan men would take turns carrying venison to my parents when I was eighteen summers.'

"'I was so comely,' the next ancient related, 'that each Clan would hold a wrestling match to choose my suitors.'

"'Ah, Sisters,' said the last, 'as a maiden I was so radiant, the Moon would not shine for envy when I walked to meet my lovers.'

"Now, as it happened, these old women were all blind – but as Raccoon sat drooling in the doorway, he didn't know this. Instead, he thought them uncommonly polite when they did not cast stones his way whenever they faced the door. Finally, Raccoon realised the truth when he saw how they fumbled, trying to pass thimbles of trader's whisky.

"Raccoon yearned as the old women drank and prepared a meal for themselves. He was becoming very, very hungry.

"When all was ready, one woman said, 'I'll leave a portion for my companion.' She leaned back to place a heaping bowl of wild rice and rabbit stew beside the wall.

"'I'll feed my old man too,' said another, as she placed her bowl near the first.

"Not to be outdone, the third placed her own supper beside the wall.

"Raccoon could restrain himself no longer. As the women continued to fill their thimbles from the whisky jug, Raccoon scurried to a hiding place behind the corn basket, where he devoured the delights in the first and second bowls. Then he hid behind the clothes chest and emptied the third.

"By now the old women had lost whatever good sense they may have ever had. Finally, they reached back to retrieve their suppers.

"'My bowl is empty!' the first shouted as she ran her fingers over it.

"'Mine's empty, too,' the second yelled.

"'Sisters, some man has sneaked into our lodge and stolen our food. Let's catch him!' said the third.

"Now these ancients were of the Whitefish Clan, just as I am," Kmonokwe said, "and so to catch the thief, they brought out a fishing net. They spread the net wide, and began to sweep it across the lodge to ensnare the man who stole their suppers.

"Raccoon was sore afraid that he would be caught, but then he thought to hold up a great clay pot as the net passed overhead. When the women felt the pot's weight in their net, they grabbed sticks and began to beat the pot until they broke it into many pieces.

"Raccoon made his escape as the women flailed, but never again was he able to steal their food. For you see, the next time he visited their lodge, they had netted a man of their very own."

## New Winter Moon: 1811
## (December 15, 1811)
## The Warriors' Lodge

"Senisqua and Shkote will live?" Kshiwe implored. Tears streamed down his cheeks. As he lay on the pallet, his right leg was suspended a little so that his wound might drain. "Kmonokwe taught you to say this?"

The boy nodded.

"And you said it right?"

Hannibal smiled and took Kshiwe's hand in both of his as if to arm wrestle.

"Where are you staying?"

Hannibal made the sign for lodge, and then tapped Kshiwe on the chest.

"My lodge?"

"Yes," Hannibal said. "Kmonokwe, too."

Kshiwe turned his face to the wall for a long while, but continued to hold his adopted son's hand.

For an hour that morning, Hannibal knelt beside Kshiwe. The Warriors' Lodge was a long cabin with a peaked roof and mud-chinked walls. Bear skulls looked down from the rafters. On this, the second day after the war party's return, the men sat in small groups. Some smoked as they gambled for trifles at the peach stone game, others shaved arrow shafts or fashioned bowstrings, and some of the older men carved powder horns with intricate designs. All listened without apparent interest to the questions the elders Maukekose and Ashkum posed to the youths in the farthest corners of the lodge. Each man knew that only time separated them from the same questioning.

# The Land Between Flowing Waters

"Mukos, what did you see at Prophetstown?" the old okama Ashkum asked of the youngest returning warrior. Ashkum sat with his back deep in the corner, wrapped in a fur cloak. Mukos faced him, forgetful of the others at his back. Mukos answered the question quietly. The others pretended not to hear.

"Mukos, what did you do at Prophetstown?"

"Mukos, do you dream of what you saw there?"

"Do you dream of what you did there?"

"What will you tell your Mother of what you saw?"

"What will your little brother say?"

"What will you tell your friends about Prophetstown?"

"What will you tell the young woman whom you hope to impress?"

"Now I ask you again, Mukos, how can you keep yourself whole with such hatred for the Long Knives in your heart?"

"Kshiwe, tell me how you killed the guard before Harrison's tent," Maukekose asked a few days later.

"Kshiwe, do you dream of killing him?"

"Why did you leave Hannibal's father behind?"

"Do you ever think of the Kickapoo lad who died beside you?"

"Why do you think the Master of Life is punishing you?"

"What will you tell your children of the fight at Prophetstown?"

"What will you do when the Long Knives come again?"

Over the next four weeks, when they thought themselves ready, the men returned to their families. But any man tempted to raise his voice, or his hand, knew that he was still troubled – and to no one's surprise, several men came back to speak long into the night with Ashkum or Maukekose.

As it turned out, Kshiwe and his friend Menomni were the last to leave the Warriors' Lodge, for Menomni would not leave Kshiwe behind. Prophetstown was not the most dreadful close combat for Kshiwe; when first he returned from Fallen Timbers, he believed that never again would he be fit to love Nanokas. This time Kshiwe lingered at the Warriors' Lodge, first because his wound was still healing, and then because a Grandmother stood beyond the Lodge fence to call that Hannibal had fallen ill, and then only one day later, Kmonokwe. The boy recovered in only two or three days, but Kshiwe suffered in great concern until, ten days later, the

# Ken Leland

Grandmother shouted that Kmonokwe had survived. That was a week ago, and he had run out of excuses.

"Your children miss you, old friend," Menomni said as they walked through the cold, shadow-casting moonlight. "It's long past time for you to see Senisqua and Shkote."

"I'll walk with you to the footbridge," Kshiwe said.

When they reached Shishibes Lake, the sky opened wide. A magnificent trail of stars stretched from horizon to horizon. A wisp of cloud, too thin to hide the waxing moon, drifted in the south. The points of the Great Bear shone like bright, shining pebbles.

"Do you see?" Menomni said, as he lifted his hand to the north and heaved a great white sigh. "Go home."

*So strange,* Kshiwe thought, as he paused to speak softly and scratch at his own lodge door.

"Welcome," was Grandmother's reply from inside.

Senisqua and Shkote flew into his arms, his daughter crying with heartbroken sobs.

"Hush. Hush," he said as he kissed her forehead four times. "I'm so proud of you. So very proud."

He lifted Shkote high and hugged him fiercely. As Shkote soared, Kshiwe saw Grandmother standing by the western wall. She was the mother of a son he had led to death in battle. Beside her was the black boy. Kshiwe spun Shkote through the air, but as he twirled, nowhere did he see Kmonokwe.

"Welcome home, my son," the old woman said, as she pulled him down to kiss his cheek. "Yesterday the Midewiwin shaman moved to the lodge of Women's Okama. They must plan the homage for those who have died."

When she stepped back, Kshiwe held out his hand to the black boy who stood gazing at the floor. "I want to thank you, Hannibal, for all you have done for my people."

The boy looked up. "Kmonokwe says the Neshnabek are my people now."

"Do you understand what she means?"

"Yes," the boy said as he ran into Kshiwe's arms.

# The Land Between Flowing Waters

## Tuesday, January 14, 1812
## In a Cocked Hat

The front doorbell jingled, and a gust of frigid air swept into the Niagara Dress and Tailor Shoppe. Janie Roberts looked up from the fabric table to see General Isaac Brock stoop as he entered, holding his staff officer's hat. The two steps up to the fitting room floor shook as he stomped snow from his boots.

"Good morning, Mrs. Roberts. I've...well, I've come on business."

"Good morning, indeed, General Brock. Please come in. May I take your hat?" Janie asked.

"Oh, Mrs. Roberts, I most certainly hope you will," the General said as he extended the battered black felt crescent.

"Of course, of course," Janie said, now holding the disreputable chapeau. She turned to call up the stairs, "Miriam, General Brock's here."

"Who? Oh Heavens," came the faint reply.

Brock smiled weakly as scampering feet descended from the second floor.

"Oh, my," Miriam Lockwood breathed on reaching the bottom step. Her braids were coiled fashionably at the back of her head.

"I hope I've not come at an inconvenient time," Brock said.

"No, no, of course, not. How may we help you?"

The women stumbled into one another. Miriam firmly caught herself before dropping a curtsey to the red-faced, grinning Brock.

"It's my hat. It's old and limp and an embarrassment. I've only just written a request to military stores, but nothing can come from home till the fall. God knows what will happen between now and then, and I'll be stuck in this dreadful old thing."

Janie held out the offending haberdashery.

"Hardly calculated to inspire confidence, is it?" Brock said.

"Well, it is very much the worse for wear," Miriam observed as Janie gave her the scarred felt hat. "We don't have this material in stock. We'd have to order it from London, just as you have."

"I feared as much. I tried on two or three new ones from the commissary, but they're all too small. Now the men are joking that their General has a swelled head. I suppose they're right."

"There are new hats at the fort?" Janie asked.

"Yes. Do you suppose you could stretch one to fit?"

"No," Miriam said, "but if we could cut the fabric apart, I'm sure we could make a new, larger one."

"Marvelous! Simply marvelous," the General said. He glowed at Miriam.

"If you would please sit down," Miriam suggested, "I'll get a measuring string."

Janie led Brock to a cane-backed chair near the bay window. The chair creaked as his weight settled. Miriam wrapped a knotted string round the forehead of an immensely pleased general, and showed the measure to Janie. The women looked at each other for a moment, and then broke into giggles.

"I told you, ladies. I get the same reaction wherever I go."

Since Brock showed no desire to leave, Miriam and Janie supposed themselves obliged to invite him for tea. As they sat in the upstairs parlour, Janie's two-year-old son, Ethan, pulled a platform horse across the floor in a determined attempt to terrify Miriam's cat.

"I was thinking of you particularly, Mrs. Roberts, as I walked down from Government House today," Brock said.

Janie glanced at him in surprise.

"A delegation of black men came to me yesterday. I don't wish to cause either of you any concern, but they presented me with a petition to form a Coloured Corps, a black militia company for active service should...well, should matters with the people to the south become a problem. As I say, I don't wish to frighten either of you."

"General Brock," Janie said, "Miriam and I are Loyalists. We don't frighten easily."

"Indeed. Remarkable, but I thought as much. Well, Mrs. Roberts, happy as I am that any Upper Canada residents show such devotion to the King, almost certainly I will grant this petition. I told them so." Brock glanced at Janie in anticipation. "But perhaps this is not news to you, Mrs. Roberts?"

"No, it's not," Janie replied. Miriam's demeanour showed that she was aware of the petition as well. "My brother, Matthew Benjamin, is acquainted with the authors of that petition."

"Your brother, Mrs. Roberts? I believe he is the owner of that fine brace of draft horses I see on the streets of Niagara almost every day, is he not?"

# The Land Between Flowing Waters

"He is. My father has given over the freight service to Matthew."

"Your brother, Mrs. Roberts, from what I've seen and heard I judge him to be an uncommonly skillful driver. Do you suppose he would be willing and able to teach others to be the same?

"Drive draft horses?" Janie asked.

"Yes, draft horse teams, to pull caissons and heavy field pieces. Would you please pass a word to your brother, Mrs. Roberts? I would speak to him, in private, as soon as possible. If he's of a mind to serve the King, creating a car brigade – horse-drawn artillery, you know – it would be a signal benefit to the cause. I mean the cause of this province still existing past the end of summer."

Janie was thunderstruck. As Miriam led Brock downstairs, Janie gazed through the parlour windows to the snow-draped trees outside. *Alex is right*, she thought. *Something dreadful is coming. And Alex is right about the General, too. Somehow Brock makes you want to try to stop it.*


"My dear, Miss Lockwood," Brock said as he paused and turned before the front door.

Miriam wished to hurry back to speak with Janie, who was clearly upset, but she waited on the top step. For these moments Miriam was at eye level with the general.

"Yes?"

"I've heard that the Lockwood women are sublime dancers."

"I beg your pardon, General Brock. Dancers?"

"Perhaps I should be asking your father..."

"About dancing?"

"No, my dear Miss Lockwood. It's just that we have met socially, in your father's home, and you are of independent means, and are..."

"Of a certain age..."

"A most wonderful age to a man of my age."

"If you are looking for a dance partner, General, I shall introduce you to my sister Ruth, should the opportunity arise." Miriam was smiling now, directly into the General's beaming countenance. "Still, you have heard correctly; the Lockwood women love to dance."

"The next subscription ball is in two weeks."

66

"And each time I see you there General, you seem somewhat uncomfortable."

"Most perceptive. I come alone, as you know, my dear Miss Lockwood, and every debutante and dowager supposes I'm pining to dance. With them."

"And you are not," Miriam laughed.

"Exactly."

"So, you would ask your 'dear Miss Lockwood', who is happy to dance, to defend you from other ladies who would drag you onto the floor. Is that to be my service to the Crown, General Brock?"

"My dear...Miriam, if I may be so bold, you would not need to drag me anywhere. I would follow most willingly. Would you accompany... or should I speak to your Father? John Ellis is at the farm now. I could..."

"Of course, visit your son at our farm. And tell my father I've consented that you escort me to the subscription ball. Father will be flabbergasted – and happy too, I imagine."

## Friday, January 31, 1812
## The Subscription Ball

Jeremy Roberts moved the card table close to the upstairs fireplace, then played at solitaire while Miriam and Janie primped. But both women were ready, and becoming anxious, when General Brock finally arrived at nine o'clock, almost half an hour late.

Together they made the short, dark walk through ankle-deep snow to King Street, then one block south to Freemason Hall. In torchlight at the hall's entrance, sleighs manoeuvred to deposit Niagara's late-arriving gentry for the night's festivities. Snowflakes drifted down, unnoticed, as the finely-dressed formed a receiving line for Brock and his party.

"Good evening, General."

"A fine evening, Sir. Hello, Mr. Roberts."

"Evening, Sir."

"Good evening, General Brock, Miss Lockwood."

They mounted the wide front steps, then up again through the painted plaster stairwell to the hall, now cleared as a dance floor. Near the door, servants tended refreshment tables loaded with pastries, meats and festive beverages. Music swelled from inside, as musicians held forth from a dais at the far end of the hall. Two

# The Land Between Flowing Waters

rows of dancers stretched the length of the floor. An English country dance was in progress as lines of partners advanced and retreated, then broke into fours to swing partners merrily to the music of violins and trumpets. Jeremy and Janie soon broke off to join the revels as, arm in arm, Brock led Miriam in a slow procession around the hall.

As Brock steered her through the crush, every eye was upon them, every official eager to pay his respects. Brock's grip on Miriam tightened at the approach of each family with an eligible daughter, each ageing squire grown too stout to accompany his wife onto the dance floor.

"We've come late, General Brock," Miriam murmured into his shoulder.

"*Mais non*, Miss Lockwood. I, and therefore you, are never late – or only fashionably so. Ah, Miss Lockwood, I'm sure you've met the Chief Justice," said Brock as he began the next round of introductions, "and his lovely wife, Marie."

Half an hour later the first circuit of the hall was complete, with many names and introductions confused or forgotten. Miriam whispered again, "So many, all at once. Don't you find this a bit...intimidating?"

"I've grown accustomed, Miss Lockwood. But, if it helps, recall that you have doubtless seen some of these worthies in their small-clothes. And I'm sure they cannot say the same of you."

Miriam laughed.

In a lovely blue silk gown, Miriam held Brock's hand as they led the promenade in a regal minuet. From the corner of her eye, Miriam saw her brother standing near the musicians' platform. As they swept by, Lockwood's smile was broad and delighted, but it became rather fixed at the passing of the enchanting black woman and her companion. Miriam saw her brother head for the rum punch table as Janie and Jeremy Roberts bowed to one another at the minuet's conclusion.

"Your brother is finally here," Brock said as the dancers applauded the musicians. Miriam could barely hear him. Brock leaned in closer.

"Please stay with Mrs. Roberts. I shan't be away for very long."

Miriam watched as her brother and Jeremy Roberts followed Brock from the dance floor.

# Ken Leland

Upstairs, the small walnut paneled office of the Master Freemason was crowded. Major Branson, an officer of the 41[th], stood at attention in the centre of the room. General Brock balanced on the corner of the office desk with folded hands. Aide-de-camp Major Glegg twirled a quill pen behind the desk, prepared to note any orders for Major Branson. Roberts and Lockwood stood at their ease by the window, pretending disinterest.

"As I'm sure you are aware, Major Branson," Brock began, "The chain of command in this expedition is, let us say, unusual."

"Yes, Sir," was Branson's only reply.

"And because it is unusual, I've asked Major Glegg to put your orders in writing, to protect you should there be any misunderstanding at a later date that I may not be available to untangle."

"Yes, Sir," was again the reply.

"Major Branson, you will leave tomorrow morning in command of two fatigue companies of the 41st and two pioneer companies of the Lincoln County Militia. As we discussed, your mission is to build a series of courier trails through the back country, linking Lake Erie to the Dundas Road. Mr. Roberts will accompany you, but he is not under military discipline. His duties are ostensibly those of a surveyor, and he will assist in laying out the trails, but his other duties are similar to those of Captain Lockwood. And Captain Lockwood is, to put it bluntly, a spy – answerable only to Major Glegg here, and ultimately to myself. Captain Lockwood will be dressed as a civilian, and will come and go at his own discretion. Mr. Roberts may accompany him at any time. Major Branson, your orders will include my instruction to hold yourself ready to assist Captain Lockwood in any manner he may request.

"It's important this last part appear in writing – to protect you if matters should go awry." Brock paused to gauge Branson's reaction. Clearly, the officer was appalled by the irregularity implied.

"Rest assured, Major Branson, we would never have chosen you for this endeavour if we felt you unequal to its subtlety."

"Yes, Sir," Branson barked.

"You will leave tomorrow, one hour after reveille," Glegg concluded. "Your orders will be handed to you as you pass the gate."

"Sir!" Branson turned and marched from the room.

"Major Branson's a bit nonplussed just now," Brock said to Lockwood, "but there's no one I'd like better at my back."

"And by the by, Captain, you needn't worry. I'll see Miss Lockwood home safely."

Lockwood descended the stairs, but Branson was nowhere in sight. Up ahead, Roberts had already reached the doors leading to the dance floor, where Miriam and Janie stood together. Music poured forth, a waltz. As Roberts approached, he held out his hand to Janie, but she brushed past him and walked down the hall to Lockwood. When Janie found Lockwood's eyes, she pressed her palm against his chest.

"He's not a soldier, not as brave as you," Janie said quietly, her eyes unwavering. "Alex, if you still care for me, bring him back. I beg you."

Janie returned quickly to her husband. As they left for the dance floor, the anger in Roberts' glance was unmistakable. Lockwood leaned against the wall, unable to move or think.

"If you still care for me..."

Miriam hurried to her brother. "Alex, what's wrong? What did she say?"

"Nothing. Nothing. Just to look after Jeremy."

## Big Bear Moon, Third Quarter: 1812
## (February 5, 1812)
## Hannibal

The Elders say I can name myself – everyone does – and if I get tired of that name, I can change it to something else. I'd call myself Tom's Son, but no one here knows my real daddy, and sure as shootin' somebody'd ask me what 'Tom' means. Lots of folks have a hard time saying Hannibal, and I don't know what it means. But I'll just wait till something special happens, and I can call myself by that.

Now it gets real cold at night. The little lakes are frozen so hard we walk on them. Kshiwe took me out on Shishibes, and we cut a hole with a tomahawk. We didn't stay out too long, 'cause it gets dark early, but we took home three big fish. Senisqua and Grandmother cooked them up last night.

# Ken Leland

This morning Mukos came by, with three rabbits he snared. He handed them to Senisqua, and then he turned round right quick and went out the door before she could say thanks or anything. Mukos comes by a lot. Most times he says he's come to teach me something. He asks Kshiwe real polite, but Kshiwe is most always grumpy about it. I don't know why because I know he likes Mukos. But then my father, I mean my adopted father Kshiwe, gives in and Mukos and I go sit in the sun to carve a bow or fletch arrows. I've got a good bow now because of Mukos. I've got bird arrows and deer arrows and fish arrows I can't use till summer comes. At first we'd shoot at grass targets, but now I go out to look for pigeon or quail or turkey, if I'm really lucky enough to find the tracks. Mukos is alright, but we all know why he visits. He hardly ever says anything to Senisqua, but she always sits where he can see her, and if we're outside in the sun, she brings us sassafras tea.

Shkote isn't afraid of me anymore. He never saw a black person before, and all those times I went round with Kmonokwe, he thought maybe I was a demon she'd conjured to help her. Some stories the Neshnabek tell are real scary for little folks. Now Shkote chases after me when I go bird hunting, and we've got a trap line for mink and muskrat on one of the little creeks round here.

The other boys tease me some, but I got a bloody nose only that one time. When they thought I didn't know how to talk, they'd say some silly stuff, but now I can outwrestle all but the biggest ones. But mostly they want to race, if the snow's not too deep. On the short I can beat 'em every time, but in a long race – say all the way round the lakes –I start out real good, but they always catch up by the end. The last few days since the lakes froze, we've been making a snow-snake run. Out on the lake we make a real long groove in the snow, and then water it so it freezes hard. Then we take a fishing pole and slide it down the groove. Farthest wins!

I don't know why Kmonokwe don't stay with us anymore. Grandmother says Father had a companion and baby boy, who died before we got home – got here, I mean. I think folks all got the whooping cough, but Kmonokwe doesn't understand me. She says it's one of the bad spirits settlers brought to kill the People. She stayed with us for a time, but right before Kshiwe came home, she left. Maybe they don't like each other. But I like her just fine. She lives with Women's Okama now, and I go see her there almost every day. She's teaching me about plants and roots and medicine prayers.

# The Land Between Flowing Waters

## Monday, February 10: 1812
## The Letter

"Good day, Mrs. Roberts. Compliments of Major Glegg."

The young subaltern stomped back down the snowy path to Front Street as Janie closed the door. She recognized the handwriting and tore open Jeremy's wax-sealed letter.

My darling wife,

I am so very ashamed. Captain Lockwood explained what you said to him the night of the subscription ball. Your concern for me is most touching, and I am terribly sorry my heart was filled with jealousy. There was a time when you – but now I believe that has all changed. Somehow I must prove I'm not the bumbler you suppose. But I forgive you. Indeed there is nothing to forgive, and I most humbly beg you will forget my suspicion.

A few days ago near the Welland River, Alex fell through the ice. We fished him out, along with a Quaker lady. But he must really be more prudent if he expects to roam about all on his own.

I'll send my letters with the supply sleds as they return to Fort George, but please don't worry if I miss a time or two. The roads (ha!) are sometimes nearly impassable.

Your devoted husband,
Jeremy

"Miriam! Miriam!" Janie shouted up the stairs. "Jeremy saved Alex on the ice!"

*****

Jeremy Roberts and Captain Lockwood were riding near the head of the column. Snow showers drifted fitfully from an overcast noonday sky. Major Branson's command of nearly two hundred men, on foot and in sleighs, stretched along the Welland River for half a mile.

"Do you see them, Captain Lockwood?" Branson called out.

"Yes," Lockwood answered. Three men on the opposite shore had been shadowing the column for the last few miles. "I'll ride ahead and see what's doing."

Lockwood hoped the watchers would not notice a single man detach and race ahead to the ford. He was dressed in snug, well-worn farmer's garb, but no one would mistake his golden-brown stallion for a plow-horse. He crossed the Welland on the ice and began to work his way along the western bank. Lockwood stopped on the deer path he had been following and listened. After a time, the watchers appeared. They were dressed as drably as himself, but each carried a rifle balanced on his saddle. From time to time they stopped to peer across the river, then they plodded forward along the trail. No one seemed to notice him until he called out.

"Hello! I've lost my way. Do any of you gentlemen know where the ford might be?"

The first man reined up with a start, but the second raised his rifle to fire. Lockwood rolled off his saddle into the snow before the rifle cracked. The riders plunged past as he ran into the brush pursuing the spooked stallion. As he stumbled through the snow, Lockwood could imagine Major Glegg laughing.

After discovering that the stallion would stand only if he approached with an outstretched, cupped hand, Lockwood mounted and galloped after the ruffians, who turned west on the frozen road leading away from the ford. They rounded a bend and were already disappearing from sight when Lockwood reached the road. Major Branson's advance party was crossing the river. Despite his better judgment, Lockwood cantered on alone. As he neared the bend he feared an ambush, so he slipped into the snow-carpeted forest to cut across. Among the trees, he stopped again to listen. There was a faint cry from far ahead. *Oh, damn*, he thought, *what's that?*

When he burst back upon the road, he saw the spies riding up into the woods on the far side of an open hillside. At the bottom was a wooden bridge over a stream. The bridge railing was broken.

From somewhere a woman was screaming, "Hah! Hah! Hah! Get up, horse!"

Lockwood hurried to the bridge and looked down. A light sleigh had plunged onto the steep, stone-faced creek bottom. The sleigh was smashed. A mare struggled to rise from the wet, icy chute, but the broken sled pinned her down. A woman, dressed in a long grey overcoat, tried to free the horse by yanking desperately at the harness clasp. Her face was bleeding. Her blue bonnet floated in the water cascading into a pool below, and her coat and dress were soaked.

"Be careful! I'll help," Lockwood yelled as he leaped out of his saddle and fought through the knee-deep snow to reach her.

The frightened mare screamed as she tried to escape. The woman pulled at the clasp-pin, but with every tug the sleigh slid a bit farther down the rock face. Just as Lockwood waded into the stream, the pin came free. The horse lurched to its feet – but the ruined sled, freed as well, scraped down the rock. The woman reached out to steady herself, but the sleigh gave way and she fell, face first, into the pool below. In horror, Lockwood watched as her fall drove her into the water, then deep beneath the covering ice.

He scuffled down into the pool. The icy shock was stupefying, but his boots found the creek bottom. Howling, he stood as the water sloshed against his chest. He fought past the floating debris toward the sheet of ice and pushed against the thin edge, breaking the ice as he groped below it with his hands and feet. Where the ice was thicker, he bludgeoned it with all his strength to force his way forward. Blindly, he reached out and down into the water. He screamed with pain and cold and fear, wrenching up his arms to lift away a thicker sheet of ice.

Something, a hand, clutched at his coat. He grabbed the fingers to lift the woman. Her desperate thrashing splashed his face with burning cold as she fought her way to the surface.

"I say, down there!" called a familiar voice. "Do you folks need some help?"

Major Branson, Lockwood was learning, could be a master of understatement.

\*\*\*\*\*

"Now, Dinah," Henry Babcock said to his younger daughter, "there's a thing called modesty. Go upstairs now and help thy mother and Patience. This brave young man is like near to frozen."

A squad of Redcoats had brought home the Babcocks' nineteen-year-old daughter, Patience, along with the dangerously chilled man who had pulled her from the creek. Henry Babcock could not imagine how Patience's sleigh could have fallen from the bridge, but there was no time to ask as her mother hustled Patience upstairs and into bed.

Henry Babcock thanked the soldiers profusely, but then firmly closed the door on them. His sons Hopestill and Nathan dragged the stricken young man to the parlour sofa.

# Ken Leland

"Hopestill, get some towels, and thy small-clothes and socks," Henry Babcock commanded, "and the bed warmers. Nathan, bring down as many blankets as Mother will allow. Now, Mr. Alexander...Lockyer, was it? Let me help thee out of these frozen clothes."

"Tha...Thank you, Sir. I'd b...be most obliged," Lockwood answered through clattering teeth.

"Henry Babcock, I am, young man. No Sirs in this house."

Lockwood still shook uncontrollably as Hopestill helped him into a third pair of dry socks. While young Nathan swaddled him in blankets, Lockwood watched the grey-bearded Henry Babcock build up the fire. Lockwood recognized him as one of the Society of Friends Elders at the worship service in Niagara. Lockwood lay back on the sofa and closed his eyes in exhaustion. As he drifted away, the family gathered in the kitchen to discuss Patience's remarkable experience.

Mr. 'Lockyer' spent three days in the Babcock household – the first and most of the second day in a deep, dream-filled sleep, and the third in ravenous hunger. The lady-of-the-icy-pool, as her siblings had taken to calling her, descended from the second floor late in the third day, but only after sending her brothers and sister Dinah ahead to ensure that her rescuer was properly attired to receive her.

"Thanks to thee, Hopestill, Nathan, and Dinah."

"Awwwww," Dinah groaned.

"And thanks to close the door behind thee," Patience directed.

In a long grey dress, housecoat, slippers, and two blankets, she seated herself far across the parlour, just inside the passageway between the front door and kitchen, where she could not be surprised by the entrance of any family member.

"I'm told, Mr. Lockyer, that I owe thee my life."

Lockwood cleared his throat. This brazen beauty with curly brown hair clearly remembered him from the Niagara service.

"I'm not sure I would owe my life to a man with as many secrets as thee, Mr. Lockyer, but there it is, and so my thanks. I'll pray for thee too, as I suspect thee might be needing it." Patience Babcock rose from her chair and shuffled to the stairs.

"I did not come here, Miss Babcock, to lie to or deceive anyone," Lockwood replied indignantly. "Yours was the nearest house, and Major Branson believed we were both near death from cold."

"I suspect thee have something to do with those ruffians who ran me off the bridge, Mr. Lockyer. But why thou stopped, and not they, I don't know."

"Be assured, they are no friends of mine."

She paused, her foot upon the first step. Lockwood watched her waiting there for some time, perhaps as she counted to a hundred.

"And so thou can see why my name is ever a trial and a lesson to me, Mr. Lockyer. I should have come with grace and true gratitude, but instead...well, thou art not a Friend, and I've no right to judge. Despite all, I'll not tell Father there is a soldier in the house. But I pray thee never to say so, for it would cause us great trouble at Monthly Meeting."

"I will leave in the morning, Miss Babcock."

Later that night, in their bedroom, fourteen-year-old Dinah could contain herself no longer. "Patience, art thou keeping a secret from Mother and Father?"

"Yes."

"Oh, Patience! Who is he? Where did thou meet him? Is he thy beau?"

"Dinah, thou art profoundly silly. He will be gone in the morning, and I'll never see him again. Not that I'd ever want to."

"But he saved thy life! How could anything be more...more..."

"Breathe not one word of this to anyone, little sister, lest trouble come to us all."

## Saturday, February 29: 1812
## Another Subscription

It was long past three in the morning, but there were still a few couples on the dance floor when General Brock and Miriam Lockwood left Freemason Hall. As Brock was about to whistle for his cab, Miriam touched his arm.

"It's not far, Isaac. Send your driver home."

They walked arm in arm through the freezing night. Brock held her tight as they crossed the frozen road.

# Ken Leland

"It's Leap Year," Miriam said. "I was born on Leap Year Day."

Brock smiled broadly behind his scarf. "And so, my dear, that means you are what...six or seven today?"

"Seven." Miriam laughed and held him closer as they neared her house.

"I'll find you a present, and come back for lunch," Brock said.

"Oh, no. Your present for me will be inside," she said, firmly steering him though the front gate. "Upstairs in my bedroom. That's the only present I want."

At midmorning, when Mrs. Roberts arrived at the shop, a letter from Jeremy hung from the door knocker. Miriam was nowhere in sight. Janie opened the letter and read:

My dearest Janie,

I receive your letters with great joy, three or four with every delivery. I'm also glad you are starting to feel more yourself in the morning. I remember it was much the same with Ethan.

I confess I've no idea what has become of Captain Lockwood. He was with us for some of the time while we cut a trail to Port Albino, but when I saw him last, he was in the company of an old Indian reprobate. That was at the Grand River.

After we crossed the Grand at Cayuga, Major Branson divided the expedition into four company sized fatigues. I work surveying routes for courier trails reaching north to the Dundas Road. We will continue west to a place called Culver's Tavern, then perhaps as far as Long Point. Time and weather determine all.

I've no idea how I'm to help Alex when he's never here.

Please give my regards to Miriam. All my love to you my darling wife.

Jeremy

"Where are you Miriam, you slow coach?" Janie called up the stairs. "Your brother's run off with the Indians!"

# The Land Between Flowing Waters

*****

Captain Lockwood stabled his horse in the barn behind the Cayuga general store. He had slept there for a week in a weather-tight feed room, and broke his fast each morning with a Haudenosaunee grandmother who lived beside the hamlet's grist mill. Dressed in his usual farm garb, Lockwood lounged on the general store's front steps as Major Branson led the fatigue companies over the ice-bound Grand. Folks from the Nations, and a few settlers who lived nearby, watched as they passed. One or two cheered; some laughed. Lockwood paid the troops no mind, but scanned the sparse crowd for a group of three well-armed farmers in weatherbeaten fur hats. He had watched each day for one or another to come to the general store, but was always disappointed.

"I'm surprised you're sitting here, and not riding with your friends," said a quiet voice.

"I..." When Lockwood turned, he saw an Indian on the steps just behind him – or, the speaker might have been Indian from his dress, if a native could speak faultless English with the faintest Scottish burr. The man was thin and fit, in his middle years with grey starting at his temples. As he walked downwind to tap the dottle from his pipe, Lockwood saw that the man was tall and likely very strong.

"Major Glegg described you pretty well, young man. I'm John Norton." He held out his hand. "Pleased to meet you, Captain Lockwood."


In late morning, Lockwood and Norton rode northwest along the river beneath white-barked sycamores. As they neared Brant's Ford, Lockwood could hear the sound of Haudenosaunee women singing.

"The Clan Mothers are arguing," Norton chuckled, as they reined in their horses to listen. The women were inside a whitewashed chapel a hundred yards from the river.

"A beautiful argument," Lockwood mused.

"That's in the Onondaga language," Norton replied. "The next might be in Mohawk or Seneca, or maybe a hymn in English. When they can't see their way, they sing – sometimes for hours."

"What's wrong?"

"Oh, about what you'd expect," Norton said. "We're almost home. I'll tell you over coffee and brandy."

Norton's farmhouse was spacious, built for councils and entertaining. Its mistress was a young, breathtakingly beautiful, Delaware woman. As she slid the library door closed, Norton poured from a steaming china pot.

"Tell General Brock that emissaries from our Brothers below the lakes have just arrived. They beg us to stand aside when the Long Knives invade."

"I beg your pardon!" Captain Lockwood sat up in astonishment. "Why would you even consider such a thing?"

"Normally, I wouldn't – but there are many who will. The Clan Mothers are trying to decide."

Lockwood stared out the window in dismay.

"Captain Lockwood, consider our position. The Haudenosaunee below remain on their lands only at the sufferance of President Madison. If we in Upper Canada fight the Yankees, it will be bad for our Brothers. The Americans might demand they fight us or lose their homes. Brother fighting Brother for the benefit of the Long Knives – the Clan Mothers will never stand for it."

"What can General Brock do?"

"In the end, maybe nothing. I'll not lead warriors against our own People."

"What if they refuse to fight beside the Americans?"

"Then General Brock can hope for our help."

"What else must we do?" Captain Lockwood asked.

"Brock must show he has a chance to win. There are so many traitors in Haldimand County, in Norfolk and Oxford, even in the towns – and the Friends and Mennonites will not raise their hands, not even to defend themselves. The war may well be over the moment the Yankees cross the border."

# Chapter Four
# Decisions

**Full, Trout Moon: 1812**
**(March 28, 1812)**
**The Grave House**
**Hannibal**

The snow's melting fast now. The red buds are all swollen so you can tell they're almost ready to make leaves. Last night my foster father, Kshiwe, told us about how his grandfather would slash a tree just deep enough so sugar water would drip into a bucket. Then women empty the sap into a boiling kettle and you get a fine, sweet syrup. Boil all the water away and you've got maple sugar. There was syrup on the General's table when I was a slave at Harrison's plantation, but I never did see how to make it. Father and I mended our buckets and now everyone's going to the sugar bush.

My Father thanked the grove for its gifts before we hung baskets or cut any firewood. Shkote helped us drag dead wood back to Grandmother and Senisqua who kept the fires going.

After a couple of weeks, the snow was gone and the clay pots were full up. It was about then that Mukos made Father angry.

Mukos came to us one day after we got home from the sugar bush. For a long time he stood outside the open lodge door waiting to be noticed. All of us inside could see him, but Grandmother said nothing, and so I just sat quiet beside her. Senisqua looked at Father, then at Mukos, then back to Father before going to sit by the south wall, her back turned. I guess Shkote didn't know what to do because he scooted outside to play. Finally, Father gave in.

# The Land Between Flowing Waters

"Welcome, Mukos." Kshiwe sat with crossed legs beside the hearth, facing the eastern door.

"Honoured, Uncle," Mukos said. He knelt across the fire from Father, but he didn't even look at my sister. "My parents told me. Women's Okama and Kmonokwe say the grave-houses should be made ready in ten days."

"Yes, in ten days. I'm thankful, Mukos, that this sad task does not fall upon your family, upon your shoulders."

Mukos didn't say anything for a long while. "Uncle, I would..."

"Hannibal, Shkote and I will build the grave-house for Nanokas and Mishomes. Your help is not needed. It is not appropriate. You are not a part of this family. You never can be."

I could tell Father was very angry and upset. Senisqua bent to the floor and hid beneath a buffalo robe. She didn't make a sound but I could see the robe trembling.

"Uncle..."

This time the silence lasted forever. Father just looked at the fire.

"Uncle, Senisqua and I ask if somehow there could be a way for us. We know we are both Bear Clan, but..."

"No! It is shameful." Father shook his head. "Don't you think I've asked myself, again and again? Both of you must put it aside."

Then Father turned his back. "Don't come again to see Senisqua."


Our village cemetery is a little west between the river and the last lake. The next morning, Father gathered up a stone mattock, an iron spike, and a heavy wooden mallet, and we went to build the grave-house. I carried cattail mats to sit on and Shkote brought the trader's axe. We squished along the muddy trail with lots of other men on the way to the oak grove. The forest is open there and you can see for a good way all around. The trees are big and far apart. Shkote and I held hands but we couldn't circle a tree trunk even half way round. The ground is crunchy from last year's acorn caps, and above, the branches have only a few brown leaves.

"Shkote," Father said, "Choose an oak that Nanokas would like for shade on a hot summer's day."

And so we wandered until Shkote found a tree even bigger than all the rest. I spread the mats and we knelt there facing the oak. Father prayed aloud, explaining and asking for permission.

Then we began to dig. There was mud but the ground below was frozen. I held the spike and Father whacked it with the big mallet. Shkote tossed the clods away till we dug a trench a little longer than a man is tall. The three of us worked in the frozen mud all day, most to sundown, but when I stood in the trench, it was only a little deeper than my knees.

"Good, that's deep enough," Father said. "Tomorrow we'll make the grave-house."

The men chipped planks for the graves. Then we made a box almost as high above the ground as the trench was deep. Planks and staves made the sides and the top.

On the tenth day, everyone got up real early. It was grey and rainy but the Grandmothers brought out all the people who died and laid them in a circle beside the corn fields. So many died in the winter! When Kmonokwe and I went to the lodges trying to help, I saw some dead folks, but Grandmothers always took them away. Some people, like Father's companion and baby boy, died even before we got home.

The bodies were wrapped, some in cloth, some in furs. Kshiwe knelt in the rain to draw back the cover from one face. The bulge beneath the blanket was a little baby, cradled in the woman's left arm. Father sat there in the drizzle for a long while. Kmonokwe and the Elders called out prayers to the Master, prayers of thanksgiving and remembrance, prayers of consolation, prayers of hope for better days.

Then all the People walked in single file to the cemetery. The bodies were on travois because there weren't enough pall bearers. At the oak grove, I saw three strangers standing quietly as we passed, their muskets grounded, their forearms resting on the muzzles.

I led the horse to the grave-house we built. When I unhitched the poles, Mukos came. Father stared at him but we needed help to lift Nanokas into the grave. Finally, Father nodded.

"Mukos, I would be most grateful for your help."

Together they sealed the timber box.

Shkote tied a white mink pelt to the top of the funeral pole and Father set the pole up high beside the grave. All across the oak grove, all those little flags dripping in the rain.

# The Land Between Flowing Waters

## New, Maple Sugar Moon: 1812
## (April 11, 1812)
## The Emissaries

"Dear Brothers, I grieve for your losses. The Master of Life has gathered thirty-one of your beloved to the Land of Peace. But in your village, many yet stand to face what is to come."

So the Emissary spokesman began his address that night in the Warriors' Lodge.

When the People of Shishibes Lake had gathered, Pipe Carrier brought forth the feather-garlanded calumet. He filled the bowl and lighted it so that rising smoke might carry each person's thoughts to the Master. Maukekose spoke the opening prayers as the pipe was passed, first to the three visitors, and then to each of the villagers. Kmonokwe led the responses.

All but the youngsters were crowded inside the Lodge. Outside in the red-clouded evening, half-naked youngsters laughed and swooped like mosquitoes between the muddy fields. Inside, Wabameme of the Marten Clan, emissary of Main Poche, stood at Okama Menomni's gentle urgings to speak the news he carried to all the Neshnabek.

"Brothers, the news I bear is simple and dire. By the waning of the Strawberry Moon, war will spread across Turtle Island. The Long Knife chiefs prepare to attack the King's People above the lakes. They make no secret of their plans."

From the smiles creeping across the faces of Ashkum, Maukekose, and several others, it was clear that not everyone supposed this news was unfortunate.

"Brothers, I admit I feel no sorrow that the newcomers will once again fall to killing one another. Main Poche is with the English across the Erie Lake. Tecumseh was there too, but now he travels to the Mississinewa for a conference of all the Nations. The English promise to arm all who stand with them. Governor Harrison says he will do

# Ken Leland

the same if we join the Long Knives. So it is as in our grandfathers' time – we must decide what to do, even if it is only to stand aside."

Wabameme sat then, and listened quietly throughout the night as the villagers passed the speaking feather from hand to hand. Wabameme had heard it all before – at Pierishe Village, at Winamac, at Aubbeenaubee, at Tiosa, and at Five Medals. He would hear the arguments for days and days more as he carried the news west to the Kankakee and Illinois Rivers. In the end, most People would decide: the English must show us they are willing to fight. It must never again be as it was at Fallen Timbers, for the King to abandon the Nations to the Yankee armies.

"Walk home with me, Kshiwe," Kmonokwe said.

Pink dawn coloured the tree-line as the villagers left the Warriors' Lodge, south to the river, east and north to the lodges beside the string of lakes. As the weary scattered to their homes, Kshiwe and Kmonokwe walked west on the elm-sheltered trail to the causeway. Menomni's footsteps approached from behind, and with a "May the Master bless you," he hurried on with a smile. Kshiwe was stiff from sitting all night on the wooden lodge floor. *Kmonokwe must be sleepy*, he thought, as they ambled slower and slower till they were quite alone on the path. She wandered close to brush against his shoulder, but then veered away, like a sleepwalker. Eventually Kshiwe realised she wanted him to take her hand. After that they went on together, arms entwined, down the path to the shallows between the lakes. The footbridge was bathed in mist as the sun rose above the trees.

On the opposite shore was a white carpet of trillium. In the face of a cool spring breeze, they meandered along the trail toward the home of Women's Okama. Then Kmonokwe stepped in front of Kshiwe, as if to block his way. He bumped into her, and suddenly his arms were holding her upright. Kmonokwe embraced his neck and snuggled close to kiss his ear.

"What have you told Nanokas?" she asked.

Indeed, Kshiwe had knelt beside his companion's grave for hours yesterday, recounting every moment since Kmonokwe appeared in the lodge at Prophetstown.

"Everything I can remember."

Kmonokwe leaned back only far enough to look in Kshiwe's face. Her belly and hips pressed against him. "And?"

85

# The Land Between Flowing Waters

"She laughs and teases me. She asks why we live apart."

Kmonokwe nestled against him for warmth and rested her head on his shoulder.

"A good question," she murmured. Then, "You owe me a favour."

"I owe you far, far more than that," Kshiwe said as he caressed her shoulders and back.

"You owe me six days. Together. At Maxinkuckee Lake. We will make two travel lodges – one for the children, one for us. Yes?"

He kissed her eyes. "Yes."

"We have a lot to decide."

# Ken Leland

## New, No Snow Moon: 1812
## (May 10, 1812)
## Maxinkuckee Lake

Kshiwe hobbled the horses so they might graze in the forest beside Maxinkuckee Lake. Then he, Kmonokwe and the children looked out from the grass-covered beach. The lake was a bowl, so wide that the far shore was blue with haze in the sparkling morning light. The water was clear and brilliant, and cattails lined the shore. Shkote kicked off his moccasins, but could only bear to dip his toes before coming away with a shriek.

The beach was long untended. Willow and cottonwood saplings grew up between the ribs of abandoned canoes.

"Such fear there must have been," Kmonokwe said as they walked through the debris.

"No one has been here for many years," Kshiwe speculated.

"We were. Toghtarask and I came here," Kmonokwe said. Then she turned to grasp Senisqua's hand. "That was before you were born, my dear."

Kshiwe was careful to look anywhere except at the woman he'd grown to love. *Who was Toghtarask?* he wondered.

"Come, everyone. I'll show you where my parents lived," Kmonokwe said.

"Is it safe?" Kshiwe asked. Shkote and Hannibal hovered a little closer as they walked the long-forgotten path up to the village site.

"Of course it's safe. I loved everyone here."

The day was cloudless and bright. A light breeze swept in from the south, over the vast lake and up the gentle slope to the open forest. The wind, fresh at their backs, urged them onward into a pasture. The children scattered into the yellow expanse. The lodges had long since collapsed to leave dark ovals of rotting bark and branches. Last year's waist-high grasses were broken, falling into the new green carpet. The children spread out, stalking through the empty field. Red-winged blackbirds trilled from leaning lodge poles, and quail sprang into the air.

"Here it is. This is where my parents lived," Kmonokwe said, her arms spread wide in the midst of a blackened space. She knelt then to pick at bits of wood covering the ground.

"Children," Kshiwe called, "Go find a place to build our lodges, down closer to the lake...away from all this." He stooped then to gather Kmonokwe into his arms, and held her close as she cried.

# The Land Between Flowing Waters

"Smallpox," she sobbed. "It took everyone."

After a time, she leaned back to wipe her eyes. "Only their bones remained – my father, my mother. Toghtarask built one grave-house so they might rest together."

In a small copse of young maples, not far from the lake, the children pulled a sapling-top to the ground and staked it to make an arch. Another sapling formed the second arch, and another, the third. They used reed mats to make walls. Senisqua helped the boys, but when they were almost done she moved away a little to build a shelter of her own. Kmonokwe and Kshiwe worked together, but before long she said to him, "Kshiwe, find a spot where Shkote can fish. Take Hannibal hunting. Let the women do their work."

In the late afternoon of the first day, Kshiwe and Hannibal lay downwind, in ambush beside a deer run. They'd made a blind from brush a dozen paces from the trail, and they crouched there in silence. It was Hannibal's first chance to use the deer-arrows he made with Mukos.

Kshiwe's lance lay on the ground between them, but he made no move to grasp it as a yearling buck appeared. He only raised his finger to point towards the head of the trail. Slowly, the yearling drew even with the blind. Its head was down carelessly to sniff the ground. Hannibal trembled as he shifted onto his knees, drew, and loosed.

The stone-pointed arrow struck deep, just behind the front shoulder. The yearling surged forward in leaps as if unwounded, but as Kshiwe shouted, "Quick, your knife!" the deer fell onto its side, gasping, with a blood-speckled muzzle.

Hannibal bounded from their hiding place, straddled the deer and instantly slashed its throat.

"We thank you. We hunger," the boy said as the buck's spirit fled its death throes. "Father!" he shouted then in celebration.

"And did you make him carry the carcass all the way back?" Kmonokwe asked Kshiwe.

"It was only a yearling," he replied. "He was so proud."

It was long past sunset. As they sat outside, the stars sparkled in a moonless sky. Kmonokwe drew the striped blanket-coat around her shoulders and called to a sleepy Shkote. She pulled the boy onto her lap and wrapped him into her coat. Senisqua joined them, stood close, and then leaned in to pat her little brother's head. Across the campsite, Kshiwe and Hannibal knelt beside the fire-frames, curing the last of the venison strips.

"Will you tell us a story tonight?" a tired Shkote asked Kmonokwe.

"Your brother can tell you again how he killed the deer," she said as Hannibal approached, "and you can tell him how you caught the buffalo fish we had for supper."

"Good night, Mother," Shkote said as he struggled up from her lap to grab his brother's hand. "You tell me a story," he said to Hannibal as he pulled him towards their lodge.

Senisqua reached down to help Kmonokwe to her feet. "I'm glad we are all together now," Senisqua said as she turned to her own bed.

Then Kmonokwe slid into Kshiwe's arms. She kissed his lips, his eyes, embracing him with all her might. She pressed against him as he ran his hands over her back and hips.

"My love," she said, "it's cold. Come to bed."


Kmonokwe laid the coat aside as Kshiwe searched through his cartouche for flint and file. A stream of sparks bled from the iron onto the pine shavings in the hearth. The smallest flame caught, and then spread, light leaping outward to the hearth stones, to the fur pallet, to Kmonokwe.

Kshiwe watched as she slipped off her blouse and threw it atop her coat.

"Kmonokwe! How lovely you are."

She smiled at him and loosened the belt at her waist. Her wrap and small-clothes fell away. These too she tossed aside.

"Oh, Kshiwe. It's cold in here too."

"Then come to me." Kshiwe held out his hand to her.

"Oh, yes. But lie back now," she said.

Kmonokwe bent to loosen the shirt ties at his throat. His eyes followed her every movement, unblinking. She opened the silver clasp holding back her hair, then raised both arms, lifting her breasts before him. She smiled, for surely his eyelids now would break. Her hair fell down around her. He pulled his shirt over his head. When he was free, he fell back onto the furs.

"Kmonokwe, you are so very, very lovely."

# The Land Between Flowing Waters

Kmonokwe bent to pluck the ties at his waist. She pulled away his clout and leggings, then caressed him between her hands as he gasped and quivered at her touch.

"You are very lovely, too," she said.

His fingers came up to touch her face, to stroke her neck. He kissed and fondled her. Kmonokwe sighed – how long had it been since she had known such... Swaying, breathing deeply, she was beginning to feel a little dizzy. Kmonokwe was lost in pleasure as his fingertips brushed across her belly. Her breath shortened into soft whimpers. *O most wondrous...*

"Kmonokwe."

"Mmmmm?"

"Please."

She moved to straddle him. She knew he was on the edge of urgent need. Kmonokwe began to move above him. *Amazing, amazing*, she thought as Kshiwe clasped her with a sharp cry.

"My darling, Kshiwe. My dearest," she said aloud as she kissed his face and neck and thought, *You wonderful man, you feel just like Toghtarask.*

She rested upon his chest as he told her how much he loved her, how beautiful she was, how so very incredibly beautiful she was. And she did not doubt his love.

"Stay with me. Stay with me," she whispered.

Breathing deeply, again she raised herself over him. Kshiwe's hands drifted along her ribs, and as she moved her spirit drifted, dreaming in love and boundless affection. The man beneath her was her friend, her companion, the most wonderful father of her children – the man who pleased her, body and soul. Now her breath was coming in forceful, shortening gasps, her body tensing, tighter and tighter. She pushed down hard and trembled in a long surge of delight.

They were quiet for a while.

"Oh. That was wonderful," she sighed.

"Is it always like that for you?"

"No, just sometimes. Don't worry."

Kshiwe soon fell into a dream.

*Toghtarask*, Kmonokwe thought happily, *somehow you've found your way into this man. But I know Kshiwe loves me, so it doesn't matter. Sometimes I will see you, feel you my love, and sometimes Kshiwe. Maybe Nanokas lives in me. It doesn't matter. It just doesn't matter.*

# Ken Leland

The next day Kshiwe and Kmonokwe lounged in the lee of an outcropping boulder, a few-score paces uphill from their campsite. In the distance the lake waters were grey and wind-torn, and beside them, on the hillside, May-apple fronds bent in the wind. Kshiwe sat propped against the stone. Kmonokwe reclined between his legs, resting her back upon his chest. Her striped coat covered them both in the blustery light of early afternoon.

"May I ask you a question, my love?" Kshiwe said.

"Only if you don't fear the answer," Kmonokwe replied.

"Who is Toghtarask?"

"Who was Toghtarask." She twisted back to kiss his cheek.

There was a hint of relief in his voice. "Who was Toghtarask?"

"The most wonderful man I have ever known, save for you." Beneath the coat, she moved his hands to cup her breasts. "My companion, gone to the Master's Village almost two years now."

Unspeaking, they watched from afar as Shkote clambered among the boulders with his fishing pole. After a while he gave up as the south wind drove chilling spray into his face. Hannibal was out of sight with his bird arrows, hunting for supper. Senisqua had stretched the deer hide on a frame, and they could see her sheltering behind her small lodge as she scraped the skin. She had promised Kmonokwe a pair of knee-high decorated moccasins for winter.

"Senisqua and Mukos have a difficult problem," Kmonokwe commented to Kshiwe.

"You know of this?"

"Everyone does. You only have to watch them."

Kshiwe growled in her ear.

"You realise Mukos' parents are helpless. There is nothing they can do. He's a disobedient, disrespectful, and shameful young man."

"You're right," Kshiwe agreed.

"But, my love, there is something you can do to your disobedient, disrespectful, and shameful daughter."

"I'll not beat her. Never," he replied. "That's as unnatural as marrying within the Clan."

"If you wish to help them, you must disown her."

# The Land Between Flowing Waters

Kshiwe was astonished. "No! It would break her heart." He turned her shoulders to face him. "Kmonokwe, how can you suggest such a terrible thing?"

"Have patience. Women's Okama told me Nanokas came from Five Medals Village."

"That's right. It was my mother's village, and she knew Nanokas' family. She chose Nanokas for me."

"And the people of Five Medals are Wolf Clan?"

"Yes. Yes they are."

"This is how you may help Senisqua and Mukos. Go to the people of Shishibes Lake and say that your daughter disobeys you in her love for Mukos, that she does not respect your judgment, and that she is shameful for wanting to marry a Bear Clan brother. Say that you disown her and that you will return her to...does she still have blood kin at Five Medals?"

"Her grandparents."

"Say you will return her to her grandparents. She is Bear Clan no longer. She is Wolf. Then Mukos can sit outside the grandparent's lodge till all the streams run dry, and finally bring her home."

"No one will be fooled by all that, especially when they come back together," Kshiwe said.

"You're not out to trick anyone, Kshiwe, only to give your daughter a chance to love Mukos as I love you."

Kshiwe considered for a long time, and in the end he decided. "It's the only way for them, isn't it?"

"Are we agreed then?" Kmonokwe asked. "Our first journey will be to the Elk Hart River to meet Senisqua's grandparents."

"And where else would you have us go?" Kshiwe laughed.

Kmonokwe stood. "To our bed. I want to work my magic on you again before we talk about that."

During the night, the wind shifted to the southeast to bring warmth instead of cool lake breezes. Morning sunshine soaked the land, driving away the last spring chills. Kshiwe carried his shirt in one hand as he and Kmonokwe walked along the shore. Shkote and Hannibal romped naked through the ankle-deep shallows, howling in the splashing cold water. From higher on the open treed hill, Senisqua watched them all, and then, when her father waved, she returned to her work decorating a small birch box with dye and quills.

# Ken Leland

"You have children?" Kshiwe asked Kmonokwe as she led him by the hand. They followed an overgrown trail that wound gently uphill to the east.

"You know well that I've borne children."

"Yes, my love," Kshiwe said, "but, I mean, where are they?"

"Walpole Island."

"Where is that?" he asked.

"You know that the Erie and Huron Lakes are connected, by a great river called the Detroit?"

"I've not seen the Detroit, or anything north of Erie," he said.

"Walpole is in the northern part of that passage, on the King's side of the river." She walked backwards now, both hands extended to him on the shaded path. "I have two grown sons. The elder's companion will make me a grandmother before the end of summer. And I have a daughter, about Senisqua's age." She turned then to go on alone. "I will leave for Walpole in a few days."

She listened. The warm, soft breeze rustled the new-growing leaves overhead, but that did not hide the whispered "No!" She looked back.

"By what right, my love, do you tell me 'No'?" she asked.

Kshiwe was transfixed, his face contorted in disbelief. "I...by no right...but how can you leave?"

Kmonokwe approached but did not reach out to him.

"Surely, you will come back to us," he said. "Bring your family to Shishibes Lake. We cannot live without you. I cannot."

Then Kmonokwe leaned in and wrapped her arms around him. "This is my last visit here. I will not return."

"But why?"

"Dearest," Kmonokwe asked, "what would happen if Horse Soldiers came riding now into our little camp?"

"But...that won't happen. I promise we're safe here."

"I want to believe you, but you know it isn't true," she said.

Kshiwe scowled at her.

"My love, if Long Knives came, you would be dead in ten heartbeats. And what would happen to precious Senisqua, and your friend Kmonokwe? As you lie bleeding your spirit into Mother Earth, the soldiers would use us until we were dust."

"No. It won't happen!"

"And dear little Shkote, what of him? He would be sabre practice."

# The Land Between Flowing Waters

"I will not listen to this." Kshiwe whirled and began to stalk back down the trail. Kmonokwe ran after and clutched at him.

"And your black son. What will they do? Kill him? No, they will truss him across a horse and carry him away – to be a slave again."

Kshiwe broke free of her and began to run down the trail. Kmonokwe fell to the earth and called to his fleeing back.

"What did you promise the boy? What did you promise his father at Prophetstown?"

A hundred paces on, at the bottom of the hill, Kshiwe slowed and stood with his fists driven into his waist. He kicked and stomped the tussocks there as she watched. There were incoherent screams of rage, a long howl of "No!", then repeated shouts of "How can she say such things?" and finally some tears he tried to hide.

One high cloud after another swept over the hill to cool her skin. After a while she saw Kshiwe sit down and wrap his arms around his knees. Seemingly, he stared at the lodges, toward his children in the valley below. Eventually, she saw him turn to find her on the trail above. Then he slumped down again, but this time facing uphill.


Kmonokwe did not raise her eyes as he approached. His shadow covered the grass beside her.

"You said, 'your friend Kmonokwe'."

She sighed. "And so I am. Should I be more?"

"I love you. I cannot live without you."

"I feel the same," she said as she looked up into his face.

"We will go to every lodge to say it."

"Yes, to every lodge," she agreed.

"We will be companions, forever."

"Forever," Kmonokwe vowed as she stood.

"Then we will go to the Elk Hart and on to Walpole. All of us."

"Yes," she said. And then with a little smile, "it will be as you say."

They held each other tight. After a long time, she patted his bare back and leaned out of his embrace. "Now let us go to the grave-house to tell my parents."

# Ken Leland

## Monday, May 18: 1812
## The Sawmill

Climbing roses clothed the picket fence beside the Niagara Dress and Tailor Shoppe, and on the front lawn, Janie Roberts sat on a padded bench beneath a shade tree. On her belly she balanced thread and scissors as she sewed buttons to a man's swallow-tailed coat. On the bench across the gravel path, Miriam Lockwood hemmed a camisole as white petals floated down from the pear tree. Janie's two-year-old son Ethan, with trowel and wooden bowls, dug in the vegetable garden beside the house.

Baby stretched inside her. Janie reached down to massage the spot as she absentmindedly gazed across the road to the tree-lined beach. Light sparkled from the waves on Lake Ontario.

"Hello! Hello!" It was John Ellis, pounding down the sidewalk. His adoptive father, General Isaac Brock, was not far behind.

At the call of "March" John slowed and held open the gate for his father, then John rushed to hug Miriam.

"Hello John," Miriam said as she kissed his cheek.

"Grandma Lois asks you to come for Sunday dinner."

"I'd love to," Miriam said as Brock came to stand beside her.

"Father's bringing dinner!" John crowed.

"From the Commissary," Brock said with a depreciative wave.

"That's very thoughtful, Isaac." Miriam reached out to him.

Janie glanced at them with a warm smile. *Finally,* Janie thought, *Miriam has a man who gives her the independence and respect she craves. The General and his Lady, the townsfolk are saying.* There were people, she knew, who lifted their noses to sniff at the lack of a wedding band, but many others were happy that the middle-aged general and the handsome spinster had found each other.

Miriam glowed as Brock fondly picked pear blossoms from her braided hair. John crossed the path to gaze shyly at Janie's swollen belly.

"And Grandma wants you to come too, Mrs. Roberts – and please to bring Ethan, because Grandma misses him."

"I'd be most glad," Janie said with a wince as the baby turned over.

"What?" John asked in alarm.

"May he?" Janie asked Brock.

95

# The Land Between Flowing Waters

"Of course."

Janie took John's hand between her long, elegant fingers, and pressed his palm against her abdomen. "Wait just a moment. Baby doesn't like lying on that side for very long."

Soon enough, she flinched again.

"Oh! I felt that," John said in wonder. "Is it a boy?"

"Maybe," Janie said. "Ethan's in the garden. I think he's digging a hole to China."

John kissed Janie's cheek before running off.

Brock came to Janie. She patted the bench for him to sit beside her.

"Mrs. Roberts, I'm certain your husband is alright," Brock said as he slipped a letter from his waistband. "Major Branson has written this note to you."

Janie noticed the unfamiliar handwriting as she broke the seal.

My dear Mrs. Roberts,

Your husband and Captain Lockwood will be unable to communicate with you or Miss Lockwood, possibly for several weeks. Please do not be alarmed.

Both have left the expedition I command. In the guise of civilians, they hope to discover the identities of certain traitorous ruffians known to be operating in the vicinity of Twenty Mile Creek.

My most respectful regards,
Major W. Branson

Janie clutched the letter in fingers that suddenly felt cold.

\*\*\*\*\*

The bridge over the headwaters of Twenty Mile Creek was barely five yards long. A ramshackle tavern lay on the opposite side, almost lost among the trees. The shin-deep swamp, laughingly called a road, petered out just past the saloon as it split into ever smaller muddy rivulets that disappeared west and south into the forest. It was a grey, misty afternoon, but a score of horse-carts and filth-speckled nags were tied to the hitching post outside

# Ken Leland

Twenty Tavern. The publican took his ease outside, alone on the porch of his own establishment.

Muffled voices could be heard, but the common room was empty. A squint-eyed man in dirty trousers sat beside the back room door. A shotgun was balanced across his knees.

The door was slightly ajar. Inside a meeting was in progress. The room was crowded; men in rough, homespun clothes sat on benches along both sides of a plank table. Other men leaned against the wall. The air was foul, but the windows were closed. At the head of the table sat Assemblyman Elijah Mason, a tall, stout, middle-aged man with a florid complexion and a quick smile. Mason was the representative for the riding of West York, and he was running for reelection to the Sixth Parliament of Upper Canada. The men in the room supposed themselves to be workers in his reelection campaign.

"Some of you are too young to remember," Mason glanced at a couple of young toughs leaning against the wall to his left, "but it's easy to point a man's mind where it's got to go."

Neither of the young louts blinked an eye. The one with sandy hair pulled out a foot-long pig stabber and began to pare his grime-encrusted nails; the dark-haired one gripped his rifle barrel. The other men in the room were older and similarly armed. A few snorted in amusement. One farmer spat tobacco juice through gapped teeth onto the floor and grinned at scoundrels across the table. Many seemed to remember well enough.

"Most times," Mason said, "all you got to do is pile some dry brush under the corn crib. Make it look like maybe the wind rolled it there. But folks know. A man'll call his neighbours, and they'll stand around and jaw about it. 'Who done that? Who's got it in for me?' But they always figure it out right quick – which side the butter's on."

Mason looked as though he might say more, but thought better of it. "Mr. Benson here will tell you when and where. Good day, gentlemen."

Mason shook hands with every man before leaving, a silver crown warm inside each handshake. Benson, a thin, hard man with three days' growth covering the scar below his right eye, moved to the head of the table as the door closed. During the Revolution, Benson had led a Safety Committee that promoted terror and intimidation against those still loyal to the Crown. To Benson, the present and yesteryear were much the same.

"Now, you men know it ain't always as easy as Mason says. Sometimes you got to spark a chicken coop, or fire a barn like we

97

did to the Sloans a couple weeks ago. A lantern through the back door with folks asleep upstairs is mighty powerful too, but you got to be careful not to annoy the Tories too much. They's right mean bastards when they get riled, and there's lots of them – some places, but not here. We'll run 'em out, just like we did before, and all those bloody Redcoats with 'em."

The young pig-stabber and the dark-haired rifleman stared at each other. Benson picked up his mouldy fur hat and jammed it on his head.

"The election's three weeks from tomorrow, so sleep late mornings. There'll be work to do at night. Now let's roust that innkeeper – the whiskey's on Mason!"

As darkness fell, the two young hooligans staggered from the Twenty Tavern. They seemed surprisingly drunk on the few drinks they had actually consumed. As they wandered up the trail to the sawmill, each straightened and breathed deeply to clear his head. The sandy-haired ruffian glanced around to ensure they are alone.

"My God, Alex. Those men are traitors! They're gonna kill somebody if we don't stop them."

"You're right, Jeremy. You've got to find Major Branson. Tell him to get a company of militia down here and arrest the bastards."

"Ho! You think I'm leaving you here alone? No, we'll go out together, Alex."

"And what will we tell Branson if we both leave? That some farmers threatened to burn their neighbours' corn cribs? Don't you see? One of us has to stay, go on a few raids, see who does what and write it all down."

"Alex, you're a damned blasted fool. You'll get us killed!"

"Branson can't arrest them without evidence. I've got to stay, or these men will go free."

*****

The day's last sunlight streamed through the western windows, into the yellow-painted farm kitchen.

"Mother, the neighbours have agreed," Henry Babcock said over supper. "Three weeks, Fifth Day, there'll be a barn-raising for the Sloans."

"Poor folks," his wife Margaret said. "Does anyone know how the fire started?"

Henry sighed and leaned back. On his left Patience and Hopestill both looked up with interest, but Nathan and Dinah still attended to their soup. He looked down the table to Margaret and combed his beard with his fingers.

"The men are talking about patrolling the roads at night."

"Father!" Hopestill said. Nathan and Dinah looked up.

"Tell me please, Husband, how that will not lead to violence!"

"I'd not go armed..."

"Father!"

"... or even carry a snake stick. And no, Hopestill. Thou and thy brother will stay home to look after the farm," Henry continued. "I could put a cot on the back porch. The boys could take turns sleeping out there...and listening."

"And I inside the kitchen door all night, watching over them," Margaret said.

Henry frowned. It was exactly what his wife would do. The silence at table stretched on for a while.

"I can see thee hast already done some thinking on this," Margaret offered quietly, "but it is a matter for the Business Meeting on Third Day. Pray, Husband, let there'll be no patrolling until then. Not until there is a sense of the Meeting."

Henry knew she was right, but The Peace of Christ did not require a man to lie down a victim. A magistrate could be found to enforce the law.

Henry looked at Patience. He had never gotten a full explanation of her near tragedy in the winter. Somehow, he thought, her problems were linked to the ruffians in the neighbourhood. Nevertheless, she was defiantly closed-mouthed. Her temper, her independence – how like her dear Mother. Now Patience was gazing at him with those open, determined eyes he loved so well. He sought to break the mood so he passed the cornbread and laughed.

"Ye will never guess who was at the sawmill this afternoon."

There were no takers and so he continued with a twinkle in his eye. "T'was the young man who saved our Patience-of-the-icy-pool. He's working there."

Two days later, Henry Babcock, Patience and the boys drove the heavy wagon to the sawmill on Twenty Mile Creek. Henry did not find it untoward that Patience should wish to thank young Mr. Lockyer again, but he was surprised at how long she primped before declaring herself ready. She wore the same long blue dress and spring coat, the same dark bonnet over her brown curly hair. Still, something about her demeanour gave the air of...well, Henry wasn't sure, but something about it all reminded him of days long ago with Margaret.

After the spring melt, the millpond was high against its banks. The saw's screech could be heard far down the muddy road on this warm May morning. The lumber yard was filled with last year's timber, dried and prime for cutting. While Hopestill and Nathan drove the wagon away to be loaded, Henry Babcock went to the manager's office to arrange future deliveries. On her own, Patience wandered into the saw room. The man she sought stood by the governing lever for the vertical saw.

"Good day, Mr. Lockyer," Patience shouted over the ripping din.

Lockwood turned in surprise. He wore a straw hat and a sodden plaid shirt, both pasted with yellow sawdust. His pants were oilstained, and he was covered in sweat. Patience could not tear her eyes away.

"Miss Babcock! I did not imagine..."

He looked positively startled. Patience put her hand to her ear and motioned for him to come outside. He called to an oddly familiar, sandy-haired stranger holding a log roller to take his place at the governor.

Patience saw her father watching through the office window, but she continued around the sawmill to a platform over the millrace. She glanced down into the green water surging along the wooden box onto the drive wheel, then turned, and was most pleased to see that he had followed.

"I wanted to thank thee, properly and humbly, as I should have done before," Patience said. "And to tell thee that I am praying for thee..."

She saw his jaw set and the quick shake of his head.

"No, I'm sorry. That didn't come out right."

Her eyes implored that he not be angry. "I mean, I am praying for thee in a generous and heart-felt way, for the good of thy soul. I am determined to think well of...everyone...as we are all God's children."

This time his look was quizzical.

"No, that's not quite right either. I mean, I wish thee good in everything."

Now his brow was beginning to lift and there was a ghost of a smile.

"And I'm praying in thanksgiving to the Lord, because thou hast left the soldier's life of violence and become..." she looked about somewhat at a loss, "....become a sawyer."

She saw his total confusion, as if she had suddenly spoken in an unknown language, but still he made no reply. Desperate at his reluctance to confide in her, Patience blurted the sentence she had practised so long. "She must be very proud that thou hast left the army. Is she here with thee?"

Lockwood could not restrain himself. "She?"

"Thy wife." Patience steeled herself to see him nod in agreement. She had memorized what she must say immediately after that nod.

"The lovely brown-haired woman who sat beside thee at the Niagara service. Thy...wife?"

"That was my sister," Lockwood smiled. "I have no wife."

"Oh! That's wonderful," Patience gushed in relief. "I mean, it's wonderful thou hast a sister. Truly. Wonderful."

Patience supposed the worst was over. There was only one plank more in her construction of a new, favourable understanding of him. "That night at Niagara, I too was most upset, as I think thee must have been, that the sandy-haired man..."

Patience momentarily lost her train of thought.

"...that the sandy-haired man would presume to flaunt that poor woman's slavery at a Friends' service. Surely, thou too wert appalled by the effrontery. Thou couldst not stop staring at her."

The plea in her eyes was beyond mistake. Lockwood's head was reeling. He would not lie to this remarkably deluded young woman, but he could hardly admit the truth.

\*\*\*\*\*

The sliding panels were closed, separating the women and men at Third Day's Meeting for Business. In segregation, both men and women were freed from ties of affection and posture to seek the Lord's Counsel. As usual, Mrs. Rogers had asked the women of Lundy's Corners Meeting to quiet their hearts and minds. For twenty minutes not a word was spoken, not a sentiment expressed, until Mrs. Wilson spoke clearly from her seat along the wall.

"'Except the Lord keep the city, the watchmen waketh but in vain.' Yet it is needful for me to endeavour to keep in the watch tower, yea, to dwell there whole nights."

*It was clear enough,* Mrs. Rogers thought, *where Emily Wilson would stand on the issue of Quaker men patrolling to guard the community against outlaws.*

There was barely time to close devotions before a grandmother in the first row was on her feet. "Emily Wilson, I cannot agree with thee quoting Elder Cadwallader in such a fashion. Every counsel she has ever given is based squarely upon The Peace. That night in Niagara, she was being...poetic."

Several voices murmured in agreement.

Margaret Babcock looked to her daughters beside her in the long row of unpadded wooden chairs. Patience and Dinah were rapt in attention as the discussion began.

"The Sloans may have lost their barn, but they aren't Friends."

"The Sloans, like ourselves, are Children of God."

"Everyone must be prepared to witness against evil."

"We must stand aside to preserve The Peace."

"Those supporting the Americans know we will not bear arms. They'll not harm us."

"'Do the work of an evangelist – make full proof of thy ministry.' To do less than protect our neighbours is moral cowardice."

"We gave our support to the King and his government so that we might come to Upper Canada."

"The men must go unarmed."

"Should Friends patrol with those who do bear arms?"

"The government exempts us from the militia."

"We are not exempt from fines for not serving!"

"Are we exempt from ruffians?"

"'O Love Divine! A ray wherefrom warms the breast, inflames the heart of the true Christian, to make him love his enemies, and do good for evil.'"

"What should we do if, in Conscience, a soldier flees from violence and asks to shelter among us?"

Margaret was astonished to see Patience beside her, standing to speak for the first time in a Meeting for Business. It was an important question, Margaret thought. One perhaps that would take many Meetings to resolve, but what on earth could have prompted Patience to ask it?

Mrs. Rogers ruled that the question was too complex to be decided quickly, and suggested it be laid over till next meeting. Mrs. Rogers then asked the Secretary to find a consensus on patrolling.

In writing, the Secretary sought to express the sense of the Women's Meeting. As the women waited, the Men's Business Meeting droned on beyond the wall. The Secretary's first attempt at expressing consensus failed, as did the second, but the third – calling on the men to patrol unarmed and in sufficient numbers to witness safely against evil – was passed and slipped through the opening between the panels. And thus, the men came to know the Lord's Will, as seen through the eyes of their mothers, wives, and daughters.

## Thursday, June 4, 1812
## The King's Birthday
## Janie Roberts

This is perfectly ridiculous. I may be more than eight months along, but everyone supposes I am a glass bottle liable to burst. Glegg can hardly restrain himself. He keeps peeking at me with those worried smiles.

"Major Glegg, I assure you the carriage springs are very comfortable. Aren't they Miriam? So you needn't worry. Really."

"Well, if you're quite sure, Mrs. Roberts. It's truly a lovely day, and we are most pleased you insisted on coming."

Glegg, Miriam and I are in the second carriage on the country road leading south out of Niagara. Our fathers, Ben and Asa, are in the lead carriage with General Brock and John Ellis. Today, the King's Birthday, is a bright warm day, and on June 4th men always come together for militia service. The First Lincoln Regiment, some 500 neighbourhood loyalists, is mustering in a newly mown hayfield. The Light Artillery and the Coloured Corps will maneuver with them. General Brock is attending so that he might watch and encourage, for today our militia will go through their paces with a purpose, perhaps for the first time since the Yankee Rebellion.

# The Land Between Flowing Waters

All the way out of town our fathers regale the General with stories of Butler's Rangers and the old war, but, thank the Lord, both are too old to serve again, even if they are full of advice. From time to time my father's laughter floats back to me as we pass orchards and cow pastures. Up ahead, a volley of musket fire crashes. Fifes and drums are playing. I watch John Ellis bouncing up and down in the General's carriage ahead of us.

"Miriam, they're having the time of their lives."

Miriam nods and holds out a parasol to me. "Please, Janie. Now will you take this?"

I open it if only to hide from the Major's nervous glances.

"Look, Miriam! There's Matthew."

My brother is riding lead on what Glegg says is a nine-pound artillery piece. I can see four men mounted on the six horses pulling the limber and cannon. Two more men cling to the limber's bench for dear life, as they dash madly over the hayfield. Five more teams follow in my brother's wake. As the Light Artillery careens away, the 1st Lincolns march into position. At the far end of the field all six teams unlimber, then in dumb show, they load and prepare to fire. The men let out a yell instead of firing precious powder, and then everyone scrambles to retreat halfway back up the field. Again, they hurry through the pretense of loading and firing before skedaddling – this time to the cheers of the 1st Lincolns arranged in three long rows.

Now the Artillery is hurtling toward the militiamen. There is a break in the infantry line, and the guns wheel into it. They spread out and pull to a stop. In a score of heartbeats, the Lincoln's Colonel is raising his sword. When he brings it down, all along the line the militia sergeants scream, "Fire." This time a wall of gunsmoke leaps out. The tree-line reverberates as five hundred muskets and six cannon let loose a roar I will never forget. Afterwards, the cheering is as loud as the volley.

Glegg, bless his heart, twists around, expecting, I suppose, to find me fainted dead away.

"Mrs. Roberts! Are you all right?"

"Thrilling, isn't it?"

I stand and cheer.

"My Lord," Asa Lockwood shouts above the din. "We could have used something like that."

"Napoleon showed us," is Brock's reply.

# Ken Leland

*****

A few minutes later, Asa and Ben stand alone beside the lane leading into the militia grounds. The forty men of the Coloured Corps are moving down the lane at the quick–march, led by a white Captain and Lieutenant, both mounted.

"Reckon those men know better than most why they're here," Asa says of the black infantry.

Ben glowers for a moment then speaks his mind. "I don't see why they got only white officers."

Asa is about to agree when he notices one of the soldiers. "Ben, who's that white-haired old man in the third row? Is that Pierpoint?"

"You're right, that's Richard Pierpoint. He's joined again!" Ben said. "Damn, he's older than the both of us put together. Makes me ashamed to be standing here, he surely does."

"Can you still march like that, Corporal Benjamin?" Asa asks, waving toward the men moving smartly across the hayfield.

The Coloured Corps take position to demonstrate a quick-paced picket advance maneuver.

"Well, I could try, Lieutenant Lockwood."

"Neither could I," Asa admits.

"I suppose they'd laugh at us."

Ben thinks for a while as the Coloured Corps advances in three staggered waves to kneel and fire, then reload as the next wave passes through their open ranks in a rush.

"Asa, we wouldn't have to run or even walk fast if we were behind a parapet."

They watch as the Corps marches back from the end of the field to the playing of "Grenadier's March."

"When Sarah and Lois and the children are safe," Ben says, "You and I, Asa, we'll come back – back to Fort George, south bastion, rifles with sixty rounds."

"Agreed."

The men stare at each other for a moment. Ben sticks out his hand. "I'll be proud to stand with you one last time."

"Not as proud as me, Ben."

By the early afternoon, the militiamen are exhausted. Major Glegg tells the officers to gather their men around General Brock, who stands bareheaded in his landau. Over 500 men with sweat-covered faces congregate quietly in a circle centred on the General.

# The Land Between Flowing Waters

The second carriage, with Janie, Miriam and John Ellis, is an island surrounded.

"That was fine," Brock says in a voice that carries. "From what I saw today, I know your officers are pleased. And if they're not, you tell 'em to come speak to me." A ripple of laughter spreads outward. "But don't you think I'm preaching Yankee rebellion. You do what your officers say and you'll make your families proud."

They are smiling now. Brock knows the men are listening.

"Yesterday I got a New York City newspaper. This is what Jonathan is saying about us in Congress."

He makes a great show of squinting and holding the paper at arm's length. "It says here: 'There is a great object to be attained by war with Great Britain. We can estimate not only the benefit to ourselves, but also the injury to be done to the enemy. The conquest of Canada is in our power. I verily believe that the militia of Kentucky is alone competent to place Upper Canada and Montreal at the feet of President Madison.'"

The men turn to one another. Brock tosses the newspaper onto the carriage seat behind him.

"This man who says he's going to march over us – after today, I think I'll write this man a letter. I'll say that maybe he can march over me." Brock slaps his modest paunch with both hands. "I'm not quite as fast as I used to be."

Gentle laughter swells around them. Janie looks merrily over to an ashen-faced Miriam.

"But sure as sunrise after a long stormy night," Brock shouts, "I know Jonathan won't march over the Light Artillery!"

The artillerymen send up a piercing cheer.

"And I know Jonathan won't march over the Coloured Corps!"

Old Richard Pierpoint waves his hat and leads his company in three rousing huzzahs.

"And as God is our strength, Jonathan won't march over the First Lincoln!"

The men explode with cheers.

Janie is weeping in pride, hope and resolve.

Miriam weeps in fear for her dear general.

\*\*\*\*\*

# Ken Leland

## Janie Roberts

In the middle afternoon, as the militiamen scatter to homes or taverns, we drive along back-country lanes toward River Road. Brock wants to take his son to the Lockwood farm before returning to Niagara. Brock and John Ellis ride with us. This time Glegg is in the lead carriage with our fathers.

As we near the Niagara River we see the steep, almost perpendicular, heights that rise three hundred feet above the plain. The escarpment's top is a broad oak forest. The north side is almost bare, strewn with massive boulders. The village of Queenston lies at its base, the last landing place for ships before the Falls. After making the turn north onto River Road, we are only a few paces from the gorge. Brock motions for Major Glegg to proceed, then asks our own driver to pull over.

"John," Brock tells his son, "Please stay here. There's something I would show the ladies over by the river. We won't be long."

Miriam is as mystified as I am. Brock climbs down to assist her, and then, as I approach the carriage step, he reaches up with both hands to carry me to the ground like a leaf in the breeze. The three of us walk through the trees toward the brink. Dark grey clouds are gathering, and a streak of heat-lightning flashes noiselessly, high above the eastern shore. Brock turns to us and takes Miriam's hand.

"There is something I saw in Europe, years ago. When an army marched out to meet Napoleon's hordes, civilians would gather at the battlefield's edge. It was absurdly dangerous."

I am appalled by the very idea, and drape my arm over Baby.

But Miriam says, "Isaac, I can help. There will be wounded."

"Please, no. I will be in command. If I'm fearful for your safety, I might...do you understand?"

Miriam lowers her eyes and grips his hand. "Yes, I do. You must make no mistakes because of me."

"But there is something I beg of you."

"Yes?" Miriam says.

"From now on, keep John close at the farm. Before the attack comes, take him and your parents far away."

Brock turns to me. "Mrs. Roberts, if the Americans can force their way across the river, the black families must flee."

# The Land Between Flowing Waters

"We know."

"Talk with your fathers," Brock tells us. "They are stout-hearted men, full of good sense. Tonight would not be too soon to start making plans for escape."

Brock sighs and studies the thunderheads roiling over Queenston Heights. "There was much in the New York paper I didn't read out today. It says that Congress plans to arm half a million men for war. I have 1500 regulars to guard a border of as many miles. We will do our best..."

"But we must pray that God grants us a miracle," I say.

That evening in the shop, Miriam and I swear that when the time comes we will lead our families to safety, but then we will return to Niagara to help. I know Miriam thinks I'm mad, but in a month or so Baby will be born, and I'll carry him in a sling. There will be a lot I can do.

# Ken Leland

## Full Strawberry Moon: 1812
## (June 25, 1812)
## The Prairie

Senisqua's father, Kshiwe, told her that it would take two days to reach Five Medals Village.

She rode a placid brown mare through the forest. Here the trail was broad and clear, but lonely. Kshiwe scouted ahead on foot with his hunting bow. His powderless musket was strapped to Senisqua's travois. Just in front rode her foster mother, Kmonokwe, whose travois poles scraped over the earth leaving two endless, shallow gashes. Senisqua's mare plodded dutifully between the traces as she scanned the forest. On every side enormous oaks, sugar maples, and hickories rose until lost in the unbroken canopy. The underbrush was barely knee-high in this shaded world, and she could see for many paces between the standing giants. Just behind was her little brother, Shkote, mounted on a black-and-brown stallion that Father rode at need. A little farther in back of the slow-moving column was Kshiwe's black foster son, Hannibal.

The trail angled north and a little east between low rising rock-strewn hills. All morning they crossed streams and creeks flowing south or west, but just before midday they came to a creek flowing steadfastly northward. Senisqua had never seen such a thing, and she called out to Kmonokwe as their horses splashed across.

"Some day when it's cold and snowy," Kmonokwe replied, "I'll tell you the story of the land between flowing waters."

Senisqua looked with new eyes. Yes, this place where the waters changed direction must have powerful spirits.

The family travelled at an unhurried pace to the scrape of sliding litters. Woodpeckers knocked, red squirrels scolded, and partridges drummed in the distance, but somewhere beyond the hills on the right Senisqua sensed movement as crows complained and set flight from treetops. Behind her, Hannibal was too inexperienced to notice, but sometimes she saw Kmonokwe glance furtively to note the flight of yet another bird.

"Father," Senisqua asked as they rested at midday, "who shadows us in the south?"

Kshiwe chuckled. "I suspect it's Mukos and his friends. Someone's been there since we crossed the Yellow River."

Hannibal looked surprised, and a bit annoyed at himself for not noticing.

# The Land Between Flowing Waters

Father glanced at Mother before saying, "South is the more dangerous side. The Horse Soldiers at Fort Wayne are only two days away."

Later that afternoon, the lonely forest path had grown even wider.

"Mother," Senisqua said as she rode beside Kmonokwe, "Father would never have banished me if not for you. I owe you my thanks."

"Hah!"

"Truly, he would never have done it – even had it been his own idea."

The day after Kshiwe and Kmonokwe had gone to every lodge to announce their marriage, they sought out Mukos and his parents to give a careful explanation of why Kshiwe was banishing Senisqua to her grandparents at Five Medals.

"Senisqua," Kmonokwe now asked, "did Nanokas tell you about the herbs a married woman needs for good health?" They talked of things that women must know, while Shkote hung back farther and farther until he could pretend to hear nothing.

The day grew uncomfortably warm, and mosquitoes more troublesome, as they skirted a cedar swamp. Senisqua nodded in dreams of Mukos, as her mare plodded on. Afoot, Hannibal was tiring. As the sun slanted deeper into the west, the trail ran beside a swift-flowing stream. When the horses descended a short, steep hill, Kshiwe was waiting for them at a traveller's camp. A cool northern breeze blew down from the treetops, and the stream pitched noisily over a rocky ledge into a wide pool. In the din of falling water, Kshiwe signed that they would stop for the day. Shkote whooped and jumped down from the stallion to rummage for his fishing line. Hannibal trudged into the clearing and collapsed on the grass beside the fire-pit.

"We can go swimming after Shkote catches supper," Kshiwe said to Hannibal.

The boy mumbled something. Then he rolled over and began to snore.

Senisqua dismounted and watched Kmonokwe walk into her father's embrace.

"The days are so long now," Kshiwe said to her. "We could travel for a few more hours, but this is a nice spot."

# Ken Leland

On the trail it is a daughter's task to gather firewood, but even as Father was saying, "Senisqua, I'll fetch the wood," Kmonokwe was beckoning. "Come daughter, help me put up the lodge."

At the back of the camp, farthest from the waterfall, were bare saplings already staked. Mother sorted through the mats on the travois and finally pulled out Great Grandfather's black ironwood lance. She leaned it against a tree.

"Senisqua, I'm sure it must be the Shishibes hunters, but..."

She was right. These were not days to take chances.

## Senisqua

In the morning, after I bathed, Mother braided my hair beside the pool.

"Kshiwe says we'll be at your grandfather's village by noon," she said. "This is my wedding present to you." It was a fine silver clasp for my hair, one I had seen her wear. Then, reaching into a bundle, she brought forth a doeskin dress, sun-bleached almost white, with beaded leaf patterns in green and gold.

"The dress is from Mukos' mother," Kmonokwe said, as I held it out in great admiration. "For six days before we left, she worked until sunset to finish it. Put it on to show your father."

We got a late start, but even my brothers thought I looked nice. They were not as happy when Father said I must sit quiet to stay clean while everyone else packed.

It had been two hours since sunrise prayers and an hour more on the trail, yet I had not seen any sign of our shadows in the south. The day was warming quickly, with a wind that barely stirred the leaves. There was a trace of smoke on the air, but surely we were far beyond our shy friends' campsite. Maybe we would finally meet other travellers.

"How far is it to the Elk Hart River?" I called as Mother rode before me.

"I've never travelled this way," she said. Then she raised her arm to point to a brightening above the trees. "It can't be too far. We're coming to a prairie."

Indeed, now the land was almost flat and we could see ahead through the forest for many paces.

# The Land Between Flowing Waters

Hannibal heard it first – something rushing toward us from the south. He called to Mother and ran forward to stand beside us with his bow nocked. Father heard it too. He came sprinting back down the trail, shouting for us to loosen the travois from the horses. I jumped down just as two riders splashed across a shallow creek far out to the right. Mother grabbed the ironwood lance and stood beside Hannibal.

"Daughter," she directed, "mount behind Shkote and ride clear."

The stallion pranced, but I calmed him and jumped up behind my little brother.

"Who are they?" Shkote kept asking. I could only see the two but I scanned the forest all around. If it was an ambush, there would be more.

The two men plunged toward us, uttering no cries, waving their bows high in the air. As I pulled the reins to flee, Shkote shouted, "Neshnabek!" Father and Hannibal both lowered their bows as the riders signed "Friend."

"War Leader, it's us," one of the young men panted as they jumped down to stand trembling before my father. Yes, they were Mukos' friends from Shishibes Lake.

"Oh, War Leader," the other said, "we didn't do it! We didn't do it!"

"What are you talking about?" Father asked. "Where are the others?"

"Mukos has set a guard along the prairie," the first answered.

At the same time, the second was blurting, "Mukos says you must ride back as fast as you can!"

They were frightened. Mother put the lance away and started searching for her medicine packs. Father turned to her and stamped his foot. He does that when he thinks he is being pushed too hard, too fast. "Woman, what are you doing?" he shouted, and then to the young hunters, "Is Mukos War Leader now?"

"No, Kshiwe! No," they both answered. "Someone has burned two settlers' farms on the prairie, but it wasn't us, War Leader."

"Show me," was all Mother said.

"Woman, where are you going?" Father snapped as she climbed back onto her horse.

Mother rode off, her heels kicking, and the travois lurched back and forth across the trail behind her. The hunters rode in pursuit. Father started to run after them, then he turned to shout, "All of you stay here!" before joining them at a dead run.

After a moment or two, Hannibal looked up at me. "If people are hurt, Mother will need me." And then he jumped on the second travois horse to follow her.

Shkote and I sat atop the stallion, abandoned.

My little brother turned in front of me. "We have the fastest horse. We can ride away if there is danger."

"I'll not leave them," I said more bravely than I felt. Besides, Mukos was up there somewhere. We turned to follow.

There were two smoldering farmsteads on the prairie. As we came out of the forest, I saw Mother dismounting near the first burning cabin. Hannibal was right beside her.

"I tried to stop them," Mukos was telling Father at the prairie's edge.

"So you say."

"No, truly, War Leader. They just wouldn't listen."

"Then, Mukos, you are not alone," Father said as he saw us riding up. "No one in my family pays attention to me either."

"But now, you men really must listen," I heard him say to the half-dozen young hunters who gathered round. "Some of you must find the raiders' tracks, and the rest watch for Horse Soldier patrols. This smoke can be seen from a long way."

"Uncle..." my lovely Mukos began, as both he and Father looked my way.

"Lead the scouts, Mukos. It's the best way to protect us all." Then Father turned to me as the young men rode away and said, "Keep your brother back."

What was Shkote not supposed to see?

I rode more slowly then as Father ran onto the prairie. Ahead, a few hundred paces from the trees, was a broken fence line.

"Senisqua, look," Shkote said as a dozen crows struggled up from the ground. In the field were two oxen, and also a milk cow and her calf, all hacked to pieces. Their entrails were strewn over the pasture. Their heads were mounted on the fence with the eyes gouged out. Shkote flinched as we rode by. Who would do such a wasteful, stupid thing?

At the first farm, the hay-barn had burned fiercely to leave only piles of drifting grey ash and glowing beams. The stallion snorted as the wind drove clouds of smoke toward us. The horse danced aside until we could see the blazing farmhouse. Its chimney stood, but the roof and log walls had fallen into a pile of flames. The house was no bigger than our lodge at home. Father stood as close as he dared. "I can't see any bodies," he called out. Mother had already dashed ahead.

We rode behind the house where the dug well was broken up, its timbers cast down inside. A dead cat was nailed to the outhouse door. "Maybe the people got away," my little brother whispered as I clutched him tight.

"Mother's at the next farm. Stay here," Father shouted as he hurried ahead.

The next cabin was a hundred paces away, hidden by roiling black smoke. As Father ran towards the darkness, I could see him studying the grass. I heard Mother shout to Hannibal. Father disappeared as he plunged deeper into the smoke. Shkote and I galloped after him.

Choking and coughing, we burst through. My brother grabbed my wrist and pointed toward two settler men, mounted upright, thrust atop jagged fence posts. The men were naked, their bellies slashed open to let the purple ropes inside hang down into the dirt. Their genitals were torn off and stuffed into open mouths. The tops of their heads were white bone ringed in blood. The eyes stared across the yard to their women.

Now Shkote vomited over my leg. The half-dozen women and girls were bare, their arms and legs staked wide over the grass. Their breasts were gone, their sex gone, their bellies gutted, their insides piled on the ground beside them.

The stallion shied and reared at the odour, and we fell. Shkote landed on top of me, crying and terrified. Mother was yelling for Hannibal from somewhere close by, behind the second farmhouse.

I tried to cover my little brother's eyes as I pulled him away from the bodies, toward the house. Its door was broken and lay upon the ground. Only two walls were burning. The sod-covered roof had collapsed in a dusty heap. There was a child's white doll lying in the weeds beside the door. I pulled Shkote nearer to try to distract him with it – but as I reached down I saw it was an infant boy, his head crushed, his body opened up like a fish. Mother was screaming now, and Father rushed behind the ruined cabin. I stumbled after.

Behind the house were seven children, some tied to posts, some impaled upon tall stakes. Fires glowed at their bare feet, the naked bodies blackened, the skin burst. I buried Shkote's face against me as Mother and Hannibal kicked ashes from below the child at the end. Mother was shrieking that he was still alive.

It was a boy of eight or nine. His hair was burned away, and his arms and chest were scorched bright red. His feet were baked until only bones and gristle remained. His little sex had melted away. Mother struggled to lift him but she could not. Father had to pull him off the stake.

Mother knelt to hold him tight. As I lay prostrate upon the earth in horror, she intoned death prayers to the Master of Life.

Hannibal kept begging Father, "What can I do? What can I do?" But Father could say nothing and just kept shaking his head.

Somehow the boy was yet alive. He blinked as Mother cradled him. His mouth opened and closed but he made no sound. His limbs shook and his back arched. His head lolled back from Mother's breast.

"Father! Father!"

I crawled to comfort Hannibal, but he had lost all control. He snatched Father's hunting knife and ran toward Mother.

"Master, forgive me!" he wailed, as he cut the boy's throat.

The young men returned as Mother held Hannibal's hands. Perhaps she feared he would harm himself. Everyone else gathered around Father.

"They came from the east," one of the Shishibes Lake trackers said. "Fifteen or twenty on ponies."

Father only nodded.

"The tracks are fresh, heading south. We followed the trail, but they broke apart in every direction."

"They'll reunite in a day or two, to strike again," Father said.

"Uncle, we must leave right now," said my beloved Mukos. "We saw no one, but Horse Soldiers must be patrolling the prairie."

"Yes, but where should we go?" another hunter asked. "We can't lead soldiers to Five Medals, or back home. Even Long Knives can follow a trail like that," he said pointing to the travois.

"Burn the litter poles," Father decided. "Take what we can and throw the rest in the fires."

"Kshiwe," Mother said quietly.

"But don't leave any medicine packs behind."

The young men hurried to do his bidding. When all was ready, Father called out again as he jumped onto the stallion. "We will follow the raiders' trail and split apart where they did."

# The Land Between Flowing Waters

"Hannibal comes with me," Mother said as she pulled him onto the horse behind her.

"Senisqua, you and Shkote will ride the mare. Come with me," Father said. "Mukos, the young men must disguise their tracks in the forest before going home."

My beloved did not seem at all pleased to leave us, but he would not speak against my Father.

We rode over the raiders' path. The torn sod from their hoof prints was unmistakable. With my left arm I held tight to the sniffling Shkote. Mukos rode beside me, speaking of what I already knew.

"Senisqua, we will return home to warn Okama Menomni. But then I will come back for you."

"I know," I said.

"Never doubt me. Watch for me every day."

"I will."

"I love you," he whispered.

I wondered, how could he love a smoky, bedraggled, vomit-covered wretch such as I? Yet he said he did.

"I feel the same."

A few hundred heartbeats to the south, the raiders' tracks splashed apart like water droplets beneath a falling stone. Each of our hunters took a different direction; one rode south by southeast, another due south, and my brave Mukos waved as he headed southwest. Soon only my family remained.

Hannibal, deep in anguish, rode behind Mother as she turned to the northwest. His arms clutched her waist, and he buried his face against her back. She had rescued Great Grandfather's lance and carried it in her right hand. The medicine packs were draped over the horse's withers. The path Mother chose would take them back into the great forest on the near horizon. Shkote and I followed Father into the southeast, across the prairie.

"Woman," Father called out.

"Yes, my wonderful man?"

"Try to heal our son."

"I will," Mother answered.

"Can you find Five Medals Village?"

"It's on the river, isn't it?"

"Yes," Father replied softly to placate her. Then, "Woman..."

"Yes?"

"I love you more than words..."

"... more than words can say," they finished together.

"Five Medals, then on to Walpole Island," Father shouted as Kmonokwe galloped towards the forest. We all watched her go.

Eventually, Father turned to me and pointed to the southern tree line. "Senisqua, can you see the broken pine?"

"I see it." Here the prairie was like a wide river flowing across the earth. It was a long ride to the other side.

"Aim for the pine. I'll circle around to find you in the woods behind it."

I held Shkote as we flew. Father ranged ever farther to the left as we crossed the green river.

It was not even noon. We waited near the broken pine, watching and listening in the gloom. Here the forest possessed little of the majesty of the northern trail; the trees were shorter, the undergrowth more apt to clutch and tear. Father soon appeared, but he stopped at a distance and signalled that we should advance alongside one another. I lifted Shkote onto the mare before me.

"Little Brother," I whispered, "Help me make the least trail."

We travelled slowly as Shkote pointed to stretches of drier ground, to expanses of flat rock, to deer trails. Far out on the left, Father did the same. By early afternoon, he waved his bow high overhead. 'Water' he signalled, and he guided the stallion into it. A little farther on, Shkote sighted the same creek and we too entered to pass downstream. I could see Father ahead of us, his horse walking quietly, barely splashing. The creek bottom was mostly gravel and, in places, sheets of tan-coloured stone. No trace remained of our passing.

The banks were lined with black willow, beech and cottonwood, and the stream was only a few paces wide and almost knee deep. We rode until mid-afternoon, following the winding stream east and north, back toward the prairie in a great loop. When open sky loomed ahead, Father waited for us beside a willow. As we came near, I listened hard to hear his words.

"After dark, we will cross the prairie again. This stream will lead us to the Elk Hart River. Try to get some rest for later."

I guided the mare up onto the bank and jumped down. "Father?"

# The Land Between Flowing Waters

"Mmmmm?"

"I would bathe, if it's safe."

"I suppose. Shkote, let's see if there are any strawberries or mushrooms hereabouts."

I stepped from my moccasins and waded into the stream. The water was clear and surged over smooth stone. It was cool, but I could bear it. I stood there gazing sadly at the smudges, soil, blood and vomit that marred the once-beautiful gift. I pulled the dress over my head to the smell of burned wood and flesh, to the stench of my own revulsion. Once free, I threw the dress into the stream and watched it float away. Only moments later, I splashed after it frantically. How would Mukos feel if I just cast away his mother's present? I examined the stitching, the beading, the blood-and-vomit-covered skirt. Then I knelt in the water to rub it carefully against the stones.

*Spirit of this Water*, I prayed, *wash away the black stains of destruction, the smell of defilement. Rinse away all evil. Let the love in this creation shine through once more.*

I rose and draped the sopping doeskin over a bush before returning to sit in the stream. I cupped water in my hands to lave over my face, my shoulders and breasts.

*Spirit of this Water*, I prayed again, *wash away my fear and weakness. Cleanse my mind, my spirit, my body. Make me worthy of my name. Make me worthy of love.*

I lifted my arms to tease out the now tangled braids Kmonokwe had fashioned only this morning. I held her silver clasp tight in my hand as I bent low. My hair flowed in the current as the Spirit swept away all care.

"Splash around or something, so I know you're there," Father called to me.

I whacked the stream a great joyous smack, sending spray high onto the bank to wet the willow's bark.

"That's better."

The water was no longer chilling. "Father?"

"Yes," he answered from somewhere behind the willow.

"How can men do such things? I know you could never..."

"No. But then, I still have some hope."

"Hope?"

"If a man loses all hope and falls into despair, then, perhaps, he will do what we saw today."

"But Father, why should we ever despair? The Master always holds us in his arms."

"That's true, but some people forget. I think a good man who deals in horror is filled with despair. He believes his family, all his People, will be trampled into the dust and there is no way, short of terrible deeds, to stop it." Kshiwe snorted in frustration. "I've been wondering about this all day, and I'm tired of running in circles. Ask your Mother – she can say it better than I."

"Mother?"

"Yes, dear one," the spirit of Nanokas answered.

"How do you keep Father from despair?"

"By loving him, by respecting him, by not asking for what he cannot give. We are trying."

"You mean Kmonokwe?"

"Oh, yes," Nanokas said. "We are both trying to keep him safe."

"Is that what I should do for Mukos?"

"Yes, dear one."

"Then I will."

"What's that?" Kshiwe called.

"Oh, nothing, Father. I was just talking to Nanokas."

*****

Hannibal was deeply downcast and sorrowful that he had killed the settler child. He could not bear to look at Kmonokwe for shame at what he had done, he who hoped to be her Midewiwin initiate in healing.

"Listen to me," Kmonokwe said as she gripped her foster son's shoulders. "I would teach you something."

The sun was sinking. They had not eaten since breakfast and his mother made no attempt to prepare food for the evening. After fleeing from the desecration on the prairie, they had wound through the forest, riding in a tiny creek until they came to a beaver dam. There, Kmonokwe would not allow her son to wallow in sadness but hectored him into the deep pool behind the dam to bathe. Afterwards he was cold and miserable. She wrapped him in a blanket and made him sit beside her at a small fire. Then she took firm hold of his chin, raising his face to stare into her eyes.

"Now, tell me," she said to Hannibal. "Do you ever dream of your black father, Tom?"

"Yes," he moaned.

"Often?"

"Not every night, but a lot."

"Who else?" she demanded.

"My grandmother, and my mother, almost as much as Tom."

"Where are they? Where are these people you dream of?"

Hannibal looked at her in confusion. "They're all dead."

"But they come to you just the same."

He nodded.

"Good. Seek the boy you killed. If you can stay awake, try to talk to him. But maybe he will come in a dream, or maybe a spirit will guide you to him."

"A vision?"

"I know Kshiwe has been preparing you," Kmonokwe said. "I wish he was here, but you must do your best alone."

"I have to fast," the boy said.

"We haven't eaten since sunrise. You have already begun."


### Full Strawberry Moon: 1812
### June 25, 1812
### Five Medals Village

"King George calls us to war. War! War! Warrrrrrrrr!"

Kshiwe improvised loudly in the night. He sang out 'war' in a strangulated, breath-exhausting howl, and then dropped into a deep rumble to repeat the phrase "calls us, calls us, calls us, calls us." *It would sound much better*, Kshiwe thought, *if I had a hand drum and the children joined in, but Senisqua is too shy and Shkote too sleepy.*

The stallion picked his way between marsh pools. Fireflies twinkled, frogs creaked and cicadas screeched. Bats swooped low over the water. Owls hunted.

"King George, King George, King Geooooooorge."

# Ken Leland

"Peace, Brother," said an aged voice from the darkness. "The Drum Society has heard your approach since moonrise. Already they argue over who will tell you the bad news about your singing."

Flint scraped against iron. A torch flared to light the path through the bog – then, farther out, another torch, then a third and a fourth.

"Welcome," the old man said as he reached up to take Kshiwe's hand. "Welcome to Five Medals Village."

Kmonokwe and Hannibal had not yet arrived.

All through the night Kshiwe stared at the guest-cabin ceiling, listening to the sleeping children. Where was Kmonokwe?

At daybreak he arose and walked back toward the river. The village lay at the edge of a prairie, with the tree-lined river some two hundred paces to the south. Fields of corn and squash extended down to the trees. The village corral held mostly mares with foals, and yearlings. Many of the men, Kshiwe surmised, were away. At the corral he found Nanokas' father watering the horses.

"Grandfather!" Kshiwe exclaimed, as he embraced his father-in-law.

"Welcome, my son. I heard you'd arrived. Did Nanokas come with you? It's a perilous time for visiting."

"I knew she was gone," Grandmother said, as she cuddled Shkote on her lap. Kshiwe and the children had gathered in the grandparents' small cabin in the centre of the village. The grandparents insisted that the children leave the guest-house to join them.

"Since Winter Moon, Nanokas has come to me in dreams," Grandmother said. "She was never sad, but wistful sometimes. And now and then, she was merry when we remembered things from when she was little."

Grandfather sat up and stared at her.

"I didn't say anything to you," the spry old woman admitted as she reached out to her companion. "Maybe there is such a thing as bespeaking a misfortune, but you felt it too, didn't you, my love?"

Grandfather nodded.

Senisqua held her grandfather's hand.

"Mother is with me every moment, whenever I turn to her," Senisqua said.

# The Land Between Flowing Waters

"But I still miss her," Shkote sobbed against his grandmother's breast.

"Kmonokwe's a Midewiwin, you say?"

Kshiwe and Grandfather stood on the low riverside pier where more than a dozen canoes were tied.

"It is the Master's gift, Grandfather. Somehow Nanokas lives in her. You'll feel it too."

"The Mide's bewitched you, my son," the thin old man said as he eased his aching bones into a canoe. Then as they cast off, he added, "Well...maybe she'll bewitch me too."

The current was slow, and Kshiwe let the canoe drift in bright sunshine. Kmonokwe, he supposed, would appear on the river trail – but there was a chance she and Hannibal would cross the upper prairie to arrive from the north, or even strike the river south of the village. Kshiwe longed to go in search of them, somewhere, but decided to trust in Kmonokwe's skill to find the way.

Willow branches hung down like ropes to trail their narrow leaves in the water. Grandfather dozed atop an old trader's blanket. With a hand-line, Kshiwe pulled in a dozen fat buffalo fish before beginning a slow paddle back to the village.

As they walked past the corral, Kshiwe asked, "When did the young men leave?"

Grandfather shifted the heavy fish-string from his right hand to his left, then back again. "A score of Main Poche's warriors came ten days ago. They knew of the two settler families squatting on the south prairie. They said we must destroy the interlopers. Five Medals told them no, but a few of our young men didn't listen. You saw what happened."

"So now scouts are watching for an attack," Kshiwe concluded.

"Five Medals has gone to the Long Knife Okama at Fort Wayne," his father-in-law said. "I hope he comes back alive."

"Senisqua," Grandmother said, as she spread the green-and-gold beaded dress across a table. "This is very fine. It is a wedding dress. Has Kshiwe brought you here to find a companion?"

"Grandmother, his name is Mukos. He promised to meet me here. I know he will come soon."

# Ken Leland

After repeated apologies for the absence of so many hunters, the Women's Okama of Five Medals Village hosted a welcoming and consolation feast, at which Nanokas' life was remembered in loving detail. Late into the night, aunts, uncles, cousins, friends, and acquaintances came to sit beside Kshiwe and Senisqua to wipe away their tears with stories of grace and praise. Mercifully, Shkote was allowed to play on his own with the other children. As dawn broke, Kshiwe lay in the guest lodge, worried by Kmonokwe's continued absence.

Kshiwe passed his second day at Five Medals Village in increasing anxiety. He walked beside the river, listening for any sound of Kmonokwe's approach, praying that nothing was amiss.

It was mid-morning on the third day that word came of the approach of a woman painted in the green and red stripes of a Midewiwin, and of a black boy, sprinkled with the green spots of an apprentice healer.

Finally, finally. Now it was clear. Hannibal was the cause of the delay – the prayers and rituals required of his new vocation explained all.

Villagers lined the trail from the river. Smiling, Kmonokwe rode her mare as Hannibal walked in front, the reins draped over his shoulder. The younger villagers were frightened, just as Shkote had been months ago, supposing that the apprentice was a demon the Mide had conjured to do her bidding. The older boys looked at Hannibal with curiosity as he passed.

"Welcome, Revered Mother."

"Welcome, Mide."

Kmonokwe bent to touch the uplifted hands of the mostly naked youngsters. Their mothers smiled, seeing that the Mide loved children. There would be no hesitation in coming to her for advice, prayers and medicine.

Kmonokwe scanned both rows of upturned faces along the village street. At last, she saw Senisqua and Shkote on the steps of a small cabin with an older couple. They waved and shouted "Mother" with special meaning. *Oh, thank you, Master of Life,* Kmonokwe thought. *That means...Oh, yes! There he is, my wonderful man. My Kshiwe.*

He stood silent and straight with folded arms. On his face there was such love, such admiration.

# The Land Between Flowing Waters

Up ahead at the council circle she saw a tall, stout woman, doubtless the Women's Okama, and beside her were elders, grandfathers and grandmothers.

"We are glad you have come to us," Women's Okama said as she dismounted.

"I am Kmonokwe of the White Fish, and this is my apprentice, Hannibal of the Bear. We will do our best to help any who come to us."

For a time more Kmonokwe would have to be the confident, skillful healer, the fount of tradition and piety. For a little longer, though she ached to fly into Kshiwe's arms.

In the guest-lodge that afternoon, Kmonokwe told one worried mother, "Your son's leg is fiery and swollen because there are still splinters deep inside. They must come out. My apprentice will lance the gash, cleanse it and apply a poultice."

Hannibal nodded. "There will be some pain," he told the boy. "You'll have a chance to be brave."

Then to a new mother, "You're right, Daughter. It's too soon to have another child – maybe in four or five years. Powdered snakeroot will bring your flows each month. Drink the tonic before each new moon."

Then to an elder, "Your morning cough is the Master's way of saying tobacco is a sacrament, not a pleasure to be too much indulged."

And in the early evening to Senisqua's grandparents, "Our beloved Senisqua has given her heart to Mukos of Shishibes Lake." The old folks glanced at one another. "He is young, but a skillful hunter, and already his friends trust his judgment. By now you have guessed the problem; he is Bear Clan, as she is. But there is a way to help them, if you agree."

That night, Hannibal snored lightly by the guest-lodge door. In the bedroom, Kshiwe kissed the tip of Kmonokwe's nose as he lay with her.

"Kshiwe," she whispered.

His tongue traced her eyelids, and then he tugged at her earlobes with his lips. When Kmonokwe tilted her hips upward, Kshiwe raised himself above her with straightened arms.

"Please, my love!"

# Ken Leland

Kshiwe felt her hands, her fingers stiff and splayed as the palms travelled down his back. He rocked slowly, hardly moving at all. Kmonokwe was balanced on the brink of delight. Kshiwe held her there. Tenderly.

"Oh, Kshiwe, now!"

Kmonokwe wrapped her legs around his hips to pull him deep inside. He gasped as she clutched him. Hers was a long happy moan.

Kmonokwe slept and dreamed in the warm, humid night. Kshiwe lay facing her, his arm across her bare hip, their knees touching. Both were startled into wakefulness by a loud cry.

"Kshiwe, Kmonokwe, wake up! Long Knives are on the way!"

Naked, Kshiwe grabbed the ironwood lance and rushed to the door. Hannibal was there before him, guarding the entry with his hunting knife.

"Are they attacking?" the boy asked of the men standing outside in the moonlight.

Kshiwe shifted him aside gently. On the path, he saw Mukos and the Shishibes Lake young warriors, and beside them was Village Speaker with the veterans.

"Mukos, what have you done!" Kshiwe exclaimed.

Village Speaker clasped Kshiwe's arms in greeting. "No need to growl at him, War Leader. All of us thought the Wolf Clan might welcome help."

Kmonokwe came to the doorway, her long hair falling over bare shoulders, a blanket clutched to her breasts. "What news, Speaker?"

"Revered Mother," Speaker said with eyes wide. "We met Five Medals Okama on the trail. He says Horse Soldiers and Long Knives are approaching, no more than a hard day's ride from here."

She nodded. Already there were shouts between neighbours as torches flared throughout the village. Then she spoke.

"Kshiwe, my love, you might want to dress before going off with your friends."

# The Land Between Flowing Waters

## Saturday, June 27, 1812
## The Barn Raising

It was warm and misty on the morning the Babcocks stopped at the lumber yard. Patience's curly brown hair framed her face as she beamed down at the man she called Alexander Lockyer. Patience's father was on the driver's bench beside her, and from the wagon bed her brothers watched with impish grins.

"My brothers will come for thee around eight, First Day morning, Mr. Lockyer," Patience said brightly. "In Meeting thou must sit with Father and the other men, but I promise they don't bite."

Lockwood managed a weak smile as the Babcocks drove out onto Creek Side Road. He pulled down his straw hat and wandered back to the sawmill cutting room.

Later that evening, Jeremy Roberts and Alexander Lockwood saddled their horses in the paddock. They faced another night of skulking through the countryside with Benson's ruffians, burning chicken coops and dodging local patrols.

"Alex, what happens if Patience tells her father you were an army officer?" Roberts asked. "If word got round to Benson we'd be in big trouble."

"If she wanted, Patience could have said something long before now."

"She thinks you deserted. That would make you a hero to these Bedlamites, and you'd be the talk of the town."

"If that happens, let's hope Benson sees it that way too."

The sound of galloping horses came from the road. Roberts cinched his saddle with a worried look.

"Hell hath no fury...Alex, you've got to string her along, least till we can get out of here."

"We're after Henderson, Lauder, and Wainwright," Benson announced. His henchmen had gathered in a lonely elm grove beside a backwoods trail.

Clouds covered the sky, leaving barely enough light to guide their way. Roberts counted twenty-four riders in the circle around Benson. Roberts and Lockwood could name them all.

"They all went to militia muster, and that's not smart," Benson declared. "Tonight we'll burn their hayfields."

Benson divided the men into three groups, with Roberts riding in Benson's squad.

"Everyone got flint and iron? Right. Let's go."

Roberts rode next to last along the country road. Frogs croaked in the swamps. Trees loomed darkly overhead. More than once, men cursed at the sting of a low-hanging branch.

Dogs barked over to the left. *There's a farm over there somewhere,* Roberts thought. Over the weeks, they'd killed a dozen guard dogs.

Benson led them for another twenty minutes but then called a halt. "This is the Wainwright place," he whispered. "See the lane?"

There was a jagged picket fence along the road, breached by a wagon gate.

"The hayfield's on the left. Burn it all."

The raiders pushed over the fence to lead their horses through. The drying alfalfa was raked into a dozen windrows that stretched from the road up to the farmhouse.

"Hurry up. Spread out," Benson hissed as the first few men knelt to start fires. "Roberts, follow me to the house. We'll fire the top end."

*Bastard's brave enough,* Roberts thought, as he galloped after.

Benson jumped down. The farmhouse was a grey blob, just a few score paces ahead; the barn and outbuildings were even darker. He fumbled for his iron file. Flames were already leaping high back by the road. There the raiders struggled to mount horses frightened by the quickly spreading blaze.

Benson knelt, and then sparks fell onto tiny dry leaves to explode with a sweet aroma. After a few scrapes, Roberts' pile caught as well. Smoke billowed into the midnight breeze. A bright, shadow-casting glow sprang up to illuminate the field as Benson hurried to fire the next row. From the farmhouse, dogs began to bark furiously.

"Go get 'em," someone bellowed, and then a rifle shot.

"Ride!" Benson yelled to Roberts.

In the burgeoning light, Roberts could see two black shapes racing toward them. Benson shot one dog when it slowed to circle. The second leapt immediately, and dug its teeth into Roberts' shoulder. The impact knocked him into the burning stubble. Shrieking, he rolled over, forcing the hound into the nearest flames. When its fur began to burn, pain overcame rage and the dog released its grip.

Roberts staggered to his feet. The hound had shredded his shirt with raking claws and teeth. His left shoulder was bleeding and torn. He freed his knife, but the dog had had enough and was already streaking away. The horses were gone. Benson was gone.

Someone was shouting from the farmhouse. At the sound of a second shot, Roberts ran. Serpentine flames soared into the night, up and down the hayfield. Roberts plunged through a row of dying embers to reach the tree-line and the road beyond.

The raiders were gone. They had abandoned him.

He was mad as hell.


"I'd still be wandering lost if you hadn't found me," Roberts told Lockwood just after sunrise. Roberts lay abed in their room at the sawmill. Lockwood dabbed at his cuts, scrapes, gouges and burns with twice-boiled water and salve.

"At least your horse came back," Lockwood chuckled, then sobered. "I'll take you to John Norton. The Haudenosaunee will help you back to Niagara."

"No, Alex. Miriam will have conniptions if I come back without you. Just make up some cockamamie tale about me falling against the saw."

"I've got to stay longer, Jeremy. Assemblyman Mason is their leader, but we haven't any solid evidence against him."

"Alex, I'm tired of doing shameful things for Benson and Mason. And I'm tired of hiding my face so that Quaker girl doesn't get suspicious. One way or another, we've got to get out of here – and soon."


*****


On the morning of the Sloan barn raising, the Babcock family woke early. By sunrise, they and their neighbours for ten miles around were on the roads. Patience and little sister Dinah sat cushioned in straw across from Hopestill and Mother in the wagon-bed. Nathan was on the driver's bench with Father.

Despite the hour, Patience brimmed with anticipation. The man she knew as Alexander Lockyer had promised to meet them at the Sloan farm.

# Ken Leland

*Alex works so hard at the mill,* Patience thought. *Father says Alex always looks tired in the morning, and is exhausted by afternoon. Maybe he's not sleeping well.* She envisioned sliding into bed beside Alex, running her arm across his bare chest, lifting her leg over his to press against him. Patience blushed, and then glanced over to see if Mother had read her thoughts.

Margaret had quietly advised Patience some days ago, "He's not a Friend. Don't set thy bonnet for him."

*But I can make him so,* Patience resolved. *A Friend by convincement is good enough for the Elders. For three weeks, Alex has sat beside my father and brothers at Meeting. After supper last Seventh Day, Papa asked if Alex would read a copy of 'A Friend's Journal.' And he took it home!*

*I can teach him what it means to be a Quaker. He can come to the house. He can come to supper. He can come to me.*

*Yet he is so guarded. He thinks twice before saying a single word. But he smiles ever so sweetly when we meet. I would kiss him for every smile, but we are never alone.*

*He tells me of school when he was a boy, and of his father's farm and his wonderful sister, Miriam, and her business. What an accomplished woman! I wish I could meet her. But never a word of the army. I'm sure he is hiding here. Why else would such a thoughtful, intelligent man spend his days in a sawmill?*

*Will he ever confide in me?*

*How can I hold him?*

*Doesn't he know how much I care?*

The rising sun burned away the early morning dew. Gigs, buggies, carts, and farm wagons streamed onto Twenty Mile Road from every direction, making a procession half a mile long. The wagons were loaded with tools, picnic baskets, blankets and garden vegetables. Grandparents and young people, fathers, mothers, babies and children, scores of neighbourhood families converged. Down the back-country road they came, to turn at the maple-shaded gate, past the cattle pasture and cornfields, onward to the heart of the Sloan farm. As they came, children and young folks waved and called to their friends. Dust drifted lazily from horse-drawn wheels into the bright morning sky.

The Sloan farmhouse was nestled in a hickory grove. People jumped down from the wagons; men and older boys greeted one another with warm handshakes. The bearded, plain-clothed Friends mixed easily with their neighbours. Hopestill and Henry paused to strap on leather tool-belts before joining the stream of men heading uphill to the building site. They found Alex waiting for them beside the path. He was surrounded by half a dozen young men from Lundy's Corners Meeting, all loaded with saws, adzes, pulleys and rope.

"Alex, I'm glad thou hast come," Henry Babcock said, as he reached out to grasp his hand.

"I wouldn't have missed it for the world."

Both Babcock and Alex looked back toward the wagon where Patience stood. Ringlets of curly brown hair escaped her grey bonnet; a matching apron covered her plain, ankle-length dress. With one hand braced on the wagon-bench she stooped to descend, but feeling Alex's eyes upon her, she glanced up and blushed. Her heart soared.

The cluster of young women waiting on the ground to receive her turned to follow her gaze.

"'Tis Patience's beau," one young Quaker wife confided gaily to a neighbour.

"A fine figure of a man, I think," another giggled, as she took Patience's arm.

"I hadn't noticed," Patience replied.

The cluster of chatting women gravitated toward the Sloan summer kitchen, where Patience's mother and Dinah had already forged ahead. At the farmhouse, women, whether clad in simple dress or more colourfully, embraced one another. Babies and growing children were admired. The outdoor summer kitchen was already bustling. Grandmothers baked bread, biscuits and cakes. Young wives and daughters organized food and necessaries for the communal dinner to be served at noon, while girls guided the youngest children into the hickory grove for games, songs and crafts. A bell began to ring slowly. The women trooped off to join with their men to begin the day.

"May God prosper what we do here," a Methodist Elder intoned to the gathered families.

"And God protect everyone as we work," came a Friend's contribution.

"Amen," concluded two hundred voices.

A fiddle player struck up 'The Duchess of Brunswick' as the construction foreman urged, "To work!"

A hundred men wandered over the building site, inspecting lumber and materials. The remains of the burned barn had been carted away and the site cleared for rebuilding. The foreman allowed the men to satisfy their curiosity before he clambered onto a shoulder-high pile of sawed lumber. He clanged the dinner bell twice as heads turned his way.

"That there is Mr. Sloan," the foreman said of a white-haired man standing beside the timber pile. "You all know him, and when we're done he'll be mighty grateful. But meantime, we don't want to worry him none bout men fallin' offen the roof or gettin' brained by loose hammers. Everybody's got to look sharp what they're about.

"Now, you all know me, and most of you worked with me before. All those barns we built are still standing, by the way. I'm the boss, and anyone who doesn't agree is welcome to go fishin'."

There were smiles all around.

"Like I say, first we got to raise the main posts. That's heavy work, and we'll need most everybody on a post. Then we lay the ground-sill, and tenons for the second floor and the roof. We can do that in teams of twenty or so. If we can get the braces in by noon, we'll finish a barn today."

There was a round of applause and a few emphatic "Yessir"s.

As the men began to take up position around the first massive walnut post, Henry Babcock spoke quietly to his twelve-year-old son. "Nathan, we're in for some real heavy lifting here, so you got to stay back if you want to watch. Then you go find the roofers and learn how to make shakes. That's your job for today."

"Yes, Papa."

Nathan knew the barn at home had three or four leaky spots, and Father had promised Nathan could fix them once he could make cedar shakes.

Forty men took position on both sides of the thirty-five-foot-long post. Alex and Hopestill, opposite Mr. Babcock, strained as the post began to rise from one end. Teams of men pulled with ropes attached securely to the top, while other men with push-poles guided the post into its vertical seating. By the time the post was erect, the young men were puffing.

"Seven more to go, boys," Mr. Babcock said. "Don't wear out too soon."

For the next hour and a half, the men laboured mightily as the fiddle player moved on to "Fanny Fairer than a Flower" and "Lovely Nancy." Before the morning sun truly began to sear, the skeleton of a barn took shape. Nathan had long since disappeared to work with the roofers. Four-score men swarmed over the barn frame as it began to grow.

"Heads up, Alex." The rope team was lifting yet another beam.

With pulleys attached to upper-level tenons, men on the ground raised braces to the second floor. Alex and Hopestill cat-walked on horizontal cross-timbers to auger and then pound the braces into place with six-inch wooden dowels.

"Anybody thirsty?" one young man called down from a roof tenon. Now the fiddler was playing a shivaree tune, "Come Haste to the Wedding." Young women and wives carrying water buckets were making their way up the incline from the well-house. Even from a distance, Alex instantly spotted Patience's grey bonnet.

"We thought you'd forgotten about us," called one grandfather.

"It's about time," another man groused.

"Who's got the beer?"

Husbands and fathers joshed as water mugs passed from hand to hand and then rose high into the air. The women seemed well pleased with the attention they attracted.

"Hold tight, Alex," one young Quaker husband teased.

Patience came to stand almost directly below Alex, holding her arms high across her forehead to shield her eyes from the sun. Her dress strained across her lifted breasts. She found Alex's eyes with ease, and with a half-smile she stretched up to pass a tin mug to a young neighbour perched on a second-floor beam. When he drained the cup she refilled it, and with a negligent wave motioned that it should go higher – to Alex. The joker on the roof level began to sing in appreciation.


"Come haste to the wedding ye friends and ye neighbours,
The lovers their bliss can no longer delay..."


Patience shone in the sunlight.

Alex clung to a brace-beam, vowing somehow to make things right with her.


Later that day, all gathered for the feast the women had prepared.

"Lord, we thank thee for the fruits of the field and orchard, and for the dear hands that prepared it. Keep us safe all this day to do thy will."

# Ken Leland

"Amen."

In the shade of hickory trees, grandparents, men and youngsters tucked into fresh bread and butter, ham, roasted chicken, potato salad, greens, berries, and cakes. Ever watchful for platters growing lean, the farm women hovered. They snatched only hurried bites themselves, between trips back to the summer kitchen for seconds and thirds for the labouring men. The chatter of neighbours, the cries of children, and the music of the fiddler filled the copse with sounds of joy.

Little sister Dinah, holding a pitcher of milk in one hand and a pitcher of water in the other, filled glasses as she moved along the saw-horse tables. Patience, wielding an enormous coffee pot, leaned in gracefully to fill cups up and down the rows of country folk.

"Thank you, Patience."

"Most kind, dearie."

"Where's the cream?"

"Thank thee, darling."

This last was from her father, seated with two other Elders. As she leaned past his shoulder to pour, from the corner of her eye she saw her brother Hopestill's outline across the table – but she steadfastly refused to look at the figure beside him. Then she straightened, and she did look – openly and steadfastly.

Alex lost any thought of eating. His open hands lay beside his heaping plate. His eyes were fixed on her. He even forgot to smile.

*Be mine*, Patience thought, *and thy heart will never hunger.*


In the late afternoon, Nathan worked with a heavy hemp rope looped under his arms for safety. He and half a dozen young men nailed rows of shakes over the barn roof. The walls were complete on three sides now, and the fourth was well in hand. Inside, stairs rose from the first to the second level, where floorboards were nailed in place. Hopestill and Alex roamed the building site, looking for final tasks, finding less and less to occupy their hands.

The sun was coasting downward and the fiddler running out of tunes. At early dusk, Farmer Sloan rang the dinner bell slowly to call the families to receive his most sincere thanks.

Before he could begin, Nathan called out from atop the barn roof. "Who's that?"

A score of men were riding up the lane. The crowd turned to watch as they arrayed themselves between the farm house and the newly finished barn. As the men waited, a handful of girls herded toddlers and youngsters from the grove in a wide circle to stand with their parents. Everyone recognized Assemblyman Elijah Mason when he urged his horse a few yards in advance of the others.

"Good evening, neighbours, " he said. "It's good to see you all here today. Neighbours helping neighbours – a fine thing it is to rally round those who've seen misfortune."

Old Mr. Sloan stepped forward. "What do you want, Elijah Mason? The polling's not till next week."

"Well, there you have it, Mr. Sloan. Sharp as a tack you are. Yes, I'm electioneering and no mistake."

"Reckon we can make up our own minds," the foreman declared loud enough for all to hear.

"Indeed, you will," Mason replied, "but I've brought a bit of news that might help to make your decision a little...well, easier, let's say."

"And what's that?" asked the fiddler, with a derisive scrape with his bow.

"War! Yes, that's the news. It's all over Niagara."

The farm people turned to one another. A murmur swept through the crowd.

"President Madison's declared war! The Americans are comin' to run the Redcoats out!"

The murmur turned into a storm.

"Benson!" Mason commanded.

A rifle shot startled the people.

"They're comin'. The Yankees are comin', right soon – maybe next week. But you got to get smart right now," Mason announced.

"What you mean 'smart'?" someone challenged.

"Hell's a poppin', boys! The Injuns are on the war-path. When the Tories call the muster, a smart man will get lost in the woods. A smart man will keep his head down and his mouth shut. A smart man will still have his hair, his farm and his children this time next week. That's what smart is.

"A new day's comin', folks," Mason crowed. "You gonna live to see the dawn, or be buried in the night?"

*****

# Ken Leland

The next morning, Captain Alexander Lockwood and Jeremy Roberts resigned their employment at the sawmill and rode to the Babcock farm.

"Hello, Dinah," Lockwood said as he stood just outside the porch door. "Is your father at home? May I speak to him?"

Leaving the door open, Dinah sprinted for the back kitchen yelling, "Papa!"

"He's here! Alex is here," she said as her father rose slowly from the breakfast table. Then Dinah charged upstairs, where she found Mother and Patience with a bedsheet stretched between them. The boys, she supposed, must be out weeding the cornfield. "Momma, Alex is all white in the face. He's come to ask for Patience's hand. I just know it!"

Margaret Babcock breathed deeply and, in straight-backed dignity, began to descend the stairs. Patience, trembling, followed her with one hand on the rail and the other on her mother's shoulder. Dinah floated behind.

In the hall downstairs, Mr. Babcock tucked in his shirt and lifted his chin before advancing to the front door. Margaret, Patience, and Dinah followed him onto the porch.

Alex was standing by the swing. Patience saw a stranger holding two saddled horses in the yard. No, not a stranger! She knew him; it was the sandy-haired man from the winter Meeting in Niagara – the man who sat beside the beautiful black woman. What could he possibly be doing here?

But now Alex was speaking.

"Mr. Babcock, I've come to tell you the truth."

"No," Patience said, so quietly that only her mother heard.

"I'm Captain Alexander Lockwood, not Lockyer, of His Majesty's Royal 49th Regiment of the Line. General Brock sent..."

"No!" Patience raged. "Not another word!"

She rushed to grab Alex's arm and pulled him down the front steps. With an angry glare at the lone man in the yard, she dragged Alex out of sight behind the wagon shed.

Everyone heard Patience's infuriated scream. "How can thou treat me so?"

Mrs. Babcock moved to aid her daughter, but her husband reached out to her. "Let them sort it out."

# The Land Between Flowing Waters

Patience launched a whole-hearted, roundhouse punch. Alex made no attempt to dodge. Her fist smashed against his mouth, and sent his straw hat tumbling. He staggered. Patience pushed Alex hard onto his back in the tall weeds. She straddled his chest and grabbed two handfuls of his hair. Blood began to ooze from his lip.

"No more lies!" she shouted. "No more secrets! Thou will tell me all, right now!"

"I will, Patience. I promise. I am Captain Alexander Lockwood of His Majesty's..."

"I heard that part," she growled – then noticed that blood was dribbling down his chin. "Oh, thy poor mouth," she said. With a pang of conscience, she loosened her grip on his hair.

"General Brock sent me as a spy..."

"A spy?" she said dabbing one finger at the wound.

"... to identify the outlaws and their leaders."

"And now thou knows. We all know."

"When I return, it will be with troops and a magistrate's order to arrest them all."

"Thou never fled the army?"

"No."

"Always a soldier – ever loyal and true?" she scorned, still wondering how to staunch the trickle of blood.

"Yes."

"And when thou took Father's copy of *A Friend's Journal*, was that a sham as well?"

"No! Not entirely. A lot of it was interesting."

She bent to kiss his bleeding lip. He reached up to caress her.

"Interesting is enough for now," she conceded.

She sat up to see whether they were still alone. The sandy-haired man in the yard, and the woman, then leapt to mind. Patience considered for a moment.

"The handsome black woman at the Niagara Meeting: is she thy sister's business partner, Janie?"

"Yes."

"Tell me."

"Janie and I are lifelong friends."

Patience slapped his chest. "Tell me all of it!"

"We've loved each other since childhood."

"Oh," Patience moaned in dismay.

"Janie is married to the man I came with today."

Patience took a few seconds to digest this. Then she brightened. "Then thou canst never have her," Patience said, with some satisfaction, from her perch atop his chest. She looked down to study Alex more closely. "But thou loves her still!"

Alex would not meet her eyes. She bowed to kiss him once more.

"I'm sorry for thee," she whispered, "but thou must leave now."

Alex only looked at her.

"When thou art reconciled to Janie's choice, I am here," Patience said. "When thou art sick of horror and war, turn thy heart to me."

As Captain Lockwood and Jeremy Roberts rode away, Patience trudged up the porch steps.

"Patience, thy lips are bleeding!" her mother exclaimed.

"It's not my blood," Patience said. "Mother, I'm going to my bedroom. I'm going to bar the door to cry and grieve and pray. Dinah will have to sleep on the couch tonight."

\*\*\*\*\*

"My God, it hurts worse than Ethan," Janie Roberts wailed.

Miriam and Sarah held Janie beneath each arm as they walked her from the bedroom, out into the hall, and back again. Janie's white muslin gown was blotted in sweat. Her nipples were swollen, leaking and sore. Last evening, Miriam had insisted Janie stay over even though the labour pains were then far apart. Her water broke in the night. Now it was almost noon. Old Doctor Kerr sat downstairs in the fitting room, drinking tea, just in case something should go amiss.

"Eeeeeeeeee," Janie screamed, as a long tearing pain ripped through her womb. While she grasped the tall bedpost, she tottered, legs bowing and wobbling in her agony. She held on weakly. Darkness swam at the corners of her eyes. The sheets, rumpled and stained, were strewn across the bed before her. "Don't let Isaac bring you to this," Janie gasped to Miriam.

"You're close, Janie. So close."

Miriam's voice came from a great distance, even as she clutched Janie's left arm. Sarah supported her on the right. Janie clung to the post, dizzy and swaying.

# The Land Between Flowing Waters

"You must walk again, my dearest. Come, let's go look at the wisteria out the front window," her mother encouraged. The three women turned back toward the sitting room as Janie staggered between them and breathed deep.

"Where's my man when I need him?" She turned to ask Miriam. "Where's Jeremy? If he's going to do this to me, at least he could have the courage to watch."

"He's safe with Alex," Miriam assured her. "They'll be home soon."

"Men! They're perfectly worthless. Never. Here. When. I. Need...Eeeeeeee!"

Now the sitting-room window was far away and so small. How could it be almost dark outside?

"Worthless! Worthless!" Janie panted. "I need them now!"

"You're almost there. Almost there."

"Miriam!" Janie clutched her friend's arm to keep from collapsing. "Where is he? Where's Alex? I have to tell him...I have to tell him..."

"Later. He will be here later, Janie."

"I'll catch the baby," Sarah said, falling to her knees before Janie. "Miriam, you've got to hold her up from behind, just like we did with Ethan."

Janie began to push. There was nothing she would not do to end the pain.

"Eeeeeeeeee! Eeeeeeeeee! Eeeeeeeeee!"

"It's coming. It's coming," her mother said from miles away.

"It's a girl! A perfect little girl."

# Ken Leland

## Full Strawberry Moon: 1812
## (June 27, 1812)
## Refugees

"Grandfather, my name is Mukos. I am Bear Clan of Shishibes Lake. I've brought three horses."

There were hours still before daybreak. Torches burned along the Five Medals Village paths. People called out to one another and rushed from place to place, hurriedly loading travois with food and belongings. Thrilled to hear Mukos' voice, Senisqua peeked out from between her grandparents to see him in the moonlight. He held the horses' reins, each with a litter already lashed in place.

Shkote, her little brother, squeezed past to ask, "Mukos, is it true? Are the Long Knives coming?"

"Yes, Shkote. There are too many to fight. We must leave before dawn."

Grandmother stepped out to take Mukos' hand. "Senisqua has spoken of you."

"Honoured Grandmother, tell me how I can help."

The village emptied before sunrise.

The People fled to the northeast. Mothers and the aged led horses pulling heavily laden travois. In the hours of darkness, boys and girls walked close to their mothers as the long file crossed the grasslands. Then as sunrise brightened the east, youngsters chased each other the length of the column. The younger men, including the Shishibes youths, scouted in advance of the slow-moving caravan. Less than three-score warriors screened the rear from pursuit. Two hundred refugees moved at a steady, walking pace across the prairie toward the lightly wooded hills.

At the end of the first day, Mukos returned with five fat rabbits and a turkey. From campfires all around, families watched unobtrusively as he placed the game in Grandmother's hands. The bounty rested there only moments before Senisqua gathered it up and moved away. She skinned and prepared the meat so that Grandmother might contribute it to the communal stewpots.

Mukos then walked ten paces, as if to Grandmother's front door at home, and spread his blanket upon the ground. He sat facing outward into the crowded camp. Families all around

139

# The Land Between Flowing Waters

noticed, nodding and smiling at the suitor come to wait upon the grandparents of the dazzling young Senisqua.

As the Strawberry Moon rose in the east, Senisqua prepared a bed for her grandparents beside the fire. She cast aside rocks and twigs, and then she used a small mattock to break and loosen the soil. She spread the bedrolls, side by side, on the ground between her own place and Mukos, but in such a way that she could still see him.

Kmonokwe was close by at the hearth of Women's Okama, watching it all. Kmonokwe wished that, instead of being on guard, Kshiwe was beside her to see his daughter courted in the old way. But they had given up that right. Grandfather had proclaimed his adoption of Senisqua; she was Wolf Clan now.

After supper, little ones gathered around Kmonokwe as she told how Turtle, Partridge, and the Wolves went hunting for winter meat. Later, after the story was ended and a hush fell over the camp, she lay alone watching the stars.

Mukos waited until everyone seemed to be asleep before rising to rejoin the scouts.

Mukos found Hannibal nodding beside the embers of Youth Leader's fire.

"*Bozho*, Brother," Mukos said as he cleared the ground for his bedroll.

"I see you, Mukos – just barely," Hannibal replied with a sleepy smile.

"Are you joining us tomorrow?" Mukos asked.

"No, I'll return to the warriors before dawn."

Why a boy two years younger than himself rode with the veterans was a mystery written on Mukos' face.

Hannibal explained. "Revered Mother has taught me how to treat a wounded leg or arm, how to staunch a sabre-cut or set a broken bone...what prayers to say if there is a belly-wound."

Mukos nodded. "Then you've already learned a lot. Someday you'll be a great healer."

Hannibal paused before asking, "Where are we headed?"

"Pathfinder is taking us to an Odawa village on the Huron River."

"Where is that?" Hannibal asked.

"Twelve, maybe fourteen days away."

"In the King's country?"

# Ken Leland

"No," Mukos said. "I don't think it's so far away as that. I will ask." Mukos considered the apprentice healer. "And I will ask him where Walpole Island is."

The days of travel stretched on.

Each morning, after sunrise prayers and a quick breakfast, the main column of old people, mothers and children began another long march. Pathfinder left signs or stationed scouts to lead the People through the wooded hills and across the prairies. Kmonokwe rode beside Women's Okama at the head of the column, ever watchful for the fork-braced branch, the twisted handful of long grass, or the solitary scout framed against an evergreen on the horizon. And at the end of each day, Mukos brought food to Senisqua's grandparents. Then he sat until long after dark at a place where Senisqua could admire the shape of his back, which she did with great longing.

In late afternoon of the fourth day, Grandfather called Mukos to walk aside with him, a little way up a sloping hill beside the night's camp. From there, Mukos could see Senisqua also seated in conversation with Grandmother.

"Mukos," Grandfather began, "Your intentions are clear and honourable, but I fear that Senisqua is still too young and inexperienced to be your companion."

"Grandfather," Mukos said patiently, for he knew the roles each must play in the marriage negotiation. "It is true that Senisqua is young, but you know that she is quick to learn. Nanokas, your daughter, taught her much, and now Revered Mother guides her."

"Hmmmm. But perhaps Senisqua is too impatient. Such a young woman often is, wanting much from her companion, too soon."

"Grandfather. Senisqua's hand is ever open. She thinks not of what she wants, but of what she can give to others."

"Yes, you're right Mukos. I, too, have seen this."

Grandfather was silent for many moments. "A young man longs for the delights and warmth of a woman, one who knows how to please a man. Grandmother believes there is much Senisqua has yet to learn. A kind widow, there are several among us, would please you very much."

"Honoured Grandfather, I know as little as Senisqua. We will learn together."

# The Land Between Flowing Waters

Grandmother sat silently lacing rawhide into the seams of a pair of moccasins. When she finished one, she handed the other to Senisqua.

"Granddaughter, can you see my companion and Mukos talking, on the hill behind me?"

"Yes, Grandmother."

"Do you know what they are talking about?"

"Me. Us, I think."

"And what should I do now?" Grandmother asked.

"You should try to talk me out of marrying him," Senisqua confirmed.

"Senisqua, I want you to think of the day, many years from now, when your own daughter says to you, 'There is a man.' I want you to ask and answer all the questions you will ask of her."

"I will."

"There is only one thing more. Does he treat you as you would wish – even when he is angry or tired, when he is worried or afraid, when he is confused or ashamed? Think on this for a few more days."


On the fifth day, word came from spies left behind that the Horse Soldiers had swept through their village, burning the buildings and destroying the crops. The next morning when Kmonokwe rode out, she overheard a young mother and child leading their horse out onto the trail.

"Mother, where are we going?" the little boy asked.

"We go to find a new home, one so far away that the settlers will never come to find us."


It began to rain on the seventh day.

Tired, dirty and bored after the heat and stress of travel, the younger children revived and pranced naked as rain drops began to fall. But light grey clouds gave way to flashing black thunderheads, and the wind rose to lash the trees.

Kmonokwe shouted to Women's Okama. "Shelter! We need shelter."

Rain fell like a river pouring from the sky. Lightning streaked above, the great noise fairly beating upon the ground. Mothers and grandparents grabbed the little ones to carry them to wayfarer trees, huge pines with branches bending low onto the forest floor. The dancers celebrated no more, but complained of needles scratching their legs and chests beneath the water-soaked pines. Kmonokwe's skirt was a sodden blanket against her legs, her hair a stream overflowing onto her blouse.

"Everyone will be ill tomorrow," Women's Okama called against the storm.

"We need mats, travel lodges, a way to get dry," Kmonokwe said.

The Thunderers rumbled.

Just before dusk, Mukos and all the scouts brought bails of cattail stalks, gathered from the shallows of a nearby lake. The women rushed to weave them into waterproofing to line shelter roofs. When Senisqua finished the first mat to cover Grandfather's lean-to, Grandmother embraced the young couple.

"Thank you, my son. Thank you, my daughter."

Then, looking in surprise at the bright, sparkling Senisqua in the pouring rain, Grandmother exclaimed, "There, I've said it, haven't I? Well, I can't take it back. I love you both."

Then she kissed Mukos and Senisqua on both cheeks and it was done.

# Chapter Five:
# It Begins

### Sunday, June 28, 1812
### Coming Home

Jeremy Roberts' mood brightened every mile they rode closer to Janie. He and Captain Lockwood had left Niagara months ago in winter; now, on a sunny, hot morning, Roberts and Lockwood were riding east along Lundy's Lane toward the stupendous falls on the Niagara River.

"So Patience bloodied your lip!" Roberts laughed.

"Yes, she did that."

"Not a very Friendly thing to do, was it?"

"No," Lockwood smiled, his voice barely audible above the clop of their horses' hooves. "But she apologized. Twice."

"Did she now?"

"Hmmmm."

Not for the first time, Roberts considered the benefits to his own marriage if Lockwood should become captivated by the young Quaker woman.

"Still," Roberts said, "I supposed that's over now – you telling her father you're a soldier and all."

Perhaps it's over, Lockwood mused, though Patience's last words still echoed through his soul. "I am here... turn thy heart to me."

*All I have to do,* Lockwood thought, *is foreswear the life I lead, the life I'm proud to live.*

*God help me, she might be worth it.*

# The Land Between Flowing Waters

*****

Proclamation to the People of Upper Canada

Isaac Brock, Esquire
President, Administrator of the Province of Upper Canada

To all whom these Presents shall come, greeting.

Whereas on the seventeenth day of June last the congress of the United States of America declared that war then existed between those States...and the United Kingdom of Great Britain...I do hereby strictly enjoin and require all His Majesty's liege subjects...to manifest their loyalty by a zealous co-operation with His Majesty's armed forces in defense of the province, and the repulse of the enemy. And I do further require and command all to be vigilant in the discharge of their duty, especially to prevent all communication with the enemy, and to cause all persons suspected of traitorous intercourse to be apprehended and treated according to law.

*****

As Lockwood and Roberts neared the river, farms became more numerous, but stretches of forest still covered much of the land. Seldom was more than a quarter of a two hundred acre farm cleared for crops. As they rode, that perishingly hot morning, occasionally they saw farmers armed with shotguns or rifles lounging a few dozen paces back in the gloom to watch the road.

A canvas-topped Conestoga creaked down the lane. The oxen moved at a walking pace. Two young children, a boy and a little girl, looked out from the back wagon-gate. With a shy smile, the girl slid down to hide, leaving only her fingertips showing. Lockwood could see furniture and bedding stacked inside the wagon.

"Hiya," the boy challenged, as he balanced on the gate to kick his heels.

"Hello," Roberts replied. "Where you goin' today?"

"We're fur Black Rock."

"Joel!" The boy's father leaned round from the driver's bench with a worried expression. He relaxed after seeing two young men in farm jackets slowly overtaking them.

"Morning," the man said tentatively. His bonneted, gingham-clad wife glanced toward the strangers but said nothing.

"Morning, folks," Lockwood replied.

"Thought maybe you was more of them Provincials," the man said.

"Provincials?"

"We run across some earlier. They'll probably take that rifle offen you, Mister. Took my shotgun, they did."

"Really!" Roberts said with a raised eyebrow.

"We's gittin'," the boy announced, popping up from behind the driver's bench.

The father's smile was weak and anxious. "You all have a good day," he said as Roberts and Lockwood rode ahead.

"Yankees going home." Roberts spat in the dust.

"Better they leave now," Lockwood said.


They overtook another wagon just before reaching Portage Road. The wagon was crowded with one set of grandparents and half-a-dozen children.

"You men heading for Black Rock?" the father asked, just before taking the right-hand turn.

"Niagara," Lockwood replied quietly. "The Queenston ferry is closer, you know."

"Can't get down the mountain. My brakes ain't fur shit," the man said as he pulled his team to a stop.

With a glance at Lockwood's rifle, the driver asked, "You fellows know anything about Injuns hereabouts?"

"Injuns?"

"Heard they's scalping folks," the man said. "If you men was to be riding to Black Rock...well, I guess you ain't."

Lockwood and Roberts took the left-hand turn. The rumble from the Falls and its rainbow rising in the mist were just a few hundred yards away. But then Roberts rode back to the refugees.

"There are more families coming up the lane behind," he told the driver. "You could wait and go together, if you're that worried."

# The Land Between Flowing Waters

"Damned nonsense," Roberts growled as he and Lockwood cantered north.

As they approached Queenston Heights, the road hugged the precipitous, hundred-yard drop to the river below. The Heights were cleared for wheat and corn fields except along the tree-lined northern brow. There, beneath the oaks, was a long abandoned military camp – a cantonment of ramshackle cabins and stone ovens. From the top, they saw a line of wagons waiting at the village wharf. A ferry plied the waters over to New York State. The men leaned back to let the horses pick their footing on the long, sloping descent to the village.

"I can hardly believe it," Roberts said, nodding at the wagons far below. "It doesn't seem real."

"Getting out," Lockwood said.

They were almost at the bottom when they heard gunfire.

"Haw!"

Lockwood spurred the golden-brown stallion into a hard gallop. Roberts followed close.

At the angle where the main road branched was an artillery park, and beside was it a bivouac for militia. Janie Roberts' brother, Sergeant Matthew Benjamin, was standing guard beside the horse lines. Lockwood waved his straw hat to attract Benjamin's attention.

"Captain Lockwood, Sir! Ain't seen you for a month of Sundays!"

"Sergeant!" Lockwood called using the voice of command. "Who's firing?"

"I think them troopers down by the dock, Sir," Sergeant Benjamin called back.

A few men from the Light Artillery and the 1st Lincolns began to gather round. Several who recognized the long-absent captain explained to others who the 'farmer' in the straw hat really was.

"Who's in command here, Sergeant?"

"Colonel Claus, but he ain't here, Captain. Want me to roust up the Major?"

Lockwood shook his head. "I'll send Mr. Roberts if I need help."

Captain Lockwood and Jeremy Roberts cantered along Queenston's main street. The shopkeepers had taken cover when the firing began. Carbines were still popping along the dock. The refugee families lined up for the ferry hid beneath their wagons or behind stone walls. From atop the incline leading to the water, Lockwood saw a half-company of mounted troopers firing short muskets at the opposite shore, four hundred yards away. The very young lieutenant in the light-blue uniform of the Provincial Dragoons had lost control of his men.

"Report, Lieutenant!" Lockwood barked as he rode in. "What's going on here?"

"Sir!" the young officer said before wheeling his horse to face what looked like a straw-hatted rustic. "Sir?"

"Captain Lockwood of the 49th. Who are you firing at?"

"Those People, Captain." Across the river a score of brown-clad New York State Militia scurried for the tree line.

"Cease fire," Lockwood commanded. "Get behind a stone wall. Now!"

The troopers knew 'the voice', and holstered their carbines.

"Who are you?" Lockwood asked as they rode behind a warehouse.

"Lieutenant William Hamilton Merritt, Sir. Colonel Claus ordered us to guard the ferry, but Those People keep sneaking down to shoot at us."

"Well, Lieutenant Merritt, if any of Those People have a long rifle, you'll be explaining a dead trooper to his father. Maybe even your own."

"I'm trying to follow orders, Sir."

"Commendable, but stupidly done."

"Yes, Sir. There must be a better way."

"There certainly is. Borrow, Lieutenant Merritt – mind you, I said borrow – five or six sets of civilian clothes. Post sentries behind trees to watch who comes back on the ferry. Surely we don't care who leaves. Send everyone else out of range."

"Yes, Sir!"

"And hurry these damned Yankee farmers back home as quick as you can!"

"I'm a fish out of water," Lockwood told Roberts as they rode out of Queenston. "I'll stop by the farm and get into uniform."

"Janie's due – past due, I imagine," Roberts said as they rode. "I'll go on into town after we get to your father's place."

149

# The Land Between Flowing Waters

The River Road to Niagara had been settled by Loyalists for almost thirty years. Though the road was lined with pin-oaks and maples, here the woodlots were smaller. Most of the land was given over to crops, pastures, and orchards. Lockwood knew every family, every field, every tree, as did Roberts.

When they approached the sharp curve just before the Lockwood farm lane, a single young Haudenosaunee warrior came round the bend at a dogtrot. A bedroll was strapped across his bare back. His face was painted half red, half black, streaked vertically between the eyes and down the nose. His feathered scalp-lock bounced in the breeze. Behind him at a hundred paces came a line of warriors in pairs, a stream of war-painted, almost naked men armed with muskets. The line stretched beyond the bend and out of sight. Lockwood and Roberts yielded the centre of the road.

"*Shekon tsia,*" Lockwood called out in greeting as the first young man trotted by. Lockwood took off his straw hat and swept it low in gratitude. Some of the older warriors nodded, but most looked straight ahead as they pounded down the road. John Norton ran with the last few Grand River warriors.

"*Niawen.* Thank you," Lockwood called as Norton slowed and approached them.

Major Glegg is at Government House," Norton said with a smile, "but General Brock is in York."

"Thank God you've come!" Lockwood said.

"We're only a hundred. For now. We'll camp in the cantonment on the Heights." Norton studied Lockwood's companion. "Would you be Jeremy Roberts?"

"Yes."

"Glegg mentioned you're a father. Don't know if it was a boy or girl."

Roberts whooped and lit out for Niagara.

Lockwood reached down to take Norton's hand "Bless you, all your People. Niawen."

When Lockwood reached the farmyard, General Brock's young ward, John Ellis, was leading two milk cows from the barn.

"Hello, Captain," John called out. Then, to Asa Lockwood, who was coming from the wheatfield, "Grandpa! Look who's here!"

"Glad to see you," Asa said as he embraced his son. "Are you home for a while?"

Asa wiped his eyes.

"Yes, Dad – for a little while. How's Mom?"

"We're all fine, Alex. Lois is in the house." Then, looking at his son's filthy, worn, work clothes, he added, "Your uniform's clean in your closet upstairs."

Captain Lockwood, resplendent in the red officer's jacket of the 49th Regiment, stood with his mother on the front porch. They watched as John Ellis drove the buggy down the farm lane to River Road, carrying a load of clay milk jugs and dozens of eggs cushioned in straw-stuffed boxes. John was on his way to make Sunday deliveries in Niagara.

"That was my job!" Lockwood laughed as he draped his arm over his mother's shoulders.

"Alex, we've already got the big wagon packed." Lois spoke quietly.

"What in the world are you talking about?"

Lois shook her head. "Asa buried the good dishes and cutlery in the apple orchard – third row, fourteenth tree – you remember, the one that almost died from the ice storm?"

"Mom?"

"Ben and Sarah are ready, too. All we've got to do is grab John Ellis, Miriam, Janie and the babies, and head out."

"Babies?" Lockwood asked.

"Janie has a beautiful little girl now. Where's Jeremy?"

"He's probably already with her."

Asa came out onto the porch and Lockwood asked, "Dad, are you leaving?"

"We've got to be ready if the Yankees get across the river," Asa said. "Lots of folks, Loyalists, are already in the bush."

"I...well, you're right. It might happen."

"Before you go to town Alex, there's something you should know."

Lockwood glanced anxiously at his father. "Yes?"

"Miriam has a beau."

"What? Why, that's wonderful news, Dad! Who is it?"

"I think it's wonderful too, but I'll let Miriam tell you all about it."

# The Land Between Flowing Waters

Half an hour later, Captain Lockwood stood at attention in Major Glegg's office on the third floor of Government House.

"The General's in York. He has to sort out the new Assembly," Glegg said.

"One of them is a traitor. Assemblyman Mason is talking treason."

"Hah! He's not the only one, Captain. But at least you have evidence against him."

"Major Glegg, do I have to wait until Brock returns?"

"No. General Sheaffe and I are delegated to run things military; Colonel MacDonnell looks after the Provincial side. So...you and Mr. Roberts must swear out complaints against every man jack of them. Come to me for what you need, and then go arrest the lot."

"I met a Provincial Trooper on the way in, a Lieutenant Merritt. Says he wants to do his duty."

"Remarkable! He's yours if you want him. I'll clear it with MacDonnell."

"Sir? Is Major Branson still at the fort? I want to thank him for all he did for Mr. Roberts and me in the winter."

"Brock sent him with reinforcements for Amherstburg. He left a few days ago. Just one more thing, Captain Lockwood." Glegg paused and took a deep breath. "You might want to say hello to your sister Miriam first thing."


Jeremy Roberts dashed up the gravel walk to the Dress and Tailor Shoppe. He burst through the front door shouting, "Janie! Miriam!"

Miriam hurried out from the work room.

"Is Janie here? Where's the baby?" Jeremy demanded as he clasped Miriam under the arms and swung her in a circle.

"Jeremy, she's here," Miriam said breathlessly. "Your daughter was born a week ago."

"Daughter!" Jeremy charged the stairwell.

"Where's Alex?" Miriam called.

"He's right behind me."

"Oh."

Miriam sat in the display room, gazing out the bay window to the lake beyond, and thought about what she would say when her brother arrived.

# Ken Leland

Janie Roberts woke from a nap at the sound of her husband's voice downstairs. Their daughter lay asleep in the basket beside her. Janie was propped almost upright by three pillows. Her hair, washed and straightened, was swept up into a bun atop her head. Her white nightgown was low cut and loosely gathered over her swollen breasts. She reached across to the hand-towels Miriam had stacked on the night table to wipe perspiration from her face and neck. She glanced down at her daughter as footsteps raced up the stairs and abruptly stopped. There was a soft knock on the bedroom door.

"Jeremy?" she called.

He came in, beaming.

She held out her hands to him as he leaned in to kiss her forehead, then he sat on the bedside to kiss her cheeks, her beautiful broad nose, and finally her lips. His arms scooped her from the pillows to hold her close as he said, "I love you. It's been so long. Darling Janie, how are you?"

"A little sore," she said falling back out of his embrace.

Then, seeing his face, she said, "Oh, I love you too, my dear. But look! Look who we have now!"

She tilted the basket so he might see his daughter.

The little one slept, her jet-black hair straight against her scalp, her tiny fingers clenched with thumbs tucked in. Eyes shut, she arched her back with a soundless yawn at her father's touch.

"She'll be hungry and awake, soon enough," Janie said.

"She's an angel. We'll have to think of a name." Then he bent to kiss Janie's glistening shoulders.

"Your hair's so long," Janie said, as she raked her fingers through the shaggy locks at the back of his head. Gently, she gripped his hair to guide him lower to kiss the tops of her breasts.

Jeremy pulled down her white cotton gown. He ran the tip of his tongue over each swollen nipple as Janie caught her breath. White droplets formed and he licked them away. Janie fondled the bulge at his groin. His hand drifted lower, sliding down over her belly, but then Janie flinched.

"Oh, Janie, I'm sorry," he said abashed. "I didn't mean to hurt you."

"I'm still so sore. I want you but...I can't."

Jeremy started to sit up.

"No, darling," Janie said. "Don't leave. Lie down with me." She nuzzled his nose, and then breathed sweetly in his ear as she unbuttoned his trousers. "I've missed you so," she whispered. Her long, slender fingers made a warm, welcoming sheath as Jeremy shivered in her grasp. She caressed him gently.

Between Jeremy's soft moans, she could hear voices through the open window, below in the front garden.

Urgently, Jeremy kissed her forehead, her eyes.

She listened. *He's here*, Janie thought, *just outside.* She rubbed her face across Jeremy's unshaven cheek. "I've missed you so," she said again, as he gasped and pulsed in her hands.

Later, Janie stood at the window and gazed out into the fading afternoon as Jeremy slept beside their daughter. The garden was empty, the white gate closed.

*Where has Alex gone?* she wondered. *To the docks, to spill himself inside some trull?*

*How sad we are.*

*Oh, how we have hurt each other.*

### Third Quarter, Strawberry Moon
### July 3, 1812
### A Call to War

Hannibal scraped at the outer bark of a black willow. He had gathered herbs and roots all morning, but it was only now, when his hatchet slipped against the jagged bark, that he chanced to glance across the Huron River. There, on the opposite bank some forty paces away, was a figure almost hidden in the brush. *Well,* Hannibal thought, with some impatience at his carelessness, *if the stranger meant harm, I would be dead by now.* Hannibal walked to the water's edge. Facing the thicket, he signed as he spoke.

"*Bozho*, Brother. I am Neshnabek, Hannibal of the Bear Clan. I'm gathering medicines."

A youth, hardly older than himself, rose from concealment. "I am Odawa, Sheyoshke – Bird Flying Fast – of the Crane."

To Hannibal's ear, he spoke with an accent, but understandably.

"No one told me the Neshnabek were black," Sheyoshke laughed.

"And no one told me the Odawa were slow-witted," Hannibal replied smiling. "I am adopted, of course."

# Ken Leland

"What medicine comes from the willow?" Sheyoshke asked as he waded chest-deep into the river, his bow held high.

"I make a powder from the inner bark. It's good for body pain and headache."

"You are a healer then?"

"I have a Midewiwin teacher, Kmonokwe of the White Fish."

"Our village would be happy if she came to us. Is she nearby?"

"Yes. We travel with the Five Medals People. Our Pathfinder and Okama are probably in your village already," Hannibal said.

"Then I'll take you there, Brother. A messenger from Tecumseh came in the night. We are gathering to hear what he has to say."


The aged Ojibway messenger stood motionless in the glen. Odawa People had gathered from small summer camps strewn at a distance, north and west along the Huron River. The Neshnabek refugees joined in the expanding circles of elders, hunters, women, youths and children, some six hundred souls in all.

There was a small fire at the centre of the council circle. A Neshnabe youth sprinkled it with fresh bits of cedar bough and tobacco until the aroma drifted across the clearing. The Odawa Calumet Carrier raised a pipe to the Master of Life, then lowered it to Mother Earth, and finally offered it to the Four Winds. Kmonokwe led all the People in opening prayers.

Afterwards she quickly told the story of how the Odawa, the Neshnabek, and the Ojibway joined to become the Three Fires of the Anishnabee. She did this so the children might know that the strangers among them were their Brothers.

The Ojibway elder, bare-chested, painted in red and black stripes, strode forth into the blazing summer sun so that all might see and hear him. His voice carried even to the small children playing in the trees beyond the outermost ring.


"The Long Knife chief, General Hull, leads two thousand soldiers. His army approaches the Maumee River. Already the women and children of the Wyandot and The Three Fires are fleeing. Hull comes to fight the King's People across the Detroit River.

"Brothers, I ask you. When he has finished with the King's People, what will he do?

# The Land Between Flowing Waters

"Honoured Elders of the Crane, the Bear, and the Wolf, hear me now. I bring the words of Tecumseh, the Shawnee war chief. He sends this message to all the Red People of Turtle Island. Hear his words! This is his message:

"Today we met together in solemn council. We are not here to debate whether we have been wronged and injured, but by what measures we should avenge ourselves, for our merciless oppressors, having long since planned out their proceedings, are now making attacks upon those of our race.

"But have we not courage enough remaining to defend our country and maintain our ancient independence? Will we calmly suffer the white intruders and tyrants to enslave us? Shall it be said of our race that we knew not how to extricate ourselves from the three most to be dreaded calamities – folly, inactivity and cowardice?

"What need is there to speak of the past? It speaks for itself and asks, "Where today is the Pequot? Where the Narragansett, the Mohawk, Pocanoket, and many other once powerful tribes of our race?" They have vanished before the avarice and oppression of the white men, as snow before a summer sun. In the vain hope of alone defending their ancient possessions, they have fallen in the wars with the white men. Look abroad over their once beautiful country, and what see you now? Naught but the ravages of the destroyers meet your eyes. So it will be with the Three Fires! You too will be driven away from your native land and ancient domains as leaves are driven before the wintry storms. The white usurpation in our common country must be stopped, or we, its rightful owners, will be forever destroyed and wiped out as a race of people.

"Brothers. Sleep no longer in false security and delusive hopes. Our broad domains are fast escaping from our grasp. Every year the white intruders become more greedy, exacting, oppressive and overbearing. Do they not even now kick and strike us as they do their black slaves? How long will it be before they will tie us to a post and whip us, and make us work for them in their cornfields, as they do them? Shall we wait for that moment, or shall we die fighting before submitting to such ignominy?

"Brothers. Have we not for years had before our eyes a sample of their designs, and are they not sufficient harbingers of their future determinations? Will we not soon be driven from our respective countries and the graves of our ancestors? Will not the bones of our dead be ploughed up, and their graves be turned into fields? Shall we calmly wait until they become so numerous that we will no longer be able to resist oppression? Will we wait to be destroyed in our turn, without making an effort worthy of our race? Shall we give up our homes, our country, bequeathed to us by the Great Spirit, the graves of our dead, and everything that is dear and sacred to us, without a struggle? I know you will cry with me:

"Never! Never!

"Then let us by unity of action destroy them all, which we now can do, or drive them back whence they came. War or extermination is now our only choice.

"Which do you choose?"

*****

Two days later, Kmonokwe faced the array of Odawa and Neshnabe warriors. The men stood quietly, Hannibal and his young Odawa friend Sheyoshke among them, awaiting her final benediction. Two dozen large canoes floated by the riverbank, ready to carry them to the lands below Fort Detroit. Behind her stood the hundreds of family members they would leave behind. Kshiwe and his small band of warriors were on Kmonokwe's right, near the water. At the last moment, Mukos hefted his bow and bedroll to cross from Senisqua's side to join them. Senisqua's face streamed with tears but she tried to smile.

Kmonokwe stood rigid, locked in ceremony by so many eyes, struggling not to be swept away in despair. She walked to Kshiwe.

"I have failed us," she whispered. "I have brought us to ruin, not safety. Had I but listened to you, we would be happy at Maxinkuckee Lake."

"My love, where is there safety for us, for our People?" he asked.

"Nowhere," her voice broke. "But you must come back. I have no life without you."

She turned then to the open ground between the warriors and their families. She raised her arms and prayed aloud:

# The Land Between Flowing Waters

Master of Life, hear our prayer.
Protect us from fear. Strengthen our hearts.
Grant us victory over our merciless enemy.

Shield us from their eternal malice.
Save us from destruction.
Bring us to a time of peace.

\*\*\*\*\*

Day ended. The northwest wind faltered, then faded away at moonrise.

A willow tree stood on the river bank. Muskrats slept among its roots. Its trunk was wider than a man could stretch out his arms, and its branches rose above all others.

A grey lynx sprawled in the willow, resting its chin on gathered paws. Its hind feet hung down to straddle a limb. The cat's tufted ears swiveled, and its bright yellow eyes blinked.

The river was alive in the night.

A boar raccoon, an old and massive grandfather, woke from his nap. He limped down to the stream. The first finger on his left paw still ached from the snapping-turtle he'd surprised sleeping on a log. Head to the ground, his haunches riding high, the raccoon loped slowly through the tall weeds at the water's edge, looking for easier prey – a tasty frog or water snake. From higher on the bank a river otter twitched his whiskers at the raccoon's passing, but soon resumed munching on a catfish. The boar paused then, and hearing the whining snuffle of his own kind, he rose on hind legs. There, digging for mussels in the muddy shallows, was a sow raccoon and her kits. Five kits, one for each of the codger's long clawed fingers, even the achy one. The small, inquisitive balls of grey and black fur were his, he supposed, but he had paid them no mind after the fierce joy of their making. Their mother saw him. Screeching viciously to warn him away, she shielded their progeny behind her, each kit making the whining coo of submission, of distress.

*Ah, well,* the old boar thought, *she's not as powerfully desirable as I remember. And one of those fluff balls will come by some day, demanding I move on. Not likely! Somewhere there's a joke in all that. I'll puzzle it out later.*

He heard a soft, hollow thump. Grandfather raccoon turned to gaze out across the moon-white water. Canoes floated there, tied together in a long chain with humans riding inside. Most were asleep, lying back on bundles, but in the nearest he saw a youngster rise to point up into the willow.

"Sheyoshke! There are eyes glowing in the tree."

"Go back to sleep, Hannibal. You're only dreaming."

Before dawn, the winds gathered. Clouds swept in from the west to hide the setting moon. Rain fell in torrents. In the storm's fury, the willow branches strained but did not break. Riding the wind, the lynx waited until, somewhere far downriver, a great tree limb did break and fell into the river. The cat yawned as the storm faded.

*****

"*Bozho*, Brothers. The Long Knives are camped only an hour downstream."

Hannibal awoke, wet and aching from sleeping in the waterlogged canoe. A white man speaking Odawa had called to them from the shore. Behind him among the trees were smoking campfires and the shadows of many people.

The war-band landed to walk among the rain soaked exiles. Hannibal and Sheyoshke took up the medicine packs and followed. In the growing light, the warriors wound past overturned travel lodges, collapsed shelters and broken tarps, all casualties of the storm. Here a bewhiskered man in sodden clothes mended a broken cord; there two men in work-trousers strained to straighten a shelter. On the left, a young father in a leather hat carried his daughter to the women at the communal fire; on the right, splashing in a grassy rain puddle, was a collection of little boys.

Now warriors were breaking away, striding off to help one family or another. Forgotten, Hannibal and Sheyoshke looked around, unsure of what to do. Kshiwe and Village Speaker were already rebuilding a shelter. Mukos, Youth Leader and the other young men were heading into the forest to hunt game. Odawa were wading into the river with fishing nets.

Hannibal watched as the Okamas took counsel with the white Elders.

"General Hull stopped by us yesterday," one old man was signing. "They stripped our gardens, looted our barns, and frightened the women. So we left."

# The Land Between Flowing Waters

"Are the Long Knives still there?"

"Yes. Their wagons are too heavy; they're trying to strengthen the bridge."

There were many families here, drying out. Beneath a lean-to, Hannibal saw a woman in a long cotton dress with a naked child lying limp in her arms. As he approached, her tears fell upon the boy's chest. Hannibal motioned for Sheyoshke to follow, but Sheyoshke stopped short to watch. When Hannibal knelt, she was wiping the boy's face with a corner of her skirt.

Hannibal searched for the words and then asked, "Is your boy sick? Maybe I can help."

The woman glanced fleetingly at him, but did not reply. Thinking he must have spoken in Neshnabe, he tried again. This time in English, for sure.

"Can I help? Is the boy sick?"

*"Mon fils a une fièvre."*

And then she began to sign, with great skill, and Hannibal understood. Sheyoshke moved to join them when he realised she was Canadienne.

Hannibal searched through his medicine bags for powders to treat the child's fever. *How surprising,* he thought. *The Nations and these settlers are friends.*

*****

A broken catalpa limb, longer than a settler's wagon, drifted downstream around the narrow island. At one end, the limb's white flesh was torn by the windstorm. At the other end, a canopy of large green leaves floated both above and below the water line. Those above cast shadows, those below fluttered to disguise that which was lower still. Wedged securely, an arm's length above the current, rode a squirrel's nest of bone-dry twigs. The great limb began to spin, ever so slowly, as its torn leading edge glided noiselessly into a bed of cattails. Then, unnoticed but in plain sight of a long wooden bridge, the limb shuddered to a stop.

The tramp of many feet came from the bridge. By the hundreds, by the thousands, armed men in blue and brown trudged northward. Tree trunks, newly set into the riverbed, supported the bridge as wagons rumbled across. In the middle of the span was a timber pier. A great pile of white-skinned driftwood, accumulated over years, lay tangled in its crosspieces.

# Ken Leland

Kshiwe floated beneath the catalpa branch as water flowed over his shoulders. He leaned back against the current, bracing the limb so that it might not drift away. Broad leaves shaded him from view as he counted the army wagons, and then the bawling cattle. The squirrel's nest holding his flint and file was jammed between the branches just above his head.

Hannibal and Sheyoshke hid on a tree-covered hillside overlooking the bridge. They peeked out from a gap beneath a fallen log to watch the army pass. In its vanguard was a shoeless black man in a worn, walnut-dyed shirt. He pulled a pack-horse behind a blue-coated, mounted officer. With disappointment, Hannibal watched the ragged stranger cross the bridge and disappear from sight.

The boys were amazed by the passage of thousands of soldiers, of wagons, and last of all, drovers herding cattle. Happy to tread no longer on wooden sills, the cattle lifted their tails to add to the vileness of the muddy road.

The Shishibes Lake war-band lay hidden in the brush between Hannibal and the bridge. The warriors were invisible. The Five Medals men waited just across the road. The Odawa warriors lay in ambush on the north side of the bridge. Finally, the sounds of the army faded. Only a corporal's guard remained behind on the southern approach to the bridge. They wore brown homespun jackets, floppy leather hats, and white shoulder belts. On the far side was a second squad of militia.

The catalpa branch lurched and then floated with the current. Hannibal forgot to breathe as his father maneuvered the limb toward the pier and the mound of driftwood there.

Two soldiers wandered onto the bridge as the branch drifted. A redbird's song was answered on the far shore. One soldier paused to loosen his fly, and a thin stream of urine shot out over the railing. A second guard leaned over to stare into the water. Hannibal heard him shout something to the corporal about fishing.

The catalpa floated closer until its jagged stump wedged in the brush. The leafy end revolved slowly, coming to rest beneath the bridge. There, in the shadows, the squirrel's nest rustled, but instead of falling into the water, it rose imperceptibly to the driest portion of the piled driftwood. After a few moments, there was a spark and a feather of smoke.

# The Land Between Flowing Waters

Flames spread upward through the pier. Seeing heavy smoke swirling downwind, the corporal shouted for his men to extinguish the fire. Soldiers from both sides ran towards the middle of the bridge. The Long Knives peered over but seemed confused.

At a shouted signal, the Neshnabek on the southern approach screamed for all they were worth. Waving tomahawks in the air, they charged from concealment onto the road. They came fast, but the soldiers had enough time to become thoroughly terrified. The northern bank seemed clear and so the militia panicked in that direction. Only the corporal raised his pistol to fire at their attackers; the rest threw down their muskets to run the faster over flames lapping up between the sills. Once across, the soldiers sprinted for their lives through the mud.

Up on the hill, Sheyoshke dragged Hannibal to his feet, and both snatched up their bows and medicine packs. As they careened downhill, Hannibal scanned the road for anyone who might be hurt. Then he saw Kshiwe treading water.

"Look for a powder horn," his father called.

In the quickly spreading flames, the warriors advanced only far enough to gather up the weapons left behind. War cries came from the Odawa waiting in ambush, farther up the road. A towering black cloud rose to mark the burning bridge.

The Long Knives would not find it easy to come this way again.

## Monday, July 13, 1812
## The Long Distance War

At his father's farm, Alexander Lockwood had just finished sweeping out the wheat bin. With the front and back doors open, a cooling early evening breeze flowed through the barn. To a farm boy, the odour of manure from the cows was barely noticeable. Lockwood leaned against the door that overlooked the apple orchard and the golden field beyond. The wheat harvest would begin by the end of the week – Lockwood only needed to feel the air and watch the sunset to know there'd be no rain before then. While he lounged, bats took flight from the rafters, soaring out against the purple-streaked sky, plunging and twisting to snatch insects from the air.

Lockwood and Roberts had worked at Government House comparing notes as they drafted charges against the ruffians at Twenty Mile Creek. It was exhausting work that promised to stretch on for days. Roberts, home and most happy in Janie's arms, was by turns supercilious and condescending to Lockwood.

The Roberts had named their baby daughter Anna. Lockwood was surprised how much he wanted see the little girl, but he made excuses to stay away. He could not trust himself in Janie's presence.

At the beginning of the following week, General Brock returned to Government House. It was the hottest day of summer so far.

"The latest reports are almost ten days old," Brock said, "but General Hull was marching north, just a few miles from Detroit with an army of militiamen and regulars. He comes to invade our western counties."

"You know his orders, Sir?" Lockwood asked in amazement.

Lockwood stood at ease in the stifling heat. All the third floor windows were propped open, but there wasn't a breath of air. Major Glegg sat behind the small secretary's desk, twirling his quill pen with a mischievous grin.

"No Captain Lockwood, but a boarding party from Fort Amherstburg captured a ship carrying his luggage, and General Hull's papers were in his travel chest," Brock explained. "He comes with three regiments of Ohio militia, a company of Dragoons, and the U.S. Fourth Regiment – good fighters; they destroyed Prophetstown last fall. He will have about 2500 men at Fort Detroit."

Brock leaned back to fan himself with the report. With a broad smile he asked, "Tell me, Captain Lockwood. Saddled with twenty-five hundred hungry, complaining, lawyering Yankees, wouldn't you be desperate to kill somebody?"

Glegg chortled.

"He'll invade," Brock concluded. "Why else would he come with so many?"

Lockwood reached down to touch the general's desk. "I'll raid them, bleed them on the King's Road. It's the only way east from Amherstburg. I can recruit 200, 300 Loyalists on the way. Let me try, Sir."

"General Hull will hope to raise the back country; using the same banditti you and Mr. Roberts are drafting charges against."

Lockwood paused to think again. "No, you're right General. We have to go after the outlaws first. The civilians are balanced on a knife edge."

# The Land Between Flowing Waters

"And the Haudenosaunee teeter on the same blade," Glegg added. "John Norton says that Hull is trying to sweet-talk them from us."

Brock sighed. "Lockwood, are you quite sure you haven't got two or three twin brothers hiding in your father's barn? I certainly wish there were more of you; I hardly know where to send you for fear of not having you somewhere else." The general propped his boots atop an open drawer.

"I'll do my best, whatever you decide," Lockwood said.

"I'm sure you will."

Brock sighed again as he gazed out the window onto Queen Street. "You know, Captain Lockwood, every day John Ellis comes home from the farm with another story of milking cows or selling eggs or cutting wheat."

"He's part of the family, like another grandson."

"Family." Brock sat up and paused to look carefully at Lockwood. "You've been away so long on duty. Are you aware that my son is starting to think of your parents as family, as grandparents? And he views your sister Miriam with great affection..."

Brock came to a complete stop, and then added, "As do I."

"Miriam has explained this to me, Sir, in the same terms."

"Yes. Well. Just so. Perhaps it's too soon to speak about this."

"Perhaps, Sir, there is no need. I wish only for Miriam's happiness. And I know she is happy."

"I assure you, Captain, our wishes – yours and mine – are in complete accord."

Again, Brock lapsed into silence. "I cannot leave for Amherstburg until after the Assembly meets at York on the 27th."

Then, he decided. "Major Glegg, please take note of Captain Lockwood's orders. He is to continue writing affidavits and swear out charges as promptly as he and Mr. Roberts are able. And Lieutenant Merritt is to train the Dragoons as quickly and efficiently as may be. Captain, you are to keep busy and await further developments."

Glegg slapped Lockwood's shoulder and led him off to lunch, laughing, "They also serve, my boy, who only stand and wait."

# Ken Leland

## Sunday, July 12, 1812
## Invasion

The British province of Upper Canada lay on the eastern shore of the Detroit River. In 1812, the land and its people were quite unlike what they would later become.

In the north of Essex County was the Thames River. Navigable by sail for some twenty miles from its mouth at Lake St. Clair, the lower reaches of the Thames were sparsely settled by a few Loyalists and scattered Canadiens whose roots in North America began in the *ancien regime* of New France. The newly established outpost of Baldoon lay a dozen miles north of the Thames on Bear Creek. Unaccountably situated in malarial marsh land, the tiny Scottish community had struggled for survival since its inception in 1804. Farther east along the Thames was the pacifist Christian and Indian community of Moraviantown; then came the hamlet of Delaware, and finally the village of Oxford, around which white settlement was thin but growing with American immigration. The King's Road, a glorified forest trail, paralleled the Thames until it intersected another dreadfully bad road, Dundas Street, midway between Delaware and Oxford. It was Dundas Street that led directly east toward Lake Ontario, and ultimately to the provincial capital at York.

But except for this ribbon of settlement along the Thames, settlers considered the interior as unused and uninhabited – it was in fact the home and hunting grounds of many First Nations People.

In 1812, comfortable travel in Upper Canada could happen only on water. By descending the Thames westward, one approached white civilization as represented by the settlements along both sides of the Detroit River. Below Lake St. Clair, the King's Road became increasingly passable as it bent south to skirt the Detroit River's eastern shore. Here were century-old farms. Their narrow fronts abutted the river and stretched back to create thin, long fields reminiscent of France. That summer, windmills twirled slowly to grind what was expected to be the best harvest in years. Southward, almost opposite the Fort and Town of Detroit, was the village of Sandwich, where some 300 Canadiens lived in frame houses among two churches, a court house, a jail and a school, as well as businesses that included a shipyard and warehouses for the fur trade. Its largest home was the mansion of the Baby scion, Colonel James Baby, whose ancestors had grown rich in the Indian fur trade. The Huron Chapel was nearby, and to the west was a village of Mississauga Ojibway.

Proceeding south over the Turkey Creek bridge, the King's Road led to the farming community of Petite Cote, past granaries, windmills, straw-thatched farmhouses and well-tended gardens, before broaching upon a prairie and the Canard River. This prairie extended below the Canard Bridge for a hundred yards, only to give way to forest. The Huron Reserve lay in the forest, four miles above the town of Amherstburg, which was the administrative centre of the Western District of Upper Canada. A garrison town of taverns and shops, Amherstburg was home to 200 Loyalists families and a few blacks who had escaped slavery by crossing into Upper Canada. Fort Amherstburg, at the town's northern edge, was an almost indefensible earthen work, guarded by 250 regulars of the 41st Regiment. The grounds of the fort included a military dockyard which was the home port of the 18 gun HMS *Queen Charlotte*. The British Indian Department Council House was nearby.

From Amherstburg, the King's Road extended farther south to the mouth of the Detroit River and past the New Settlement on the southern border of Essex County. The New Settlement was a farming community founded by Loyalist veterans of Butler's Rangers. As the road bent eastward over the Lake Erie shore, it again devolved into a forest path through First Nation lands. To the western settlers of Upper Canada, civilization was this thin crust, this rim of land between flowing waters.

\*\*\*\*\*

On Sunday morning, July 12, 1812, 180 men of the Ohio Third Regiment refused to cross the Detroit River, though the passage was completely unopposed. The reason reported for this refusal was that, by Ohio State Regulations, militiamen were required to serve only on United States soil. Perhaps it is to be supposed that this portion of the Third Ohio was composed principally of lawyers, or of cowards, or of those with scruples against what they were being asked to do – or perhaps all three.

In any case, the willing that remained attached to General Hull, after a large detail had been sent to guard Fort Detroit and patrols detached to keep the supply roads open, were sufficient for an invasion force of about 1000 infantry, regulars and militia. Those soldiers crossed in small boats from a point below Belle Isle and landed about two miles upriver from the village of Sandwich.

# Ken Leland

John Hunt, an American civilian of the town of Detroit, considered it a marvelous sight: "My blood thrilled with delight when I saw...the march of that fine army, with drums beating and colours flying, with the gleaming of bright muskets." Colonel Cass of the Ohio Second Regiment planned carefully to be the first soldier onto enemy soil. He carried a flag of 18 stars onto the eastern riverbank, around which soldiers clustered to cheer the great deeds they were about to accomplish.

Moments later, General William Hull splashed ashore to proclaim, "The critical moment draws near!" This battle cry was hardly inspirational, but it was wiser than almost anyone credited. For indeed, those who planned the invasion supposed it would be largely unopposed – a mere matter of marching, involving little or no risk. Would it, then, be a bloodless incursion by a people already raised to an elevated rank among the citizens of the world? An effortless conquest by a nation afforded a greater measure of peace, security and wealth than achieved by any other? How could, why would, anyone resist such an invader?

*****

Colonel James Baby and his brother Francois watched as Yankee boats landed that morning. Sheltered behind Francois' now empty house, they noticed an ill-favoured man running up the beach with a large flag. He impaled its staff into the sand and then crowed loudly as blue-clad officers and brown-jacketed militiamen clustered around. A stout, aging, General Officer was assisted by juniors as he limped along rows of cheering would-be conquerors. Boats were landing now by the dozen. Hundreds of armed men swarmed ashore to form a battle line. The men near the flag were hectored into position.

"*Je regrette*, Francois," Colonel Baby said to his younger brother. "I think the Americans want your house. We'd better leave."

The brothers ran to their horses in the front yard. They crossed King's Road, then galloped along the dirt lane between narrow, golden wheat fields. 500 Canadiens of the Essex County Militia, untrained farmers, shopkeepers, voyagers and fishermen, stood in ranks in a woodlot behind the fields. Stolidly arrayed before them were two red-jacketed British companies, 100 men, of the 41st Regiment of the Line, commanded by Major Willard Branson. From horseback, Colonel Baby could see gaping holes in the

# The Land Between Flowing Waters

Essex's ranks; indeed, men in leather hats and work pants were slipping into the forest even as he watched.

"Major Branson!" the Colonel shouted. "Those men are deserting."

"Yes, Colonel," Branson agreed. "They've been sneaking away all morning."

"We have to stop them!"

"How, Colonel, short of killing them?"

Major Branson waited as the Colonel and his brother fumed. After a few moments the Colonel came to the only possible conclusion.

"We have to withdraw, Major. These men will not stand."

"Yes, Colonel. I think you're right."

"How can we get them down to Fort Amherstburg?"

"You lead. We'll follow as a rear guard," Branson said. "Tell your militia the Yankees won't get past us."

Colonel Baby was embarrassed, particularly as he was required to leave in a few days for York to serve as the Assemblyman for Essex County. There he must face General Brock to explain how his command had not fired a single shot in defense of Upper Canada.

But surely, it was clear for anyone with eyes to see – the province was as good as lost. American victory was inevitable.

*****

The sun blazed that warm Sunday afternoon. 100 sweating men of the 41st followed Branson down the King's Road. They marched, not in step, but at least in rows, behind the 500 nondescript militia, or what was left after the most recent desertions.

The militiamen shambled aimlessly, a Sunday procession that had lost its way. They balanced weapons on their shoulders, lessening the chance of killing a neighbour accidentally. Squirrel guns and muskets, a few blunderbusses and the odd rifle slanted carelessly toward the burning sun. A few carried halberds, long heavy lances fitted with axe-heads. These legacies of New France were for use against slashing cavalry sabres, but no one knew how to use them properly.

Men of every trade, except arms, wandered down the dirt road. They were clad in floppy leather hats and homespun shirts. Some were barefoot, having already discarded ruined leather shoes. Others wore moccasins. Their officers wore red sashes without insignia; some carried a sword or pistol.

Colonel Baby, in a fine blue coat and white crossed belts, rode at the head of the column. He watched grimly as dust-devils swirled on the road ahead. How could he ever explain this disaster?

A few houses came into view. As they trudged past Sandwich, a number of militiamen cast longing eyes toward the village. Women, families, stood outside in back gardens as their men passed. One militiaman dashed for home. Two more followed. Only one returned when Colonel Baby fired his pistol into the air.

"Stay together," the Colonel bellowed, more in hope than in expectation.


"Look at 'em, John," Private James Hancock said quietly to the next soldier in the 41st ranks. "Them Frenchies ain't the Old Guard, now are they?"

"Nappy'd put 'em afore a firing squad, he would," Private John Dean agreed.

"So it's up to the old 41st again." Hancock sighed.

"It is that," Dean said.

"Course, you can't blame 'em.... Much."

"Not too much."

"Canadiens won't fight for King George," Hancock opined.

"Nope. Not even on a good day," Dean answered.

"And, they ain't gonna fight for Jonathan."

"Lord, no!" Dean avowed.

"Still..."

"What?"

"There ain't enough of us, is there?" Hancock mumbled low.

"Maybe the Injuns'll fight with us," Dean said.

"Lord God o' Mercy," Hancock growled. "If they go agin us, we're all dead."


When the British contingent cleared the village, Major Branson ordered a mounted squad and a lieutenant to lag a mile behind. Branson did not expect an active pursuit in this heat, particularly with the Yankees still flush from their easy crossing.

# The Land Between Flowing Waters

But they would follow soon enough, and someone would have to stop them.

"Dismantle the bridge at Turkey Creek," Branson told his officers.

It was whistling in the dark, he knew. Soldiers could wade the creek; it was only waist deep. But cannons would need a bridge. Did Hull bring cannons? Branson wondered. Probably not. Not yet anyway – but there were plenty at Fort Detroit. Maybe the 41$^{st}$ had a day or two more until the Yankees came rolling down the King's Road.

*****

The invaders were more ambitious that day than Major Branson supposed. From his new headquarters in Francois Baby's mansion, General Hull ordered teams of agents into the Thames Valley. These agitators would carry printed proclamations of America's good intentions, and offer paroles to anyone hoping to avoid violence. Elements of the Third Ohio rode northeast toward Baldoon in pursuit of Ojibway rumoured to be hostile. Armed patrols fanned out into the hinterlands to reassure the white residents of America's benevolence. Hull ordered a contingent of the Fourth Regiment, his only regular army unit, to procure food in Sandwich. When the army arrived at Detroit, quartermasters had brought provisions for four weeks, with the expectation of continual replenishment from Ohio. But the first resupply train was stalled somewhere between the Maumee and Raisin Rivers. American forces in Upper Canada would have to depend increasingly upon the generosity of the locals.

*****

"Collette," her father shouted from the garden, "Run tell Maman. There's Yankees on King's Road!"

Collette was surprised to see her father, Pierre, come home early that morning but, even so, he wouldn't take Collette and the boys to church. Papa said something about Colonel Baby and where all the Sandwich men were supposed to be.

Marie, her mother, must have heard him shouting. Maman was already on the back steps pulling little Robert out of the wash barrel and screaming for footloose Jean and Rene to get home.

# Ken Leland

Collette could see a line of blue-jacketed soldiers running through the wheat fields north of town, heading for the river wharf. Another blue line was trotting down the road, towards the windmill. From the garden Collette could see its great canvas vanes turning slowly.

## Colettte

Our neighbour ran in from the street and called out to Papa, "Where's Monsieur Bouchard? There're soldiers at his mill."

"I don't know," Papa answered. "He was still with Colonel Baby when I left."

Then Papa ran up the road to the grist-mill. Papa helps M. Bouchard sometimes.

Maman and the women on our street gathered at the corner to watch the soldiers up at the mill. They were yelling at people but we couldn't understand what they said. A tall officer in a black hat was waving his arms at Grandpere Leblanc. Grandpere knows a little English, I think. The officer struck him in the face when Grandpere gave an answer he didn't like. Then the soldier waved his arms some more, and his men broke down the mill door. They took M. Bouchard's wagon from the shed, and his horses too; then they started heaving the flour bags into the wagon.

Papa watched the soldiers for a while, but then Maman called for him. Maman yelled for him to hurry, but he kept looking back at Grandpere Leblanc. Two soldiers held Grandpere by the arms, and again the officer was saying something and poking him in the chest. The women and children all ran home as the soldiers escorted Grandpere down the road. He called out to each house as they passed.

"Everyone must stand in their front gardens." Grandpere's voice was a trembling, high-pitched quiver. "They want to see all the men!"

Papa ran to the Naults next door. Maman was beside herself, but Papa wouldn't listen to her. Little Robert was so frightened at Maman's screams, he peed himself down her dress. Pretty soon Henri Nault, our neighbour's oldest boy, just a couple years older than me, he came running out to stand with Madame Simard, just across the road. Her husband Giles was still with Colonel Baby. Papa knew she'd be standing alone when the Yankees came.

# The Land Between Flowing Waters

"They want every man to sign a parole," Grandpere explained.

Soldiers were going from house to house now as Grandpere talked to Papa. There were women trying to block the doors of houses without men, but they just got pushed to the ground. Then the soldiers went inside and began carrying out any food.

"What's a parole?" Papa asked, wary of the squad of armed men in our own garden.

"It means you got captured by *cet batard*," Grandpere said, as he gestured toward the Yankee officer, "and you can't fight them in future."

"And if I don't sign?"

"Then you're their enemy. They'll strip your garden and empty the root cellar. Maybe they'll burn your house."

Already the sky above the mill held a great black cloud.

Maman begged him, so Papa asked, "Where do I sign?"

When the soldiers left our village that evening, they nailed a paper to our front door. I kept it because I knew someday, someone could tell me what it said.

Inhabitants of Canada!

After thirty years of peace and prosperity, the United States have been driven to arms. The injuries and aggressions, the insults and indignities of Great Britain, have once more left them no alternative but manly resistance or unconditional submission.

The army under my command has invaded your country, and the standard of union now waves over the territory of Canada. To the peaceable, unoffending inhabitants, it brings neither danger nor difficulty. I come to find enemies, not to make them. I come to protect, not to injure you.

Separated by an immense ocean, and an extensive wilderness from Great Britain, you have no participation in her councils, no interest in her conduct. You have felt her tyranny, you have seen her injustice...I tender you the invaluable blessings of civil, political, and religious liberty, and their necessary result, individual and general prosperity...that liberty which has raised us to an elevated rank among the nations of the world, and which has afforded us a greater measure of peace and security, of wealth and improvement, than ever yet fell to the lot of any people.

Remain at your homes – pursue your peaceful and customary avocations – raise not your hands against your brethren...the arrival of an army of friends must be hailed by you with a cordial welcome. You will be emancipated from tyranny and oppression, and restored to the dignified station of freemen.

Had I any doubt of eventual success, I might ask your assistance – but I do not. I come prepared for every contingency. I have a force which will look down all opposition, and that force is but the vanguard of a much greater. If, contrary to your own interests and the just expectations of my country, you should take part in the approaching contest, you will be considered and treated as enemies, and the horrors and calamities of war will stalk you. If the barbarous and savage policy of Great Britain be pursued, and the savages be let loose to murder our citizens, and butcher our women and children, this war will be a war of **extermination**....No white man, found fighting by the side of an Indian, will be taken prisoner – instant destruction will be his lot....

I doubt not your courage and firmness – I will not doubt your attachment to liberty. If you tender your services voluntarily, they will be accepted readily. The United States offer you peace, liberty, and security. Your choice lies between these and war, slavery and destruction. Choose then, but choose wisely.

By the General W. Hull
Head Quarters, Sandwich, July 12, 1812

### Thursday, July 16, 1812
### First Blood

His saddle creaked as Major Branson shifted uncomfortably. He'd been on horseback since dawn, and the afternoon was well advanced. Branson doffed his crested black hat to mop his brow. *Everything seems to fall on the 41ˢᵗ*, he thought. *Colonel St.*

# The Land Between Flowing Waters

*George is too fat and too timid to take the field. He cowers at Amherstburg and goes nowhere a wagon can't take him. And the Indian Department is commanded by an eighty-year-old who stays at home shuffling papers.*

*Lord! It's up to me and these Indians I can't even understand.*

The towering beech was good cover as he scanned the tree line. A war-band led by Tecumseh and Main Poche were out there, somewhere in the waist-high grass. Not an hour ago, fifty warriors jogged onto the prairie and simply disappeared. *Are they still there?* Branson wondered. *Or am I the only man between Jonathan and the Canard River Bridge?*

At noon General Hull ordered a portion of his invasion force to pursue the British. The Yankees proceeded south on King's Road, past the farms and orchards of Petite Cote. As Branson waited beneath the beech tree, he could see three American companies emerge to form a double line on the prairie before the Canard River. With their officers riding slowly in front, skirmishers dashed forward into the high grass. Two, maybe three hundred, militia advanced towards Branson.

Branson rode promptly back to the Canard. Perhaps they could stop them at the bridge. A squad of British lookouts ringed the northern approach. The First Company's lieutenant came out to meet him.

"Are the planks gone?" Branson asked.

"Yes, Sir. We're building a breastwork on the south bank."

Beyond the bridge's empty skeleton, Branson could see the Essex County militiamen stacking thick planks into a shoulder-high barrier.

"Good. Maybe they'll stand behind three inches of solid oak," Branson chuckled. "But if they don't, keep First Company behind the wall. *Queen Charlotte* will blow Jonathan to hell if he tries to cross."

The British schooner was anchored at the river mouth, 300 yards away. She carried ordinance of eighteen 24-pounders.

"Your orders, Sir?"

"Hang on to this crossing, Lieutenant. There's nothing else between you and Amherstburg."

"Defend the river," the Lieutenant called out to the observation squad, then swam his horse back across the Canard.

174

Now there was firing out on the prairie. Branson wheeled and returned to the beech tree. *Well, well,* he thought, *Tecumseh's still here.* Branson could see warriors popping up from cover to fire at the advancing pickets. A bugle call sent three companies of the Ohio Second Regiment rushing forward to drive off the Indians. Outnumbered, Tecumseh's men sprinted out of range as Branson galloped in pursuit. They would rendezvous at the Canard's first ford, nearly five miles upriver. Branson's 2nd Company was already there.

Private James Hancock lay snoring in the grass, his head resting on a tussock. A few feet away, Private John Dean woke from the sun burning his face, or maybe it was the Lieutenant screaming his name. Dean sat up reluctantly. The jar of whiskey they'd shared for lunch might not have been one of his better ideas. Yes, the Lieutenant was definitely exercised about something – but he sounded a long way off. Dean crawled over to shake Hancock awake.

"Lieutenant wants us," Dean said. "Guess we're in trouble."

"Lemme sleep," Hancock mumbled.

Dean glanced around. The sun was blazing, the yellow grass swaying. They were alone.

"Squad's gone."

"What?" Hancock yelped. He started up, but then held his head.

The Lieutenant called their names again. Dean staggered to his feet and faced the Canard to search for the officer. Yes, there he was on the far bank, yelling to wake the dead and pointing back at the prairie. Private Dean turned. There was a company of Yankee militia, double-timing down the road, less than 100 yards away.

"Time to go, Jamey, me boy," Dean urged as he dragged Hancock up. "We got visitors."

"God of Mercy," Hancock said when he made it upright. "Where's the squad? Where's the firing line?"

"Cross the river, old son. Come on."

Both grabbed their muskets and stumbled towards the bridge. Their pursuers were less than 50 yards behind when they reached the missing sills of the dismantled bridge.

"Swim for it!" the Lieutenant yelled as he edged backwards toward the plank wall. The Canadiens and the 1st Company peered over the sills, silently pleading for Dean and Hancock to save themselves.

# The Land Between Flowing Waters

"Lord, John," Private Hancock breathed. "I can't swim."

"Jamey, you know I don't even wash."

Hancock's only reply was a sickly grin as they turned to face the Yankees. The closest stood only twenty yards away.

"I'm sorry, Jamey," Private Dean choked. "You been a good friend to me."

"The same. The same."

"Throw down your muskets," the Yankee captain commanded. A dozen militiamen stood ready with weapons raised.

"Now! Surrender!" he screamed.

Clutching his musket with white hands, Private Hancock shook his head. Private Dean could only stare down at the dusty road.

"Fire!"


*"Diable de chien!"* Behind the wall, a Canadien growled and raised his rifle as both the infantrymen were flung to the ground by the fusillade. Others gasped in horror as the squad of executioners ran forward to plunge bayonets into Hancock's body.

He lay on his back. The dreadful wound in Hancock's throat had killed him instantly; or perhaps the fatal blow was the gaudy red hole centred in his chest. Surely he was dead, or nearly so, but the militiamen stabbed him repeated so that they might boast of having killing a Redcoat.

Dean was obviously still alive, moaning piteously from a broken leg, a broken arm, and other bullet wounds that somehow missed vital organs in their passage. There was a bounty for prisoners, and so two non-coms grasped his arms, even the broken one, and pulled Dean away from the blood-crazed militiamen.

Firing was general now from Canadien militia at the breastwork. Buckshot could barely reach the near riverbank; musket balls flew erratically among the Ohioans over two hundred yards away – and so it was only the rifleman who killed a soldier plunging his bayonet into Hancock's mutilated body.

The men of the First Company of the 41st, friends and comrades of Hancock and Dean, grimly held their fire at the centre of the barricade. Endlessly, they were drilled to fire only on command, in devastating volleys. To aim at and kill an individual, even in the heat of battle, was not in their ironbound training. But now, if there had ever been any doubt, they vowed silently not to give way before this pack of murderers.

# Ken Leland

From the river mouth, the first ranging cannon shot from HMS *Queen Charlotte* flew long. The invaders fell back quickly. The second 24-lb ball bounced through the space they vacated. A broadside was never loosed as the Yankee militia company, with the broken Private Dean in tow, disappeared from sight.

*****

Five miles inland, well beyond the *Charlotte*'s cannons, the Canard riverbank sloped gently to a wide, shallow ford. Major Branson was slow in arriving. He had paused on the way to watch the Ohioans diverted east from the bridge. It was almost sundown, and the Americans were nearing the ford.

Tecumseh's small war-band had already crossed the river. As Branson rode down into the open shallow bowl that was the ford, he could see warriors taking positions behind trees on the far bank. The British infantrymen of Second Company were a thin red line standing in the open, 50 yards from the water's edge. Halfway down the northern rim, Branson reined in to look back. He imagined the Yankees marching over the rim in a line much longer than the 50 Redcoats. From the rim it was 250 yards, through scattered trees and boulders, down to the river. What could draw the Yankees closer, Branson wondered, into killing range of the British muskets?

Branson rode slowly through the knee deep ford, another 50 yards, and then up the slope to Second Company – 350 yards, all told.

"They're ten minutes behind me, Lieutenant."

"Yes, Major."

Branson glanced back. The Lieutenant's pistol could barely clear the river's width; the infantry muskets would not reach even halfway up the far slope. The Indian warriors had taken sheltered positions closer to the water – Indians never fought in the exposed ranks of regiments of the line.

"Where's the Canadien militia?" Branson asked.

The beat of approaching drums came from the opposite shore.

"At the tree line," the Lieutenant said as he gestured to the south 100 yards away. "Tecumseh and Main Poche are up there, too. They're doing some trading."

With a sinking in his guts, Branson wheeled behind the regulars and galloped for the trees. Francois Baby, the Colonel's younger brother, stepped out, whipping his sword through the weeds.

"You must speak to them, Major," M. Baby complained. "They want to take our only rifles."

Branson dismounted and plunged into the woods. There he found a hundred Canadiens sheltered behind boulders and logs, just as the warriors had positioned themselves down by the river. *At least they're facing the enemy*, Branson thought. He wandered through the brush, past the white-faced farmers and shopkeepers. A shouted argument drew Branson farther along the line.

Main Poche and a Canadien voyager were screaming in each other's faces. Main Poche held his own musket level in his one good hand, balancing it over his opposite wrist. He kept thrusting the musket into the chest of the voyager. The voyager was shaking his head, yelling, *"Non! Non!"* He refused to give up his rifle in exchange. Tecumseh was engaged in a similar test of wills with a rifle-carrying hunter.

The Yankee drums were louder now. In the fading light, Canadiens around Branson stood cautiously to stare across the river. A long brown line was marching into view at the top of the far ridge.

"Imbecile!" Main Poche screamed before following Tecumseh back toward the river.

A rifle company of Americans jogged down the slope. They took firing positions among the trees, far from the ford itself, and began taking pot-shots at the red line of British regulars. Major Branson was on his horse in only moments, but already half a dozen of 2nd Company were down. As Branson hurtled toward the regulars, Tecumseh was shouting to his warriors, orders that could only mean 'Withdraw!'

The men of 2nd Company were falling, dying. Their Lieutenant ordered a volley before he fell backwards into the grass. It was pointless. Muskets could not reach Yankee riflemen 300 yards away.

"Retreat," Major Branson ordered. "Bring the wounded."

Branson rode at a canter behind the regulars as they struggled up the slope to the trees. At every moment he expected a rifle bullet in his back. The Redcoats carried their dead and wounded as they ran.

In the twilight, they staggered into the woods. Those unencumbered knelt and turned again to face the enemy. Behind

Branson, Francois Baby was pleading, with some success, for the Canadiens to fall in among them.

Jeers and catcalls came from the enemy riflemen. Tecumseh listened to them for a while and then, as the darkness grew, he smiled broadly at Main Poche and began to sign. Main Poche scrambled along the British line to send a handful of warriors crawling into the night to watch the ford. When he came back, both lay down to sleep, snoring lightly until moonset.

Insults, songs, and dubious noises floated through the darkness from across the river. Tecumseh and Main Poche awoke and searched the pitch-black sky. Branson, supposing that something was afoot, kept his men rigidly silent.

"Stay. Watch," Tecumseh managed in English. Then he and Main Poche disappeared in opposite directions along the river.

"They go across?" Francois Baby whispered to Branson.

"*Oui, je pense ainsi.*"

To Major Branson's surprise, the enemy retreated just after dawn – carrying with them half a dozen dead riflemen, their throats cut.

## Wednesday, July 29, 1812
## The Fight against Treason

In the growing morning light, Captain Lockwood, Jeremy Roberts, and Lieutenant William Merritt prepared to ride out from Fort George with 40 Provincial Dragoons. They carried arrest warrants for two dozen outlaws.

Major Glegg called out to them from across the parade ground. When he reached Captain Lockwood, he passed up a handbill and then distributed a fistful among the Dragoons.

"Those people are spreading this trash everywhere east of Sandwich," Glegg said.

The troopers clustered round men who could read Hull's Proclamation. A few minutes later Glegg asked, "Well, gentlemen, are you frightened by the Exterminating General?"

"No, Sir," Lockwood answered firmly as he returned the crumpled broadsheet. He twisted in the saddle toward the troopers.

"Any doubts? There's no turning back once we pass the gates."

# The Land Between Flowing Waters

Lieutenant Merritt turned to the Ensign, who glanced at the Colour Sergeant. The Sergeant looked at the Bugler, who considered the Corporal, who studied the men in the patrols.

"Sun's up, Captain. Time's a'wasting," the Corporal advised.

"Lead 'em out, Sergeant," Lockwood ordered.

No man remained behind.

\*\*\*\*\*

Deep in the forest, a dark-haired man in a straw hat knocked at a plank door. Smoke rose from the cabin's stone chimney, and embers floated down onto the grass-covered sod roof. A baby's shrill complaint and the aroma of breakfast bacon seeped through the planks.

Four Provincial Dragoons were hidden from the woman inside. They stood with their backs flush to the outer wall. Others waited at the windows. Again, the dark-haired man knocked, and at last the door opened a crack.

"Good morning, Mrs. Stiles. Is your husband at home?"

"Who's askin'?" came a timorous reply from inside. A barefoot slattern in a filthy dress peeked through the gap.

"I rode with your husband and Mr. Benson this spring. I've some news for Mr. Stiles."

"He ain't t'home," she said as the opening began to creak shut.

"Do you know where he is, Mrs. Stiles?"

"No."

She made to lower a thick, wooden bar, but Captain Lockwood was not to be denied. He rammed the door wide with his shoulder and grabbed the woman's arm as she turned to flee.

"Come!" Lockwood shouted. The Dragoons rushed in, carbines at the ready. Now the woman was shrieking for fear of bloody murder.

"Where's your husband?" Lockwood demanded as she twisted in his grip. "Damn you! Stop kicking."

The woman turned to scratch his face. Two troopers grabbed her from behind as the rest milled through the filthy cabin, looking beneath the bed and in the travel chest.

They brought forth her children – a girl of four or five, a bare-bottomed toddler, and a squalling infant. Mrs. Stiles was on her knees now, begging.

"Please don't hurt 'em! We ain't never done nothin', I swear it."

"I know very well what your husband has done, Mrs. Stiles. I have a warrant for his arrest."

"Please don't hurt him! We needed the money."

"Where is he, Mrs. Stiles?"

"I don't know, I swear don't!"

"We're going to find him Mrs. Stiles – and if he resists, we'll kill him. If he surrenders, he'll live to see you and the children someday. What will it be?"

"He run off to Delaware Town. That's all I know."

"Why in the world would he do that, Mrs. Stiles? Run from a fine home and lovely lady like yourself? I think you're lying." Lockwood turned to Lieutenant Merritt. "Tie and gag her. Put her in the wagon. Give the children to the neighbours."

"No! No! Please, I ain't lyin'. He's gone to Delaware Town with the rest."

"But why, Mrs. Stiles?"

"There's Yankees comin' up the Thames. They're goin' t'raise a rebellion. Please, please don't take the chillun'!"

"Lieutenant, give the little ones to men who are fathers. But keep that woman quiet till we can get her into gaol."

*****

A sandy-haired man in faded, mud-stained trousers strolled slowly into the tavern. An oversized hunting-knife hung in the sheath at his belt.

The Thames River Tavern was crowded, but the stranger found a seat at an empty table near a tall window. Two-score boisterous patrons pounded the long oak table in time to "Yankee Doodle." More leaned against the bar in the smoky saloon, where the tapster and his wife poured with abandon in the warm, midsummer afternoon.

Shouts from a scar-faced man named Benson were lost in the drunken chorus as he waved a handbill in the air. At an island of calm, over by a side window, two well-kept men wearing pistols sat at a small round table. Between them was an empty chair. On the table were quill and ink, a blotter and a stack of printed sheets. A man named Stiles wrapped his arm over a farmer's shoulders, and steered him towards the empty chair. The men at the writing table spoke earnestly, patted the farmer on the back, and read the printed sheet to him. Then one pointed to the line where he might make his mark. Stiles brought a large whisky after the name was printed clearly below the X. Blotted and then creased, the document found its way into the man's grasp. He staggered away to his friends at the bar, whisky in one hand, military parole in the other. He was safe from the coming war.

Stiles went in search of the next traitor to the King.


The sandy-haired stranger stared out the tall, porch window. He watched four men in farm clothes ride in. Each carried a short musket. They hitched their horses to the front railing but did not enter. Instead they gathered round the checker-board on the tavern porch. A hay-filled wagon was parked just down the road, where half a dozen field-hands slept, and at the dock a score of men, all carrying the same short muskets, had just landed from the river ferry.

"What's your pleasure?" asked the harried pot-boy who came to take the stranger's order.

"Got sompin' to eat?"

"Stew."

"What kind?"

"Hog. Groundhog and carrots."

"Two bowls and a tankard of beer. Two glasses."


After a few minutes, a dark-haired man in a battered straw hat entered, to sit at the window-table with his friend. He carried a long sack that clanked as he slid it under the table. They ate without saying a word, oblivious to the commotion behind them.

"It's all over but the shoutin', I tell ye," Benson was promising anyone who would listen. "General Hull's got the Redcoats on the run. He'll be here in a week."

"You men what join us," Stiles was saying, "you'll be the first in line. Freedom! Just like before. We do what we want."

"The Canadian Militia's done for. The Tories are runnin'. Good times when the Yankees come! And they're comin', don't you doubt it," said one of the well-kept men at the side table.

"We arrest the sheriff and magistrate, and the Tory militia officers, too. Round 'em up and hold 'em till Hull comes. Every man who helps gets shares."

Another man slipped into the empty chair at the writing table.

# Ken Leland

By the tall window, the sandy-haired man began to rummage through the sack beneath the table. Seemingly, he found what he was looking for and he glanced at his companion. Then the dark-haired man nodded, took off his straw hat and calmly sailed it out through the window onto the dusty road.

The men down by the dock began a silent scramble up the riverbank, running for the tavern. Each wore a red handkerchief at his throat and carried a loaded carbine. The men sleeping in the wagon were awake now, similarly armed. They jumped down to join the rush to the tavern door. Sandy-haired Jeremy Roberts pulled a long iron bar from the sack and smashed out the front window. The men on the porch were already dashing though the front door, carbines at the ready. From the alley came the sound of men breaking down the back door.

Lockwood pulled his cavalry sword from the bag and brandished it toward the crowd. Kicking aside the broken glass, Roberts stood beside him, holding the iron cudgel high over his right shoulder.

"I am an officer of the King!" Captain Lockwood bellowed to the muzzy patrons. "You're all under arrest."

Astounded, the inebriated mob turned to face the intruders as more armed men poured through the door and broken window.

"Get 'em!" Benson screamed, as he shoved an unarmed man toward the sabre. The two well-kept men at the small table yelled "Charge!" and pushed forward a knot of farmers. Suddenly, almost thirty drunks were surging toward the front door.

Carbines fired. The wounded and frightened screamed as they stumbled into the troopers and began to grapple.

Lockwood's sabre swept out, forcing two men to dodge aside, but just behind them was a man aiming a pistol. Roberts swung the long iron bar, and the pistol discharged into the barroom floor. Off balance, Roberts stumbled across Lockwood's guard, directly into the line of charging men. As he fell among them, someone snatched his hunting knife. With a downward sweep, the attacker slashed Roberts' back, leaving a bloody streak from shoulder to waist.

"Help!" Roberts yelled from the tangle on the floor.

The knife-wielder raised his arm to strike again, but Lockwood transfixed him, driving the sabre into his throat. Roberts was covered in a torrent of blood when the sabre twisted free.

As more troopers poured inside, Lieutenant Merritt led a charge against the men escaping through the side window.

# The Land Between Flowing Waters

Lockwood slipped in Roberts's blood, but righted himself and roared. Without looking down, he lunged into the retreating line of traitors.

"Lie down!" Lockwood screamed at the men cowering among the tables. "On the floor! Now!'

He swung the sabre at waist height, slicing open the stomach of one fool too slow in following orders. Then, with another bellow of "Lie down!" he sliced open the scalp of a farmer who had only fallen to his knees.

"Extermination? God damn you bastards, I'll show you extermination!"

Lockwood raised his sabre to butcher a whimpering lout lying at his feet, when arms clutched his waist and hands rose to block his sword.

"Captain! Captain!" Lieutenant Merritt pleaded in his ear. "It's over! They've surrendered."

The traitors were on the floor, some crumpled at odd angles, many weeping from wounds and terror.

\*\*\*\*\*

*John Norton's Journal*

"Brothers, the People of the great King are our old friends, and the Americans are our neighbours. We grieve to see them prepare to imbrue their hands in the blood of each other. We have determined not to interfere; how could we spill the blood of the English or of our Brethren?"

So said Arosa, of the Seneca below the Lakes, three days ago. The Six Nations there are surrounded by strong enemies, and have no choice but to stand aside in this war. They beg us to do the same. And not one day later, word came to us that General Hull with a thousand men has crossed the Detroit to take possession of Sandwich.

Though the People are sore divided, I have decided to volunteer with the British to defend our homes. Thus I went to General Brock this morning at Onondaga Village to explain my intentions. He has asked me to collect whatever men I could to take up a position at the mouth of the Thames River. There we will endeavour to prevent the American army from obtaining supplies, and observe their movements. The General said that the Dover Militia and a company of the 41$^{st}$ will meet us on the river at Oxford. I, and twenty others, took our leave before noon.

On the trail, shortly after we left the Grand River, we met a handful of Warrow's People. They are Huron from the reserve near Amherstburg. They say it is true that Hull has crossed the river, and that he has persuaded many Western Nations to stand aside. Only Tecumseh of the Shawnee, and Main Poche of the Neshnabek, fight for the King at Amherstburg, but with less than 200 men. I am ashamed to see that the words of the enemy are everywhere so eagerly received. They have won more through deceitful speeches than by hard fighting.

My small war-band arrived at Oxford near midday. As expected, we found Major Chambers with a company of the 41$^{st}$, but I was much downcast to hear that the Dover Militia has refused to march to our aid. Indeed, the settlers of Dover seem in revolt, refusing even to defend themselves against the invaders.

It was only a little later that much more agreeable information arrived from the northern lakes. Fort Michilimackinac has been captured from the Americans. A company of Royal Veterans and 400 Ojibway and Western Nations have taken it without firing a shot. The Ojibway runner who brought us the news is much fatigued, so Major Chambers has sent riders to General Brock at the Grand. One of our Mohawks is already on his way to Amherstburg. This is the first bit of good news I have heard for a very long time.

*****

Lieutenant Merritt's Dragoons returned home along the forest road leading to the Grand River. 35 banditti chained in iron cuffs trudged between the second and third hospital wagons. Guards rode beside them as the column proceeded at a walk. From horseback, Lockwood climbed into the first wagon to speak with the wounded Jeremy Roberts. Jeremy lay face-down, on a pallet cushioned by knee-deep straw. Three other wounded troopers shared the luxury.

"We captured Stiles and most of the rest, but Benson and those two Yankees are missing," Lockwood said.

# The Land Between Flowing Waters

"What you gonna do with these traitoring sonsabitches?" one trooper asked.

"Hang 'em in the woods," Lockwood declared flatly.

There were sharp barks of laughter.

"You wouldn't do that," Roberts said, as with a wince he raised his head to scan his friend's face. Roberts was wrapped from armpits to waist in a bed-sheet. Between his shoulder blades, the bandages were brown with dried blood.

After a long pause, Lockwood said quietly, "Back in the tavern, I thought you were dead."

"Hah!" Roberts scoffed. "You hoped I was."

"No. No, I didn't. Your wife would never forgive me."

Lockwood cast an odd expression at the other wounded, perhaps only then remembering they were scarcely alone. Then he crossed from the moving Conestoga back onto his horse.

"I'll come by to see you again at suppertime, Jeremy," he promised.

*****

Jeremy Roberts was bored, and despite the soft pallet, he ached and was feverish. But beyond all that, he was proud of himself – and with good reason. Lockwood had seen the pistol deflected as Roberts destroyed the hand that aimed it, and Roberts had seen the ghastly, throat-pierced corpse of the man who knifed him, collapsing onto the barroom floor. After Lockwood's quiet word to the Colour Sergeant, the news spread instantly throughout the company: Roberts had saved Lockwood's life.

It seemed unlikely they would ever speak of it, to each other, to Janie or Miriam, or anyone. And somehow, Roberts thought, that was the way it should be.

Hours later, the column again came to a halt, jarring Roberts from a fitful nap.

"For Heaven's sake, why's he stopping now?" was the querulous lament from the first medical wagon.

They had reached the Mohawk Chapel on the Grand River. In the snows of last February, Lockwood had heard the Haudenosaunee Clan Mothers sing for wisdom in this small, high-peaked church. Now, in summer, the women at the heart of the Six

Nations stood motionless on the chapel steps to watch the column pass.

Captain Lockwood handed his reins to Lieutenant Merritt and then walked into the soaring pines. One solemn Grandmother in a beaded sash stepped out to meet him. A younger woman in a full flowing skirt and blue blouse followed at her elbow. Lockwood bowed – how could there be any other greeting?

"*Niawen, Akhso. Niawen* for coming to speak with me." The young woman began to whisper in the Clan Mother's ear.

"We, the King's People, are standing on our feet now."

The red-coated Lockwood pointed out toward the traitors sprawled exhausted on the road.

"No longer will we suffer our enemies to make trouble among us." Lockwood bowed again and said, "may the Great Spirit guide your deliberations for the good of all your People."

Lockwood then stood aside so that they might see the prisoners and the Dragoons who guarded them. The Clan Mother glanced at the translator, speaking only a few words.

"Mother asks if that is all you have to say."

"Yes."

Clan Mother turned again to her translator.

"Mother asks if you have any advice, any counsel for us." This time the young woman in the blue blouse smirked. Lockwood suspected a trap.

"I am only a warrior. I would not presume."

The slightest of smiles played on the old woman's lips. She walked forward and reached out to him. Taking one hand, she patted his wrist and spoke briefly before turning back to the Chapel.

"Mother says your modesty is most becoming, and quite appropriate for a white boy. Bring your good manners to us any time."

Then the young woman laughed at him, open mouthed, and shook her hair as she hurried up the steps in the Clan Mother's wake.

There were still two hours before sunset when the prisoner column arrived at the Onondaga Council House. There was a tightly-spaced, militia bivouac 100 yards to the south. This was the overnight resting place for some 200 men of the 5th Lincoln and 1st York. The soldiers accompanied Brock on his westward dash to

# The Land Between Flowing Waters

Fort Amherstburg. Despite the urgency, the relief forces had diverted to the Grand so that Brock might try to head off the growing threat of Haudenosaunee neutrality.

Lockwood could see more than 100 unarmed, unpainted warriors milling in the gravel courtyard. Lockwood sighed with relief as he noticed General Brock and Major Glegg detach from the crowd waiting by the Council House.

"Lieutenant Merritt," he warned, "it's time to report to the General. Keep your wits about you."

As the senior officers approached, Glegg was chuckling and trying to count the outlaws under guard out on the road. Brock studied the medical wagons.

"Well, Captain Lockwood," the general said, "You'll be the second bit of good news today."

"Sir?"

Glegg couldn't contain himself. "The Royals and 400 Indians captured Fort Mackinac, without firing a shot!"

"When?" Lieutenant Merritt blurted.

"Almost two weeks ago. Word just arrived," Glegg bubbled.

"Report, Gentlemen," Brock ordered quietly.

Lockwood nodded at the young lieutenant. "We served arrest warrants on 21 banditti, Sir. Sorry, but some got away."

"I'd say you have more than thirty over there," Brock said as he nodded toward the road.

"We'll have to swear out some more warrants when we get home, Sir."

"That's fine work, Lieutenant Merritt. I'm more than pleased. You have my sincere thanks." Then, turning to Lockwood, he asked, "Where's Mr. Roberts?"

"With the wounded, General."

"Wounded?"

"Four in all, in the first wagon."

"Don't get lost, Captain," Brock said. "I'll need to talk with you in a bit. Lieutenant Merritt, please introduce me to your wounded troopers."

When he returned, Brock found Lockwood and Glegg outside the Council House. "Captain Lockwood," he said, "Let's take a walk down to the river."

# Ken Leland

Lockwood and Brock wandered by the low broad building, nodding to warriors and war leaders who sat smoking in small groups. The sun was sliding lower.

"*Shekon. Shekon tsia,*" Lockwood murmured as they walked among them.

"You speak the language?"

"Dreadfully," Lockwood said. "When I came here in the winter, I lodged with a Cayuga grandmother who tried to teach me manners. She complained she didn't have much to work with."

"Hah!"

"Mr. Roberts is too badly injured to return to the field for a while," Brock said. "We'll turn over outlaw hunting to someone else."

"I understand, Sir," Lockwood replied.

"Glegg's been asking for you – to run errands and move mountains. Come with us to Amherstburg. By the way, that's a request, not an order. We'll keep you busy."

"I like being busy, General."

"Good."

They followed the wooded path toward the river where Haudenosaunee paddlers lounged in canoes at a small pier. The officers stopped short to speak in private.

"We've also received the most disheartening news. The Essex County Militia is deserting in droves."

Lockwood doffed his hat and ran his fingers through his hair. "We need companies of Loyalists. I can sort the men – go to the New Settlement on Lake Erie to find them."

Brock nodded with a ghost of a smile. "And we're stalled here," he confided. "We're waiting for the chiefs to make a decision that just doesn't come."

"What's wrong, General? I saw John Norton with 100 warriors on the River Road, not a month ago."

Brock sighed. "I asked Norton to go to the Lower Thames, to try to protect the settlements there. He left this morning. He's disgusted by all the vacillation, and has only a couple dozen warriors."

"But why are the chiefs wavering?" Lockwood asked.

"General Hull has sent messages that the British will desert them, like before," Brock said. "Even the news about the capture of Fort Mackinac hasn't helped – they won't recommit. It's the Clan Mothers. They're the real power here, and they doubt us."

"Thank God I didn't try to give them any advice," Lockwood breathed in relief.

"What! What have you done?" Brock demanded.

"Nothing, Sir," Lockwood stammered. "Or, at least, not very much. I just stopped at the Chapel to explain about the prisoners."

There was the sound of singing on the forest path behind them. A straight-backed woman in a long skirt and blue blouse glided toward them. As she approached, she broke into a full faced grin.

"Good evening, General Brock. Captain Lockwood."

She stared openly at Lockwood as she sidled past, then she broke into pealing laughter. She shouted in Mohawk to her escort waiting on the river. Several warriors smirked; a few waved at the officers before pushing off from the pier. Sitting in the centre of the first canoe, the woman grasped the gunnels and rose onto her knees to call, "Remember, Captain. Keep standing!"

Brock snorted. "She seems to enjoy a joke at your expense, Captain. Who is she?"

"I met her at the Chapel, Sir. She's the translator for the Clan Mothers."

A shout came from the direction of the Council House. Glegg was pounding down the trail. Winded, he stooped to rest with his hands on his knees.

"General," he gasped. "The chiefs...have decided...You'll like...what they have...to say."

## Thursday, July 30, 1812
## Lean Times

"The foragers are back!"

The news flashed through General Hull's headquarters at the erstwhile Baby mansion. Blue-jacketed junior officers rushed outside, through the trampled gardens down to the King's Road. There, 200 men of the Third Ohio and a long line of mismatched farm wagons and carts rolled into sight, loaded with flour, dried peas, salt pork, whiskey and blankets, and at the end of the convoy were hundreds of sheep on the hoof.

Hull's Quartermaster of the Army of the Northwest reached up to shake the Commanding Officer's hand as the wagons rumbled by.

"Thank God. We're getting mighty hungry down here. Where did you find all this?"

"Grist mills. Shops and stores. Farmhouses. The sheep are from Baldoon."

"Generous, were they?" the Quartermaster chuckled.

The officer laughed and threw a handful of provisions receipts high into the air.

"Take 'em or leave 'em; it's all the same," he crowed as the pay-bills fluttered down unheeded onto the muddy road.


## Collette


"Pierre," Maman yelled, "*Les bâtards reviennent.*"

There were soldiers in brown jackets and some in blue, too, wandering up from the river dock.

Maman found Papa and me at Monsieur Bouchard's mill. Papa was trying to save some of the unburned timber in hopes of rebuilding.

"Collette," Maman told me. "Take Robert."

I put Robert across my shoulders and he whooped when we started to run back home to find my brothers. But before we got even halfway, we could hear people screaming at the end of our street. Soldiers were breaking into the houses. Papa stopped suddenly and grabbed Maman by the arm. I stumbled into them, but then he grabbed me too. He was very angry, and afraid I think.

"Go back and hide in the mill," he said. "Don't let the soldiers see you."

Then he took Maman by both shoulders and said to her, "I'll find the boys. Don't let the soldiers see Collette. *Comprenez-vous?*"

Maman nodded, and then together Maman and I went back towards the grist mill. Grandpere Leblanc was shouting that the soldiers were drunk. Our neighbours called to us to come inside, to help them keep the soldiers out, but then we heard two shots from down the street and everyone ran into the tall corn.

# The Land Between Flowing Waters

Maman and I hid in M. Bouchard's stable. We climbed a ladder into the haymow, where Maman found a pitchfork. We lay down in the smelly hay next to a crack in the wall where we could see out to the road. Little Robert was frightened now and began to whine. That worried Maman because she could see soldiers at Madame Simard's house. I could hear Mme. Simard shrieking with a terrible fear, but Maman wouldn't let me see. Pretty soon Mme. Simard stopped. Maman would only tell me, "They went inside."

After a while Maman saw Jean and Rene, coming up the road looking for us. Jean is ten and Rene is almost fifteen. They both looked scared. I climbed down the ladder to whisper to them before they could pass by, and they came up to sit with us.

"*Où est votre père?*" Maman asked.

Rene said Papa found them in our house, but that they ran out the back when soldiers came to the door. Papa stayed behind. Maman was shaking now, and I played with Robert so he wouldn't see. Rene climbed back down and found an axe and a hatchet on the tool bench. He gave me a hammer and I let Robert play with it.

A streak of sunlight was coming through the wall. Rene looked out and said there were soldiers coming up the street toward us. They were singing and yelling, saying bad things in English, I think. Robert began to cry when he heard them. Jean told him to shut up but that only made Robert cry harder.

Maman was white-faced. Even in the gloomy old mow I could see how afraid she was. I could hear them now, just outside. Jean and Rene crept over to the ladder. Maman scooped Robert from my arms. Then she pulled down the bodice of her dress. Robert was weaned a year ago, but he remembered. He snuggled against Maman, and then we began to pray.

*****

"Ride ahead, Captain Lockwood," Major Glegg ordered. "The General wants to see all the Dover Militia, assembled at parade, in a half an hour."

Lockwood galloped ahead of the long mounted column that followed Brock from the Grand River. They rode past scattered farms in the hardwood forest. As Lockwood pounded down the dirt trail, farm children ran out to see him, wives looked from cabin windows at the sound of pounding hooves.

"Brock is coming! Brock is coming!" Lockwood shouted it to everyone he saw. *It can't hurt*, he thought.

Indeed, as the rumble of 200 riders grew in the distance, men came to stand by the road as red-coated officers, and then Provincials, swept by.

"Come on!" the Provincials shouted. "Join us!"

Farmers, hunters, woodsmen, fur traders – each turned to wife and family in the swirling dust. Time and again, a woman held out her hand to touch her man, only to see him turn and sprint to the barn to saddle his horse. The line of riders grew as neighbours hailed friends from the flying column.

Dover Road led past a mill, a church and country store, down to the dock in the sheltered harbour. The sun was setting, but hundreds of people came to the hillside above Lake Erie. Word had spread before Lockwood like ripples from a boulder plunged into a pond.

The crowd gathered in front of the store's long porch. Sparks rose from bonfires, and torches guttered in the dying lake breeze. Men stood closest in a great arc; women and children were at the fringes of the crowd.

Glegg and Lockwood, their uniforms glowing in the firelight, stood together at the bottom of the porch steps. The crowd before them was cautious and sombre. Less than two days ago, these same militiamen had refused an order to march to the Thames; most had refused even to muster. Surely, some were traitors, spies or American agents. What would Brock tell them?

Lockwood glanced back at the sound of men moving behind him on the porch. Lieutenant Colonel John MacDonnell emerged first, closely followed by Brock. MacDonnell was a tall, thin man, Brock's aide-de-camp for the Provincial Militia. He was 27 years old, of Scottish descent, a loyal Assemblyman and the recently appointed Attorney General.

General Brock strode to the edge of the steps. He took off his black crescent officer's hat and began to speak quietly but firmly. Suddenly, Lockwood realised that someone in this crowd might try to kill him, but Brock's voice calmed his fears.

"Good evening, men. My name is Isaac Brock."

A good-natured chuckle spread through the crowd at this artless beginning.

"I bring you best wishes from those who have joined me tonight. Here you see the 1st York."

# The Land Between Flowing Waters

Brock waved his right hand toward the provincial troops standing in rows.

"And beyond them are the 5<sup>th</sup> Lincoln. Wave your caps men, so the folks at the back can see you."

The militiamen smiled at the attention. A few doffed their hats to hoist them atop musket barrels. Again, quiet laughter came from the wary men arrayed before Brock.

"These men have ridden a hundred miles in the last three days. We have a hundred more to go. West. To Amherstburg. I will tell you why we do this."

There was silence. Faces in the crowd glinted, upturned in the torch light.

"You have all heard that General Hull has crossed the river. You have seen his proclamation. Many of you have seen his agents on the roads, in the taverns, perhaps even in your homes."

Men glanced anxiously at their neighbours.

"I ask you now to turn from these vipers who speak sweet words but intend evil. They have told you many things that are simply not true. There are, as the Nations say, bad birds among us."

Brock's voice rang out. "General Hull's minions have told you that the Nations will not fight, that they will stand aside, perhaps to fall upon your families when your backs are turned – but I bring you news. The Nations and British arms have just captured Fort Mackinac. The truth is, the Nations will fight with us to protect their homelands as we fight to protect ours!"

In the silence, Brock paused to take a deep breath, to let that sink in.

"You have heard that our militia will not fight – but the 200 men of York and Niagara, standing before you, give it the lie. They are only a small part of the King's loyal subjects who have taken up arms. Men stand ready to defend our borders at Kingston, at York, at Niagara. But it is at Amherstburg that the enemy tests our courage."

Again, Brock let silence reign, only to break it with a determined appeal.

"The people of Baldoon and Sandwich and Amherstburg are hoping, praying, for our help. Their homes are being looted, their farms are burning. Their need is urgent.

"Before you stand men of York and Niagara. We leave at midnight to throw the invaders out.

194

"I ask you now. Will you join us?"

Not a man spoke in that assembly of hundreds.

Lockwood looked at Glegg. Both climbed the steps to stand at the General's shoulders. Lockwood looked out, worried and anxious that there were numerous armed men in this motionless, silent crowd. Some men leaned with both hands resting atop long rifles, staring at the ground; others traced the Milky Way in the moonless sky. In the firelight, Lockwood saw a young man toward the back raise a musket, but as Lockwood stepped in front of Brock, he could see that the rifle was held aloft like a beacon.

"I'll go," the young farmer croaked.

Faces in the crowd turned toward him. Brock heard him, too, and lifted his hand in return.

"Me, too, General."

The crowd turned toward another man standing near the porch steps.

Now the men were looking to each other; finding brothers, fathers, neighbours, friends, nodding to each other, and then raising their rifles too.

"I'll come."

"I'm ready."

"We're with you, General."

"First Norwich is ready, General Brock."

"Throw the bastards out!"

"Hurrah! Hurrah! Hurrah!"

Brock raised his hat, but quickly turned to shake Colonel MacDonnell's hand. Brock ducked his head as he walked back into the general store. MacDonnell motioned for quiet.

"Lieutenants of Militia, form your companies! Report the muster in one hour."

"We'll need as many boats as you can find," Glegg said to Lockwood as they stood in the shadows beyond the bonfires. "Seaworthy would be best."

## Collette

The last quarter moon is rising now. It casts a white gleam upon the water. Madame Simard's husband, Giles, is a fisherman, away serving with the militia. We have borrowed his boat to sail for the Huron Reserve.

Our house was broken by those searching for riches we do not have, but at least they didn't set it afire.

*Les bâtards* on the road were drunk, but, *Remerciez le Seigneur,* they passed us by as we hid in the stable. After we hurried home, we found Papa in the kitchen. He was moaning and could not walk. His face was bleeding. They had kicked him many times as he lay upon the floor. Maman and I carried him to bed and then she ran across the road to Mme. Simard.

Maman would not let me come. She said we were leaving, just as soon as Papa could walk, and I should get the boys ready.

Tonight we brought Papa in a wheelbarrow to the wharf. He still can't walk. We have made a pallet for him beside the mast. Jean and Rene are with him. Maman and little Robert are in the bow with Mme. Simard.

Mme. Simard cries. She cannot stop. Her face is all bruised and she holds her middle like she has a belly ache. She will not look at us. She whispers for her husband, Giles.

Henri Nault, our neighbour's oldest son, is at the tiller. I sit beside him to scan the shore. Henri keeps looking at Mme. Simard and then at me. He wonders if I know what happened to her.

I know.

Half an hour ago, we found a British ship anchored at le *flueve* Canard. A guard boat filled with Redcoats hailed us, but then they waved us onward.

We sail close to shore now. There is a little creek just ahead.

I reach out to grab a tree branch as we glide into the stream. There are Indian warriors on shore. One holds out his hand to me.

*"Nous avons besoin d'un docteur."*

# Ken Leland

## Sunday, August 2, 1812
## The Western Shore

"A Kentucky long rifle could kill you right now," Kshiwe said as he clapped his hands with a sharp smack.

Hannibal collapsed to the forest floor like a falling walnut. "Father!" he gasped.

"Well, I thought you ought to know," Kshiwe said, as he lay at ease behind a majestic tulip tree. The rest of the Shishibes Lake war-band smiled and looked away.

"Kmonokwe would be most unhappy," Kshiwe sighed. "All that hard work to make you a healer, wasted."

"How could I ever explain it to Senisqua?" Mukos teased. "Her brother dead, because he forgot to keep his head down."

"Please. You're embarrassing me," the now fourteen-year-old Hannibal complained.

"Oh, I was just saying," Kshiwe continued. "Be alert. Be thoughtful."

A snicker came from beneath a log shaded by a blueberry bush. Sheyoshke had propped a small, forked branch on the bush's lowest limb so he could watch the Frenchtown Fort, 200 yard away.

The village on Raisin River was a 100-year-old mixed Canadien and Three Fires community of farmers and fur traders, clustered around a Catholic chapel and a windmill. On the north side of the Raisin, the Americans had built a fort – two log blockhouses outside the opposite corners of a stockade. A striped flag hung motionless from the nearest blockhouse, where loopholes pierced the walls. Sentries paced the firing-walks in the burning sun. On the western wall an officer raised a spyglass to study the tree line, but then finding nothing, he continued his rounds.

The fort's southern wall was the fourth side of a cattle pen, built of solid timbers piled chest-high. After spending dawn in a treetop, Kshiwe knew the pen held about 300 cattle and 100 packhorses. Now, at midday, the cattle lowed, complaining of the heat. A line of drovers carried water buckets up from the river.

In July the local villagers had fled at the approach of General Hull's army, whose soldiers promptly ransacked their unattended homes and gardens. The villagers fled again in early August when a supply column of 200 men arrived – but instead of continuing north, the column took shelter in the stockade to wait for an armed escort. The Nations controlled the road.

"Someone's crossing the river," a scout warned from his perch high in the tulip tree.

A dozen troopers galloped over the Raisin River Bridge to enter the stockade.

"Northbound riders, looking for a change of mounts," Kshiwe surmised. "Let's greet them when they come out."

Musket balls and arrows flew from both sides of the road. The dispatch riders went down like leaves blown in an autumn wind. Most of the Horse Soldiers were dead before they hit the ground. Kshiwe dashed out with his hunting knife to finish a blue-jacketed officer. The man was screaming in dreadful agony. Kshiwe cut his throat then turned away.

There were two-score warriors milling about on the road. Scalps were quickly taken, though after the fusillade no man could say with certainty who had killed which enemy. Village Speaker pulled a black leather pack from the back of one of the dead.

"What are they carrying?" Kshiwe asked.

"Papers, folded and sealed with wax. Messages," Village Speaker said holding up two handfuls. "I think the Redcoats would be pleased to see these."

"Let's take them to Brownstown," Kshiwe said. "Maybe we can hail a British patrol boat from there."

\*\*\*\*\*

*John Norton's Journal*

Our war band is moving swiftly along the Thames River. I am glad that hopes are rising among the loyal after Fort Mackinac was captured. Near Oxford, we found that the local militia had attempted to arrest one of the American agents at his house. He escaped, however, and we found the militia company too drunk to stand from the whisky the traitor left behind.

Leaving the militia to their carouse, we met with Munsey and Ojibway villagers who, though engaged in completing the summer harvest, promised to follow us to the defense of the Lower Thames. True to their word we resumed our journey next morning and the forest resounded to the War Song. At Moraviantown, the people told us of General Hull's foragers stealing flour and grain from their mills. They expressed great joy at our appearance as it was expected daily that the Ohioans would return to continue their deprivations. Here, too, some armed men joined us as we headed west.

At noon, word came of American agents on the river. We pursued them eagerly, and near dusk we sighted them. At our approach, they landed on the opposite riverside and fled through the fields into the forest. We soon lost their trail in darkness. Still, we were not too disheartened because that evening in camp, messengers from the Three Fires People at Walpole and the St. Clair River found us. They vowed that a hundred warriors would take up arms if the Six Nations would join the fight. I sent back word that the Haudenosaunee were already on their feet and that they should meet us immediately at McGregor's mill near Chatham.

All the next day at McGregor's our war band increased by the hour. We have spent the day making bows and lances. McGregor has given us his supplies of ammunition and gunpowder. He says if we do not take it, the Americans will. There is hope the King will repay him, but none that President Madison will. I have sent word to Amherstburg that there are 300 warriors waiting to meet the Americans, either here on The Thames or at Amherstburg at need. I hope that General Brock will reply soon.

\*\*\*\*\*

That evening Kshiwe's war party fell in with Tecumseh and two dozen Shawnee, waiting in ambush on the road near Brownstown. Kshiwe and Village Speaker took council with them. Mukos, Hannibal and the other warriors crouched in a circle at a respectful distance, but close enough to see and hear what was said.

"Militiamen are marching down from Fort Detroit," Tecumseh said, as Main Poche translated. "They come to escort the supply train stalled at the Raisin."

Main Poche had a small clay whiskey jug. Kshiwe seemed to stare at the fire, but from the corner of his eye, he could see the man's withered, misshapen left hand clutching the bottom of the jug as Main Poche raised it to take a drink. A bandage, caked with dried blood, was wrapped around his neck. There were old scars, white streaks across his chest and arms. Of battle, no one supposed this man ever made an idle boast. He lowered the jug. Main Poche thrust it toward Kshiwe, prepared to take offense if it was rejected.

"I would then sleep through tomorrow's battle," Kshiwe said carefully. "I've promised the Master of Life never to taste whiskey until the settlers are gone from our lands."

"Ho! You sound like Tecumseh here," Main Poche crowed. "All the more for me." Then the scarred Neshnabe war leader stumbled off into the forest to relieve himself.

Tecumseh sat cross-legged beside the fire, casting the merest glance as Main Poche staggered away. Tecumseh was a quiet man of middle age, thin and plainly dressed, with leggings and bare chest.

"Main Poche is the most dangerous man I have ever known," Tecumseh signed in the firelight. "He will wake in the morning, ready to kill."

"I always have a headache," Village Speaker signed.

"Ho! So does he. So does he."


At dawn, fog rolled in from Lake Erie.

Tecumseh and Main Poche had positioned their small war-band along a creek in a shoulder-high bank of cattails. Here the road was only a wide trail of muddy, broken grass that oozed into, then out of, the lily-covered stream. Kshiwe's Neshnabek knelt in the cornfield on the lake side of the trail; the Huron River Odawa lay concealed in the brush to the west.

A game trail looped behind the cornfield towards the lake. Kshiwe placed Mukos and the other young warriors there, along with Hannibal and Sheyoshke. Mukos supposed the youths were being sheltered once again from hard fighting. Seeing the unspoken complaint in his son-in-law's face, Kshiwe mused aloud that it would be very bad if the Long Knives encircled them. Mukos placed the youngest of all, Sheyoshke and Hannibal, on the opposite side of the trail behind a log, only paces from the lake.

A faint breeze brought swirling mist. Hannibal hid the medicine packs, and then helped Sheyoshke cut brush to cover the log. The boys lay down to wait.

They were so far from the main road, Hannibal was sure the ambush would be over even before they could run through the

200

cornfield. The fog above them was a thin blanket, reaching up only as high as a cottonwood. He gazed through it up to the open sky. Later it would be hot. Hannibal drifted away with a high floating cloud. He awoke when Sheyoshke tapped the bottom of his foot.

Somewhere in the distance, a horse snorted. A moment later, a swinging bayonet scabbard thunked against a wooden canteen. The slog of many men approaching on the main road was unmistakable.

Hannibal snatched up his bow. There was someone riding down the side path, straight for them. Already Sheyoshke was poised with arrow nocked as the first rider came into view. It was an officer. A silver chain decorated his tall dark hat. A sabre dangled from his hip. His carbine was balanced over his left arm. Behind him came a second Horse Soldier with a short musket, and third, a black man riding a mare.

In surprise, Hannibal lowered his bow even as Sheyoshke signed, "Get ready."

The black man was unarmed. He wore grey pants and a dirty walnut-dyed shirt, and his feet were bare in the stirrups. He glanced from side to side, just as the soldiers did, obviously uncomfortable on the fog-shrouded trail.

Hannibal thought it must be the same man he had seen crossing the Huron River Bridge.

As the officer passed, Hannibal turned to Sheyoshke and signed "Third," then pointed to himself.

He dashed out onto the trail, past the second rider, and on to the black man, screaming, "Get down! Get down!"

Hannibal's words were lost in a crash of musket fire sounding from beyond the cornfield, as Tecumseh and Main Poche sprang the ambush on the main road. On the game trail, Mukos' warriors fired a heartbeat later. At a glance, Hannibal could see the officer with the silver chain falling. The second Horse Soldier reined sharply but arrows found his back and leg as he, too, tumbled from the saddle. Hannibal threw up his arms to frighten the black man's horse. There was hardly any need, as the mare was already rearing, pitching her rider into the brush.

"Stay down!" Hannibal yelled, as the man rose to scramble back down the trail. Hannibal tackled him, and both collapsed into the muck.

"You're safe! Don't get up," Hannibal shouted, even as the man kicked him in the face.

# The Land Between Flowing Waters

On the main road, war cries flared to be answered by terrified screams. The Long Knives were fleeing northward.

"You're free! You're free!" Hannibal insisted.

The man stopped struggling long enough to look down in astonishment at the Indian, he supposed, who was wrapped around his feet.

Mukos found Hannibal and Sheyoshke sitting on the chest of the second Horse Soldier. He was breathing, just barely, and crouching beside them was the slave.

Mukos examined the wounded white soldier and the unharmed black man. "What do you intend to do with them, Little Brother?"

Hannibal gulped as the other young warriors paused to listen.

"I...I'll practise healing on the Horse Soldier. If I can save him, I'll trade him to the Redcoats for a musket."

"And the black?"

"He's my captive too."

"Alright, Brother, but Kshiwe may have something to say when he gets back."

The ambush had turned into a rout, as the militiamen took flight in horror. Tecumseh and Main Poche led the warriors in pursuit, but it was too late for the younger Neshnabek to follow.

The boys and their black captive carried the gravely injured soldier to the stream to cut away his clothing. An arrow was lodged deep in his upper back and another protruded from his right calf, but the musket-wound in his abdomen concerned Hannibal the most. Kmonokwe had taught him healing prayers for belly wounds, but Hannibal did not suppose they would work on white folks.

Hannibal sent Sheyoshke running to the nearest farmhouse to beg for a blunt, round-edge table knife. Mukos watched as Hannibal worked frantically, but after a while Mukos wandered away. The boy seemed to know what he was doing.

When Sheyoshke returned, Hannibal was ready to remove the arrow from the soldier's back. Hannibal pressed the torn flesh away as he teased out the arrowhead. The second arrow was more difficult – when he tried to withdraw the shaft, its stone notches snagged on the leg muscles. Sheyoshke held tight as, instead, Hannibal plunged the arrow all the way through the leg. The unconscious man groaned as they broke the shaft and removed the pieces.

Hannibal filled the back and leg wounds with a paste of white pine and wild cherry bark, but the belly-wound was the most dangerous. The bullet had passed completely through the right side. It seemed to be draining well. Hannibal leaned forward to sniff; any hint of gut, of excrement, meant death. No, there was nothing but the smell of fresh blood. In relief, Hannibal began to mix another poultice.

"What you doin', coon?"

*Oh, Master of Life! He's one of those*, Hannibal thought, as the Horse Soldier struggled to clutch his arm weakly.

Hannibal searched for a moment then said, in English, "Saving your ass, cracker."

"You shut the..."

Kshiwe had returned, and now both he and Mukos were walking toward Hannibal and his prisoners. The Horse Soldier's eyes widened as first Sheyoshke, then Kshiwe and Mukos, came into view.

"Is he giving you trouble?" Kshiwe asked his son.

"Oh, Lord. The Injuns got me."

"Yes, we do," Hannibal agreed.

"Are they gonna burn me?" he asked as he collapsed back onto the grass.

"Not 'less you piss me off," Hannibal said.


After the ambush, Tecumseh and Main Poche's warriors remained behind to block the road from Fort Detroit. Kshiwe's war-band trekked south to Brownstown. Pulled on a travois, the wounded Horse Soldier was too frightened to complain. At Brownstown, they found Huron villagers embarking with all their possessions. Red-coated soldiers helped the refugees into a flotilla of small craft, while a larger ship armed with cannon guarded the evacuation.

From the pier, Major Branson noticed the Neshnabek warriors emerging from the forest. The warriors stopped and began to gesture towards the wharf. Branson doffed his crescent hat to fan his face while the warriors debated. Then Branson walked out part way in their direction, raised his hand, and simply waited. The warriors had brought a wounded Yankee. Even more curious, Branson thought, was the young, mostly naked black boy who stood next to the travois. An older black man stood behind the boy.

As the Huron climbed into their boats, they noticed the newcomers but did not hail them.

"Monsieur Boucherville," Branson called to his green-coated interpreter. "Who do you suppose these people are?"

"Redcoats," Kshiwe said, gesturing toward the pier. "King's Warriors. Don't you think?"

"I suppose..." Mukos allowed.

"I've never seen a King's Man," Village Speaker added. Nor had anyone with Kshiwe.

"Maybe we should just leave the Horse Soldier and the letters, and go," offered one of the other men.

"They don't seem to be very interested in us," said yet another warrior as the boats pushed off.

"The soldier with the crescent hat keeps looking this way. The man in the green coat too."

"Hannibal," Kshiwe called, "Bring out the travois where the Redcoat can see your captive. The mail bags too."

"Father," Hannibal asked as he led out the horse onto the beach. "Is that King's Country over there?" Hannibal pointed to the blue-hazed forests across the wide river. Hannibal's black captive was looking that way too.

"I think so. Now come back and stand with us," Kshiwe said.

The two white men began walking slowly across the beach.

Branson stopped a score of paces from the bandaged American militiaman. There were five black leather pouches in the sand beside him. One was left open so Branson could see the dispatches inside. The black boy who brought out the travois was again standing among the warriors. His face and bare chest were covered in green splotches.

"Green war paint?" Branson wondered.

"Three Fires Healer," Boucherville corrected. "*Tres jeunes cependant.*"

HMS *General Hunter*, the 12-gun British schooner, heeled to starboard as she raced eastward in pursuit of the evacuation convoy. Hannibal was thrilled as he clutched the lines to keep from sliding across the wet, slanting deck. He sang at the top of his lungs, a song his black father had taught him about following the drinking gourd in the night sky.

Kshiwe, Mukos, and the black man braced themselves against the ship's railing. It was a very long swim to shore.

"Are you a captive?" Boucherville asked the fiercely grinning Hannibal.

"Oh, no. This is my Indian father," Hannibal said pointing to Kshiwe. "My mother – my Indian mother – she's my teacher. She's Midewiwin."

As they overtook the slow-moving eastbound boats, *General Hunter*'s crew took in sail until she wallowed in long rolling waves.

"Is it true, Mr. Boucherville?" Hannibal asked. "Are black folks really free in King's Country?"

"*Mais oui!* Of course it's true."

\*\*\*\*\*

Kshiwe shouldered a fine new long-rifle in the woodlot behind Boucherville's trading post. He squeezed off a round, and broke the small clay disk swinging from a tree branch. Mukos also had a new musket, and they practised firing at clay targets.

"Major Branson was happy for all the captured mail," Thomas de Boucherville said, "but now he has to find men to read it all!"

Boucherville lounged at a long wooden table with Hannibal beside him. He traded furs with the Three Fires People from both sides of the river, and spoke their language with ease.

"Will they torture the Yankee?" Kshiwe asked as he sighted at another swinging target.

"Probably not."

Crack! At 75 paces, the disk exploded.

Kshiwe glanced at the fur trader. "No, they won't. He has nothing to tell. Why bother?"

"What will happen to the black?" Kshiwe asked.

Hannibal looked sideways at Boucherville.

"He was a slave, not a soldier. He's free now."

Crack! Mukos made a black walnut jump from atop a fence-post.

"Good. That's good," Hannibal said. "But how will he eat?"

"He could work in my store, or on any of the farms. With a war on, crops are languishing in the fields."

"Work for hire?" Hannibal asked.

"*Mais oui!*"

Kshiwe raised his new rifle once more. Hannibal waited until he, too, made a walnut streak off into the high grass.

"Father, I'm going back with you, back across the river," Hannibal said. "Sheyoshke can't tend the wounded alone."

"I'm going too," Boucherville said. "I'm Major Branson's interpreter. He's taking Redcoats over to fight with Tecumseh. General Hull has to have those provisions at the Raisin or the Yankees will starve on the vine."

*****

Headquarters
Banks of Lake Erie
15 miles S. W. of Port Talbot
August 11, 1812, 6 o'clock p.m.

General Orders:

The troops will hold themselves in readiness, and will embark in the boats at twelve o'clock this night precisely.

It is Major General Brock's positive order that none of the boats go ahead of that in which is the Head Quarters, where a light will be carried during the night.

The officers commanding the different boats will immediately inspect the arms and ammunition of the men, and see that they are constantly kept in a state for immediate service, as the troops are now to pass through a part of the country which is known to have been visited by the enemy's patrols.

A Captain, with a subaltern and thirty men, will mount as picket upon the landing of the boats and a sentry will be furnished from each boat, who must be regularly relieved to take charge of the boats and baggage, etc.

A patrol from the picket will be sent out on landing to the distance of a mile from the encampment.

By order of the Major General;
J.B. Glegg, Major, A.D.C.
J. MacDonnell, P.A.D.C.

# Ken Leland

## Alexander Lockwood

"Away all boats, Lieutenant Lockwood!" Major Glegg shouted the order to me, and we cast off.

There is no word whether Fort Amherstburg is already besieged. We set sail at midnight with resolution but also with the prayer that we are not too late.

John Norton reports from the Thames that the Nations flock to his standard. Glegg says we must remember to provide Norton with a flag at the first opportunity, and that my sister and Mrs. Roberts could sew a nice one for him. I reply to Glegg that if he should somehow fall overboard, we are probably close enough to shore that we need not stop to fish him out.

Glegg and I found a nice single-masted freighter for General Brock. We detailed twenty militiamen as crew. Colonel MacDonnell kept station with us all during the night in an overloaded fishing smack. Try as we might, we could only find seaworthy craft, of any description, to hold about 300 men. The 1st York and 5th Lincoln are with us still, along with two companies of Dover men. At dawn, small boats follow behind us like a clutch of ducklings.

Captain Chambers' company arrived at the lake just before we embarked. General Brock has ordered him to bring the remaining militiamen overland.

The wind is fresh from the northwest, and all morning it has slowed our progress. We row incessantly a few hundred yards offshore, and our hands are covered in blisters. A little past noon we arrive at a great point of land, a peninsula called Point aux Pins. Here the lake is quite shallow. A vast marsh of cattails and lily pads lies across our bow. The point extends to our left, into the heart of the lake and out of sight.

"Shall we go around?" Colonel MacDonnell calls to us.

The General raises his telescope. "It's not too wide," he decides.

"Straight through," he calls. "Follow me."

We enter the morass. For a hundred yards, the beating, struggling oars propel us, but soon the men must stand and push. We use the oars as poles, to thrust us forward another few feet with every concerted shove. It is still more than 200 yards to open water when we are mired and cannot budge. When I look back, there is a long line of boats strung out behind us, floating in the water trail we have forced open. It will take hours, maybe days, to back up and find our way around the point.

"That's fine work men. You've done your best," Brock says to the exhausted crew. He takes off his fine leather boots and throws them in the bottom of the boat. He tosses his bright officer's jacket atop the boots, and slides down into the knee-deep mud.

"Look, men! We're floating higher already."

Then he leans heavily against the stern. Glegg is over the side, and complaining of the squish between his toes, before I can tie a rope to the bowsprit. Then I'm into the marsh with everyone else to pull the boat forward.

MacDonnell watches us from the next boat behind. He tosses away his own boots.

"Men," he shouts, "This is where we get out and push!"

\*\*\*\*\*

On the morning of August 9, British forces sailed for the Brownstown pier.

Hannibal wrapped his arm around the mast as the ship heeled from the brisk northwest wind. *General Hunter* and a flotilla of freight canoes transported Major Branson and three companies of the 41st, along with a small contingent of Essex County Militia. Standing clear of *Hunter*'s crowded deck, Branson trained a spyglass on the western shore. Word had come from Tecumseh that a large contingent of American regulars and militiamen were marching south, to open a way for the supply column trapped at the Raisin River stockade.

Amidships, sheltered by the mast, Kshiwe and Mukos sat cross-legged on rings of coiled hawsers, cradling two small casks of gunpowder and sacks with pots of white and black war paint.

Thomas de Boucherville in his green cloth coat huddled from the spray and counted his rifle cartridges for the third or fourth time. A chin-strap held a black leather cap tight to his head. Sprigs of basswood tucked in the hatband marked him as a King's Man. The leaves whipped in the breeze.

Branson snapped the telescope closed. As *Hunter* pitched and rolled, he lurched through the crowded deck to the small group next to the mast.

# Ken Leland

"Landfall in fifteen minutes, Boucherville. There must be 100 warriors at the dock."

Kshiwe and Mukos rose to peer over the ship's railing.

"Keep track of where I am," Branson said to Boucherville. "At need, I'll send you with messages."

"Yes, Major."

Branson teetered away on the rolling deck, but then returned. "The boy knows the languages, yes?"

"*Mais oui*, Major."

"I can't be sure," Branson said as Hannibal listened closely, "but he might be safer with you than the Nations – a second messenger. What does his father think? Will the boy help us?"

Though Hannibal pleaded with his eyes to be allowed to stay with the warriors, Kshiwe's nod was final. Hannibal would be a messenger in this fight.


On reaching the Brownstown shore, Kshiwe and Village Speaker stood facing each other. Other Neshnabek and Odawa warriors stood in pairs as the Redcoats and Canadiens found places to nap in the shade.

"It's going to be like that, is it?" Village Speaker sighed when he saw the pots of black and white death paint in Kshiwe's hands.

"No, no. There's just no more red left."

Each warrior carefully painted half his partner's face white and the rest black, vertically between the brows, then white on the opposite side of the bare chest and back, and black for the rest. They stood back to admire their work.

"You look truly terrifying, Kshiwe!" Village Speaker chuckled. "Even Kmonokwe would run from you."

"Hmmmm. If you say so."


A repeated staccato yipping echoed through the forest. Warriors snatched up their weapons; soldiers began to strap on their packs. Branson, Boucherville and Hannibal trotted out onto the muddy road at the top of the empty village to meet the messenger.

"Major, he says the Long Knives are like a cloud of mosquitoes."

Boucherville translated as the young Shawnee painted in red and white slashing stripes bent double with hands planted on his knees. "He says they were almost at the Ecorces River when he started. He ran very fast."

"How far away do you think?"

"Eight, ten miles at least."

The messenger spoke again as Hannibal edged close to listen.

"The Yankees have two cannon. Many Blue Coats, many Brown Coats. A few Horse Soldiers." Boucherville paused as the Shawnee fought for breath.

"Tecumseh asks you to come quickly. Alone he can only annoy them. Together we can kill them all."

Branson turned to Hannibal, but the boy was already sprinting for the Three Fires warriors.

"Lieutenants," Branson called to the Redcoats forming up on the beach, "Line of march. We're heading north at the double."

Warriors spread out in an arc centred on the soldiers. Branson led them forward at the quick march, but half an hour later his face was dripping sweat. Here the road was but a broad quagmire from recent showers. Clouds hung low making a hot, wet oven.

"Lord of Mercy," Branson gasped as they crossed a creek. "What is that dreadful smell?"

"Something's dead," Boucherville said as he held a towel over his nose. "A lot of somethings."

"Yankees," Hannibal said quietly from just behind. "Tecumseh and Main Poche ambushed them here five days ago."

Just ahead, a score of rotting, naked bodies hung in the trees. Vultures had found the softer outer parts; rats the inner.

"Leave them," Branson shouted as the soldiers slogged by, shuddering in disgust. "We'll bury them later. And a lot more."

A second Shawnee messenger arrived just before noon.

"The Yankees are about two miles ahead, resting at a village called Maguaga. Tecumseh has laid a trap."

Below Maguaga, a tall cornfield grew west of the road. From there, the road continued through two low hills, forming a ravine through which the Yankees would surely pass. Trees and brush shaded the road along both sides of the ravine. In the cornfield, Tecumseh waited in ambush with 100 warriors.

# Ken Leland

Branson arrayed the three Redcoat companies in the centre, and interspersed the Canadiens among them. Main Poche and the Neshnabek held the right flank, nearest the lake. Having learned from experience at the Canard, Branson directed the soldiers to crouch behind logs and trees, just as the warriors did. With the steady Redcoats anchoring the middle, Branson hoped that the Nations on the right and left wings might sweep around to attack the Yankee column in the sides, after they blundered into the British roadblock. Unable to go forward, Branson supposed the enemy would buckle in terror from the Nations' flanking attacks, and would be swept back north toward Fort Detroit. A bugle call would be the signal for an advance by the centre, to push the enemy out of the bottle and send them fleeing.

It was a good plan, with Tecumseh and Main Poche in accord. But as they settled in to wait, Branson was surprised by the last-minute approach of reinforcements, a fourth company of the 41st. The company had arrived at Fort Amherstburg only that morning, and been forwarded to Branson's assistance. American drums beat in the near distance as 60 more Redcoats came jogging up the road. Branson hurriedly sent word that the newcomers should simply strengthen the centre of the line; there wasn't time to plan anything more elaborate as blue-coated Yankee Horse Soldiers rode cautiously into view.

A hundred Three Fires warriors glided silently through the wooded ravine. Village Speaker paced Main Poche to ask, "What are your plans?"

"Scream, then go in and cut their throats."

"Simple enough, even for me," Village Speaker said, with a smile he was careful to hide.

On hearing this exchange, Kshiwe stopped to wait for the Shishibes Lake band to catch up.

"Mukos," Kshiwe said, "Tell the men to keep an eye on me. Go where I go, forward or back. Be alert."

The Three Fires warriors ran down the hillside, into the brush along the muddy road. As American drums pounded, a handful of mounted Yankees plodded down the road. Behind them came blue-coated regulars, marching in columns on each side. Militiamen in brown filled the middle of the road.

"The Bluecoats are strong fighters," Kshiwe whispered to those around him. He remembered them from the battle at Prophetstown. They would not run at the first volley. They would charge the warriors' roadside position.

# The Land Between Flowing Waters

Tecumseh's men lay in the cornfield west of the road. With a sinking belly, Tecumseh saw the enemy in three columns, the nearest wearing blue. Well, it couldn't be helped. Maybe the Brown-coats in the middle would flee, and the sides fall back to shield them. It was the best the Nations could hope for. Tecumseh raised his rifle as a cavalry officer, with three jaunty plumes in his hat, rode in to scout the tall corn. Tecumseh waited until the man's eyes grew wide at what he found there. Then Tecumseh killed him.

From behind a log on the hillside, Boucherville heard the first shot. It was followed instantly by a ragged volley from warriors on both sides of the road. Hannibal crouched beside Boucherville with an arrow nocked. Boucherville sighted over his rifle but waited for Branson's command. Boucherville watched the militia in the centre; they weren't running from the war cries. Well, they were running but not in terror. Their officers yelled and they formed a square. In only moments, they were moving forward again at a measured pace. The Yankee wings pushed outward on both sides, into the cornfield and opposite into the brush-filled berm.

The Blue-coated regulars fired at opportunity, not in volleys. There was no breeze through the ravine, and gunsmoke accumulated with every shot. Two cannons rolled up beside the Yankee square.

"Fire!" Branson screamed. British whistles blew all along the line.

Hannibal flinched as a wall of lightning leapt toward the Yankees. He popped up to send an arrow arching into the square, then quickly nocked and loosed another before Boucherville pulled him down behind the log.

The Yankee square responded, aiming a volley into the bank of smoke ahead. Most of the volley passed over, clipping leaves and small branches from the trees above the British line.

Boucherville aimed at an artillery gunner, but he ducked quickly after firing. The Redcoats around him struggled to reload, unaccustomed to sheltering behind logs and trees. Boucherville simply rolled onto his back to break a paper cartridge into his rifle's muzzle, then rammed home the ball and powder with a paper patch. Lying on his back, Boucherville reached up to brace his rifle on top of the log, guessed the angle and pulled the trigger.

The rifle bucked and fell down on top of him. He grinned at Hannibal and began to reload.

The noise was deafening and continuous. First one, then the other Yankee cannon fired, sending dozens of musket balls spraying through the trees.

*This isn't what I'm supposed to be doing,* Hannibal thought, as yet another round of grape-shot brought down a green shower. He grabbed the strap of his medicine pack and dragged it closer. *Where are Kshiwe and the Shishibes Lake men? Who's already hurt?* he worried. Hannibal glanced at Boucherville, and then struck out to make his way across the road to the opposite side of the ravine. Redcoat soldiers were too busy to notice as he sprinted along the line.

White smoke obscured everything beyond twenty paces. Bullets flew past as Hannibal ran. A heartbeat before the next cannon blast, Hannibal dove behind a tree trunk. There he found a young British officer, his head slumped forward, the back of his neck a mass of gore. A bullet had knocked out two front teeth on its way through the mouth and out the back of his neck. He could live only a few moments more. Hannibal cradled him, and after saying a quick prayer into his ear, he hurried toward the Three Fires position.

As he crossed the road, there was a rolling bellow from the hundreds of Yankees down in the glen. They broke the square and charged. A bugle call echoed from the British line.

Nearby, the British captain with the late arrivals turned to a sergeant, "Did you hear the bugle? It must be the Retreat."

"Fall back," the captain ordered. "Retreat in squads. Return fire as you go."

"No. No," Hannibal yelled. "It was the Charge."

But no one listened as the company abandoned its place in the very centre of the British formation.

The next captain in line was befuddled. He did not charge, as he knew was the plan, for he could see that his left flank was now uncovered. And before he had a chance to make up his mind, his men were shouting about movement on the wooded hill to their right.

"Yankees!"

Redcoats were already firing at shadows on the smoky hillside. Some of the hillside figures stopped to fire back.

"It's Main Poche! Cease fire!" the officer yelled.

# The Land Between Flowing Waters

But if Main Poche had been driven back, soon enough his company would be flanked on the right. With a gap on his left and Yankees advancing on his right, the captain ordered a withdrawal before his part of the line could be engulfed.

Hannibal stood watching as the Three Fires warriors retreated across the hill. If Kshiwe, Mukos, and Village Speaker were alive, they were with them. The nearest British company was carrying its wounded away. The centre of the Redcoat line was evaporating. Hannibal ran back to try to find Boucherville.

"Oh, *mon ami*, I lost track of you," Boucherville said with a sigh. "But Hannibal, you must leave now. *Les bâtards* will be here in a few moments."

Blood streamed from the Canadien's brown hair, down his face onto his green jacket. The British position was abandoned, but somehow Boucherville had been left behind.

"You should never have raised your head," Hannibal whispered as he dug through his medicine pack for bandages. "We have to get away."

"Brownstown? Too far," Boucherville gasped weakly.

"We can't stay here," Hannibal said as he dragged Boucherville to his feet. "We must hide."

Hannibal and Boucherville were wet, and surprisingly cold. They lay sheltered beneath a giant willow tree, in a cave cut by a shallow stream. Inside it, dust drifted down to where they crouched in mud. There was space for one, but not both of them, to lie down. After propping Boucherville's head on his medicine pack, Hannibal kept watch through the screen of dangling roots to the creek beyond.

The Battle of Maguaga had lasted less than half an hour, but for half an hour more Hannibal and Boucherville listened to receding gunfire as the Yankees pressed Tecumseh's warriors farther and farther to the west. After that, silence reigned until finally Yankee voices could be heard, ranging along the stream in search of enemy wounded. Pickets stood guard on the stream bank, sometimes walking above their heads. Militiamen bathed, cooks drew water, and after supper men relieved themselves in the stream. As the sun set, Boucherville began to moan drowsily. Hannibal took dry bark from his stores and made him chew the bitter strands until he fell asleep.

Hannibal prayed.

All night, a yellow-eyed lynx lounged unseen on a branch high above, twitching his ears and smiling.


"Thomas, wake up! The Long Knives are gone."

In the morning light, Hannibal leaned into the hollow beneath the old willow. Boucherville groaned as he crawled out on hands and knees, his heavily bandaged head aching. Hannibal helped him climb the stream-bank, and then took his arm as they crossed the empty battleground.

"Did the Yankees go south?" Boucherville moaned. "To the Raisin?"

"No. They went back north."

"A miracle. We won by retreating!"

The road was too dangerous, and so they crept through the trees to a lakeside footpath. As they made their way slowly towards Brownstown, they found a string of abandoned Canadien farms. Most had been looted.

Boucherville was weak and dizzy. If he walked more than a few hundred paces, his heart raced and blood spread wider across the towel wrapped over his head wound. He had to rest on almost every farm porch.

It was close to noon when Hannibal heard a redbird calling.

"Mukos!" Hannibal yelled.

The young man, followed by Kshiwe and the rest of the Shishibes Lake warriors, glided watchfully into the farmyard.

Hannibal buried himself in his father's arms.

"We missed you," Kshiwe said as he crushed the boy against his chest. Then Kshiwe noticed the bandaged Boucherville, who was trying to sit up.

"But I can see you've been busy."


While two warriors took Boucherville to the Brownstown pier where they could hail a passing British patrol boat, Kshiwe led the war-band south.

"Kmonokwe sent word," Kshiwe told Hannibal. "She has joined the other healers."

"Are Senisqua and Shkote with her?"

"Yes. Let's go find them."

# The Land Between Flowing Waters

The Huron River camp was crowded with Canadien and Neshnabe families. Dogs and children romped, making this place of pain a bit more cheerful, if noisy. Now there were companions and grandparents, come to nurse the warriors. All too many men were wounded in the fighting that had continued for over a month. Healers passed from one lodge to the next bringing food, medicine and prayers. Hannibal and Kshiwe glanced into each shelter as they searched along the river trail. Finally, Hannibal spotted Kmonokwe in an open lean-to beside the river.

Kmonokwe, in a long skirt and loose white blouse, knelt to change the dressings on a warrior's broken leg. With her face painted in the red and green strips of a senior Midewiwin, she looked up at the shout of "Mother!" Hannibal rushed to greet her. She opened her arms wide, but Hannibal stopped short and carefully took both her hands.

"Mother, I am glad to find you," he said gripping her fingers. "I've worried so. Am I saying the prayers right? Am I mixing the medicines as you taught me? I'm trying very, very hard."

Kmonokwe clasped him tight.

"My son, you're growing up," she choked, and then wiped her eyes on her sleeve. She brushed her fingertips over the bright green paint on his face. "We can use your help. There are so many wounded here."

Hannibal stood aside when he saw Kmonokwe glimpse the figure standing at his back. Kshiwe was there, painted as the black and white image of a winter demon.

"Oh, my love. You do look dreadful." Now her tears were streaming.

"But that's the idea." Kshiwe smiled, and walked closer to stand before her.

"Come to the river. I'll wash all this away," she said gliding her hands over his greasy chest. "Then I'll love you with all my might."

## Thursday, August 13, 1812
## Fort Detroit

"Gentlemen! From the moment I saw the Union Jack still flying over Fort Amherstburg, I've known what to say to you. There'll be only thanks and praise from me," General Brock announced.

216

# Ken Leland

Colonel MacDonnell, Major Glegg and Captain Lockwood stood near the open headquarters window as the noontime sun streamed onto the floor. In a ring of chairs, Colonels St. George and Procter – each stouter than the other – the wizened Colonel Elliott of the British Indian Department and Major Branson of the 41st Regiment, were seated in the middle of the room. Fresh from a bath, in which he'd left a thick deposit of mud, Brock leaned on an empty chair-back, his hair dripping wet.

"But now you must tell me what's happened, what our Exterminating General Hull has been up to, and how we can force him to surrender in the next three days. The threat at Niagara demands that we end the business here as soon as possible."

Brock's words took Captain Lockwood's breath away. His mother, father, Miriam and Janie, and yes even Jeremy, were all there at Niagara – while the army was here, half a world away. Victory at Detroit in three days? Impossible!

The officers' reports came in turn with Colonel St. George leading off. "The Yankees bombarded Sandwich when they crossed the river..."

"Canadien militiamen deserted in droves..."

"Privates Hancock and Dean were the first casualties, executed at the Canard while the First Company..."

"Desertions stopped after the Americans began looting and burning..."

"The Yankees withdrew to Fort Detroit a week ago..."

"They're starving..."

"After Fort Michilimackinac surrendered, most Nations declared for the King. John Norton is bringing..."

"A Shawnee chief named Tecumseh has hit them again and again..."

"We retreated after the fight at Maguaga, but their regulars had enough. The Yankee supply train is still at the Raisin River Stockade," Major Branson concluded.

"Thank you, most profoundly. Thank you all." Brock's smile was as wide as the river outside. "But our work here has just begun. For tonight's supper entertainment, I want a plan for the subjugation of Fort Detroit – to be accomplished by Sunday morning. Then we'll hold a Thanksgiving Service."

The meeting adjourned. The officers left shaking their heads.

217

# The Land Between Flowing Waters

"Is he serious?" Lockwood asked Glegg, as they followed MacDonnell outside and across the parade ground. MacDonnell glanced back at Glegg expectantly.

"Oh, yes. He's most serious. The Yankees here must be defeated quickly. The war will be won or lost in the next three days."

They walked on, lost in thought. Finally, MacDonnell turned to face them.

"My friends, you both smell like swamp rats. I'll pour baths if you'll return the favour."

It was mid-afternoon when Tecumseh and his war chiefs crossed the Detroit to meet with Brock. Glegg and Lockwood were ready to record Brock's orders as the warriors filed into the meeting room.

Tecumseh was about thirty-five years of age, of moderate height and oval face. His bright hazel eyes beamed with cheerfulness and conviction. He wore a jacket and trousers of deerskin, and his moccasins were decorated with porcupine quills.

Brock stretched out his hand to Tecumseh. An Indian Department translator stood at the general's elbow.

"My officers tell me you are the reason General Hull is locked in his fort, not celebrating a conquest."

"There are many who helped," the translator related, as Tecumseh motioned to the chiefs behind him.

"You all have our great thanks," Brock said nodding to them. "It is my intention to defeat the Yankees in three days. How can we do this?"

"Ho! Here is a man to lead us to victory," Tecumseh beamed.

As the Nations plotted with Brock how to take Fort Detroit, Lockwood wandered in the stifling heat of early evening. Glegg had made Lockwood promise to return with a pot of fish stew if the meeting dragged on much longer.

As the sun scorched the tree line, Lockwood strolled to where the *General Hunter* was docked. There, lounging on flour barrels and coils of rope, were dozens of armed warriors painted in vermillion, white, black or combinations. Lockwood swept off his hat and inclined his head before sitting cross-legged at the pier's edge. He looked down into the water, sighing at the long, sleek shapes darting below. *Oh, for a fishing pole*, he thought. After a minute or two, Lockwood noticed an exchange of vigorous sign-talk among the warriors. There were two youths, both with shaved heads and brisling, feather decorated roach-locks. One of the boys was black.

Lockwood pretended to study the islands far out in the river. Instead his thoughts reeled as Matthew Benjamin leapt to mind, Lockwood's strong friend and Janie's dear brother. Then came the face of little Ethan, Janie's first-born. Lockwood swallowed hard. What was a black boy doing here? Was he a captive? Somehow that didn't seem likely, as Lockwood again glanced at the cluster of warriors. Both youths, silent as dusk, were signing now with two or three of the younger men, then presently a few veterans joined in. The discussion stopped abruptly. The black youth stared at Lockwood, while the others turned away. Then he approached cautiously.

Lockwood wondered if he had enough money to ransom him. Strangely, the boy's face and chest were covered in green spots.

The boy knelt beside him, holding out a hand line.

"I'll go dig some worms."

The boy spoke English. Surely he was a prisoner.

When the youngster returned to snag a nightcrawler on the hook, Lockwood asked quietly, "How can I help you? Are you a prisoner?"

"Oh, no," he said. "My father's coming just now."

He pointed to one of the war chiefs, painted as a winter demon in white and black, leaving the adjourned headquarters meeting.

"I was hoping you could bring my family across the river," the young man said. "Do you know how to get to Walpole Island?"

*How can I help him?* Lockwood wondered. *I don't even know where Walpole is.* But aloud he said, "I'll do what I can."

*****

On August 15, the day was overcast and warm. The Fort Amherstburg parade ground was crowded with lines of soldiers.

"Major Glegg!" Brock bellowed for the benefit of a thousand ears.

"Sar!"

Glegg stood quivering at attention before General Brock. The post's senior officers, the militia and four companies of the 41$^{st}$ were arrayed behind the general.

# The Land Between Flowing Waters

"You will deliver this note to General William Hull, Commander of the American Army of the Northwest. Soonest! It demands the immediate surrender of his person and his army."

"Sar!"

Brock leaned in to whisper, "And you have my permission to scare him as much as you like."

Glegg about-faced, and with a come-along wave summoned Lockwood and MacDonnell. The officers rode out through the gates, north to Sandwich.

As they cantered through the Huron Reserve, children came out to watch the officers, resplendent in red coats and white crossbelts. There were travel lodges among the shingled log cabins and frame houses.

"The Brownstown refugees have moved in," Glegg mused.

"No burning here!" MacDonnell observed.

"The Yankees never crossed the Canard," Glegg said.

A vast prairie began at the Canard River Bridge. The bridge sills had been replaced, and the defensive works torn down. Heavy artillery tracks had churned the mud.

"Have you gentlemen ever seen an artillery bombardment?" Glegg asked.

"No Sir," Lockwood answered.

"Not I," MacDonnell said.

"I did, just once, in the Lowlands. With the General it was, years ago. Quite a sight."

The habitants of Petite Cote had borne the worst of it. Ruined gardens, trampled fields and mangled orchards, looted homes, empty granaries, burned windmills – but the Canadiens were already rebuilding.

"They didn't ask for this," Lockwood growled.

"We couldn't protect them," Glegg sighed.

The fields and farms lay in ruins, but the town of Sandwich had suffered too: ransacked homes, gutted businesses and public buildings, the people bruised and humiliated. The Redcoats continued up King's Road.

It was two miles north of Sandwich that they met John Norton with 300 warriors at his back. As the reinforcements trotted by, the officers dismounted to wring Norton's hand and pound his back in gratitude.

"These men are not Haudenosaunee!" Lockwood exclaimed as he studied the war-band sweeping down the road.

"No. Some are Delaware, but most are Three Fires from the Lower Thames, from St. Clair and Walpole."

"Walpole?" Lockwood asked in surprise.

"Yes. It's nearby. More warriors are coming from the northern lakes, but they won't be here until tonight or tomorrow. Where is General Brock?" Norton asked.

"At Amherstburg, with 300 Redcoats and as many militia," MacDonnell said. "Hull must surrender today, or we'll kill him tomorrow."

"Truly!" Norton said in cheerful amazement. "We fight tomorrow?"

"Brock says so. But tonight, you and Tecumseh will have a chance to scare Hull to death."

Norton laughed. "A war dance?"

"Make it loud so they can hear," Glegg said pointing across the river. "If your men aren't too tired, maybe they could circle back through the woods and run down this road once or twice more. I'm sure those people are counting."

On the Upper Canada beach opposite Fort Detroit, two companies of Essex County Militiamen were digging. An artillery captain directed the embedding of 24–lb. long guns. Sweat poured from the militiamen's faces as the embrasure rose higher.

"Bombs tonight?" Glegg asked the captain.

"I most sincerely hope so, Sir. We ain't had much fun since we come from home."

"Now, I ask you, Captain. If I was to show a flag of parley down there," Glegg said pointing to the waterline, "Do you suppose anyone on the other side would notice?"

After waving a towel on a pole for half an hour, Lockwood, MacDonnell and Glegg took their places in a Yankee scow. Lockwood and Glegg sat facing the stern, their knees almost touching a blue-jacketed sergeant at the tiller.

"Come to surrender, then, have you Sir?" the sergeant asked Glegg in the lilt of the olde sod.

To Lockwood's complete surprise, Glegg's answer came in the deepest Irish brogue. "Now why would we be doin' that, boyo?

# The Land Between Flowing Waters

There's five thousand bloodthirsty savages in the woods behind your fort. Do you not know that?"

"Look, Major," Lockwood said as he pointed back to the eastern shore. "Another war party is coming in."

The sergeant turned to stare as Norton's warriors pounded down King's Road again. Lockwood wondered how many more times Norton could lead his men in a circle before the rowboat reached shore.

"But what I want to know," Glegg continued mildly, "is why a man of Eire is serving with these pro-test-ants."

"Ah well, Major. That would probably be a military secret."

"As is your proper rank, my friend?"

"Hmmmm."

"There'll be a party and dancing tonight, when it gets dark. Come down to the water and listen. Maybe you'll want to join in."

Glegg fell silent as the scow lumbered across the broad river.

On reaching the western shore, a Yankee major took General Brock's note up to the fort. The Redcoat officers sat bathing their heels in the river.

General Hull left them waiting alone on the dock for two hours as he read the following and weighed its significance:

> To His Excellency Brigadier General Hull
> Commanding at Fort Detroit
>
> The force at my disposal authorizes me to require of you the surrender of Fort Detroit. It is far from my inclination to join in a war of extermination, but you must be aware that the numerous body of Indians who have attached themselves to my troops will be beyond my control the moment the contest commences. You will find me disposed to enter into such conditions as will satisfy the most scrupulous sense of honour. Major Glegg is fully authorized to conclude any arrangements that may lead to prevent the unnecessary effusion of blood.
>
> I have the honour to be, Sir,
> Your most obedient servant,
> Isaac Brock, Major General

# Ken Leland

General Hull's reply was terse.

> I have received your letter of this date. I have no other reply to make than to inform you that I am prepared to meet any force which may be at your disposal, and any consequences which may result from any exertion of it you may think proper to make.

> W. Hull, Brigadier-General
> Commanding the N.W. Army of the United States

*****

At loose ends on the afternoon before battle, Captain Lockwood was directed to a Canadien trading post in the town of Amherstburg, owned by one Thomas de Boucherville.

"I'm told, Monsieur Boucherville, that you are engaged in the Indian trade and know the Nations well."

"That is quite correct, Capitaine Lockwood. How may I help you?"

"Friday night I met a young Neshnabek on the dock. He's black and speaks English."

"Oh yes, Capitaine. That was Hannibal." Boucherville lifted a portion of his brown hair to show a long, fiery scar over his left ear. "*Regardez.*"

"He did that?"

"*Mais non*, Monsieur! From that he saved me."

*****

It was well after midnight when Lockwood returned from the western shore on Boucherville's trading sloop. The quarter moon was bright on the water, and in its light Lockwood could see their passengers. The boy Hannibal, of course, and his father, now washed of the ghostly war paint in which Lockwood had seen him at headquarters. The father's lovely young daughter and her husband sat spooned together at the bow. Amidships, a boy of eight or nine sheltered in his father's arms. A most handsome matron laid her head against the father's shoulder.

# The Land Between Flowing Waters

There were three or four bonfires dotting the Amherstburg shore, and even from a mile out on the water Lockwood could hear the pounding of great drums. He went to stand at the prow, opposite the young couple – who ignored him, lost in each other. But the mother of this family came to grasp the mainstays beside him. She pointed at the dancers on shore, and said something gladly. Lockwood could only smile and shake his head. The unearthly sound of warriors' voices pierced the night air as Hannibal came to join them.

"She says it's a Three Fires war-song. She thinks her sons might be here."

*****

Captain Lockwood had asked to hire Boucherville's sloop to bring Hannibal's family across to Upper Canada. Boucherville could not image why Lockwood would request such a thing, but of course he agreed; Boucherville owed Hannibal his life.

From the tiller, Boucherville watched as Lockwood stood forward beside the young couple. *The girl*, Boucherville thought, *she is an angel. If I could find such a one for myself, I would sit at her lodge door until brown leaves turn to strawberries.*

But the mother – *Mon Dieu! She is a powerful witch, painted in red and green.* Boucherville shivered as he remembered when Hannibal had pushed back his hair to reveal the scar. She had mumbled a spell over him. *I will not be surprised*, Boucherville thought, *if I wake up tomorrow as a toad.*

They landed at Fort Amherstburg as the bonfires burned. The Nations were an extraordinary sight, some painted with vermillion, others with blue clay, and still others in black and white from head to foot. Boucherville smiled to himself. A stranger witnessing a war-dance for the first time would surely believe that he has arrived at the very entrance to Hell, the gates thrown open to let the damned out for an hour's recreation. It is frightful, horrifying beyond expression. The pounding of the great drums beats against the body, making the innards quiver. The high-pitched screech that passes for song brings panic to a stranger's mind. Hundreds danced wildly. *Even I*, Boucherville admitted to himself, *cannot help but feel overcome as though under the influence of some kind of terrifying spell.*

Boucherville's gaze followed as sparks leapt into the sky. The witch approached the dancers. She was motionless for a time, until

224

at last she beckoned to Boucherville. She pointed to the demons she would summon from the rings of Perdition, and he braved the Inferno.

First one young warrior, and then another, came forth. Each rushed to take her hand and embrace her.

Boucherville joined the Nations when they launched canoes a few hours before dawn. As the Native armada paddled north from Amherstburg, bomb-bursts broke the sky. British cannons roared in the darkness, lifting charges to explode in the air above the Yankee fort. *Queen Charlotte* and *General Hunter*, anchored in the middle of the river, join in the bombardment. Red flames lanced from their gun-ports. From mortars, arching bombs disappeared into the firmament only to descend with dreadful explosions upon the enemy's buildings and wooden walls. Fires glowed against the clouds, but soon sputtered and died.

Yankee cannons replied. Their fire was mainly directed at the British battery on the eastern shore, but many cannonballs fell short and geysers sprang into the air between the ships. Of those warriors with Boucherville, no one had seen such an exhibition, such a display of noise and death. In the canoes all around, everyone paused in astonishment. Then, seeing the British regulars and militiamen launching boats, they loosed war cries to urge them on, even as the Nations churned the waters to lead the westward dash. Boucherville greatly feared that the landing would be opposed by Yankee infantry, but they found the beaches empty.

Tecumseh and the other war chiefs led the charge across the narrow sand, into the brush, and then up the riverbank to the road. But the road was empty too. Warriors took up positions in a half-circle to guard the beachhead. They had landed three miles below Fort Detroit. In the grey light of dawn, bombs still burst over the enemy's works. Pillars of smoke rose from behind the log palisades.

Boucherville saw General Brock's launch plough into the muddy shallows. Brock was running through the sand before the rest of his officers could disembark. Boucherville yelled that the road was clear, and the general hurried back to direct the Redcoat companies as they formed ranks.

\*\*\*\*\*

# The Land Between Flowing Waters

Major Glegg was not pleased by Lockwood's untimely disappearance on the eve of battle, but he soon forgot his annoyance when he saw Lockwood arrive on an exhausted horse, two or three hours after midnight.

"About time you showed up, Captain Lockwood!" was all he said.

The army slept in the stone warehouses near the dock. Brock's tent was pitched at the head of Sandwich's only street, beside a burnt-out windmill.

MacDonnell, Glegg and Lockwood lounged in an old shed to escape the early morning dew.

"You know, gentlemen," Glegg began, "I just can't see why those people are so tentative. Not that I'm complaining, mind you."

"They outnumber us," Lockwood said. "Maybe Jonathan thinks he can squash us like a tick."

"No, I don't think that's it," MacDonnell considered. "General Hull isn't...well, particularly brave. Or, maybe he's just incompetent."

"Or," Lockwood offered, "maybe they're as surprised as we are to be fighting a war over...over...What would you say this war is about, Glegg?"

"Can't imagine. Their arguments are with England – not Canada."

"Doesn't seem to matter. It's us they attack," MacDonnell said, as he leaned back into a pile of straw.

The cannonade began when word arrived that Tecumseh and Norton were on the river. The 24-pounders roared, and mortar bombs burst over the Yankee fort. Lockwood was lost in awe at the spectacle. Almost immediately, the ships joined in and the concussions became unbearable. Companies mustered to board transports – sergeants screamed orders unintelligibly into the faces of deafened men.

At the Sandwich dock, Glegg and Lockwood climbed into the same launch with Brock. In dumb show, Glegg graciously steered MacDonnell to the next boat available, so that no one enemy cannonball could cause too grievous a loss. As they pushed off amidst earth-shaking gunfire, Lockwood saw the Nations paddling with a will towards the far shore.

Brock stood amidships, his lips moving futilely in the infernal din, "Follow them!"

Lockwood couldn't believe that anyone heard, but follow them they did.

Brock was halfway up the beach before Lockwood could untangle his boots and scabbard. Only moments later, the general returned with news that the way was clear, and ordered the gunners to land the light artillery.

Dawn.

Exploding bombs shattered the burning American fort, but the perimeter was deathly quiet. *Where is the enemy?* Lockwood asked himself. With rifle in hand, Lockwood wondered what to do. Native scouts were already moving up the road, and Brock seemed anxious to follow. Four companies of the 41$^{st}$ waited in ranks on the beach, and militiamen dressed in surplus red jackets came ashore with trepidation.

"Follow the General!" MacDonnell yelled to the militiamen.

*A good plan*, Lockwood thought.

In short order Lockwood found Glegg, and they both sprinted after Brock. Despite his girth, Brock double-timed up the winding country road. Artillery gunners hauled five light cannon behind him, and then the infantry companies followed at a dog-trot with rifles held high.

When they had gone about a mile, Brock stopped and shouted to Glegg, "Spread the companies out! Fifty yards between."

Before running back down the line, Glegg shouted to Lockwood, "Stay with him! Try to keep him out of trouble."

Lockwood couldn't see the fort, only the brilliant flashes above it as they again moved up the road. Tecumseh's people shadowed them on the left. Norton, too, was out there somewhere. After a mile and a half, the road began to slope higher above the river. The light grew as they neared the edge of town. The British column hurried past frame houses surrounded by fenced gardens. Then, on the brow of the hill leading to the fort itself, were two enemy cannons, posted squarely in the middle of the road. The men serving them held brightly burning fuses.

Brock bellowed, "Come on! Don't stop!"

*Is this the trouble Brock should avoid?* Lockwood wondered. He ran flat out to front the general, as little good as it would do if the cannons fired.

"Good man," Brock wheezed as he sprinted by. "Keep going!"

Behind them, the Redcoat companies advanced without hesitation – but they were lined up like bowling pins on the curving road. Still, the Yankee gunners did not fire.

# The Land Between Flowing Waters

Just ahead, the countryside opened into a broad field. Beyond that was an orchard leading to a farmhouse, 300 yards away. Brock held up his arms to motion towards the field, yelling, "Wheel left!"

There the ground dipped and they were no longer in the batteries' line of fire, nor could they be seen from the fort's walls. The heavy guns at Sandwich continued to pound the Yankee fort, as did the ships in the river.

"Did anyone remember the scaling ladders?" the General asked with a breathless smile.

Tecumseh and Norton soon joined them in the hollow.

"I ask you gentlemen to hold our flanks," Brock said. "We'll batter a hole in the stockade with the light guns."

Norton pointed toward a ravine far out on the left. "Scouts say there's someone out there. Probably an ambush."

"Find out. Send for help if you need it. Watch the rear all along the line."

*****

*John Norton's Journal*

I took the Three Fires people with me as Tecumseh arrayed his warriors in an arc behind the army. We entered the ravine with caution. It was wooded with steep sides and a shallow creek flowed down the middle. We were amazed to see smoke from a dozen small fires. Instead of Long Knives we found Canadien women and children who had taken shelter there.

As they were led away to greater safety, I extended our warriors farther to the left as Brock had directed, to a point behind Fort Detroit. There we encountered American pickets on horseback. They were waiting for another force to join them from the forest, but as we ran forward, they retreated quickly. We captured one however. He was dressed in the blue uniform of a Regular, but was so much alarmed we could get nothing sensible from him. I sent him on to Brock but there was no point. A white flag already flew above the fort.

# Ken Leland

"What are those people doing?" Brock asked his officers.

They had crawled to the brow of the hill on which Fort Detroit stood. White flags fluttered from crooked staffs above the smoldering parapets. A small contingent of Yankee officers waited at the gates, apparently for someone to escort them to the British general.

"MacDonnell, Glegg, for Heaven's sake. Go find out what they want, while I pray that I already know."

\*\*\*\*\*

To Sir George Prevost
Governor-in-Chief of the Canadas

I hasten to apprise your Excellency of the capture of this very important post: 2,500 troops have this day surrendered prisoners of war, and about 25 pieces of ordnance have been taken without the sacrifice of a drop of British blood. I had not more than 700 troops, including militia, and about 600 Indians, to accomplish this service. When I detail my good fortune, your Excellency will be astonished. I have been admirably supported by Colonel Proctor, the whole of my staff, and I may justly say, every individual under my command.

> I have the honour to be, Sir,
> Your most obedient servant,
> Isaac Brock, Major General

# Chapter Six:
# Queenston Heights

## Wednesday, August 26, 1812
## Interlude

On Tuesday night, Captain Lockwood arrived at Niagara after the victory at Fort Detroit. The next morning he went into town to report for duty. As he rounded Government House, he found a carriage and driver waiting at the front steps. He approached to ask if Brock was about to leave for the day, when he was forestalled by the General's bellow from an open, third floor window.

"A truce! A truce? Lord God in Heaven, Glegg, we don't need a truce!"

Lockwood wavered on the steps.

"What's a truce for? To let the Yankees recover their pride? I could take Fort Niagara this afternoon, with a company of washerwomen! We could burn every post and shipyard on the Lakes – set them back for years. We're ready; they're not. God damn it Glegg, Governor General Prevost is insane!"

*Perhaps they don't need to see me this morning,* Lockwood thought, as he wandered back to King Street and turned to stroll towards the lake. Townsfolk, farm families in wagons, a stream of people were headed in the same direction. St. Mark's church bell rang out a call for celebration.

"Good morning, Captain Lockwood!"

"Could I shake your hand, Sir?"

"God bless the General. And you too!"

"Hurrah!" children cried as wagons rolled by.

# The Land Between Flowing Waters

Through the park at the end of the street, Lockwood could see far out into Lake Ontario. The enemy Fort Niagara on the opposite shore was shielded by trees. He followed the happy crowd along the gravel churchyard path to the grey stone building at the centre of the woods.

"Captain Lockwood, we're happy to see you," Reverend Addison said beside the church door. "Take any pew. Folks will be pleased to share."

Inside, the stone walls were topped by a whitewashed, vaulted ceiling. The oak floor was a deep golden brown. Waist high, white painted doors faced the box pews. Despite Reverend Addison's assurance, Lockwood climbed the stairs to the public gallery where he found a railing seat. Faces glanced up. Heads nodded. Hands waved from the nave below.

The church filled slowly. After a time came the sound of wheels on the gravel outside. The bell fell silent, but there was a stir in the vestibule. Parishioners turned to watch as a general officer escorted a lovely brunette with braided tresses up the aisle to the front pew. Lockwood smiled down – Isaac and Miriam. Unbidden, the congregation rose. Someone at the back began to sing.

> Glory be to the Father, and to the Son,
> And to the Holy Ghost.
> As it was in the beginning, is now, and ever shall be;
> World without end,
> Amen.

Brock was having have his Thanksgiving Service for the victory at Detroit.

"Captain Lockwood, you must have been on your way to see Miriam," Brock said, later that afternoon at Government House. "I saw you in the gallery."

"I only arrived last night, General."

"Nothing much going on until this infernal armistice ends. Take a few days. Visit with your family, enjoy the countryside."

"If there's nothing further today, I will go to see Miriam."

"Of course. Please tell her, we'll take supper out to the farm tonight around eight. You'll join us, won't you?"

"I'll be most pleased to see you then, General."

232

# Ken Leland

"Alex!"

Miriam ran to embrace her brother as he came through the garden gate. "Isaac said you were in church. Why didn't you ride back with us?"

"You looked so happy, I didn't want to intrude."

"Nonsense! ...Well, yes, we are happy, but you're always welcome."

Lockwood leaned back out of his sister's arms to glance over her shoulder, toward the shop's bay window. Inside, behind the sheer drapes, a shadow moved. "For a moment, Miriam, when I saw you two walking up the aisle, arm in arm, I thought..."

"A wedding? Don't you think Isaac's a bit distracted just now?" Miriam smiled. Her hands still clutched her brother's arms. "Isaac's asked twice, most politely, most earnestly, but until we have peace, I'm making him wait....about that."

She blushed but Lockwood's attention was elsewhere.

Janie appeared at the door, her head up, watchful. Her straightened black hair was tied in a bun atop her head. She wore a lovely cream-coloured, long-sleeved dress, with buttons at her throat. Baby Anna fussed in a shoulder sling. Janie patted her daughter reassuringly, but her gaze was fixed on Lockwood. Descending the porch steps, she listened to their conversation. She sought his eyes above Miriam's braids, and finding them, did not let go. As she waited, he leaned in to embrace Miriam once more, and then they turned to greet Janie.

"What must I do," Janie asked Lockwood, "to make you come see us?" She lifted tiny Anna from the sling, and eased her daughter into his arms.

"I'll go make tea," Miriam announced, though neither Lockwood nor Janie heard.

"Oh! How beautiful she is," he said. Lockwood cradled Anna along the length of his left arm, holding her chest with his hand. Anna complained not at all, but opened her eyes wide at the stranger.

"Alex, who taught you to hold a baby like that?"

He glanced at Janie and asked, "Is Jeremy here?"

"All the surveyors left for Twenty Mile Creek. He won't be back for a few weeks." Janie stared at him. Suddenly she blurted, "Alex, will you be staying in Niagara? It's been so long. I've missed..."

# The Land Between Flowing Waters

"Janie, it should have been you," he said as he returned Anna gently. "You should have taught me."

Lockwood brushed past her.

"The General is coming for us at eight. I have to tell Miriam."

*****

Lockwood left his army uniform behind when he rode to Twenty Mile Creek. He was dressed in a plain white collarless shirt beneath a sombre grey jacket. A dark blue ribbon circled his straw hat, and its wide brim shaded the late afternoon sun.

Jeremy Roberts, his life-long friend and rival, stood in the wheat stubble beside the creek. Roberts stretched his back and shoulder muscles gingerly.

"Does it still hurt?" Lockwood asked, reining up beside him. The wound from the Thames River skirmish was almost healed.

"Not unless I forget and lean against a tree. Then I howl."

The Twenty tumbled down the mountain in two waterfalls. Here beside the second falls were a grist mill and sawmill. The stone wheels rumbled as they ground summer wheat, and the planking-saw screeched interminably.

"The owners want to hive off farm lots up on the escarpment," Roberts said. "Hope springs eternal. I can't guess who'll buy land 'til the war's over."

"Shouldn't take long to survey that much," Lockwood said.

"No, it won't. But we're to stake all the land between the mountain and the lake, from the Fifteen to the Twenty – and that'll take the rest of summer. Most of next summer too."

They watched the swift-flowing brook for a long time. With a splash, a trout rose to take a water-strider. At last, Lockwood sighed.

"Jeremy, I just don't know what to do with myself. I'm lost." Lockwood split a wheat-stalk with his fingernail. "Nothing seems to matter anymore."

Roberts said nothing until finally, "You're lonely. Janie says..." Roberts fell silent again and eyed Lockwood's clothes. "You must be planning to visit Patience."

"Hope springs.... Lord, Jeremy. It's no good for us. I won't leave the army until those people go back to sleep."

"Patience loves you, Alex. She'll wait."

# Ken Leland

*****

Savery Brock
Guernsey

My dear brother Savery,

You doubtless feel much anxiety on my account. I am really placed in a most awkward predicament. If I get through my present difficulties with tolerable success, I cannot but obtain praise. Were the Americans of one mind, the opposition I could make would be unavailing; but I am not without hope that their divisions may be the saving of this province. A river of about 500 yards divides the troops. My instructions oblige me to adopt defensive measures, and I have evinced great forbearance. It is thought that, without the aid of the sword, the American people may be brought to a due sense of their own interests. I firmly believe I could at this moment sweep everything before me between Fort Niagara and Buffalo, but my success would be transient...

Men of the U.S. regiments desert over to us frequently, as they are tired of the service. The militia, being chiefly composed of enraged democrats, are more ardent and anxious to engage, but they have neither subordination nor discipline. They die very fast. You will hear of some decisive action in the course of a fortnight, or in all probability we shall return to a state of tranquility. I say decisive, because if I should be beaten, the province is inevitably gone; and should I be victorious, I do not imagine the gentry from the other side will be anxious to return to the charge.

It is certainly something singular that we should be upwards of two months in a state of warfare, and that along this widely extended frontier not a single death, either natural or by the sword, should have occurred among the troops under my command, and we have not been altogether idle, nor has a single desertion taken place.

I am quite anxious for this state of warfare to end, as I wish much to join Lord Wellington and to see you all.

Major General Isaac Brock
Government House, Niagara

# The Land Between Flowing Waters

*****

"Mr. Babcock? Mrs. Babcock? Is anyone at home?"

"Alex?...Alex!"

Her long curls flew as Patience rushed onto the front porch to wrap her arms around Lockwood's neck. She kissed him emphatically, and then kissed him again most tenderly as he struggled to say, "Patience, I'm still a soldier, just not in uniform."

"I don't care. The Lord has sent thee back to me."

She gripped his hands and pulled him inside. Lockwood looked toward the dining room, then down the hall to the empty kitchen.

"Patience, where's your father?"

"He's in gaol."

"What!"

"He's been there almost two weeks."

"Where's your mother?

"I'm watching the farm. Everyone else is in Pelham Corners."

His grip on Patience's hands tightened in astonishment.

"The Elders, almost all the men, are in gaol. Families stand on the gaol-house steps, singing hymns in protest."

Patience drew him up the stairs, step by step.

"Alex, come with me. I beg thee."

Patience pulled him inside her bedroom. She pressed against him, forcing his back against the door, and kissed him until she was breathless.

"Every night I dream of you. Every morning I wake up burning."

Patience raised her arms to undo the buttons at the back of her dress. Alex kissed her forehead, and caressed her breasts until the dress fell to the floor.

"Alex, be the man I dream of."

Afternoon light streamed down upon her bed, where Lockwood lay beside Patience. He kissed her rosy neck and shoulders as she tensed, until finally she shuddered and gasped. His fingertips moved slower and then were still. She smiled happily and turned to nuzzle the tip of his nose.

"That was most wonderful," she whispered. "But now thou must teach me."

Her hands slid down to unbutton his trousers.

"My love," she said holding him, "show me what to do."

Five-score women and children sang on the steps of the Pelham Corners Gaol.

In the early evening light, Margaret Babcock saw the family wagon rolling up the street. It was her daughter, Patience – but, Lord of Blessings, beside her was that soldier, Captain Lockwood. The man jumped down, then reached up for Patience. He held her waist, and then floated her to earth like a cottonwood seed. As they approached, Margaret sighed in resignation. Her daughter needed a man, and this most likely, was to be the one.

Patience took her mother's arm and led her aside, as neighbour ladies pretended nonchalance. At the next Quaker Meeting for Business, Mrs. Babcock knew there would be no end to criticism of her headstrong daughter.

"Alex has an idea how to get the Elders out of gaol. Please listen to him, Mother."

"When should I start knitting booties?"

"What? Please, Mother. This is serious."

Patience guided her back to where Lockwood waited, straw hat in hand.

"Still a soldier – out of uniform?" she asked.

"Yes, Mrs. Babcock."

"What is thy suggestion?"

"Patience says the Elders are in gaol because they won't pay the militia non-service fine. It's up to five pounds because we're at war."

"The amount doesn't matter, Mr. Lockwood. Now the money goes to support the fighting. Before it was just...well...lunch and beer money for the King's Birthday."

"What if I paid Mr. Babcock's fine?"

"He would not let thee do that. The end is still the same: violence and killing. And besides, would thou pay five pounds for each Quaker? My Henry would stay in gaol until every last man is free."

Lockwood frowned, but he'd already guessed that idea wouldn't work. "All right. I have another idea. Mrs. Babcock, do you want your husband home beside you?"

# The Land Between Flowing Waters

"More than thou can imagine."

"Then I'll try to make it so."

Lockwood climbed the steps to knock at the gaol house door.

"What's he doing?" Mrs. Babcock asked her daughter.


"Do you know me?" Lockwood demanded of the County Sheriff.

The Sheriff squinted at Lockwood and decided that he did. "Why yes! You're that scoundrel what tricked the Quaker girl 'bout being a soldier. T'was Patience Babcock, waren't it?"

A voice called from somewhere in the back. "Alex? What art thou doing here?"

The gaol was filled with dozens of bearded men in plain shirts. The Sheriff was alone, but Friends were helping wash the supper dishes. There were sleeping pallets everywhere, both inside and outside the three small, unlocked cells.

"I'm trying to get you out of gaol, Mr. Babcock, and everyone else too," Lockwood announced loudly.

There was a friendly commotion at the expectation.

"Now, hold on a minute. I'll have no gaol-breaking here," the Sheriff cautioned.

"Not a bit of it, Sheriff. But you say you know me?"

"Aye, you're that Captain Lockyer or Lockwood fellow."

"Lockwood. And I'm a King's officer. You agree?"

"Oh, aye."

"Tomorrow, you and I, Sheriff, we're going to collect fines for all these men."

"I'd be glad of it! But they won't pay."

"We'll make them pay!" Lockwood shouted so all could hear. "The Sheriff and I will go to every farm, every business. He and I will agree on personal property worth five pounds – no more – and we'll confiscate it. Sacks of corn or wheat, a yearling calf, a bolt of cloth or keg of nails, whatever meets the fine. We'll carry it to Niagara, and sell everything to the British Quartermaster there. Then we'll give the receipts to the clerk at Government House as payment."

Lockwood appealed to the men. "This way, the Crown is served, but no man has acted against his conscience. All go free. Is it agreed?"

The Friends turned to one another.

"I think we should pray on it," one Elder said. "Come back in the morning, young man."

Lockwood strode out into the red-striped sunset. The families gathered round.

"Your men may never speak to me again," he said, "but by this time tomorrow, they'll be free."

## Monday, October 12, 1812
## The Twenty

Ten-year-old John Ellis sat on the front porch swing as Grandpa and Grandma Lockwood loaded the covered wagon. John rocked slowly, using a broom handle to push against the floor. Captain Lockwood's scarlet jacket lay folded on the porch rail; his scabbard belt was draped beside it. In shirtsleeves, Lockwood carried out the last of the blankets and pillows to cushion the family furniture. The wagon was nearly full.

"Miriam will cry. There's no room for the pianoforte," Lois said as she slid onto the swing to snuggle young John.

"The horses have too much as it is," Asa complained.

Lockwood trudged back to the porch and leaned against the rail. Without a word he stared at the oak swing.

"Yes. I know," Asa said to his son. "It'll be the first thing to go. Then the windows, the doors, the books..."

John began to cry.

"Hush, old man," Lois said. "The Yankees will never get across the river. Isaac won't let 'em."

Lois hugged John. "Come on, let's get the horses hitched."

"Mother, I'll do it," Lockwood said.

"Let them go, Alex," Asa said quietly. "The boy needs to help."

Clouds gathered. It would rain before noon, but the maples leaves burned bright. Lockwood drove the wagon into town to meet the Benjamins. His father Asa was on the bench beside him. Lois and John sat on a mattress inside the Conestoga. Dry leaves blew across the road.

"Janie got a letter," Asa said. "Jeremy's got a new idea where we might hold up."

# The Land Between Flowing Waters

Lockwood drove slowly past the bare peach orchard, and then turned left onto John Street. Matthew Benjamin's freight wagon was parked on the gravel driveway in front of his father's house. Janie's parents came to the doorway as Matthew unlatched the gate. Three-year-old Ethan chased a chicken under the porch. Janie carried little Anna in her sling. Miriam stood in dismay beside her travel trunk.

"Hello," Asa called. "Looks like everyone's ready."

Lois fell into Sarah Benjamin's arms.

"Don't you worry," Sarah said to her dearest friend. "We done this before, and it all turned out right."

"I know, I know," Lois admitted. "I just never thought we'd..."

"Me neither," Sarah sniffed.


The families gathered together.

"I know our fathers found that cabin on the Welland River," Janie began, "but Jeremy has an idea, too."

"What does he say, dear?" Lois asked.

Janie began to read aloud from the letter her husband had sent:


> I've put a deposit on a farm, up on the Mountain by the Twenty. Alex gave me the idea. I'm building a cabin on weekends, but till it's ready a Quaker family is happy to take you in. Alex knows the Babcocks. He can tell you all about them.


"Quakers! See, isn't that a wonderful idea?" Janie smiled.

Alex only stared at her, saying nothing.

The silence stretched on until at last Asa asked, "Well, Son, are they nice folks? Is this a good idea?"

Everyone waited. Finally, Alex took a deep breath.

"Yes. They're wonderful people. If Jeremy says they're willing, you should go there."


Together, Matthew and his father Ben inspected the wagon harness one last time.

"You remember about Siegfried?" Matthew said as he patted the lead stallion. "He doesn't like nippy dogs."

240

"Lord, Matt! *I* told you that, years ago."

"Dad, I got to report at noon," Matthew said as they stood alone. Matthew wore the blue-and-red sergeant's uniform of the Provincial Light Artillery.

Ben's voice trembled. "Keep your head down, Son. Look after your men."

"I know Dad. And you'll all be fine with the Quakers."

"Yes, you're right," Ben said as he patted Matthew's arm. "But once I know everyone's safe, Asa and I made a promise. Even old men like us don't have to take this lying down."

"Daddy, you got to be careful too."

Asa and his son walked down the road as rain drops began to fall.

"Dad," Lockwood said. "The Babcock girl, Patience, she thinks she's in love with me."

"Jeremy knows about that, doesn't he?"

"Yes, Dad. But they're fine people. You'll be safer there than anywhere else. This really is a good idea."

They walked in silence for a while.

"I forgot to let the chickens out," Asa said.

"What?"

"I forgot."

"I'll go back and open the hen house," Lockwood promised, as they turned the corner onto King Street. "Dad, you've got to stop worrying."

"Look out for yourself, and keep your men safe."

"That's what you always said, Dad. I remember."

"Ben and me. Once the families are out of harm's way..."

Father and son walked on together, but soon it was time to leave. The rain was falling harder.

As the storm gathered, Janie and Miriam whispered in the back of the jostling Benjamin wagon. Anna's tiny arm stretched over her mother's breast as she nursed.

"Ethan and John Ellis will be safe with Quakers," Janie said.

"But you can't leave Anna behind," Miriam replied. "Are you sure about coming back to Niagara?"

"I can help. Matthew, Jeremy, Alex, so many... We can't turn our backs on them."

# The Land Between Flowing Waters

*****

"Mama, Poppa, the Benjamins and Lockwoods are here!" Seventeen-year-old Hopestill Babcock shouted as he dashed up the rain-sodden farm lane.

Patience stepped out onto the porch, her long curls gathered in a kerchief behind her ears. It was two hours past dark. Torches guttered along the lane, guiding their guests.

Younger sister Dinah hovered near Patience as Mr. Roberts led the wagons into the farmyard. Henry and Margaret Babcock came out to greet their guests.

When the elderly Mrs. Lockwood descended, Patience's mother welcomed her with a kiss. As Patience stepped forward to greet Mrs. Lockwood, she wondered if this dear, white-haired woman knew that her son...that her son...Patience had no idea how to finish that thought.

Alex's father, a most handsome older man, shook hands and thanked the Babcocks profusely.

A ten-year-old boy jumped down.

"Thou must be John Ellis," Patience's younger brother Nathan said, shaking his hand. "Is thy Father really General Brock?" The boys disappeared into the night before Mrs. Babcock could admonish Nathan for his forwardness.

Mr. Roberts was at the Benjamin wagon, his sleepy son draped over his shoulder. Patience's parents came to greet the Benjamins. Dinah then took Mrs. Benjamin's arm to lead her into the house. Mrs. Lockwood and Mrs. Babcock followed.

The men gathered to take the wagons into the stable. As the second wagon moved aside, Patience saw those who had filled her thoughts – Miriam and Janie.

"Ye are most welcome. My name is Patience," she said as she held out her hands.

"Thank you. We're so very grateful," Miriam said.

"It's wonderful what you're doing for us," Janie added. "I can't begin to thank you enough."

# Ken Leland

Even in the flickering torchlight, Patience could see Janie's poise and beauty. Patience knew not whether to cry or rage at the hopelessness of her love for Alex. But then, before she could turn to flee, Anna began to fret in Janie's sling.

"Oh, thou hast a baby!" Patience said in surprise.

"Anna's a little tired from traveling all day."

"Please, please come into the house. We have a cradle," Patience said. "Could I? Could I carry her?"

"Of course! I'm worn out too."


*What could Mr. Roberts be playing at?* Patience wondered as she lay awake that night. It was late, and the house was quiet. Her sister Dinah snored softly on the other side of the bed.

*Mr. Roberts knows how I've thrown myself at Alex. But Alex loves Janie – I know he does. Can it be that Janie loves them both?* Patience was dumbstruck, but realised it might be true. Both were Janie's friends since childhood.

*Does Mr. Roberts think Janie and I will fight for Alex, and that I will win? That can't be. I'm a dandelion; she is a black rose. What possible good to him, Janie and I meeting this way?*

She heard tiny Anna crying in the night, but Patience soon drifted off to sleep.


Before breakfast the grandfathers, Ben and Asa, announced they would travel with Mr. Roberts to work on his cabin. Both were dressed in leathers, like hunters. They went to retrieve their long rifles from the wagons, and Sarah and Lois followed to bid their husbands goodbye. Patience spied from behind the sitting-room curtain and strained to hear what was said, but their words went unheard.


"You're such an awful liar, Ben," Sarah said to her husband.

Lois fumed with crossed arms. "You two are going back to Niagara, aren't you?"

"Don't tell the children. Don't tell Miriam and Janie," Asa said.

"You fought the last war. Why again?"

"Our boys are in it. We can't stand aside."

# The Land Between Flowing Waters

"I love you, you dear old fool," Sarah said as she threw herself on Ben's neck.

Lois buried her head against Asa's chest. "Don't you dare die on me."

Mr. Roberts came downstairs alone.

"Janie's still asleep," he told Patience before heading out the front door. "Anna kept her up half the night. Tell her I'll be back...well, as soon as I can."

The three men rode out an hour after dawn on Monday, October 12.

After lunch, Patience watched from the hall as Miriam and Janie talked quietly in the parlour. Later in the afternoon, when everyone else was in the cornfields, Patience minded Ethan while he dug in the flower garden. From the corner of her eye she saw the young women disappearing towards the barn. Patience scooped up Ethan, promising to show him baby chicks, then hurried after. She found them saddling horses.

Suddenly, Patience realised where their fathers had really gone.

"Don't tell me ye are for cabin building," Patience said stiffly. Ethan squirmed down, out of her arms.

Miriam cinched her saddle. "We're going back, Patience. We left notes for our mothers."

Janie adjusted Anna's sling, but before she could mount, Patience touched her jacket sleeve.

"Dear Janie, thou should not do this. Yankees could take thee and Anna as slaves."

Janie burst into tears.

"That's why my brother is fighting, why all the black men are. There will be so many hurt – but we can help. I will help."

Ethan returned, a hen tucked under his arm. Janie kissed him quickly and swung up onto her horse. "Mommy will be back soon, Ethan."

"Ye will not reach Niagara before dark," Patience cautioned.

"We'll know the roads before then," Miriam replied.

Janie leaned down to take Patience's hand.

"Never doubt him. I was wrong....." Janie looked away momentarily. "Alex will come to you when all this is over."

Miriam and Janie with Anna in the sling rode down the farm lane in the golden light of autumn.

Patience balanced Ethan on her hip as he waved goodbye to his mother. "Did you find the chicks?" Patience asked as Ethan began to sniffle.

She followed him back into the barn, but stumbled when she realised what had just happened.

*Janie gives Alex to me! But she doesn't know he still loves her.*

\*\*\*\*\*

"At least you brung your own blankets," the Fort George Garrison Sergeant said. "We muster an hour before dawn."

Jeremy, Asa and Ben spread their bedrolls to settle in for the night. Early evening rain dripped from the eves of the long, open horse stable. The walkway between the feed boxes was dry, and mostly clear of manure. Two lines of horses blocked the cold, wet wind to create an illusion of warmth.

"The barrack's full, and the mess-hall too," the sergeant said before leaving. "This is all we got, lessen you want a tent in the mud...but I don't recommend it."

Late that night in Niagara, a small group of senior officers gathered on the third floor of Government House. They waited for Brock to appear before beginning a quiet supper. Since dawn, General Roger Hale Sheaffe, commander of the recently arrived 49th Regiment, had inspected every British post from Fort Erie to Chippewa. Aide-de-Camps MacDonnell and Glegg had examined all the militia bivouacs and artillery batteries between Niagara and the Falls.

Brock worked alone in his office, penning his final thoughts for the day to his superior at Quebec City.

# The Land Between Flowing Waters

Sir George Prevost
Governor-in-Chief of the Canadas
Quebec City

The vast number of troops which have been this day added to the strong force previously collected on the opposite side convinces me, with other indications, that an attack is not far distant. I have in consequence directed every exertion to be made to complete the militia to 2000 men, but fear that I shall not be able to affect my object with willing, well-disposed characters. Were it not for the numbers of Americans in our ranks, we might defy all their efforts against this part of the province.

Yr Ob'dt Servant,
Major General Isaac Brock
Fort George
October 12, 1812

Brock laid the note aside and headed in to supper. It was late. The letter could wait until tomorrow's courier.

A little before midnight, Janie and Miriam rode into Niagara. In the moonlight between rain clouds, they opened the stable doors behind the Niagara Dress and Tailor Shoppe.

Captain Lockwood slept in his own bed that night. Lieutenant Merritt and the rest of the Provincial Mounted Squadron were bunked throughout the farmhouse and barn.

## Tuesday, October 13, 1812
## The Battle of Queenston Heights

Captain Lockwood woke in anger. It was pitch dark outside, and some damn fool was pounding on the barn with a sledge hammer.

Thump!

There it was again! The sound floated through the blowing curtains.

246

Then, after two thumps, the second almost overlapping the first, he realised it wasn't a man with a hammer.

"Merritt!" Lockwood yelled down the farmhouse hallway. "Wake up. That's artillery!" Lockwood slid into his trousers, snatched up his sabre and ran downstairs. "It's started! Saddle up, everybody! Now! Now!"

Lockwood grabbed his long rifle and cartridges at the front door, then clanged the dinner bell before sprinting for the stable. Bleary-eyed troopers began to spill from the house and barn.

"It must be Queenston," Lieutenant Merritt called as the squadron galloped down the farm lane, only to pause at River Road. There was a high wind blowing from the north.

"Captain Lockwood, there's someone on the road!" A trooper pointed to a figure approaching in the dark.

"Halt!" Lockwood shouted to the rider.

"Halt yourself, Lockwood. I haven't got time!"

It was General Brock, on the road alone.

Brock slowed for only a moment. "Wake Glegg and MacDonnell at Government House. Get Sheaffe and Norton moving. Bring everyone!"

Then he was gone.

*****

"I tell you, that's a boat," one sentry said to another in the early morning darkness.

The guards stood on the lower terrace of Queenston Heights, looking out onto the river. The moon had set hours before. Dark blobs moved on the water between the cliffs.

"My God, there's lots of 'em! The Yankees are crossing!"

The sentries blew whistles, then fired into the darkness.

In the gloom, Yankee soldiers in open boats were rowing upstream, heading for the narrow beach beyond the cliff on the Upper Canada shore. Each bateau held a score of blue-coated, United States Army Regulars. The Canadian militia sentries fired, killing and wounding a few men in several boats.

Above, on the bare north face of Queenston Heights, was Captain Williams' Light Company of the British 49th. William's 90

# The Land Between Flowing Waters

men had spent the night in wet misery. They guarded the redan, an earthen-walled battery with two heavy guns.

Provincial Gunnery Sergeant Matthew Benjamin was one of the half-dozen artillerymen on the mountainside that night. At the sound of the sentries' whistles, Benjamin awoke on the muddy ground, between the single massive cannon that threw an 18-pound ball and the squat, deadly mortar that fired 8-inch exploding shells. As the artillerymen scrambled to load the heavy guns, William's riflemen pressed forward to the redan's edge, but they could see very little except muzzle-flashes from the sentries on the terrace below.

The American landing site was upriver, beyond the curve in the escarpment's face. Once the invaders were on the Upper Canada beach, they were safe from British gunfire, but in the water, the heavy guns at the redan as well as the light artillery in Queenston Village could be brought to bear. As soon each boat landed, Yankee marksmen hurried along the beach to engage the sentries, who eventually retreated towards Queenston, only a few hundred yards away.

In the muddy redan, the artillery officer shouted. Sergeant Benjamin limped stiffly to the thigh-high pyramid of iron balls. *By golly,* he thought as he lifted the topmost sphere, *we lugged them bastards up the hill. It's gonna be pure pleasure to send 'em down again.*

After an artilleryman rammed a cloth gunpowder bag down the long barrel, Benjamin tipped in the cannonball. While a third man shoved the ramrod down the barrel, Benjamin rushed to help aim the gun. At the touch-hole, the Gunnery Officer pricked the powder bag and inserted the fuse.

"Fire!"

Oh, such a roar! Benjamin watched the water, but the blob that was a Yankee longboat just kept coming, so they made to try again. The Mortar Sergeant thought he could tell where the Yankee boats were launching, so he aimed at the far shore, where the shells burst in the air above the trees. Benjamin thought the mortar was doing a lot more good than the long gun.

Down in the village it was still dark, but from the redan they could see British musket flashes all along the wharf. And the 1st Lincolns had a 9-pounder down by the landing, blasting away. Maybe the Lincolns were doing some good too, since two or three American launches seem to fall off and drift away.

# Ken Leland

Captain Dennis of the 49th was the British officer in charge of the defense of Queenston. At his command were two companies of his own regiment, one in the village and another at the redan with Captain Williams, plus 200 militiamen of the Lincoln and York Regiments at bivouac on the River Road.

When the firing started at 4 A.M., Dennis was asleep in Hamilton House at the north end of the village, farthest from the Heights. From the east lawn, Dennis could see his sentries at the foot of the mountain firing towards the river. In the moments that followed, red-coated regulars joined in the musketry from the stone warehouse by the wharf. The first militia units began to arrive and mustered in the street – Queenston Street, that led directly to the Heights at the south end of the village. Dennis sent officers to Hamilton Cove, less than 100 yards away, to discover if Yankees were landing there. He also sent runners to the town wharf, with orders that the regulars join him at the lower terrace.

Runners reported that some boats seemed to be adrift in the river. Dennis left behind a mixed company of regulars and militia to guard the cove and began a march down Queenston Street, collecting reinforcements as he went.

Dennis' men double-timed toward the base of the mountain. "Wheel left and right when we reach the terrace," Dennis shouted to the men jogging behind.

Yankee cannons opened fire from across the river. In the darkness, women and children fled from houses on both sides of Queenston Street. Yankee round-shot and canister played against the stone wharf, sometimes bouncing up into the houses on the plain above. Waist-high rock walls surrounded many homes, but still, people were rightly terrified and headed for safer ground beyond River Road.

"We'll push them back across the river," Dennis encouraged the 100 men who followed him through the press of fleeing civilians.

The lane from the wharf met Portage Road at the base of the Heights. Dennis led his men to the intersection, where 50 regulars waited in a battle line. Dennis extended the line with his reinforcements, and then leapt out in front to lead the way across the narrow flat ground.

Ahead, there were moving shadows at 100 yards. Companies of American infantry had climbed up from the beach. In the darkness, they were advancing straight for Dennis in a double battle line. The Light Company, up in the redan, started to fire down the slope at the invaders.

# The Land Between Flowing Waters

Before Dennis could react, the first row of Americans came to a stop and fired a volley at 75 yards. Dennis went down, shot through the lower leg and left arm. Wounded men screamed all around. The British line staggered, and then replied with a ragged volley of its own, only to be hit again moments later by the second American line. The Light Company poured down volleys into the gloom, only guessing at the American advance from muzzle flashes.

On the terrace, the British line faltered and began to give ground. They dragged their dead and wounded as they retreated toward a stone wall at the village edge. The American infantry found themselves sheltered only by darkness, facing men behind a wall and snipers on the hillside to their rear. So the Yankees retreated too, back across the terrace and down the steep embankment to their initial landing site.

It was a few minutes later, at about 5:30 A.M., that General Brock arrived – quite alone – after riding hard through the night from Niagara.

*****

Lockwood and Lieutenant Merritt galloped into Niagara only minutes after meeting Brock on River Road. A strong, cold wind blew from the lake, masking the sound of artillery at Queenston. It was still quite dark, and as yet no one seemed to be awake either at Fort George or in the town, so Merritt's troopers split up to raise the alarm. Lockwood angled towards the Indian Council Hall. On King Street he found John Norton sprinting toward the Haudenosaunee camp.

"Norton," Lockwood yelled, "That's artillery at Queenston!"

"General Sheaffe is awake," Norton answered. "We march on his orders."

The Nations' camp was in turmoil. Women packed food and lit torches as warriors prepared for battle. The men stripped to loincloths and paired off to apply paint. From across the Commons, Lockwood heard bugles at the fort. Now lanterns were appearing in town.

Lockwood hurried anxiously through the camp. On the dim path leading to the Council Hall were a handful of Haudenosaunee Clan Mothers, arrayed in a line. Men adorned for battle quietly

250

approached one or another. At the elbow of one Clan Mother was the young translator Lockwood remembered from the Grand River. He watched as she cupped a sea shell in both hands. From it, streams of smoke from burning sweet-grass whipped through the air. The Clan Mothers bathed the men in the purifying smoke as they prayed.

Turning, the young translator noticed Lockwood standing aside. She stared at him and then looked again. Finally, she shook her head in dismay. She hurried over to grab his arm and pulled him before the Clan Mother who washed his head, his heart, and his body in smoke.

"*Niawen*," Lockwood choked gratefully.

The young woman only thumped his red jacket with her fist. "This is a target," she said. And, with a smile, "Keep standing."

Then she pushed him away with both hands and turned to the next man in line.

Grey light grew in the east as Norton's war-band gathered. A courier from the fort galloped across the Commons. As the Haudenosaunee waited, a boom echoed from American Fort Niagara across the river. Moments later, three more sharp detonations sent cannon balls flying toward the town. The British 24-pound guns on Fort George's eastern bastion crashed in reply.

The courier reined to a stop before Norton. "General Sheaffe says to march for Queenston as quick as you can." Lockwood pulled himself into the saddle. "Reinforcements will be right behind you," the messenger said.

*****

Miriam woke screaming when a cannon ball struck her neighbour's chimney. Janie ran from the back bedroom and both peered out the second floor window. Two red blurs darted through the sky to land somewhere on Queen Street.

"Get Anna," Miriam gasped. "We're for the cellar."

They ran into the kitchen and pulled up the trap door. As they tumbled down the steps, the guns from Fort George spoke in defiance.

*****

# The Land Between Flowing Waters

Dawn began to light the river valley. Brock had established his headquarters on the Hamilton House lawn. There he found Captain Dennis, his left arm wrapped in a torn bed sheet and his bleeding right calf tightly bound.

"Captain Dennis," Brock said, "You should be with the Surgeon."

"I can still fight, General."

Brock turned to Colonel MacDonnell, who – along with Major Glegg – had arrived only moments before. "MacDonnell, send Lieutenant Merritt's troopers for the Grenadier companies at Chippewa. They must hurry."

"General!" a messenger called as he sprinted up the slope from the river. "Yankee bateaux are heading for the Cove!"

Brock turned to Glegg. "Take a bugler. Bring the Light Company down from the redan. Williams isn't doing any good up there."

"Sir," MacDonnell asked, "will the main attack be at the Cove?"

"It has to be," Brock replied. "They can't get up the mountain. They're trapped on that beach. So come on, Dennis. Let's welcome our visitors to Queenston."

At 6 A.M., in growing light, four American longboats were heading for the cove's small pier. Perhaps they were being swept there by Niagara's strong current, or perhaps it was the commanding officer's intention. In any case, an American force of slightly more than 100 regulars was spotted by the guards Dennis had placed at Hamilton Cove earlier in the morning. This perhaps accidental attack distracted British attention from the Yankee soldiers farther upstream who had, in fact, found a trail to ascend the Heights.

As the longboats approached, the American oarsmen fought steadily against the back-current along the shore. Dennis clung to the wheel of a 9-pounder. Behind him was a collection of British regulars and an under-strength company of Lincoln Militia, concealed high on the riverbank above the wharf.

"Hold your fire. They're working hard to get closer," Dennis ordered.

The enemy spotted the British ambush just as their boats ground ashore. Men not plying oars raised muskets as Dennis brought down the slow-match to the cannon's fuse. Canister-shot tore into the first boat, killing or wounding everyone aboard.

"Fire!" Dennis yelled.

# Ken Leland

The British volley brought down most of the enemy before they could step ashore. Bodies of the dead and wounded littered the shallow water. A few Yankee muskets replied, but this fight was already over. The battered invaders raised their hands in surrender. Loyalist militia scrambled down the riverbank as regulars stood guard above. The quick were sorted from the dead, and after only a few minutes, a file of prisoners began the long walk to captivity at Fort George.

When Glegg returned to Hamilton House with the Light Company, Brock ordered Williams to reinforce the seemingly threatened Cove.

"I'm going up to the redan," Brock told Glegg and MacDonnell. "It's getting lighter. Maybe I can see what's happening across the water."

"Sir, do you really think..."

"Stay here should something interesting occur," Brock directed with a smile. "I'll be back in a moment."

Alone, Brock trotted up the street, heading directly for the Heights. On his left, he could see American artillery flashes from two different batteries on the eastern shore. Shot and grape fell heavily on the Canadian side. Several abandoned houses had already collapsed into the street. As he passed, a militia 9-pound gun on the wharf was hit, killing two of the gunners and leaving a third screaming with a severed arm.

A lieutenant of the 41st ran out from the stone wall facing the Heights, yelling, "What can we do, General?"

"I'll be back," Brock shouted as he ran to the right for Portage Road. The road was carved into the mountain's side, and he followed it up to the redan.

"General, Sir!" Gunnery Sergeant Matthew Benjamin exclaimed in surprise.

Brock plunged into the redan to collapse, winded, on the dirt embankment. There were only a handful of artillerymen left to wield the guns.

"Where are they...launching from?" Brock panted.

Matthew pointed.

# The Land Between Flowing Waters

At this elevation, Brock could see the American embarkation point in the growing light. Beside him, the mortar crashed. Brock followed the black arching shell until it burst on the far shore.

"Try dropping a few in the trees higher up," Brock advised. "Troops must be hiding there before boarding."

The Yankee bateaux still plied the river, heading upstream, around the cliff and out of sight. *Why?* Brock wondered. *Surely, there's no way...*

Shouts and gunfire erupted from the Heights above. A bullet splanged from the skin of the 18-pounder beside him as Americans scrambled down the hillside behind them. There were 200 or more.

"God help us," Brock gasped. "There *is* a way up! Come on, men!"

Brock plunged over the lip of the redan face, sliding though the scree as mud and rocks tumbled down the slope. The handful of gunners followed him across the lower terrace, sprinting for the stone wall. From there, a score of militia fired at the Americans pouring into the redan, but it was a long uphill shot.

"Who remembered to spike the guns?" Brock asked the exhausted artillerymen as they crouched behind the wall.

The men looked at each other, appalled.

"Then we'll have to go back up," Brock said. "Rest. Find a musket. I'll be back." Brock began another gruelling jog, back to headquarters at Hamilton House.

"This time I'm going to ride," Brock vowed as he gathered what men he could at the rallying point. "MacDonnell, stay here," he ordered. "Bring up reinforcements when they arrive."

Brock mounted. Captain Williams brought half his company; the rest remained to guard the now unthreatened Cove. There were also some York and Lincoln Militia in the small force that followed Brock up Queenston Street.

"Glegg, we have to spike those guns, or they'll kill Sheaffe's men when he arrives."

"I understand, General."

It was almost 7:30 A.M.

# Ken Leland

Climbing the Heights' mud-slick face was impossible, so Brock led the 50 men who followed him to Portage Road. Benjamin and the other artillery gunners saw the General dismount and hurried to join his pitiful force.

"We're for the redan," Brock called out. "Any man who reaches it, use nails to spike the guns. Jam them in the touch-hole."

Brock and Glegg led the desperate little group up the wet gravel road. More than 200 blue-coated regulars waited, many in the redan trying to shift the guns to fire on Queenston below. The rest of the Yankees formed an oblique line to protect their flank. It was this portion that wheeled to face Brock's charge. Scores of Yankee riflemen fired as the British scrambled up the road.

Brock's left hand was hit, twisting his body slightly. Immediately, a second bullet entered his right upper chest and exited from his back. He fell to the ground insensible as the remaining British soldiers rushed toward the redan.

Glegg saw Brock fall. He stumbled on for a few more paces, but he knew it was no good. All around, Redcoats were going down. The wounded screamed and writhed upon the road. The unmoving were dead. A few men escaped into the brush beside the road. Glegg turned back.

He found a young soldier already kneeling over Brock, saying, "Oh, Sir. Are you much hurt?"

But Brock was already gone.

With the help of a black artillery sergeant, Glegg carried Brock's body back down the road. The boy trailed behind, dragging their muskets. The attack had dissolved. A few Redcoats limped back down the road, following the men carrying Brock.

"Lord, save us. They killed the General!"

The news could not be hidden. Glegg and Sergeant Benjamin carried the general's body past the few militiamen remaining at the stone wall, then north along Queenston Street. Soon they stopped at an abandoned house. From the garden Glegg saw MacDonnell riding at the head of a company of newly-arrived York Militia.

"Wait here," Glegg told Benjamin, then he ran out into the road.

"What are you doing here?" MacDonnell asked in great alarm.

"Brock is dead. He's dead." Glegg reached out to clutch the horse's reins, wishing he could hold MacDonnell back.

# The Land Between Flowing Waters

The York Militia company at MacDonnell's back heard what Glegg said – in astonishment, in disbelief, and then in growing anger.

"We'll do what we have to," MacDonnell swore.

"Don't try the road. Captain Williams is in the brush to the right," Glegg advised.

Glegg and Benjamin broke down the cellar door of the abandoned house and carried Brock into the cool darkness. Along the stone foundation were empty grain sacks. They laid the body close beside the wall and covered it. Glegg rested his hand upon the shrouded figure.

"You'll be safe here, Isaac, until I can get back for you."

Tears streamed down his cheeks.

\*\*\*\*\*

"Look for a man on a horse wearing the biggest hat. Kill him. That's what I always tell the boys. I reckon we got us a British general a while ago. He was comin' up the road, just like that first bunch did, but this time there was an officer on a horse and militia behind. God, but they was angry!

"We musta had 100 rifles to knock him down. We fired purdy much in a volley – his horse went up, he came off and flopped in the mud. Some of them militia boys pulled him away, but there waren't no point. He was dead fur sure.

"Right then the Lobsterbacks jumped us from the brush. Scared the livin' bejesus out of us! Our boys run back from the redan. We couldn't get 'em stopped till they was at the cliff. Then they couldn't run no more. We turned around and – well, shit – there waren't more'n thirty, forty of them Lobsters, and we got four or five times that. We killed some. Some ran back into the bushes and we captured the rest.

"All in a day's work, I say. 'Cept, somebody spiked the damned guns.

"After that, things sorta went downhill."

\*\*\*\*\*

"Oh, Glegg," the wounded MacDonnell kept crying, "They killed the General."

Glegg held MacDonnell's hand. A stretcher was fashioned to carry him to the Surgeon. There were three or four wounds, but the worst was that his bowels were all shot away. Glegg just held his hand.

The British Regulars, the York and Lincoln Companies, everyone who was left alive retreated back through the village – not running, not afraid, but very tired and in great need of hope. And too, there was a desperate anger in every man.

"We're pulling back," the wounded Dennis ordered at Hamilton House.

Though he was senior, Glegg was in no mood to argue.

It was about 9 o'clock in the morning.

*****

Even as the cannonballs flew, Janie and Miriam felt safe in the root cellar below the kitchen. After only a few seconds, they could hear the boom, boom of the British great guns firing back. Anna was fussy with all the rumbling noise, but the women weren't afraid – until they smelled smoke.

They came up and ran into the back garden. They could see smoke from Queen Street where shells had landed. A house, three doors down, was smoldering from the back windows. Miriam couldn't imagine how the fire started; the neighbours had fled two or three days ago.

"Stay here, Janie. Keep behind our house."

"No, Miriam," Janie insisted. "This is why I'm here." With Anna in the sling, she ran after Miriam to fill buckets from the well. Janie and Miriam screamed "Fire" as they went, as the remaining neighbours converged. The burning house was empty. In the porch wall was a hole as big as a tea plate, and the hall closet too. The back wall in the kitchen was ablaze.

*****

With rifles braced against the parapet wall, Ben, Jeremy and Asa peered out toward the river. An hour before dawn, the bastion firewalk was lined by a company of Niagara militia, stiffened by men of the Veterans Battalion. The Fort George bugler was raising

# The Land Between Flowing Waters

billy-hell as the 41st Light Company and the 2nd York began to muster on the parade ground behind them. Officers billeted in town ran across the Commons as alarm bells rang.

Before all the racket started, Jeremy claimed he could hear cannon fire; but for Ben and Asa, the faint thunder from the south was lost in the wind. Asa stretched up over the parapet, trying to see any boats, but in the pre-dawn haze the river looked clear. *Surely*, Asa thought, *they will attack here.* It made sense – no cliffs, lots of beach and open ground to fight on, especially with all the soldiers Jonathan was supposed to have on the other side. But there was nothing out there today.

General Sheaffe must have thought it safe to send reinforcements, for just before dawn he and half a dozen aides rode out, down the road to Queenston. Following closely, Asa could see the Haudenosaunee trotting through the Commons on their way south. Asa smiled. He was pretty sure it was his boy riding up there in front with John Norton. Then the 41st Light and Holcroft's Artillery went out the gate with the Yorkers close behind.

As the 41st moved off at double time, Ben pointed to them and said. "Asa, we'd be fallin' down dead if we tried to run to Queenston."

Just the same, Asa and Ben were mighty proud to see 'em go.


The American Fort Niagara started firing across the river just as it was getting light. On the Canadian side, defenders crouched behind Fort George's dirt embrasures, but no shots fell among them. On the eastern bastion, British gun crews worked swiftly to swing the 24-pounders to aim at the far batteries. Jeremy watched as the first cannon fired a ranging shot with a right smart crash. It rolled back two or three paces, then the gunners swabbed and loaded and pushed her up again.

"I could do that," Jeremy told the older men.

"'Spect you could," Ben nodded as the second and third guns fired at the Yankee fort.

"Cannons are mighty heavy," Asa said.

"You must have built a barn, Mr. Lockwood," Jeremy teased with a grin.

"Yes, but that was a long time ago."

After a while the Garrison Sergeant came by. "You men see anything in the water?"

"No."

"Me neither, but the Yankees are using hot shot."

They turned to look across the parade grounds, north into Niagara. Towers of wind-whipped smoke rose from the town. The Court House was burning fiercely, and there were fires in a dozen places besides.

"Any volunteers for the fire brigades?" the Sergeant asked.

*****

After half an hour riding at the head of the Haudenosaunee war-band, Captain Lockwood was feeling rather sheepish. Norton, a man twice Lockwood's age, was keeping pace running beside his horse. The mostly naked warriors who followed with ease splashed through creeks to cool off and just kept going. By the time they reached Brown's Battery, still two miles from Queenston, Lockwood was positively embarrassed. It didn't help that Norton wasn't the oldest man among them.

The gunners at Brown's hailed them with dreadful news.

"Brock is dead. Americans are on the Heights."

Norton turned to his People to translate. There were a few firmly set jaws, but Lockwood felt as if he would surely weep. Then he thought of Miriam and...such anguish.

"This is why we have come," Norton said to Lockwood, in English. Lockwood spurred his horse to catch up as the war-band went pounding down the road.

Only a little later, they saw wagons filled with wounded, headed for Fort George. Many wore scarlet coats, others the brown of York and Lincoln militias. Lockwood could not guess who all these men would find to help them.

"Brock is dead! Americans are on the Heights!"

Next they met files of Blue Coats guarded by Canadian militia. Many were walking wounded, staggering into captivity. At Vrooman's Battery, only a mile from their goal, British and Loyalist stragglers appeared, some in the fields between the road and the forest to the west.

"Brock is dead! Americans are on the Heights!"

Lockwood stopped one deserter who limped slower than the rest, his wound real, not only of the soul.

"MacDonnell is dead, too," the man said. "There are six thousand Yankees coming down off the Mountain. They're in the forest, heading for Niagara."

# The Land Between Flowing Waters

One grinning warrior understood him. "The more game, the better hunting."

But this time the effect of the news was visible. The warriors had only just left their wives, their families in town. The men wanted to look back up the road. Some did.

Norton raised his arms.

"Comrades, Brothers – be men. Remember the fame of ancient Warriors, whose breasts were never daunted by odds or numbers. You have come from your encampment to this place to meet the enemy. We have found what we came for. Let no anxieties distract your minds. They are there," Norton said pointing to the Heights. "It only remains to fight."

The men looked at each other. Some rediscovered their resolve; others wavered.

"I don't believe that the Long Knives have come down, but we will find out," Norton said. "We will search the forest. If they are not there, we will climb the Heights. The Long Knives will not be pleased to find us behind them."

\*\*\*\*\*

At full morning light, the Yankee cannons shelled Fort George. Ben and Asa had gone to fight the fires in Niagara, but Jeremy Roberts stayed behind to serve the heavy guns. Then someone rang the alarm bell and yelled that the gunpowder magazine had been hit by heated shot.

"Roberts! Get the hell down from there," the Garrison Sergeant ordered. "She'll blow you to Kingdom Come!"

With a bayonet, Roberts was scraping at the copper sheeting on the magazine roof. A red-hot 9-pound ball was searing, burning its way down through the roof's oak planking.

"Bring me a pick axe! A spade! Something to dig it out!"

\*\*\*\*\*

The horse troughs beside the blazing Court House emptied in a trice. Constables braved the flames to free traitors locked in the gaol next door. The few townspeople left in Niagara formed bucket brigades from the nearest wells.

260

# Ken Leland

Ben and Asa plumbed the grocer's well, hauling up pail after pail to quench the flames until exhausted, when perforce they left the task to younger men. They staggered out onto the frenzied street. Smoke billowed between the buildings. People with blackened, sweat-streaked faces heaved water onto the burning dry-goods store. Men with shovels pitched mud onto the smoking timbers of the harness shop.

As they stood in the middle of the street, Ben noticed one fire in particular, two or three streets farther north towards the lake.

"Asa! Could that be Miriam's house?"

Ben and Asa headed for the Dress and Tailor Shoppe where they found a chain of people carrying water from the lake. The burning house was Miriam's neighbour. It was fully engulfed, and embers flew in the wind to threaten the nearest homes. The men found new strength and headed for the lake.

Janie was there, knee-deep in cold, pale blue water, filling and lining buckets on the beach.

" Daddy! What you are doing here?"

Ben looked at her in astonishment.

"Lord, girl! You ain't supposed to be here." Then, "Where's my grandbaby? Where's Anna?"

Janie pointed to the sling swaying from the lowest branch of a cottonwood a few yards away.

"I'll talk to you later, child," Ben growled. Water splashed from the pails onto his legs as he ran for the fire.


"Asa," Ben panted, "Your own precious fool must be here, somewhere."

They found Miriam with a shovel, pitching dirt up onto a roof.

It was almost 10 A.M.


*****


The forest was empty. There were no Long Knives on the plain below the escapement, but when the Haudenosaunee war-band reached St. David's Road, half the warriors had disappeared. Norton was not dismayed, but told those who remained to do their best – to keep their word.

The Haudenosaunee knew the Heights. Last summer's bivouac was in a stand of oaks along the northern cliff. There, some cabins, sheds and outdoor ovens served as a cantonment, and farms covered the rest. Portage Road came in from the south, from the Falls. The road skirted the 300 foot, perpendicular drop to the Niagara River. That was where, Norton said, they would find the Long Knives, among the oaks and fields.

Not far from St. David's village, there was a trail leading upwards. As the warriors rested, Lockwood lay down his long rifle and sabre. He draped his scarlet jacket over a tree branch, dipped his linen shirt in a rain puddle and plastered mud onto his white trousers. It was the best he could do to camouflage himself. Norton called out and they began to climb. Only 80 warriors followed him.

\*\*\*\*\*

"General Sheaffe, the Yankees are landing on the wharf," a bandaged but determined Captain Dennis said. British reinforcements were gathering near Vrooman's Battery, a mile from Queenston.

"Yankee looters are tearing the village apart, General."

"We'll let the 41st drive them out, then move in Holcroft's Artillery to command the Heights," General Sheaffe directed. "Where's Norton?"

"The Indians are climbing up from St. David's Road," Dennis replied.

"Good idea! We'll do that too."

\*\*\*\*\*

In the wet cold of midday, Norton led them to the Heights. The mountainside was almost vertical but it was clothed in brush, vines, and yellow-leafed trees. Lockwood clung to each bush, pulling himself another step higher, as the warriors beside him swarmed up the mudslides. An aging tattooed warrior with a missing front tooth reached back to pull Lockwood for the last few steps.

"*Niawen*," Lockwood gasped.

On top were the farms Lockwood remembered well: Chisholm's fields, the Phelps and Samuel Street homesteads. Norton led them across the fields toward Portage Road, to flank the Long Knives from the south. Here, the harvested cornfields held only broken stalks. The oaks ahead were clothed in brown as warriors spread out in a line and leapfrogged from one rail fence to the next.

At first it was quiet, though the enemy held the cantonment and the cliff edge less than a mile away. After a time came the echoes of cannon fire and musketry. The sound reverberated in the river valley, flowing up and over the hillside. Below the fight to retake Queenston Village had begun.

Norton motioned, and his people went to ground. Through the high pale grass Lockwood could see American Bluecoats lounging on the Phelps front porch, while others took their ease in the apple orchard. At the farmhouse, curtains flapped from broken windows. Norton signed that they should approach in stealth, and upon discovery, to yell like fury.

Soon enough, a soldier peering from the second-floor window screamed a warning – and such war cries they gave him back! A squad of Yankee riflemen, clutching plunder, poured from the farm house to run headlong up the road. The Haudenosaunee swept into the barnyard, firing at the fleeing raiders, who threw down plate and bedding to withdraw the faster. Two weeping women stumbled from the house, then a young boy. Norton directed they be led away to safety.

Again the warriors spread out to cross the fields, bending to the west, away from Portage Road. There was another rail fence beyond Samuel Street's wheatfield. Here the Long Knife pickets waited in great numbers. These stood firm, some running out to cover the marauders as they fled for their lives. Again, Lockwood and the rest went to ground as a Yankee volley passed overhead. While the enemy reloaded, the warriors sprinted forward to a long narrow creek across the American front. The enemy line, hundreds of blue and brown-clad soldiers, stretched for 300 yards, anchored on the river cliff to the east. Against so many, a headlong charge was foolhardy. Nor was it wise to stay where they were, since the volume of fire would surely begin to tell. Yet they sniped at the Bluecoats, stinging the beast repeatedly.

*Soon enough, they'll tire of dying and charge us,* Lockwood thought, as he reloaded and aimed at an officer in a black cocked hat. Norton signalled to circle left, and as they moved safely through the low ground, a most welcome sound fell upon their ears: a shell burst above the trees at the northern cliff edge, spraying a double handful of musket balls down into the old bivouac. This, Lockwood guessed, was where the enemy's main body was concentrated, on the hilltop just above the redan.

# The Land Between Flowing Waters

Holcroft's Artillery had fought its way into Queenston, and the battery of light guns was firing exploding canister into the trees above the Americans on the escarpment.

The Haudenosaunee ran to the very edge of the Heights, a little distance from where the Americans crouched beneath Holcroft's artillery fire. On the plains below they could see Sheaffe's soldiers following quickly along the trails the warriors had already crossed.

"Let's entertain them till Sheaffe arrives," Norton shouted.

Lockwood followed the warriors as they ghosted forward through the trees, pausing only once to rub dirt over his clothing. Once again they came to an open field. They rushed across to find the Long Knives scattered beneath the trees. With war cries, the Haudenosaunee drove them – killing some, terrifying them all, until the Yankees were crowded behind a waist-high, earthen wall. When they realised how few warriors pursued them, they began to dress their lines in preparation for a counterattack. They fired a volley and advanced in waves. The Nations fell back slowly, sheltering behind trees, sheds and cabins, in the ruins of the old cantonment. After recrossing the open field, Lockwood paused at the tree line to reload. The older, tattooed warrior who had flopped down beside him held up six fingers with a gap-toothed smile.

"By God," Lockwood muttered as he checked his priming pan, "they'll pay if they follow us across that field."

As they waited for the Long Knives to build up their courage, there was a terrific burst of fire from the right, back in the direction of the stream. It was a part of the original war-band who had now climbed onto the upper plain. Most unwisely, those warriors tried to withstand a Long Knife charge over the wheat field. Retreating now, they carried their wounded and a few dead. The warriors ran from the Bluecoats, leading them straight into Norton's ambush. A young hatless redhead, at the extended tip of Lockwood's rifle, disappeared in the crash and billow of gun smoke that sprang from the warriors' volley.

Lying in the wheat stubble, some blue figures remained unmoving. A few others crawled away wailing in dreadful agony. Across the killing field the war-band watched for any other Long Knives seeking to encircle them. None did, and so Norton's attention returned to the cantonment. British shells now burst over the Yankee positions with regularity. Even among the trees there was no safe place to hide. Again, Norton led a charge, with the most hideous screams the warriors could produce. And again, the Yankees fled to the embankment a few score paces from the precipice. Somehow they had hauled a light cannon up the cliff, and many of the enemy clustered near it. Even as Holcroft's shells burst above, Lockwood and the aging warrior hunted as a team in the cantonment, luring one Yankee after another from concealment to be killed by a waiting sniper. Again and again, they stabbed the monster. After much time, the Haudenosaunee retreated from simple exhaustion.

It was nearly 2:30 in the afternoon.

*****

In Niagara, the fires were out. The Court House was but a steaming pile of charred timber as Janie, Miriam and their fathers, Ben and Asa, wandered past the gutted shops. On the street, townsfolk were crying in each other's arms.

"This is bad," Asa said when he saw the damage, "but not that bad. All this can be rebuilt."

A drunken stranger staggered past. He turned to them. "Brock is dead. Americans are on the Heights."

Miriam stumbled in confusion, in disbelief.

Everywhere people were crying, weeping inconsolably.

Miriam screamed, then raged in desolation, pounding her fists against her father's chest. "No! No! We need him! *I* need him!" Miriam collapsed onto the ground.

"Oh, my darling girl," Asa said as she wailed at his feet. "I'm so very sorry."

Janie stooped to gather her best friend into her arms.

*****

Atop Queenston Heights, drums beat and fifes trilled. General Sheaffe was advancing on Portage Road.

A few moments later, 100 Cayuga warriors sprinted across the field to join Norton. The Haudenosaunee families in Niagara were safe.

Close behind came the Coloured Corps to lengthen the Nation's line. The Lincoln and York Regiments wheeled into position. Then came General Sheaffe's main reinforcements. Rushed from Chippewa, the red-jacketed regimental and grenadier companies advanced to the music. They marched in long double rows that stretched to the cliff edge. On the plain high above the river, the 49th anchored the right flank. The allies locked into position like a door slamming shut, a looping half circle that trapped the Americans against the precipice. They stood with muskets ready, 250 yards from the American lines as the bandsmen played – until silence fell.

General Sheaffe, on horseback in the centre, leaned forward and drew his sword.

"Fix bayonets!"

The general scanned the bright red line from left to right.

"Bugler, let it begin."

The war cries around Lockwood were terrifying.

The Haudenosaunee sprang forward and were across the open field in an instant.

There was no opposition as they surged through the cantonment, past the ruins. On the right, Redcoats and Loyalist militia lumbered forward inexorably. The Yankees, panic-stricken by the shrieking demons now circling behind them, fired one desperate volley, too high. Then they fled the oncoming vengeance.

The ring of British steel tightened to push the invaders back, relentlessly crowding them towards the precipice. The men of the 49th, Brock's own regiment, advanced along the cliff edge. The enemy huddled there in wretched terror as gore-streaked bayonets fell among them. Overwhelmed by horror, Yankee soldiers launched themselves from atop the cliff into the river far, far below.

On the left flank, the Haudenosaunee leapt upon the monster to pull it down. Norton's warriors surged over the embankment into the invaders' ranks, and butchered them with tomahawks. Enraged, Lockwood's sabre chopped at every enemy that faced him. Abject, pitiful men in blue began to drop to their knees with hands raised, but the slaughter continued. They would suffer the fate they had promised others.

American officers waved white towels, begging for their men's lives, for protection from extermination.

General Sheaffe bellowed "Stop Fire," again and again. His brigade major and aides took up the call for mercy. The senior officers struggled to stop the vengeance.

Hundreds of Americans lay trembling, wounded, or dead upon the ground.

# Ken Leland

## Tuesday Evening, October 13, 1812
## Aftermath

Captain Lockwood stared straight ahead as he stumbled past the redan. His shirt and uniform trousers were streaked with blood. A long string of wagons carrying American wounded rumbled down the road beside him. A troop of Provincial Dragoons guarded them. Lockwood reeled, almost falling into their path. A voice called out from behind.

"Captain Lockwood, are you all right?"

Wordless, Lockwood staggered slowly out onto the berm. Lieutenant Merritt rode at his shoulder for a while, until the last of the wagons began to draw away.

"Shall I come back for you, Sir?"

There was no reply.

The sun was low, a red ball gleaming among scattered rainclouds atop the escarpment. Companies of newly arriving Canadian militia waved caps and shouted in exultation as they escorted blue-clad soldiers on their way to captivity. The victorious jostled past Lockwood as he turned from the road onto the lower terrace, and alone he headed for the wharf.

There, bodies floated in the river. Broken launches and dead men lined the Niagara shore. Lockwood threw his rifle and blood-encrusted sabre upon the rocks.

He waded in.

The water rose quickly to his waist, then he faltered and collapsed, face first, into the gut-shriveling cold. Eyes open, he floated in freezing emerald. The current tugged at his arms and legs, pulling him farther from shore. Motionless, he began to drift downstream.

"Good God, Lockwood! What are you doing out there?"

Major Glegg's voice was muffled but Lockwood heard and lifted his face to gasp for air. Sergeant Benjamin splashed into the river to pull him out.

Glegg waited on the wharf until Benjamin dragged Lockwood ashore. Beside Glegg was a horse cart – but no horse.

"Come help us."

Glegg, Benjamin and Lockwood pulled the cart through Queenston Village. Brock's body was covered by a sheet.

267

# The Land Between Flowing Waters

In the village, doors were smashed, windows broken. A few houses smoldered in ruins. As they passed, red-coated grenadiers searched basements for stray Yankee looters. By the time they reached Vrooman's Battery, the Canadian wounded had already been evacuated to Niagara.

Glegg went in search of a horse.

"What's the matter?" Benjamin asked gently of Lockwood, who sat shivering in the grass.

"Him." Lockwood raised a trembling hand toward the cart. "Brock and Miriam, and...and I don't remember how many I killed."

Benjamin was silent. He threw his arm over Lockwood's shoulders and they waited for Glegg's return.


Darkness had fallen by the time Lockwood, driving the cart, reached the Commons outside Fort George.

"Where should we take him?" he asked Glegg.

"Government House. Someone will help me prepare the body."

"I could..."

"No. But thank you, Captain. I want you to find Colonel MacDonnell. If he's already dead...even so, try to find him."

They carried Brock's corpse downstairs to the broad walnut table in the survey office. Lockwood was thankful John Ellis wasn't a witness to this mournful scene. *And how terrible for Miriam*, he thought, *when she hears.*

Afterwards, Benjamin and Lockwood parted on the street outside. Benjamin went in search of his friends in the regiment. Lockwood wandered past the blackened pile that was the Court House. The street was almost empty. Trees swayed in the high wind. Later he would check Miriam's house, but just now, St. Mark's would be a quiet place to cheat the cold.

Torches flared in the church yard. Wagons. Tents. Horse lines. Soldiers were gathered at a bonfire beneath the cedars.

A scream echoed from the church.

*Dear God, they've brought the wounded here*, Lockwood realized.

He wandered past bodies lining both sides of the gravel path. *Could MacDonnell be one of them?* He pulled back each blanket. The uniforms were American blue, British red, and Canadian brown.

# Ken Leland

The flat river stones outside the church doors were awash in mud. Candlelight leaked from windows.

Inside, doctors were frantic, overwhelmed by scores of men in agony. The oak floor was stained with blood. Scents of alcohol and excrement filled the air. Wounded, broken men lay moaning in the pews. Even the gallery above had taken its share of horror. Those who loved the dying wailed. Somewhere, a baby fretted.

*A baby? Who would bring a baby here?*

The mewling came from a sling draped against the wall. Where could the mother be? Was her man here?

He pressed through the crowd, treading carefully between bodies in the aisles. In the gloom beyond the altar, a woman knelt. Her face was turned. Once her dress had been cream, but now it was blackened. She held a wounded man's hand.

The leg below the man's bandaged thigh was gone. At the stump, his life dripped out upon the floor. He was in great distress. Slowly, the woman leaned forward to touch his face, and together they began to pray. His breath grew more shallow with every gasp. She prayed still when he could not. The jacket folded beneath his head was blue.


Lockwood drew baby Anna's sling over his shoulder. Janie's head was bowed, and so he reached down to lift her up.

"Come with me."

They went out into the night. Hand in hand, Lockwood led her beside the lake. Miriam's garden gate was open, but before they crossed the yard, Janie stopped.

"Alex..."

They fell into each other's arms. He kissed Janie with hopeless joy.

"I'm so sorry, Alex. I should have trusted you." Janie clung to him with all her strength. "I'll always love you."

"It was my fault. I never should have left you behind. I'm lost without you."

"Janie, is that you? Alex?" Miriam was at the front door, framed by light.

"It's late. Jeremy's here."

269

# The Land Between Flowing Waters

### Friday, October 16, 1812
### Sileo in Pacis

Major J. B. Glegg to Justice W. D. Powell
Fort George
Wednesday Morning, Oct. 14, 1812.

My Dear Sir,

With heartrending sorrow I assume the painful duty of announcing to you the death of my most valuable and much lamented friend, Major General Brock. He fell yesterday morning at an early hour, when at the head of a small body of regular troops, disputing every inch of ground with a very superior body of the enemy's troops in the town of Queenston.

The ball entered his right breast and passed through his left side. His sufferings, I am happy to add, were of short duration. His body was immediately carried into a house at Queenston, and though we were obliged by a great superiority of numbers to leave it for some hours, it was recovered during the day when our victorious troops regained the place.

I am grieved to inform you that our gallant and much esteemed friend, MacDonnell, received a severe wound about the same time, and, having fortunately been carried to the rear of our army, he immediately received medical assistance. The wound, my dear Sir, is very serious, a musket ball having passed through his body near the navel, but it is supposed not to have injured his bladder. He was removed last night to Government House, where he received every aid and attention. I never quit his bed for more than a few minutes.

Our victory, though sadly clouded by the loss of our dear chief, has been most complete. All did their duty. The American General Wadsworth, a large body of officers, nearly 800 prisoners, the only piece of artillery which the enemy carried over, and one stand of colours, are now in our possession. The enemy's attack was confined to Queenston.

Our batteries at Niagara have done great execution. The court house and jail were burnt down yesterday, but whether from the enemy's fire or an act of some of the prisoners has not been ascertained. Their cannonading, though continued for some hours upon this place, I am happy to say committed no injury, except upon a few houses. Their fire was effectually silenced by our batteries, and their fort was abandoned. Our magazine was set on fire by red-hot shot, but was soon extinguished by the heroic presence of mind of our troops.

Half-past one o'clock.
My poor friend MacDonnell has just expired.

Major John Baskerville Glegg
49th Regiment of the Line
Niagara

*****

Surely Brock would never have wished for the spectacle to be performed that day, Friday, October 16, 1812. But perhaps he looked down to forgive his old friend Glegg, for indeed it was the will of the People of Upper Canada who gathered for one last tribute and outpouring of affection.

No pen can adequately describe the scenes of that mournful day. A more solemn and affecting demonstration has perhaps never been witnessed. Every arrangement connected with the ceremony fell to Glegg, and he anxiously endeavoured to plan the interment to be in every respect military.

It was Glegg's plan that Major General Isaac Brock and Lieutenant Colonel John MacDonnell would be buried side by side. The northeast bastion of Fort George would be their resting place. The band of the 41st, drums covered with black cloth and muffled, would play a funeral march as the mourners passed from Government House to the fort −200 First Nations Warriors to line the road in respectful silence. A picked company of the 41st, 60 men under a subaltern, and a company of militia were to come next. Then the general's horse fully caparisoned, with four grooms, followed by the doctors and Reverend Addison. Colonel MacDonnell's coffin, resting upon a black draped caisson, preceded the general's coffin, each attended by mourners and supporters.

# The Land Between Flowing Waters

Major General Sheaffe would walk near the end as the Chief Mourner, followed by officers of the government and local inhabitants.

*****

Minute guns fired in the fog.

"Asa, the hearse is coming," Lois told her husband, as they waited atop the walls of Fort George. She returned from the parapet to hold his arm. Asa blinked as mist blew against his face.

Ben and Sarah, Lois and Asa, and their children stood motionless on the battlements. The cortege proceeded through the warrior honour guard, past the sentry post, and then onto the fort parade grounds where a host of townsfolk waited in silence.

Janie Roberts held tiny Anna and leaned against her husband's side. Jeremy balanced Ethan high upon his shoulders so that he might see. Janie's brother Matthew was below, driving the caisson bearing Brock's body.

John Ellis stood between Alex and Miriam.

As the cannons crashed, junior officers carried each coffin to its open grave. Reverend Addison offered the multitude the solace of faith in a time of grief. There was one last salute, one last volley of arms, then the people turned away.

Miriam and John Ellis clasped hands. With streaming eyes, the boy stared up to her. Miriam tried to smile, but both were afraid.

Asa could not imagine what he might do to ease his daughter's pain. But he would tell John Ellis, as many times as the boy needed to hear, that he was theirs – theirs to hold, and to love forever.

## The End

# Background Sources

The following are a few of the sources which inform the writing of this novel.

## Primary Sources

Cruikshank, E. A., numerous publications and collections of official documents as published by the Ontario Historical Society and the Niagara Historical Society Museum.

Cushman, H. B., "History of the Choctaw," published in 1899 in which Tecumseh's speech is recorded.

Lucas, Robert, "Journal of the War of 1812," published in 1906.

McAfee, Robert B., "History of the Late War in the Western Country," published in 1816.

Merritt, William, Hamilton, journal written in 1814, published by the Niagara Historical Society in 1902, edited by E.A. Cruikshank.

Mitchell, Mary, "A Short Account of the Early Part of the Life of Mary Mitchell," published in 1812. The Ontario Quaker Archives were most gracious to allow me to copy excerpts from this memorial on the life and writings from which the sermon purportedly deliver by Priscilla Cadwallader was constructed.

Norton, John, "The Journal of John Norton, 1816," published in 1970.

Quaife, Milo, "War on the Detroit," published in 1940 in which is found period accounts entitled, "The Chronicles of Thomas Vercheres de Boucherville" and "The Capitulation by an Ohio Volunteer."

Richardson, John, "Richardson's War of 1812," published in 1902.

Tupper, Ferdinand Brock, "The Life and Correspondence of Sir Isaac Brock," published in 1845. A collection of official and personal correspondence of great interest.

United States government publication, "Abridgement of the Debates of Congress from 1789 to 1856," available online.

# The Land Between Flowing Waters

Winter, George, art and commentary in "The Journals and Indian Paintings of George Winter, 1837-1839," published by the Indiana Historical Society in 1948.

## Secondary Sources

Antal, Sandy, "A Wampum Denied," 1998.

Cave, Alfred A., "Prophets of the Great Spirit," 2006.

Cleaves, Freeman, "Old Tippecanoe, William Henry Harrison and His Times," 1969.

Clifton, James A., "The Prairie People," 1998.

Densmore, Frances, "Menominee Music," 1932; also "Indian Use of Wild Plants," 1926.

Dorland, Arthur, "The Quakers in Canada, A History," 1968.

Edmunds, R. David, "The Potawatomis," 1978.

Malcomson, Robert, "Burying General Brock," 1996; also "A Very Brilliant Affair," 2003.

McDonald, Daniel, "History of Marshall County," [Indiana] 1881.

Owens, Robert M., "Mr. Jefferson's Hammer, William Henry Harrison and the Origins of American Indian Policy," 2007.

# ABOUT THE AUTHOR
## KEN LELAND

After studying philosophy in graduate school, Ken Leland worked in educational publishing as an editor for a number of years, and then became a high school mathematics teacher. He came to writing, to historical fiction, somewhat late in life. He is typically reluctant even to mention his background in education for fear that readers will suppose his aim is to educate them.

Heaven forfend!

His only hope is that those who come to his work will be vastly entertained by it.

276

CPSIA information can be obtained at www.ICGtesting.com
Printed in the USA
LVOW07s0918100813

347012LV00004BA/15/P